SAVAGE SECRETS

Christi,

Enjoy Rocco + Caterina.
Go Team Titan.

♡,
Cristin

Cristin Harber

SAVAGE SECRETS

ISBN: 0989776093
ISBN-13: 9780989776097

Genres: Romance, romantic suspense, military romance

www.CristinHarber.com

Dedicated to my family for their constant support and to the readers who believed in Team Titan.

PROLOGUE

Twenty years ago…

Daddy took another step toward the men approaching their picnic tables. "No ahora." Not now. With a tight face and concerned eyes, he waved his arms in warning. "Hoy no quiero problemas." I don't want problems today.

The birthday balloons and streamers swayed in the wind rolling off the Mediterranean Sea. Caterina had seen the bad men before. They always had guns. Normally, Daddy did too. But today he didn't. His *policia* badge kept them—and their costal town—safe.

Her four older brothers wanted to be just like daddy. They were all brave and strong. When the men ignored Daddy's orders, stepping closer to the family, her brothers formed a protective ring. Their fists bunched, and their chests were pushed out. But fists versus bullets didn't amount to a fair fight. Caterina knew that much, and her family was in trouble.

The bad men were *traficantes de armas*. The gun runners. They were the evil men who brought weapons across the water in the middle of the night and made neighbors disappear during the day. Daddy and her brothers always talked about the men who left North Africa and washed up on their southern Spanish shores..

But it wasn't the middle of the night. It was her tenth birthday party, and those men weren't invited. She wanted to yell at them to go away, but her mouth was as dry as the sand between her toes. Caterina stared at the curled ribbons and bright paper covering the present in her hands. This was bad. Very bad. They shouldn't have crashed her birthday party.

A loud noise popped into the air, and her insides jumped. Everything slowed. Momma froze in place. Daddy's arms did that up-and-down move he used when telling the boys to calm down. A boat's engine screamed from the water as it raced toward the shore. Everyone looked at it except for momma, who looked at Caterina. Momma stepped close, tugging the sleeve of her birthday dress, but Caterina's feet were stuck like bubble gum to a sidewalk.

"*Por farvor,*" Momma begged. Her eyes shot to Daddy. "*Nos vamos.*"

Daddy shooed Momma and Caterina away, but they were surrounded. It all had happened so fast. Caterina focused on the boat on the beach. She couldn't breathe. New men arrived. Soldiers ran toward her birthday party with more guns.

Shouts erupted.

Spanish. English.

Caterina covered her face when the big guns fired. At the soldiers. At her family.

Daddy fell down, hands in the air like he was trying to catch the spray of bullets. Angry shouts came from her brothers and screams from her momma. One by one, her brothers went down with awful gurgling, wet noises. The whiz of bullets sliced the salty air. Standing in the chaos, Caterina uncovered her eyes and turned in a circle. Daddy. Her brothers. And her momma. All on the ground. All bloody red. Dead eyes and motionless faces.

She looked up. The soldiers were upon them with gun fire and smoke as they took down the gun runners.

Rough hands grabbed her, wrapping around her waist then pulling her tight. She couldn't move. Couldn't fight. She opened her eyes to a boy the age of her oldest brother. Not a grown up. Almost, maybe, but his dark eyes were ancient. Tears ran down her cheeks as she was carried away from her family. Still, she clutched the birthday present, the box wet from her family's blood and her tears.

The soldier set her down behind a stone wall. She just wanted it to end so she could go to sleep, wake up, and start her birthday over again. The soldier rubbed his hand across his jaw and dropped down to her height. He pried the present from her hands and wrapped her in a hug. Her tears soaked his shoulder. He smelled like her daddy's guns, sweat, and the sea water.

Still holding her shoulders, he tried a faltering smile that looked out of practice. "*Lo siento.*" His Spanish sounded funny: halting, with an accent. "*Lo que necesites, considérelo hecho. La venganza es suya.*"

She nodded, biting her lip until she tasted the salty tease of blood. His words, his promise replayed in her mind. I'm sorry. Whatever you need, consider it done. Revenge is yours. She would survive for no other reason than to ask for his help.

ONE

Rocco Savage rose from his barstool in the rowdy pub, abandoning his half-empty lager, then cracked his neck. Claustrophobia tickled the edges of his mind, and a few more swigs of beer wouldn't help. He'd learned that the hard way over the past weeks.

The rescue op had only been last night, and he was too tired to deal with the coming headache. He certainly didn't need his men to see him flail against the unreal. An invisible rope would tighten around his chest. Then the unmistakable chokehold of imaginary suffocation would take him hostage. Finally, he'd see things that weren't there. Lights and tracers. Angels and demons.

At least he wasn't home trying to convince his ex-girlfriend that he was serious about adding the ex- to her title. She didn't understand his job or appreciate his disappearing act when he got his hallucinating hiccups. The episodes had been happening ever since he'd been stabbed in a New York City knife fight. The blade had been coated in a hallucinogen. The occurrences weren't frequent, but they were enough that he needed to kick it out of his system or fess up to Jared "Boss Man" Westin that Rocco wasn't capable of performing in all conditions, at all times, for the Titan Group.

"I'm outta here, boys." He rubbed his hand over jaw. "A week in the field, and I have too many episodes of trash TV to catch up on." They'd believe that. If he wasn't hanging with Titan, he'd be chilling on his couch. He was all about the extreme opposites. Jumping out of helicopters or vegging on the couch.

Roman laughed. "I'm gonna call your girl. Tell her how much you miss her."

Rocco and Roman were the only single guys on the trip, and Roman knew damn well things had ended with Roc's ex. "Hey, buddy, she's all yours. Hot to trot, but looking for a ring. Beware."

"No way. No how." Roman drained his glass, signaling for another. "Not my style."

Hell, that was only because Roman already had eyes for a girl. She ignored him. Might've hated him, but hatred didn't slow his boy down.

With some of the team settling down, Rocco had made the mistake of trying to join them. Winters, Cash, and even Jared touted the virtues of coupledom. They came home after fighting to the death and sleeping in the dirt, then crawled into a warm bed with a hot body. Sounded like a good deal. But when Rocco tried it, having a plus-one proved nothing more than a big, fat fail.

"See you in the AM." He waved goodbye.

His men booed and hissed. *His men.* Only recently elevated to second in charge at Titan, Rocco savored the trust he'd been given. And here in London, with Jared on another job, in another country, Rocco was the man in charge. He'd do anything to prove Jared's decision to promote him right, and he'd also bust his ass to make sure the team was cool with the recent change in leadership.

"Whatever, dude." Cash stretched on his stool, dark ale in hand. "Unless you have some pretty Brit on your arm, you're leaving too early."

Rocco's pulse quickened, and an unmistakable flash of light pulsed around Cash's cowboy hat. The signs were there. Another hallucination was ready to strike. He had to roll out before lightning tortured his brain, and the streaks of color floated in the air.

He threw a hand up and waved good night. "See ya."

A balled up napkin hit his shoulder, and as Winters and Roman grumbled over his departure, Rocco focused on the door. He had to get out of the bar. Get into the muggy night air. Make it to his hotel room and crash. Sleep was the only thing he'd found helpful when his living nightmare hit. And it was a hit. Like getting broadsided by a freighter, it knocked him on his ass and made his brain stutter to a stop. It made him vulnerable, and that wasn't cool.

Vibrations in his ears. Flashing lights in his peripheral. *Nothing's there. Keep moving.*

He stumbled down a street. Street lamps reached for him. Bar signs and business placards swirled into a kaleidoscope of colors. He had no freakin' clue where he was.

Think, Roc.

London... right?

One block away from the hotel. You can do this.

Zip, zip, zip. The sounds echoed again. Curse his luck. It couldn't wait another day? When they were back on US soil? He sucked down a breath and planted his hands onto a bench then dropped onto it. Deep breath in. Out. He didn't have far to go and didn't need the attention—

"Are you okay?"

Attention like that. "Yup. Fine." He looked toward the voice, squinting against what he knew was a figment of his imagination. A woman hovered nearby. Not floating. Not standing. She glowed. Hell, he had no idea if she was there or not. But he did know this was nothing more than his mind racing through the aftershocks of a hallucinogen that wouldn't leave his system. "Just need a minute to myself, if you don't mind."

"You're not drunk, are you?"

He looked at the woman again and let her voice swirl around him, rich but soft. She was a beautiful vision. Angelic. Almost iridescent. But he knew better.

"Nope. Not drunk. Just surviving the night. Thanks." *Thanks,* if there was really someone there. Who knew? He thought she was there, but if she was, she definitely didn't glow. Not in real life. Only in his mind.

A glowing hand floated to his shoulder. "Come on, soldier. You can't be like this here."

3

Why would she think he was a soldier? Why would she try to help? *Because she's not really there.* His psyche was trying to get him home in one piece. That made sense.

Her gentle fingers wrapped with the strength of steel around his bicep and tugged him to his feet. She confused the hell out of him. As forceful as she was, the touch of her skin whispered over his like a feather. Rocco walked to his hotel. Imaginary or not, she was the strength he needed. For once, a hallucination helped. Somehow, he got into the room. He planted face first on the bed and ignored the zaps of electricity burning through his brain.

A cool cloth draped over the back of his neck. His vision was still with him, and she offered words he didn't hear over the static buzzing in his ears. But still, he somehow knew the cadence of her words and the lyrical sound of her voice was…perfect.

• • •

Ay Dios mio. Caterina Cruz pulled her dark hair into a ponytail. What had she been doing? Instinct told her to help the guy out, and if there was one thing she trusted, it was her gut. But still. Not her smartest move. His eyebrows twitched and his brow furrowed as he half led, half pointed the staggered path to his hotel room. He wasn't interested in her. Not curious as to why she'd pulled him off the street and helped him into his hotel room. Almost like she wasn't there.

He wasn't drunk, and didn't seem dangerous *to her*, despite his hardened body. His cut muscles were those of a hard soldier. Even in his vulnerable state, he wasn't one who would be easily taken down. She analyzed people for a living, studied them and made fast decisions. This man wore a knife holstered to his hip. A dark shirt stretched over his mountain of a chest. Sinewy, tanned flesh flexed in his forearms. She knew the type well. He was her people. A trained killer. An operative. Or maybe even a for-hire. For whom? Who knew? Either way, she didn't question her safety with him.

She checked his pulse then checked his breathing. Elevated, but not enough to concern her. A quick check of his pockets revealed

4

nothing to identify him. An encrypted, burner phone confirmed her suspicions. He was someone who lived off the grid.

Just like me… So why am I still here?

The man didn't matter. It was time to go, but the nagging feeling that everything happened for a reason made her look back over her shoulder on the way out. Purely professional. Nothing to do with the honey brown hair. The glance was to reassure her that she wasn't leaving a man to overdose in a hotel room. *Yeah right.*

Ignoring her training to be a ghost, she changed directions, walked into the bathroom, rubbed her thumb and forefinger together, then wrote an invisible note on the mirror.

She could call it a compulsion—a crazy one—but the need to stay with him weighted her mind and feet. She had too many questions, but her job called, so she looked at the mirror, making sure nothing was visible to the naked eye, then turned and left.

• • •

Light flooded the hotel room, and Rocco's stomach twisted. He knew he was running late before he even opened his eyes. He'd ended up in his room? Yeah, not sure how that happened. Last night's episode was the same as always but hadn't come with his usual post-hallucination frustration. He'd lost control, but the swirling in his gut smacked more of embarrassment than annoyance, and the vulnerability stung.

A knock rapped on his door. He rolled to his side. Squinting, he let his eyes adjust and rubbed a hand over the stubble on his jaw. "Go away."

"No can do, buttercup. Get your princess fanny up," Winters called from the other side of the door.

Rocco heard Cash laugh. "Roc's still sleeping?"

"First he goes home early. Next he wakes up late." Winters wasn't talking to him anymore. Good, they could go somewhere else and talk about him. No skin off his back.

"Slacker." *Bam, bam.* "I got your crack, Roc. Coffee."

5

Magic word. Coffee would be good. He'd get up for that. "Leave it at the door, Cash. Meet you all in ten."

Rocco pushed up and looked down. Passed out on top of the covers. Still wearing his boots. What was this, the aftermath of a frat party?

"You're alive. That's good enough." Winters smacked the door. "See ya."

Yeah, see ya. Go away. Rocco rubbed his temples, testing for aftershocks. His head was clear with no flashing lights or zaps. Nothing remained from his nightmare hallucinations. But something tickled the back of his neck. A thought. A hope. Maybe part of a trippy dream. Something good in the hazy torment.

He stood and dropped his head back to stare at the off-white ceiling. Nothing popped to mind. It was just another perplexing consequence of his psychedelic problem. Rocco rolled his shoulders and shrugged out of his shirt on the way to the bathroom. A hot shower and semi-decent coffee would kick start his day. He slapped the faucet handle as hot as it would go. Steam billowed into the room as he stepped out retrieve the coffee.

Two long pulls of the lackluster brew, and he closed his eyes, trying like all hell to remember the missing piece. After another sip of the coffee, he returned to the bathroom. Bad coffee wasn't doing him any favors but maybe a burning hot shower would.

He stopped short, set the coffee on the counter, and stared at the steamy mirror.

Hope you feel better, handsome.

TWO

The team thought they were on their way home, but Jared changed their plans at the last minute. They were already in London, and a special project popped up: new intelligence about a terrorist outpost location.

Fifty miles outside London, Rocco's team was ready for the danger zone. They arrived at the outpost in stealth mode, assessed the security measures at what looked like a one-man shop, and made an extraction plan: go big, get their mark, then go home after dropping him off for MI6 to work over. Rocco led them forward. He threw the explosive charge. Wood splinters rained down. Smoke stung his eyes. Its acrid taste coated his tongue, and he spit out a charred ember. Heaving a shoulder against the last barrier, he knew brute force would bring him to the target, a lieutenant who worked for El Mateperros, one of the world's most elusive, up-and-coming terrorist leaders.

El Mateperros hadn't struck on American soil, but he consistently attacked and threatened their international friends. A terrorist was a terrorist, and if that asswipe was plotting death and destruction for one of the US's allies, it was only a matter of time before he turned his attention to the red, white, and blue.

The door buckled, and Rocco cleared the threshold. He scanned the dilapidated room. In the corner, a man fitting their target's description lay on the dirty floor. They *may* have gone a little heavy on the tear gas and flash-bang explosives meant to momentarily paralyze the guy. Despite

Rocco barreling through the door, he remained unresponsive. Not good. Nothing about the job mattered if their mark was already dead.

The intelligence loss would be catastrophic. Terrorist chatter after a recent botched Algerian Combat Group—ACG—attack in London said El Mateperros and his minions were plotting something to rival their previous attacks. They wanted to save face among their radical friends.

It was enough to make Rocco sick. The bastard had to live long enough to provide details about future terrorist strikes and hopefully give up El Mateperros. MI6 had only partnered with Titan to bring him in. Very curious but not Rocco's concern. Next time, maybe Titan would get the interrogation because Roc wanted in on an ACG take down. Nothing like dismantling a terror organization.

Threading his hands into a mess of stringy, greasy hair, Rocco yanked the terrorist's head back and felt for a pulse. Faint, but there. *At least the dude's alive. For now.*

With a disgusted push, he let the man's head drop and wiped his hand across his chest. It wasn't the grit he wanted to wipe away. He wanted to remove that nasty feeling he got after touching someone who wanted to kill everything that Rocco protected.

"Target acquired."

Outside, an armored car waited. Rocco secured the terrorist's hands and dragged him into the night. He looked at the moon fighting to shine through the smoke. The back door of the vehicle popped open, and hands reached forward, grabbing El Mateperros's lieutenant. Rocco jumped into the passenger seat, and they took off, bumping and lurching through the brush.

"Guess we went a little overboard. He's still alive?" Roman growled from the dark back seat.

"Alive enough for someone to work him over."

Rocco gnashed his teeth that this job was nothing more than a grab-and-drop. Did Jared know the hallucinations hadn't stopped? Too much time had passed since New York City. No one knew he still had the trippy reactions.

"What's your problem?" Winters eyed him from the driver's seat.

Besides feeling a little unfulfilled in the terrorist nabbing department, and worrying his boss knew he still randomly hallucinated, his mind was stuck on the message scrawled on his mirror. Must've been for whoever stayed in the room prior because it couldn't have been for him. Housekeeping simply hadn't cleaned the mirror.

But… how often did someone think to leave an invisible message to be found by shower steam? Even if someone had seen him in a bad state, had been in his room last night—*Knock it off.* Rehashing it would only make him twitchy and paranoid. Well, twitchier and more paranoid.

"We're two minutes out." Colby Winters's foot slammed on the gas pedal. They drove off a rocky, Titan-made path and pushed onto a real road, heading to British intelligence's nearby ops location.

Each passing mile burned Rocco's blood. "Piece of shit terrorist."

Roman and Cash agreed from the back seat.

Winters lurched the vehicle off the road and slammed the gear shift to park. "And we're here. One MI6 black ops site for your terrorist disposing pleasure."

"Good. Let's be done with this already." Rocco kicked his door open and assessed the building: about as quaint and assuming as the last shack he'd firebombed. The difference was they knew he was coming.

The backseat door opened from the inside, and Roman pushed the barely conscious terrorist forward. Rocco let him hit the pavement then snagged him, moving toward an unassuming door. The tumblers of a high-tech security lock released and opened. Half-dragging, half-carrying the man, Rocco stepped into the facility. Still unassuming. Dirty floor. Unfinished walls. Flickering lights.

"Next room," an unseen British voice filtered through Bose-quality speakers.

"Roger that." Somewhere in this place was a top-of-the-line nerve center. How many people worked behind the scenes? How many people watched him at that moment? He'd guess a few.

Another door opened after a quick click of electronic tumblers. Yeah, this facility might look like what he'd just blasted a few miles away, but this one was the real deal. The second room's light flickered less and cast everything in an orange glow. Two armed men stood next to a blood-stained chair. About what he'd expected.

Rocco dropped his delivery, and the sack of flesh and bones thudded on the concrete floor.

"Signed. Sealed. Delivered." He dusted his hands together. "He's your problem now. Adios."

"*Adios*?" The word danced softly in the air of the calloused room. Sexy and exotic. Accented. And gorgeous. "Fine. Adios, if that's what you want."

He turned on the heel of his boot, lasering in on a shadowy, partitioned corner. *A woman?* Behind a screen, a silhouetted figure with a hand on her cocked hip stole his attention. Long legs and a pony tail stood outlined in a magnificent shadow. Holy hell. Nothing about that belonged in this room. This place was violent atrocity. She was a gauzy reflection of soft edges and a smooth voice.

Oh hell.

He hadn't even seen her, hadn't touched her—yet. But that didn't stop his gut from tightening and his eyes from popping. *Calm it down, dude.* This must have been all the adrenaline from snatching the terrorist not ten minutes before. But damn if he wasn't wishing he coulda, woulda, shoulda met this girl someplace else. He swallowed against the boulder in this throat. "What I want has nothing to do with mission objectives."

The metallic clang of tools hitting the cement floor clattered from behind the partition. She let loose a swell of what were probably curses in Spanish, then her sing-song called to him, still hidden behind the screen. "Ah, the American who plays by the rules. How interesting."

Whoa. Instant hard-on. Her accent had him hooked. What the hell was she saying, anyway? It was a rollercoaster of pissed off words, complete with rolled Rs that swayed over his senses. He wanted her to keep talking. Another step closer and he wanted to see her face. Instinct told him it would do justice to the rockin' silhouette painted behind the partition. "Says the Brit who speaks like a Spaniard." *And swears like a—*

"I'm not British."

What else could he learn about her in the next, oh, minute and a half he was expected to be here? Maybe she would keep talking. He'd jump through all kinds of hoops if that woman let loose her accent again. *Please, say something I can't understand.* "And I don't play by the rules. But you—"

She laughed, and the sound slid over his body, winding down his spine. He took in a deep breath, embracing the sensation. Her laugh was better than her words, and he wanted to make it happen again.

"Today." She was back to work. "It looks like you do."

"I came bearing a gift." He looked to the man lying on the floor. "My mission objective is complete, and your invite comes just a bit too late." He'd left a team of men sitting outside. If he didn't walk out soon, they'd make an appearance, guns pointed.

"I see."

No, you don't. You can't see anything, and I'm dying to see you.

It was just a voice. But hell. She was too... something. Rare? Offbeat? Familiar?

She worked behind the screen and walked toward the edge of the partition. Such a tease, like she knew he was ready to knock the thing over to get a good look at what housed her voice, laugh, and never-ending legs.

"Fine. Go." She shooed him away with a grand sweep of her arm. "Team Titan, off to the next job."

The sound of the Ts rolling off her tongue made his chest collapse. Ribs crumbling. Lungs deflating. A reaction based solely on intuition. "You know more about me than I know about you. Come on out of your hiding place."

"Almost done with my prep work." More of that accent that turned him on and made him unable to walk out of the room.

A pause dangled in the air. Rocco heard a zap of electricity, and bright white sparks sprayed from behind the divider. Shock therapy was in store for the man still groaning on the floor, and for a brief second, Rocco almost pitied the terrorist. Almost.

"Perfect," she whispered. More sparks. More zaps.

Without his control, his eyes slammed shut for a half second, just long enough that a cold shiver ran down his shoulders. But he had this. No flashbacks or star-sightings would happen right now. Those zaps were real as the body behind that screen. There was no way in hell this was a hallucination.

She stepped out, an image of beauty in that desolate, craptastic interrogation site. One long leg then the next teased him to the point of distraction. He followed the length of her boot, drinking in the skin tight black pants over the sway of her hips. A black shirt covered her torso and stretched over what he knew were the definition of perfect breasts. Finally, Rocco let his focus caress the curve of her lips, the deepness and darkness of her intense stare.

More than model gorgeous. More than manufactured beauty. She was sweet and sultry. A vision. Standing there, with electrical cables and a torture table at the ready, she couldn't have been more out of place. Yet this was her room. She owned it, and that kind of confidence was unshakable.

He cleared his throat. "Do you need a hand?"

"Does it look like I do?" She looked over her shoulder, smiling a half grin, clearly knowing the connotation behind his question, challenging him to say it out loud. She stopped and stared with narrowed eyes and pursed lips. Then she smiled again, nodding. "Do you believe in coincidence?"

Coincidence? More like luck, walking into a room manned by a woman as deadly and dangerous as she was beautiful and breathtaking. He heard noises from the outer room. Seems he'd overstayed his prescribed amount of time before back up was ready to check in. "Well, I'll leave you to it."

THREE

Yassine Harhour stubbed out his cigarette in a crystal ashtray. It was the third one in a row, and his patience was growing thin. His men were not often tardy. Never were they a no call, no show. His lieutenant was both. Several of his men stepped in and out of the living room of their British home base. Unvoiced concerns upped the tension. The missing man—more trustworthy than most—was one Yassine had found living on the streets at the start of the Tunisian Revolution. He'd taken him in, educated him, offered him food and shelter. His absence was alarming. This lieutenant had potential and been groomed for greater things within Yassine's flourishing network, the Algerian Combat Group. *The ACG.*

He nodded to his men. "Find out what has detained Firas."

"Yes, El Mateperros." A gaggle of men jumped into action. Even his own men feared him, but they stayed loyal. He was going to be an international player, and they wanted their slice of famous pie. Rolling another pinch of tobacco, Yassine admired his favorite view—the bucolic landscape for which the English countryside was known—and thought about the juxtaposition of cultures he'd brought together: his Spanish moniker, *El Mateperros,* his English country estate, and his Northern African combatants.

England was his favorite place to hunker down. Besides all the time spent absorbing their culture for research purposes, it allowed him to enjoy things that Northern Africa or the Middle East lacked. Fish and chips. Newsstands filled with tabloids. An entertaining Royal family. England was also strategic. Other than the ACG's bombing mishap a few weeks ago, Yassine did not believe that intelligence agencies knew he was still there, hiding in plain sight.

"El Mateperros." An up-and-comer addressed him.

"Yes?"

"Firas is gone. His outpost has extensive damage."

Yassine lit a fresh cigarette, sliding it in his thumb and forefinger. When his empire was attacked, his pulse raced, and his addiction to nicotine flared its familiar head. Saliva wet his mouth. A desire for revenge coursed violently through his blood though he didn't know the who or the why. Just that there would be repercussions.

He ground his teeth together and gave the order that earned him the Spanish nickname the Dog Killer. Revenge so great, so fantastically atrocious, that when his men killed, they left a message to others. *If you cross the ACG, no one will live to tell about it. Not even the family dog.*

• • •

Caterina drained the last of her Diet Coke and fidgeted with the empty plastic bottle. She didn't *want* to have a run-in with that soldier of a man, no matter how good looking he might've been. He defined *caliente.* Hot. Hot. Hot. Rugged and dangerous, walking in boots and camo. Her heart pounded, even now.

What was his name? Something that fit with that I'm-gonna-kill-ya look. Rambo, Iceman, Flex. It had to be uber-macho because no one walked around with a ready-to-scorch-the-earth glare unless he'd earned a good call name.

But for now, he was Handsome.

For now? She would never see him again. There was no *for now.* "Forget about him."

And now you're talking to yourself. She cursed a string of red hot irritation both at him and at herself, though she knew she should be proud that her ability to read a person had correctly identified him as the mercenary type when she first saw him hugging a park bench, messed up out of his mind.

Her eyelids sank shut, and she blew out a breath, both a little frustrated *and* a little interested. He was a little of a lot of things that she didn't have time for, especially after a very productive day. Yesterday, she'd gained new intelligence on El Mateperros. He was mostly underground, an international chameleon that intelligence communities spanning the globe had an interest in apprehending, especially after the ACG had botched their bombing in London. Thus MI6 had hired her.

It was a well-kept secret among her intel-seeking-and-sharing friends that she knew El Mateperros better than most people on Earth, a sad secret because her years chasing him didn't yield much information, even sadder because no one knew why. She'd tracked the leader's lieutenant down and told MI6 that she'd extract the information and pass it along if Titan could make the apprehension. It'd been a special request, but British Intelligence knew her well and made the arrangements, no questions asked. She could only imagine what it had cost them to hire Titan. But MI6's investment in Jared Westin's group showed two things that made her *muy satisfecha*: they were very invested taking down El Mateperros, and they wanted complete deniability for what she would do with the lieutenant.

The interrogation went well, and they now knew El Mateperros was searching for a new explosives distributor with his eye on Daniel Locke, an up-and-coming arms dealer with a reputation for being just as evasive as El Mateperros. Locke had first appeared on analysts' radar about a year ago. No one could pin point him or even find out what he looked like. Except for rumors and results, Locke didn't exist. But she could find him. The interrogation gave her enough to extrapolate about an upcoming meeting between Locke and El Mateperros. MI6 was so hungry for the ACG that they'd take the information and run with it.

Something would turn up, and she find Locke and track El Mateperros. She'd take the bastard down. It was her life's mission, the sole goal of her very existence.

Her cell phone buzzed on the floor next to the couch. She answered it before the first vibration stopped. "Yes?"

"Miss Cruz." Her British counterpart's accent didn't sound as calm as normal. "Good news and bad news."

Bad news she could handle. It was the good news that made her uneasy. It was far too early for any kind of good news. "Start with the good."

"Right." A heavy breath. "Well, it doesn't really matter. We have Daniel Locke."

"What? Why?" She gnashed her molars and strangled the cap onto her Diet Coke. The plan was to follow Locke to El Mateperros. "That sounds like 'we messed up,' not 'we have good news.'"

"Well, yes." Another heavy breath. He took what sounded like a long drag of a cigarette. "We *do* know where Locke is. We also learned that Locke was recently married. The story behind the man, if you will."

She uncapped and recapped the soda bottle. "You've said 'was' several times."

"Yes. *Was.* He *was* vacationing on his honeymoon prior to his meeting with El Mateperros. He *was* piloting a small Cessna, which crashed. When I said we had him, I didn't mean alive. Two bodies were recovered."

Caterina's heart sank. Locke was dead, and she was out an immediate way to track down El Mateperros. "But…"

"Back to where we started. No one to track to El Mateperros. I'm sorry, Miss Cruz."

What was there to say? Nothing. She had to find another way. So very close and then, poof, the closest thing she had to a—*wait!*

"Who knows he's dead?"

"What? Oh, well, no one. It was all serendipitous, really. Our timing. His demise."

Serendipitous? Not what she'd call it. "Local police think some John Doe fell out of the sky?"

"We've handled it. A MI6 clean team swept the scene. Nothing to worry about, Miss Cruz."

"I'm not worrying. I'm—" *Keeping this idea to myself.* "Never mind. Thank you for the update."

No one knew Locke was dead, and his mysterious demise played to her advantage. A smile crept onto her face. It was risky and took a major assumption as a cold, hard fact: Locke's reputation for keeping his identity a secret extended to El Mateperros, at least until they met.

All she needed was a new, *live* Daniel Locke.

She looked at the wall of photos, maps, and leads she'd tacked up. If it were a normal night, she'd pace. Thinking. Strategizing. Planning. Instead, she was casting a role in a complicated game of charades.

MI6 would never give her an agent. They wanted deniability. What about...?

A quick flip of her Diet Coke bottle, and she stared at her phone. Small world coincidences happened for a reason. Handsome was in her life because the stars had aligned, and she was meant to stumble upon a guy who could handle this job. Titan would work outside the lines. She'd known Jared Westin long enough that he'd let his man do this job even if nobody sanctioned it. Titan's man could do this. That she knew. She could read people. Hell, she'd read him and had him down to his job description with barely a shared conversation.

She tossed the Diet Coke bottle across the room. It ricocheted off the trash can rim and landed on the empty bag of Funyons. Dinner of champions—or at least of those who valued their time searching for terrorist cells more than meeting each tier of the food pyramid.

Kicking off her boots, she reached into her back pocket. Same as every day, she took out the pictures and went through them, one by one. All five of them, tattered and fingered, the edges softened by wear, the color faded.

Tears flooded her eyes. A Pavlovian response to the years of paging through them and weeping. Yes, she was still upset, still grieving, but really, she wanted vengeance. Caterina blinked her sight clear and dialed the phone number she'd memorized years ago.

The phone rang, and she held it to her ear while pocketing the pictures. A recorded message picked up. "Thank you for calling the Titan Group. If you know your party's extension, please dial it now."

FOUR

Rocco used the retina scanner then scanned his thumb to gain access to the outer hallway at Titan headquarters. He hadn't gone home, having left a very unhappy ex-girlfriend there before his latest assignment. Besides, HQ felt like more like home anyway. After jumping through a few more security hoops, he settled onto his chair in the war room and waited for the others. He was early and had planned it that way so he could drink his coffee and kick it with anyone at the office. But no one was there, except for Parker who was in full out geek-lovers-mode over some piece of techno-babble, leaving Rocco was alone with his caffeine and thoughts. Normally, that wasn't a bad combination, but the note on the hotel bathroom mirror and that sexier-than-hell interrogator were on his mind.

"Morning, roomie." Roman walked into the room.

Thank God. Someone to distract him even though he'd left Roman's only an hour ago. "Morning."

"I didn't see you this morning, thought you'd ballsed up and decided to go home and brave Barbie."

Well, his ex looked like Barbie and was about as boring and vanilla as Barbie too. "I'll deal with her later, if she's even there anymore. Threw some beers in the fridge, consider it rent."

Roman looked at the blank television. "Dude, you feeling okay? Don't you have some *Ice Road Truckers* or *Swamp Loggers* or something to watch?" He snapped his fingers. "Some other reality show crap to catch up on?"

Yeah, TV could've been a good distraction. Where was his head? Too wrapped up in a woman an ocean away in a MI6 intel outpost. Rocco took a gulp of his coffee, then tapped his finger on the table.

Roman kept going. "*West Coast Choppers.* Or is it *Orange County Choppers?* Whatever."

The remote was inches away on the table. Reality shows were his thing, but he didn't move. So there *was* something wrong with him. "Yeah, maybe later."

The door behind him opened.

Roman looked at the door then nodded toward Rocco. "Something crawled up Roc—"

"Don't care." Jared pulled out a chair and planted himself. Rocco blinked when Boss Man slapped the table. "Roman. Out."

Jared was piss and vinegar on a peachy day, so his snarl and growl didn't say much, but throwing Roman out of the room wasn't his typical MO. Boss Man didn't care what he said or who he said it in front of. Actually, he preferred an audience.

Rocco nodded 'see ya' to Roman as his buddy walked out. An uneasy ache churned in his gut. His chest tightened, and his temples threatened to throb. Rocco didn't need to have one of his crazy hallucinating episodes with Jared sitting front and center.

"Things went well with the Brits." Jared cracked his knuckles against the table. "Nothing noteworthy to bring up."

Rocco tilted his head, narrowing his eyes. "Those questions or statements?"

"Both."

"Then, correct."

Jared grumbled, probably a sound of amusement, but who knew. "I need you on a plane back to the UK. You're leaving now."

What the hell? "Wanna tell me why?"

"You've been personally requested by Caterina Cruz."

He didn't need to ask who Caterina Cruz was. The name was as delicious sounding as the voice and body. He pressed his lips together.

Rocco wanted to say that name aloud just so it could roll off his tongue. Instead, he leaned back in his chair, swallowed, and replaced her name with one boring, disinterested word. "Why?"

"Why did she ask for you? Or why are you needed for a job?"

"Both."

"Very few people in my universe have the ability to call in favors." Jared stood and paced the length of the war room. Returning, he glared at Rocco. "Very few are given access to Titan without question. She needs your butt back on a plane. You've been requested. By name." Jared sliced a glance at him. "Or at least description. Anything you're not telling me?"

Well, hell. What aren't you telling me? A lady that good-looking had Jared by the balls? No way. No one would have him by the boys except for Sugar, and Jared wasn't the type to make friends with anyone he'd bedded before his wife. But still, something made Boss Man give Caterina Cruz what she wanted, and that was extraordinarily curious.

"Roc. Anything you need to tell me?"

There was that short list of things he'd been keeping to himself, starting with deliriums and ending with black outs, all stemming from that knife coated in a hallucinogen. But now wasn't the time to bring that up. "Nope."

Jared glared. "She's not what she seems."

"What is she? MI6?"

"Independent operator with a specific focus on the gun trade in Northern Africa."

"Care to expand why a Spanish-accented operator who focuses on one of the most dangerous bevy of terrorist cells in the world is working with MI6?"

"Nope. She can explain if she wants to. Get on the plane, handle what she needs, and get home. This job is between you and me and Caterina. Understood?"

No. Not at all. "Sure."

Jared slapped the table, stood, and walked toward the door. He turned back to eye Rocco. "Nothing else?"

Yeah, I'm blacking out. Seeing stars. Hearing sounds. And a woman I can't knock out of my brain wants me to fly across the globe without giving a reason, and you're cool with it. "Nothing at all."

FIVE

The more Caterina found out about Locke's meet-and-greet with El Mateperros, the better she felt about her plan. MI6 had turned over what they'd found. Friends at the CIA and Interpol filled in a few blanks. But her working assumption that Locke wouldn't show his face to El Mateperros until they met was about as confirmed as it could be.

Even better, rumor amongst the intelligence analysts was that Locke's new wife was just as mysterious. Some had heard about her, but most didn't know she existed. Some said she was a caricature that Locke had built to protect his identity, but with a second body in the airplane crash and photographs of their matching rings, Caterina knew he'd been hitched.

And that was perfect. She wouldn't have to rely solely on her Daniel Locke. She could be Mrs. Locke. She could get in to see El Mateperros and be feet away from the bastard who'd destroyed her life. She would be able to take him out, but not before she talked to him. Touched him. Drained the life out of the man who killed her family, sending him all the way to the devil's doorsteps.

Her throwaway cell phone rang, and she glared at it, not expecting a call or trusting who might be on the other line. "Hello?"

"Caterina Cruz."

A feminine, no bullshit voice came through, and Caterina didn't recognize it. She pulled the phone back, checked the screen, but still didn't recognize the number. "And this is?"

22

"Jared Westin wanted me to call you."

Made more sense, but she didn't trust anyone. "Wrong number. Sorry—"

"Anyway. My name's Sugar. I'm supposed to make sure you have whatever you need."

Caterina didn't need cold calls from a random name-dropping woman. "I'm good. Thanks—"

"You don't need supplies?" An audible smirk wrapped her words.

"I'm fine."

"Ammo, hardware. Whatever you need."

Caterina waited, took a sip of the Diet Coke, and screwed on the top. Nice and slow. "And you are, again?"

"A distributor."

"I have enough of those. Thanks anyway."

"And Jared's wife."

She choked. Jared was married? She'd never expected to hear that. Still not sure she believed it. "As unbelievable as that might be, it'd take some balls to make up a little number like that. But I don't need anything."

"Not so fast, little senorita." Sugar bulldozed past Cat's phone call wrap up. "First thing you'll learn about me is that I call it like I see it. Second thing is, I can hook you up with any weapon you want almost anywhere in the world. I'm your ammo-freakin' fairy godmother."

Oh-kay. "Still not—"

"Why aren't you taking me up on this?" Sugar snapped.

"Why are you pressing me?"

"Because I don't know you or trust you."

Sugar blew into the phone, annoyed. "You're starting to piss me off."

She was already there. "I know the feeling. You know, I torture people for a living. Right?"

"I'm used to getting my way. You might extract intel, but you don't catch 'em. So I've got you there. I'm married to my very own pain-in-the-ass catcher. Do something I don't like, prepare to be strung up."

Caterina laughed. "Jared would never hurt me."

"Pffst," Sugar blew into the phone again. "I don't know if I hate or like you."

"Funny, I thought the same thing about you."

Sugar didn't say anything, and the only reason Caterina stayed on the phone was Sugar was married to Jared, and that amounted to some smidge of respect, at least enough that she wouldn't hang up on the lady.

"I've been called a bitch once or twice in my lifetime." She could picture a brassy woman shrugging as she said that, like she was playing down her favorite compliment. "Anyway, send me your shopping list, and I'll let you know where the pickup is."

Caterina dropped her forehead into her hands. "Not that I'm not grateful, but this is more of a one shot, one kill type situation."

"Oh, pretty little Senorita, let me explain. Whenever Titan comes calling, it's a safer bet to have boxes of bullets on hand. Just in case, ya know?"

No. She didn't know. She worked alone, and while she knew Titan stories—they were legendary—she preferred to do things her way, even with Jared helping as much as he was. "I'll keep that in mind."

Sugar scoffed. "Right. Well, it's your job and all. But you have one of my boys heading your way, and I like to keep them happy. That generally means something with a little high-caliber bang to it."

"No one's here yet."

"Will be any minute, I assume." A bubblegum pop punctuated the snarky sentence.

A twitch struck Caterina. Not only was this her job, but she wasn't thrilled that Sugar kept tabs on Handsome. Not that she was jealous. She just...didn't like it. "Soon enough."

"So he doesn't know your whole story yet, huh? Are you just going to tell him? Or feel him out?"

Caterina's eyebrows shot to her hair. "And you know the whole story?"

"Enough of it. Perk of being Boss Man's wife. I'm just looking after my boy. Not every day Titan sends someone out solo."

"He's not solo. He's got me."

"Well, I don't know you."

Caterina popped a Funyon. She still couldn't decide if she loved or hated Sugar. "But yet you'll arm me?"

"I'll arm someone working with Titan. Yes. No questions asked. And if you want some special bullet to do your one shot, one kill crap, fine. You want it painted pink and with a keepsake memorial case to remember the day, fine. You need to kill a fucker who hurt you and yours? I'm your girl."

Loved. Caterina crunched another Funyon. They thought alike, and Sugar offered her a commemorative knick knack to mark an impending day of death. That was freakin' awesome. Sugar now had a fan in Caterina.

A knock echoed on the cheap wood door of her equally cheap apartment. Her heart sputtered into a frenzy. He was there. She hadn't even asked Jared what his name was because Jared was a mind reader. Titan's all-knowing, all-assuming boss didn't need to see she wasn't one hundred percent focused on El Mateperros. Sugar hadn't mentioned his name either. Cat could ask, but her newfound respect for Sugar wasn't going to let her give the woman any kind of advantage.

"I have to go, Sugar." Caterina ended the call before Sugar could respond.

Cat smoothed her hands over her ponytail and started toward the door. She might not be one hundred percent focused, but she also wasn't about to let some eye candy of a man distract her, not until El Mateperros was six feet under. Then her life would change. She'd set up roots somewhere, have hobbies and neighbors, far more than just a Swiss bank account and a habit of eating her meals from a Quik-E-Mart.

Another knock made her jump, and she opened the door to find his hand in midair, going for another knock. His chiseled jaw flexed, and the chest muscles under his dark t-shirt somehow managed to ripple. She could have sworn to it. And if he'd been good-looking when sick on a park bench or while on the job, dropping off a terrorist to a black ops site, then now, showered, shaved, and wearing casual clothes, he was the type of striking that made shivers roller coaster down her back.

"Hi…" Maybe she should've asked Jared or Sugar for a name.

Piercing chestnut eyes cut straight through her. "Boss Man didn't pass along my name. Typical." He extended his hand. "Rocco Savage."

She hadn't been wrong. Not quite Rambo, but his name suited his body, all solid mass and cut muscle. His larger-than-life hand enveloped hers. It was rough and warm. When he shook, his whole body flexed, causing some primitive, feminine reaction that materialized in a mouthwatering need to step closer to him.

Instead, she stepped back. "Caterina Cruz."

"I did get that from Jared. Though that's about all."

Rocco walked past her, a duffel bag thrown over his shoulder. His jeans did wicked things to her imagination. She closed her eyes to stifle a gawk. No joke, those jeans and that man… no one would hold it against her. He turned around, and her eyes were still butt level. *Fabulous.* She faked a cough-sneeze and spun to make sure the door was shut—it was—because they were both operatives, and leaving the door open wasn't a move either would make, even if she had a bad habit of just throwing them open.

Her cough-sneeze evasive tactic did nothing to hide where her mind had been. It was like she'd never seen a man who radiated sex appeal before. Well, she hadn't. Not like him, but that wasn't the point. Caterina turned back around.

"Doing okay over there?" A cocky grin went with eyes that said I-know-what-you-just-did.

He didn't even pretend to have the good manners not to notice. She murmured a few words he didn't seem to understand. She took a deep breath. "Just…" She gestured to the door, and he watched her wave to the shut door. "Making sure it shut."

One side of his grin hitched, and he had a dimple. "Right. Door's shut. Check."

Caterina chewed the inside of her cheek, not to be outdone by a dimple and a smile. "*Bienvenido.*" She said welcome and that make him smile a bit bigger? She'd have to remember that information. Handsome liked the accent. *Check.* Still, she had an ace in the hole in what appeared to be their nice-to-meet-ya game. He had no idea that they'd met before Titan did the terrorist drop... but using his vulnerability as a potential one-up didn't make her feel awesome.

"Interesting digs." He walked the length of the run-down studio, eyeing the research-covered walls. Newspaper clippings from random countries. Photographs she'd collected over the course of years skipping country to country.

A pillow and blanket sat folded next to the couch. It was a meager setup, but she didn't need much. Clean clothes and a roof. Diet Coke and Funyons. But now that he was in her apartment, self-consciousness nipped at her.

Rocco pointed to the clippings tacked to the wall. Some were highlighted, and others were connected with pieces of red string. "This looks a little like the work of those serial killer types. You know? The ones who tin foil their windows."

"Serial killer?" She shrugged. She was on the hunt, and her target would eventually die. Maybe not a serial killer, but Rocco wasn't that far off the mark, though she was second guessing her plans to invite him in. "It's a temporary site. No access to a fancy Titan war room. It works for the job."

He pivoted. "You know a lot about Titan."

"I know enough." Jared thought she could do this and had agreed to send his man. No way would that have happened if she didn't have a decent chance at success. Caterina pushed her shoulders back, reaffirming that this charade was the right move. *The only move.*

Rocco circled round the room, *circled her.* The bang-bang of her heart accelerated. She felt more like prey than a ghost operative about to offer up her best plan to take out El Mateperros.

Out of habit, she stepped out of a danger zone and into the kitchenette to grab a Diet Coke. "Want one?"

"Diet? Nope." He looked at the window, studying the busted frame and lock. "Fake sugar will kill you."

Ha. "Are you kidding me?" He went along inspecting her studio, like she hadn't checked it out herself. "And what is it you do for a living?"

Rocco smirked. "I try not to get killed. Anytime there's an easy way to avoid dying, it's a no brainer."

She cracked the top of the soda and downed a quarter of the bottle, then lifted it up in a toast. "Here's to living on the edge and no brainer jobs."

A grin tugged at his lips. Yes, he liked the accent. May've even liked her. That was good news because she was about to drop a bomb.

Grin sufficiently hidden again, Rocco raised eyebrows, finally looking more interested in the job than whether or not she'd secured her studio. "And our no brainer job is?"

The bubbles tickled the back of her throat. She tried to ignore the carbonation but scrunched her nose, taking all the seriousness out of what she was trying to explain. "We're taking out El Mateperros."

"El Mateperros, huh?" He laughed. "The two of us? Yeah, okay."

She smirked at his unimpressed reaction. "You're Daniel Locke, the next big thing in arms trading and El Mateperros's next big dealer."

Rocco's don't-believe-ya grin faltered. "You're serious? The two of us and what back up team?"

"There is none." She sipped the Diet Coke this time. No need for another bubble explosion.

"And, what… You're…" He spun in a circle. The man could practically touch the opposite walls of her apartment. "My pretty friend who lives in a London shitshack, running an unsanctioned op out of a studio flat?"

Pretty? Was that him being sexist and condescending, or was he passing out a compliment? The dimple flashed again, and she decided to ignore it as a compliment. She reached into her pocket and tossed a small box his way. He caught it in a fist but didn't look at it.

"What's this?" He still didn't look at the box.

"The scariest thing I'm sure you'll ever hold." With a deep breath, Caterina smiled as sweetly and convincingly as she could. Years of that practiced look failed on Rocco. It felt like he could see straight through her saccharine charade and knew she wanted blood.

"Cute, Kitten."

Her face fell. "Caterina. Cat for short if you must."

"I like Kitten."

She rolled her eyes. "*Estás loco.*"

"Kitten it is."

Fine, be that way. "Actually, if you want to talk names, I'm *Mrs. Locke*—your wife—and you're holding a wedding band. We check into a swank hotel tonight." Shock waves scrolled across his face. Caterina loved it, tacking on a waggle of her brows. "We're honeymooning."

Color fled his tan face. Soft brown eyes panicked. That chiseled jaw dropped, and the dimple fled. But even stunned silent, mouth gaping, he still looked like his nickname.

She laughed, amused and aroused and annoyed. All kinds of opposing feelings. "Don't look so surprised. There's more to our relationship than even you know."

●●●

Hanging with Caterina in her crazytown apartment talking spy games had all been fun and games until she threw a honeymooning grenade. Then he felt like a freight train that locked its brakes, screeching and smoking and skipping off the tracks. Rocco's test-the-waters, check-out-the-girl attitude choked.

He let go of the small box. It hit the floor like it had morphed into a lead-lined anchor. Marriage was marriage, even the make believe kind. Didn't he just escape from one marriage-hungry woman? No matter how smokin' hot Caterina was or how much he loved listening to her talk with that accent, the commitment convo gave him the heebie-jeebies even if it was an undercover ruse.

Maybe he'd misunderstood. He looked at the floor, then at her. No misunderstanding. This Penelope Cruz lookalike had dropped the m-bomb, and he had been holding a ring box. He shuddered. Few things in life sounded like a prison sentence. Marriage topped the list.

One of her eyebrows arched, her dark cherry lips puckered, and whoa, was she sexy.

"So, I should call Jared? Ask for someone else to work with?"

Shake it off, man. This was a cake walk—with *her*, and no way was anyone else from Titan nearing this job. He could pretend he'd just walked down the aisle, and if he got his ass in gear, maybe this op would be all work *and* play. No complaints there. *You got this.*

"Honeymooning?" He rolled his shoulders and snapped his head back and forth like he was walking into the ring, gloves on. "We just got hitched?"

She nodded. "Ink's not even dry yet."

He narrowed his eyes on the pretty pout of her lips, then looked at the box burning a hole in the carpet. Freakin' Kryptonite. Who was Daniel Locke anyway? Rocco's specialty was logistics. He could fly anything. Drive anything. Blow walls down. Take bridges out. But playing the likes of happily ever after? Much as he wanted to see how she'd honeymoon on the job, a chance to take out El Mateperros wasn't worth blowing over some *muy caliente* pussy.

"Sounds like a good gig, but I'm not suited for this job."

His eyes slid down from her white tank top to her blue jeans. It was his favorite look. She'd be fun, a hot handful who kept him on his toes. Or maybe his back…

"You'll be fine." She took a sip of her soda. "I take your silence as agreement?"

Yeah, nope. Too busy having some kind of moral argument with myself, thank you very much. "Not really."

"Come on, big boy. Easy gig. Talk guns and pretend you don't mind me hanging on your arm."

Sounded simple coming from her. Then again, married? "Someone's going to call bullshit. It's not believable." He shook his head, pissed that he wasn't ready to fake it with a foreign beauty rockin' an all-American girl look. "I don't look like the white picket fence type of man. Call your boys at MI6. Find some Bond looking dude."

He paused. She looked amused, a smile ticking on her cheeks, like this was what she expected, and it was only a matter of time before he agreed.

"I don't want MI6, Rocco." She had have rolled her Rs on purpose. "I want you."

The words made his dick jump. Good freakin' Lord. Talk like that would get them both in trouble. All she had to do was throw in a *por favor,* and he might just pick that box of doom off the floor and slip on some new jewelry. *Shit.*

She smiled, and if any man ever told her no, he'd change his mind soon enough. But not him. Wouldn't work. He'd get them both killed.

"I don't fit the part. As much as I want to say *I do* and partner with you—El Mateperros? He's a big deal. I can't let..." *who I want to screw* "...my interest in a job overshadow what's best for the op. The guy needs justice shoved down his throat."

Her dark eyes narrowed, shooting silent missiles at him as if he was already negotiating this marriage minefield. Her interrogator side surfaced. All business. Very deadly. Extraordinarily sexy. What, a woman who could kill him slowly a dozen ways was a new turn on? Hell no. Except for the fact that he was turned on and fighting it. Hard.

Toned arms crossed against the white tank. "Daniel Locke was a wannabe international arms dealer. You think he wanted white picket fences? You'd play an arms dealer. Think about it. You know guns. Explosives."

Rocco shifted his weight. She had a legitimate argument, but she also had an insane plan. Marriage. "Okay. Point made, but—"

"*Ay Dios mio.*" She stared up at him through her dark lashes. "It's the *job.* Over the second the bastard is—in custody. Calm down."

He looked at the box again, seriously considering a closer look at it. Wait. No. He couldn't. Even if he wanted to. Undercover work when he randomly tripped his balls off? Hallucinating at a moment's notice? Yeah, couldn't happen. No way. He'd get them both killed. Or Jared would find out it was still an issue then kill him anyway for not mentioning it.

She continued. "Failing would kill us both anyway. What was that whole line? You avoid death. Don't fail, you won't die."

Exactly. They were on the same page—avoid death at all costs, and because of that, his answer was no. "Look, Caterina. I'm just saying there's gotta be at least a handful of men out there who could stand in here."

A ball-bustin' grin pulled at her cheeks. "A whole handful in the entire world, huh? Guess I am in good company then."

Already saying the wrong things and the ring wasn't even on his finger. This woman was going to trigger some flashing lights in his head if she kept needling him, all sexy and pushy and all. He tugged at his collar. His pretend marriage was suffocating him, and he hadn't even said yes yet.

Yet?

Wait. Not-uh. Not possible. Remember blackouts and fuzzy memories. "I'm just…not believable husband material."

Her eyes twinkled. Thick lashes blinked so slowly he would've sworn the move had been done on purpose. "I'd believe it."

Damn. That accent. And that mouth. The little flips of her tongue as words rolled off her lips were killing him. He was nearly ready to grab the ring box and put the job in motion. So many reasons to walk away…

"I *could.*" He shifted his weight from one leg to the other and looked around the tiny studio. She was playing him. He knew it, didn't care, kinda loved it. Maybe could work around his psychedelic complications. "That's not the problem."

She walked toward him. "I bet you could slide your hand around my waist like you'd done it so many times before."

Man, did she know what she was doing.

"Rocco? You're not up for the job?"

Where was the thermostat? It was getting warm. "I didn't say I couldn't or I wouldn't."

She put her soda on the coffee table—the last remaining barrier between them—and closed the distance, leaving a foot of space. Her spicy perfume and the kaleidoscope of browns in her eyes were the final selling points.

She knew it and went in for the kill. Soft hands smoothed against his chest, almost too delicate to interrogate a terrorist, too feminine to handle torture devices. Her eyes locked on his. The warm air felt alive. Tension burned hot, and that wasn't the threat of imaginary marriages or his hallucinations. That was intoxicating lust hanging heavy.

"What do you say?" Her fingers bent just enough to let her nails scratch the fabric of his cotton shirt, just enough so he could feel the tease on his skin. The slow scratch of her fingernails confirmed she knew torture. The move was fast enough to claim innocence and slow enough to make his entire body spring to life.

"*Por favor?*"

And there it was.

He cracked his neck and rolled his shoulder again. "Alrighty, let's do this."

SIX

Rocco had been married for five hours, and already he didn't know if he could pull off this job unscathed. Bombs, he could do. Faking a cover? That wasn't his scene. He checked the alarm clock on the night stand. Five hours and twelve minutes. Married life was going slowly, even if he was hitched to Caterina.

He'd been learning everything he could about Daniel Locke. The file and all of the lesser known details of his temporary life stared up at him. Not a ton of intel because no one knew a lot about Locke. Roc's eyes wandered. He watched the dangerous beauty he now called his wife. If ever was there a reason to go undercover, she might be it. Still, his big hairy hesitation was his mindfuck. He tried to remember every trigger he'd ever experienced before a hallucination.

So far he'd come up with...nothing specific. What had happened directly before he tripped his balls off?

Watched some TV.

Drank a couple beers.

Nothing out of the ordinary.

His warning signs were clear: the tingles across his skin and the electrical zaps in his brain. Those were the only warning shots that a spell was upon him. Funny, he got almost the same feeling out in the field when the enemy was just out of sight, but attack was imminent.

Caterina had brushed his arm hopping in the taxi from her apartment to the hotel. He'd bumped against her in the hotel elevator.

That had been intentional and all to make a pretty girl smile. It had worked, and *that* made him smile. But now, memorizing intel, his mind was numb.

Rocco glanced at the television, trying to relax. British humor wasn't his thing. Maybe it went over his head. Give him some *Tosh.0* or *Duck Dynasty* any day. He laughed. Hell, if Si and Tosh ever got together, it might be one of the funniest things he'd ever see.

"What's so funny?" Caterina scrutinized clothes in her closet like there'd be a test later. It all looked easy enough. Shirt, skirt, shoes, who cared? But with all that shuffling and studying, it was clear she wouldn't agree.

"American stuff." She didn't seem the type of take his appreciation of *Pawn Stars* and *Dude, You're Screwed* seriously. The hangers in the closet jangled as she slapped them back and forth, clearly having issues with the whole shirt-skirt-shoes debacle. "Where'd all that stuff come from?"

He hadn't checked the clothes for him but assumed he could make fast work of it. Shirt-slacks-shoes. When was the last time he'd worn slacks? Maybe never. There was a lot of personal stuff for the Locke cover. Clothes, luggage. After agreeing to newlywed status, the pieces fell quickly into place. Fancy hotel, designer duds, a bathroom counter that was covered in all kinds of girl crap.

He sat at a small table in the suite's bedroom. Caterina walked to the mini-fridge and pulled out a bottle of Diet Coke. "Can't have an empty closet and…" she mouthed silently, "have it believable."

"Right." He slapped the folder on Daniel Locke shut. It was the only thing in the room that proved he wasn't who he said he was. Rocco walked to the bathroom and pulled out a zippo. A flick of the flame, and the folder with its quick burning contents went up in a fiery poof. Smoky ashes and smoldering bits floated to the base of a massive tub.

One last look at the burnt evidence, and he started toward the door. A button down shirt and expensive-looking khaki pants hung on the wall. Not his typical wardrobe on a job, or ever. "This for me?"

"*Si.* Put it on."

Right…

35

She waited expectantly. "Any day now."

Roger that. Huh, he'd be unrecognizable in this garb. A minute later, that was confirmed. All clean cut, pressed, and ready for a dog and pony show with a terrorist mad man. If the guys could see him now, he'd catch a lot of hell.

"You got this." He glared at the mirror, giving it his best I'm-gonna-kill-you glare just prove the whole GQ look didn't take away his edge. Maybe he'd strap a knife to his ankle and add a nice Glock to his waist. Any good arms dealer would be armed. *Right?*

Adequately reassured, he turned back toward the sitting area. A silky robe hung on the back of the bathroom door, begging him to do a double take. "Holy smokes." He unsuccessfully tried to ignore it. She wasn't putting out, and he couldn't make a move. The lingerie was part of their cover and had nothing to do with what would actually take place while playing the Mr. and Mrs. act.

"Almost ready?" she called from the living room as if she hadn't been staring into her closet for hours.

He partially opened the door, and in the thirty seconds it took him to don his new wardrobe, she'd done the same thing. Bonus points to her for not preening in the bathroom for hours. Another round of bonus points because she was hovering over several handguns, inspecting her options.

One last glance at her, and he turned back toward the mirror, shaking his head at the contradictions that were Caterina Cruz. Candles rested on the tub's ledge waiting to be burned. He picked up a small glass bottle and sniffed it. This was the least Titan moment of his life. Ah hell, but the bottle smelled like Cat. *Freakin' pansyass.*

He put the bottle down before she caught him. The whole hotel suite smelled like that perfume, very… Caterina-esque. Rocco scrubbed a hand over his face and into his hair. What was his problem? *Get a grip.*

She knocked open the open door. "Hey."

He jumped, not wanting to get busted ogling bottles of girly crap. Thank fuck he'd just put that bottle down.

"Ready?"

She was stunning, and he'd never described anything with that word in his life. Her glossy lips and made up eyes were more than he could take. Gone were the jeans and tank top. All American was replaced by All Star. The clothes were probably designer, fitting for an international arms dealer's new wife. His brain scrambled because the whole expensive and extravagant thing worked on her just as well the jeans and t-shirt and her skintight black outfit from the MI6 location. Everything worked on her. "Yup. Ready."

She smoothed the side of a light pink dress the color of cotton candy. It softened her. The woman standing there wasn't a trained killer; she was…Mrs. Locke, and damn if he wasn't stoked to be the Mister.

"Everything disposed of?" She eyed the trash can.

"You checking on me, Kitten?" He had a thing about trust and respect. It drove him to join the Army, pushed him to become part of Titan and strive for leadership. Trust and respect defined his world. He needed it from the team, needed it from Boss Man, but had more or less expected it from Caterina.

She waggled her eyebrows. "Maybe."

"We're all good."

"Good." She nodded and walked toward the front of their big-ass suite. The woman who had pressed her hands to his chest and purred a request to work together had been replaced by an operative forced to wear a pink dress. She was all business and as focused as he'd ever seen her. It was hot as hell.

His neck burned. His chest tightened. Rocco squeezed his eyes shut, praying that this was an over the top reaction to the skyscraper legs parading in front of him. He followed her, his feet feeling that they'd been cemented to the floor. Each step seemed heavier than the last. Piss poor timing if this was what he thought it might be…

Caterina turned around. The fabric of her dress hugged her tight, making him memorize her every move. A blur of haze blocked his view for a hot second. He focused in again on the pink and lost his sharp line of sight again.

Zip. Zip. His ears burned with electricity. Goddamn it.

Zip. Zap. Zip.

Panic swelled, colliding with the reaction that had already started. The one that he dreaded. His palms went clammy. This couldn't be happening right now. Seriously. He'd will the insane episode away. Rocco sawed his teeth and ordered his lungs to breathe steadily.

Zip. His sight went fuzzy, and his lungs revolted, doing their spastic best to throw him in Lake Crazy. The glow from the lamps became shining orbs. The pink dress spun itself into a cotton candy frenzy. *Fuck.* He couldn't stop it and had to bolt. At least he was always a man with a plan and had booked a just-in-case hotel room a few floors down.

He could escape. Trip his ass off. Recover and rebound. It was the only plan he had, but he hadn't planned to use it this soon.

Caterina turned back to him. Her mouth was moving. The words? What was she saying? Something…was he okay? Did he need something? Her arm stretched, and he had to go. Run. Get the hell away from her. Lord only knew what he looked like morphing into crazy-man.

His numb lips moved side to side, feeling the pins and needles. "Change of plans." Did he sound as breathless as he felt? "Gotta run out for a little bit. Just a couple hours."

Not giving her a chance to respond, not that he'd have a clue what she said, Rocco brushed past her. Her intoxicating scent wrapped around him, holding him, telling him it would be okay. *Stop it. Smells don't talk.* But on this acid trip they did. He busted out the door, knowing he could make it to his hotel room and ride this trip out. The door slammed behind him, echoing like a round of applause. The ornate carpet swirled around his feet. The brightly colored patterns crept up, sliding over his fancy-dancy shoes, stroking his calves. Their touch tickled. The walls began to melt, rushing into a beige river and threatening to drown him in the hallway.

This is all a dream. All a trip. Make it to your room. Make it to your safe zone.

He'd memorized the room number. 521. Rigged the door to stay unlocked without leaving it ajar. All he had to do was make it there.

Five.

Twenty.

One.

So close, just a few floors. He ignored the elevator and hit the stairs. No way could he get into a metal box right now. He'd go insane, claw his way out as the walls caved in. Where was his room?

Say it out loud. You won't forget.

"Five. Twenty. One." With the effort required for a Tough Mudder with a hangover, he did it again. "Five. Twenty. One."

You are stronger than this. Survive this mind melt.

Do it.

Now.

And then his angel was at his side, same as last time. It was about the only saving grace he had, knowing that his hallucinations gave him a protector. With his psychedelic angel guiding him through the warping stairwell and again with the carpet that grew over him like ivy, Rocco relaxed into her care and let her save him more one time.

• • •

Yassine rubbed his hands together in the cold rain. Big Ben stood as a cultural icon. Historical. Recognizable. An attack would be respectable. He'd walked the area several times. It'd been harder to see inside the old clock tower. The pain of safety precautions coupled with the fact only native UK residents were allowed to tour had created a research stumbling block. But it was nothing the internet hadn't fixed. Podcasts and videos were posted all over the web. After watching hours of them, he'd felt like he'd walked the three-hundred thirty-four steps himself a thousand times.

Not forgetting the botched bombing a few weeks prior, he knew this was the time to go big. Authorities were scrambling. Newscasts were drooling over themselves, using the name El Mateperros every chance they could on air. Nothing like a panic to up their ratings. And Yassine had plans to up the ratings. For them. For him. For the ACG.

All he needed was for this Daniel Locke to come through with the required supplies. Using a new dealer wasn't ideal, but he'd cut ties with his usual supplier. It'd been messy. There'd been blood. Perhaps too much because his usual backups didn't step forward to fill his order.

But Daniel Locke had. The newcomer. The man who, like himself, seemed to thrive under a veil on anonymity. No confirmed reports on where Locke came from or called home. No photographs. But superior references. Those who had worked with Locke operated as if under some kind of code. They were elite members of a secret club. He wanted in that club the way he soon wanted people to recognize his face. Very badly.

Genius, really. Locke was smart.

Yassine was smart. The two could be good partners.

If Locke was the key to Yassine's successful attack on Big Ben, then they could have many happy years to come. But, if they couldn't strike a deal, or if Locke wasn't what he said he was, couldn't do what the rumor mill promised he could do, then the ACG would move on. Yassine was still working on his old distributors, convincing them future mistakes wouldn't be made and that he was a trustworthy partner. The ACG had a time-sensitive attack looming. He needed a supplier *and* a backup. Wiping a few raindrops off his cheeks, he embraced the cold rain and savored the feeling of it on his skin. Just a few more weeks before the ACG became a commonplace threat, and El Mateperros was a celebrated terrorist.

He walked by a magazine stand. The tabloids and magazines beckoned to him, and a selfish hunger urged him onward. Some organizations pushed for renewal in faith of the almighty Allah. Some strived for governmental power. Maybe a decade or two ago, that was the case for him, but then he got a taste of power and fear. When he'd earned the name El Mateperros on the banks of the Spanish coast, all had changed. Yassine Harhour was meant for greatness. Born to be famous. On tabloid covers and the lead story on nightly news segments. With the Big Ben bombing, Yassine would come out from behind his closely guarded identity and take ranks as *the* most sought after terrorist in the world.

And surely Allah could not fault him that.

SEVEN

Jared sat at his desk, his bulldog at his feet and his wife in his lap. Thelma the Bulldog chewed on a three foot rawhide that Sugar had dropped to the floor when she'd popped in. She smelled like gunpowder and perfume, a mixture he would never get tired of.

"So what are you going to do?"

It was the second time she'd asked and the second time he didn't have an answer. Doc Tuska had called him again, but not just with bad news. It'd been shit-on-the-bottom-of-your-shoes bad news. After Rocco's poisoning in New York City, he'd been hospitalized and detoxed from a mystery hallucinogen. The hospital sent it off for testing. It turned out that poison was a government-sponsored experimental drug gone wrong.

Clinical trials were brought to an abrupt halt when what was supposed to be a truth serum presented as an acid trip. But the kicker was, weeks later, almost every test subject reported full blown and random hallucinations. Some tests subjects had no recollection of what happened when they tripped, and others had varying lengths of time between episodes before it appeared to clear out of their system.

Jared played with Sugar's hair and considered whether Rocco had either not told him or didn't know. Jared had to act fast before dude got himself killed. Sugar readjusted on his leg. The little minx probably did it just to draw attention to her leather-clad legs and those spiked heels she trounced around in.

"You can't just pull him out." She popped a piece of bubble gum.

"I know that."

"But you can't let him run all over England tripping his ass off if he doesn't know."

He rubbed a hand over his eyes and into his hair. "Agreed."

"So you need to tell Caterina."

He stopped rubbing his hair, hand frozen on his scalp. It was a possibility, but how much did he know about Caterina? Enough that he could trust her with one of his men's greatest weaknesses? "That's an option."

"An option?"

"I trust the girl to a point, but giving her that kind of intel? That's a nuclear option. Last resort."

"She's trustworthy."

Jared chuckled. "Oh she is, is she? Cut this BS, Baby Cakes. How do you know that?"

"I can read people. We had a good conversation."

"And I've known her the better part of her life."

"Trust her, Jared." Sugar kissed his lips and tasted bubble gum. "Feel Rocco out, then reach out to her."

"Eh…we'll see."

She pecked him once more on the kisser and jumped off his lap. Thelma stood, ready to follow her newish mistress out the door.

"Traitor." He rubbed the dog's wrinkly head. "A few dog bones, and your loyalty waivers."

Jared picked up the phone to call Caterina. First try. Second and third tries. No answer.

Guts churning, he hung up his phone. Sooner or later, Rocco would check in, and he'd feel him out.

But just in case everything was going wrong, he picked up his phone. "Roman. Get in here."

• • •

42

It was happening. Caterina didn't know exactly what *it* was, but Rocco going from normal to nuts before she could turn around was unnerving. He'd run out the door, and she wouldn't let him get too far. She grabbed her key card then went to the door, slowly opening it and sneaking a glance down the hall. If she hadn't known better, he could've been any man hurrying through the hallway. He wasn't falling all over himself or licking the wall. But he was off, acting drugged, looking at his feet, staring at the wall, dragging himself down the corridor.

It only took her seconds to get to him, and Rocco was slowing down, clearly in another place. His eyes weren't focusing on her. His words didn't make sense. Babble, babble, some numbers, and more babbling.

"Rocco." She sidled up to him, not wanting to surprise him. Not that he would hurt her…but it seemed prudent not to sneak up on a man of his size and stature. "Roc, babe."

His head lulled in her direction. Power ticked in his jaw. Shadows danced in his eyes, but there was no recognition. The man she'd known for a short while was gone.

More babble about numbers and he threw the door open, nearly knocking it off the hinges. One hundred percent of his power twitched in his muscles. They contracted and released. His hands flexed into fists, and then his fingers splayed. Daring against danger, Caterina hesitantly touched his forearm.

"Angel," he mumbled.

She didn't completely understand his gibberish, but his eyes held her, pleading and screaming for help. How could she possibly walk away from the kind of vulnerability?

He blinked hard, scrunching his face, mumbling again. He didn't say Angel. But whatever it was, it was on repeat. He took off, several stairs at a time, and she clung to his arm, determined to stay with him. Shoot, she needed to get him back to their room. He wasn't in any kind of shape to be out.

Rocco paused on a landing. Caterina rested her hand on his shoulder, sliding it down to his elbow. Stepping forward, he moved so disjointedly that it was easy enough to pull him back to a standstill. "Hi. Can you hear me?"

His eyes focused on her, glancing at the lights and the wall behind her, then back to her face again. Sweat beaded on his forehead and temples. Relief washed across his face. The tension melted from his muscled arm.

"You're back." Raw and harsh, his words were painted in a tornado of agony and relief.

She had no idea what he meant. She'd never left, but it was a good thing, and she'd take it.

"Come on, babe. Back to our room." Tugging six-foot-something of two hundred pounds of brawny man was impossible. "Please, Rocco. You're scaring me."

Too many things could happen. El Mateperros's people could be staking them out. There was a laundry list of people who wanted to kill her. Him probably, too. To be out like this, in the open and out of control, was dangerous, and heaven help her, she wouldn't let anything happen to either one of them right now.

Rocco's forehead wrinkled in deep concentration. "Five. Twenty. One."

He watched like she should know what that meant.

"*Que?*"

Vapid stare in return.

"Rocco, what are you telling me?"

His hands found hers, bringing her alongside him. Fingers interlacing. Palms kissing. It was a handhold. A death grip. Life support. And everything in between.

He flinched at the lights, studying his feet as he walked. At the landing for the fifth floor, they stood by the door. Rocco watched the number five. *Five? Five twenty-one?*

"Five twenty-one?" she asked.

His head rolled down and up like he couldn't hold it up, but he nodded. Sort of. She opened the door, and he plodded forward, watching the numbers on each door, leaning back and growling at the wall.

He had to be hallucinating.

Finally, they stood in front of room five twenty-one. The do not disturb sign hung on the door handle. What now? They were going to scare the bejesus out of whoever—

He pushed the door, and it opened. The lock hadn't been engaged. No one screamed as he barged inside. Hulking toward the bed, Rocco got there in three long strides, tearing off his shirt, and collapsed onto the bed. She stood by the door, taking in the drastically smaller room. One bed, two windows. No baggage, luggage, or personal effects. A few bottles of water were on the nightstand.

Rocco had another room? Because of this? This, this, whatever this was. Whatever was happening to him…

Her heart sank, and her arms ached to hold up a man who easily doubled her in weight. He was too proud, too strong, too… just too much of everything to be brought down like this. So vulnerable. It killed her.

"Rocco." She stepped in, and the door shut behind her. "Is it okay that I'm with you?"

Unburying his face from the pillow, he looked up. No response. Just a look that acknowledged she'd said something. The whites of his eyes were red. The pupils fought dilation. The corners and his lashes twitched. She knew that look better than anybody. This was man under siege and out of control. Completely tortured.

She sat on the edge of the bed and cracked open a water. "Take a sip."

He did, still silent, and barely picked his head up off the bed. Power idled in his bare shoulders. The column of his neck was defined in corded strength, feeding into his shoulder blades and sculpted back. Tattoos covered each shoulder. Military. The kind that said he lived for something. He watched over others, a watcher, protector, savior, defender. Tears blurred her eyes. The tattoos spoke to her, and she couldn't even see them clearly through the burning mist welling in her eyes.

Rocco flinched. He stared at the alarm clock, then stopped, angry, apparently losing a standoff with it.

"Are you—"

He roared forward and slammed the clock off the nightstand. When it hit the floor, he growled. Deep. Guttural.

Long seconds passed as he perched on the edge of the bed. Old scars marred his perfectly carved chest. A more pronounced, fading pink scar stood out. She wanted to stare, but he dropped back toward his cocoon of bedding and pillows. He settled down, and she inched closer, testing their boundaries with a careful touch, just enough to let him know she was there, then withdrew her hand, careful not to startle him. "I don't know what to do. Tell me. Please."

Jerking his arm, Rocco's hands found hers, clasping so tight it almost hurt.

She squeezed back. "I'm here." Sighing, he went still again. Soothed. *Gracias a Dios.* "There you go, Handsome. I've got you."

Not knowing what to do, she hummed as if he really were a baby in need of soothing. Petting his head, singing a song, she prayed this would be over soon.

His breathing slowed almost to normal. He had been a mountain ready to crumble, but each limb, every straining fiber of muscle, softened and relaxed. Caterina had never been a comforter, only the opposite. Her job—she wouldn't apologize for it—had always been an outlet for the deep darkness of her own tortured, guilty soul. Besides, intel gathering was for the greater good. A bumper sticker was needed: waterboarding saves lives. Whatever. She wasn't an awful person, just a product of her environment and her obsession.

Still holding Rocco's hand in hers, a respite upon him…

He groaned and flinched away from an imaginary assault. Caterina held tight to their connection, refusing to let go, and his moan made her chest seize up. She hummed again and decided not to let go of him until this ride was over.

Being as careful as she could, she crawled onto the bed and leaned against the headboard. As if his strength had become that of the baby whose song she'd stolen, he was easy to move and reposition. His head in her lap. Her hand stroked his hair, his neck and shoulder.

"Well, Mr. Locke. Not how I pictured our first time in bed." Leaning down, she kissed his cheek. "And I hope it's not our last."

EIGHT

The starched pillow case rubbed against his cheek as Rocco worked his jaw. All his muscles were tired, and he felt as though he'd been sucker-punched. But that hadn't been the case, not if he was in this hotel room, his safety zone. It hadn't even been a day working with Caterina before he ran out the door, and if she was smart, she'd have called the whole thing off. Jared would bust his ass, and Rocco would have some explaining to do.

The alarm clock was on the floor, reading a little after midnight. It'd been one hell of a day. Red eye to London. Met up with Caterina, agreed to be hitched. Moved into the honeymoon suite, and tripped out of his mind. He'd been out longer than usual, his jam packed day probably contributing to the time he'd been knocked out.

He rolled over to his back and stared at the ceiling. Man, now that the end had arrived, he didn't want this job to be over with. Fancy clothes and the lack of C-4 had initially put him off, but it'd been a roller coaster of a day and he didn't want the ride to stop.

So he wouldn't let it. *Get up. Get moving.*

Rocco looked at his sock-covered feet and the crumpled blanket next to him. *Great.* He was getting proficient at hallucinating, to the point he was making himself comfortable. His shoes were by the bed. He got up, slipped them on, and grabbed the only remaining bottle of water. He groaned, pinched the bridge of his nose, and hit the head. A few minutes later, he was on his way back to the honeymoon suite, where his bags were likely packed and waiting. His head pounded, and he was hungry enough to eat an entire box of MREs. Stuffing his hands into his pockets, front and back, Rocco came up empty handed. No keycard. Only his phone.

He leaned against the door, feeling like the worst husband ever— worst *fake* husband ever—and pressed his forehead against the jamb. What would he even say?

"Caterina." It wasn't loud enough for someone next to him to hear, much less an angry Spanish female ready to slice his balls off on the other side of the door. He knocked, almost scared she *would* hear him and then the end would begin.

No answer.

This time, he knocked again. She should've heard that. No answer.

"Cat. I'm sorry."

Look at him, knocking and apologizing outside the door of a honeymoon suite. No way was he qualified for marriage.

"Cat. Let me in."

A bellboy or housekeeping or someone walked by, eyeing him. How pathetic.

The hotel staffer stopped a few feet away. "Are you okay, sir?"

What? Distrustful of anyone, Rocco nodded and went back to staring at the door.

"Are you…sick?"

Guess he looked worse than he thought. "No, thanks, though. Just locked out. I'll head downstairs in a minute for a new keycard." Yup, this moment defined pathetic. He'd fucked up his fake marriage and was locked out of the room before being handed his bags and booted out. No freakin' problem. He would just book it back down to five twenty-one, catch up on some *Man vs. Wild* and see what his boy Bear Grylls had to say. That guy was British. It had to be on some channel. *Right?*

Life advice from Bear would be something like survive the wild, and get out alive. All very pertinent to the woman and the job occupying his thoughts. He would order room service. Sounded like a plan. He also sounded like a freakin' chick. Christ.

"I can help you with that, if you like."

He raised his eyebrows. Still distrustful, he would've put his hand on his sidearm, but it wasn't there. "How's that?"

"If I could get your name, sir?" He unclipped a walkie-talkie from his belt. "I can confirm with the concierge and let you in." He looked at the hotel room door then at Rocco. "You look like you need a break tonight."

A break? Yeah, one of those would be handy. What was the name Caterina had used to make the reservation? Something Spanish… something she said she'd never forget. What was it? *Bingo.* "Last name de Campoamor. First name Dehesa."

A minute later, he said thanks and walked into a very quiet hotel room. "Cat?"

Nothing. She wasn't there. Guess it was easier for her to walk out then bother waiting for him to return. Knowing that crazy lady, she'd stalked down El Mateperros and was reading him the riot act, in Spanish. Then she'd string him up to a metal bar and pull out her electrical wires. She seemed to have a hard-on for taking it to Team Bad Dudes. The woman had become his definition of ideal.

He did a lap around the room. His bags weren't packed and waiting. Not that he had any personal effects, but he didn't want to leave just yet. A pink dress lay crumpled on the floor next to an empty beer bottle. Somehow, that made him miss her even more. Damn it. He'd left an ex-girlfriend at home who wanted nothing more than to create some cohabited life together. That'd been all wrong. Settling down hadn't been for him. Rocco tried. Didn't work. But now Caterina's dress was abandoned on the floor, and he'd give his left nut if she'd walk back in and finish this job with him, if she'd pretend to want to spend the night with him, if she could just lay down in his arms and fall asleep.

Rocco had several options. He could sit alone in room five twenty-one. He could go for a walk. Both of those gave him the option to map out a strategic response for when he saw Caterina. Or he could visit the hotel bar. Throwing a couple back seemed like the best idea. He hit the shower and then sulked downstairs to the bar because the mini-bar wasn't going to do it. On the way to the first floor, he passed the guy who'd let him in his room. Dude gave him a knowing glance, one that said sorry about trouble in paradise. *You have no idea.*

He rounded the corner toward the hotel's bar and grill and came up short. Closed glass doors and a "closed sign" just about tore his heart out. Couldn't even grab a beer. It was the second time tonight that he'd been hanging on a closed door. The hotel guy meandered over. Rocco didn't trust him, turned, and walked away, this time more comfortable that he did have a sidearm.

"Excuse me, Mr. de Campoamor?"

Right. That was him. Undercover work seriously wasn't his thing, and Rocco *really* didn't want a conversation. He stopped and stared back at the closed doors, willing the guy to walk away.

"I believe your wife is still in there. She closed the place down."

That got his attention. Rocco changed tactics, from ignore to inquire. "My wife?" He looked through the glass into the darkened room, and turned back. "Is in there?"

The man nodded, and Rocco couldn't figure out his MO. "Seemed like she was having a bad night too. Asked the bartender if she could stick around for a little bit."

Who was this guy? Some kind of hotel concierge couples counselor? Rocco was always ready for a setup, but the more he didn't want to trust it, the more it was too obvious not to trust. What was the likelihood that enemy combatants were waiting for him on the other side of the door? Probably nil.

There was a much better chance that there was an angry woman with a master's degree in torment and suffering plotting his slow demise. At least he'd get to see her one last time before he left or she offed him. Still, his palms tingled to make contact with the butt of his holstered gun, carefully concealed by a jacket.

"Thanks, man." Rocco nodded and pushed open the door. Quiet piano music drifted from the corner. The lights were low. He didn't see anybody. Not the enemy. Not his pseudo-wife.

"Cat?"

Nothing.

He walked through the empty tables to the deserted bar. "Caterina?"

The music stopped. He spun toward the silence, realizing the sad notes hadn't been background music. It'd been his wife. He couldn't see her, but he made his way over to the piano, hands in his pockets—a dead man walking toward a woman he didn't know nearly enough about. What else would he never know about her once they parted ways?

She sat in the middle of the bench, dark hair falling over her face and hands caressing the white and black keys. She didn't acknowledge him. He wished she'd just rip him a new one in words he didn't know, but that was just selfish on his part. He'd like it too much, and she clearly wished he'd get out.

"I got nothing. I suck. Sorry I screwed our plans." Apologies weren't his forte, but that was about as honest as he could be.

Her head tilted. The dark hair obscuring her sweet face fell to the side, and she tucked it behind an ear. Dark bags discolored the skin under her eyes. Her trademark smile and sass didn't surface. Sullen and silent. Not how he'd normally describe Cat Cruz, but there she was, looking as if her day couldn't get any worse.

Until he walked in.

Regret socked him in the gut.

She turned to him, sliding her foot underneath her on the bench. "Are you okay?"

"Am I okay?" *Hey, what's up, dick?* Or *Get lost. You ruined my op.* were more what he thought she'd say. "Just had something come up."

"Want to talk about it?"

Yeah, no. He shook his head and rubbed his eyes. "I can't get into it, but… I just had to go earlier."

She turned back to the keys and slid her fingers over them. "Sit with me."

His fingers fidgeted in his pockets. He had prepared for war. Not this. Rocco chewed the inside of his mouth. "I should get going. Jared can pull someone else in on the quick. Or, like I said before, any of those MI6 boys would cut their nuts off to play house with you."

Pretty pink lips gaped. Her eyes widened. "You're leaving me?"

"Well, yeah." Shifting his weight from one boot to the other, his hands knotted in his pockets, and his tangled mind couldn't stop thinking she was so damn beautiful. "Just assumed going AWOL meant—"

"Did you have a choice?"

"Excuse me?"

She rolled her wrist. "Whatever it is, the reason you left, did you have a choice?"

"Nope." He shook his head. Wished he did, tried like hell, but nothing helped. "No choice."

"Sit with me." Scooting over a couple inches, Caterina patted seat next to her. "*Siéntate.*"

Move over, reality shows. Spanish was now his crack. He dropped to the bench, sliding next to her. It creaked under his weight. Her spicy perfume hung faintly in the air. He wanted to lean close to her neck and breathe her in.

Caterina tapped a few keys, humming a tune. Very simple. The same notes over and over. He couldn't place it, but it sounded more familiar and comforting than anything he could remember.

"I like working with you." She sighed, leaning. Her shoulder touched his. "I don't want you to leave. But, you, what do you want?"

Nothing appropriate for this conversation. This was a land mine, especially when a slight touch made his skin warm. "Kitten…"

"I pushed you into this. I was manipulative." She banged a key. The harsh noise punctuated her word. "It's the job. My training. I do things almost without thinking. Push people even when I shouldn't. You could be home, watching your awful TV." She nudged his shoulder then dropped her chin.

"Don't knock it 'til you try it."

Her half smile and sad head shake were a punch to his gut. "You could be anywhere but here."

Her voice was like velvet, flooding his senses and causing a rush of tingles to erupt on his chest. He swallowed and didn't know what to say or where to bring the conversation. *Anywhere but here.* They were on the edge of a talk, and he'd never been one for that. He could say he'd been drugged, and the aftershocks were messy. But that would earn him pity. Or he could mention how badly he wanted to kiss her lips, taste her skin…

Cat's slender fingers drifted over the piano keys. She'd given him just enough rope to jump in deep. Or strangle himself. Either or, but jumping anywhere with her sounded fun.

"I want to be here." There. That was talking. A big explosion of honesty.

She nodded, her fingers played with more strength on the piano. "This is a good gig. El Mateperros is a big catch. Guess I can't blame you for wanting to stick around."

What? The job hadn't entered his mind. "I don't give a shit about El Mateperros."

She angled her face toward him, and the browns in her eyes intensified. "But…"

"I want to be here." His heart expanded in his chest. The beat, beat, beat thudding against his ribcage. He could barely swallow. Barely speak. All this honesty was going to kill him. "With you."

"Me?" she whispered, her fingers stopping on the keys.

"I'm here for the wrong reasons." With the tips of two fingers, he touched her wrist and skimmed up her silky forearm. Shivers bit his shoulders. Something about touching the smoothness of her skin made her even more irresistible. If he hadn't fucked their partnership up enough earlier, he was about to do it again.

"You." Rocco touched her chin, her jaw line. His fingers brushed into her thick hair, then back. Both of his hands cupped her face. "I'm here because I couldn't walk away. From you."

A sharp, little breath pursed her lips, and her eyes flashed like daggers. "You're crazy."

"About you."

The surprise and defense washed away. Her head tilted, cheek resting against his palm, a fraction of a move that weighed heavily. It was a go, the thumbs-up he didn't think there was a chance of getting. Ever. Especially after today. From under thick eyelashes, she stared up, so close and not moving. He lowered his lips to hers, and she softened. This wasn't happening. It couldn't be. He'd walked in expecting a boot in the ass and now… His hands slid down her cheeks, her neck, across her shoulders.

Caterina sighed, and her eyes closed. Touching her, causing those little erotic, enticing sounds and reactions, he'd have her on the bar beneath him before he thought better of it.

"Roc."

His lips slanted over hers. The contact was fire. Flames roared through his blood. Red wine flavored her kiss, rich and exotic. She tasted like heaven. Her mouth parted, inviting him. Their tongues met. He wrapped her into his arms. Holding her to him wasn't nearly enough. The clothes had to go. He'd die to see the naked swell of her breast push against his chest. Just the thought made his cock throb.

"About time you kissed me." Caterina twisted on the bench, straddling her legs around him and grinding against his lap.

Eating at her lips, smiling against her kiss, he needed her like he'd never needed anything. "You specialize in suffering. Wasn't going to push my luck."

One hand clutched her hair, the other wrapped around her back, holding her to him. He stood up, setting her on the front of the grand piano. The piano sounded around them in a chaotic chorus as they crashed against the keys. Her arms strangled his neck. She bit at his lip, her thighs squeezing around his hips. From this angle, even if she kept that dress on, he could—

"Everything okay in here?" A voice called from the front of the bar. The open top of the piano most likely blocked them from view. "Mrs. de Campoamor?"

The voice stepped closer, walking in and maybe investigating the crash of music. Rocco palmed the 9mm tucked in the side of his pants. Their interruption wasn't the man from earlier but some other guy about to get a mindful of "get the hell out."

NINE

The charged air hung over them. Rocco pulled back, his eyes locked on Cat's wild ones. Her lips were pinker, fuller, a testament to the last five minutes. Despite the disruption, his erection strained for escape. The khakis dug into him and weren't doing any favors hiding his arousal.

Caterina should move. He should unwrap himself from her sweet body. Give her some space, but she was a sexpot. Her eyes blazed. She hadn't relaxed her thighs, and he was just realizing she had a fist of his shirt pulled between them, holding him to her.

Rocco saw movement by the bar. It was dark and the operative in him wanted to shoot first and question later. But why shoot the poor bartender? Nothing but a headache to deal with later. Still, he never trusted face value and unholstered his gun.

"Mrs. de Campoamor?"

"She's fine." The approaching footsteps stopped. He leaned forward. "Tell him you're fine."

"I'm fine." Her voice was saturated in arousal. Strained and hoarse.

"Okay." Whoever was standing by didn't sound convinced. "If you—"

"Out. The lady's fine." Rocco was unable and unwilling to move from the embrace of her thighs. Jump starting their kiss against the piano was his top priority. The footsteps turned and walked away, and the man muttered for them to take it to their room. *Gladly.*

With his gun secured in its holster again, he bent over, brushing his lips on the softest skin he'd ever kissed, making his way up her neck and teasing her earlobe with a lick. "Upstairs?"

"Upstairs."

He pulled her against him. "Not every day I get to take my pseudo-wife to bed for the first time. All long legs and long hair. Freakin' dream come true kind of beauty."

A blush highlighted her cheeks. She looked away, and he caught her chin in his hand. "I'm serious, Cat. I've never met someone who works me up the way you do."

"It's the accent."

"It's everything."

"Not every day my tatted up, muscled up pseudo-husband wants to take me to our hotel room."

"Oh, I've—" Wait, what? "Tats?"

Her bottom lip dropped. "You seem like the type."

"To have a couple of tattoos?"

"I assume you have tattoos. All you military, black ops boys do."

"I need a second." He shook his head, feeling as if he were missing a connection. Had she checked on him? It'd be easy enough to find out his distinguishing marks, if nothing else, to assure the man who showed up at her door was who he said he was. But why lie? Why pretend she didn't know his name or what he looked like?

He took a step back, knocking into the piano bench. He looked at the piano keys. The song she'd just played tickled a memory. But what? "I need some air."

"Rocco. Wait."

He was already walking toward the door, pissed, paranoid, and pretty sure she'd been checking up on him but not fessing to it. What was the point in lying?

"Don't be like that," she called after him.

He turned, eyeing her suspiciously. "I don't care that you checked up on me."

Her bottom lip dropped. "You don't?"

"But why lie about it? Why the whole 'I don't know your name' bullshit?"

"Oh." She ran her hands into her hair, pulling it off her shoulders. Shaking her head, she dropped it back, stared at the ceiling. "Checking up on you before you arrived—got it."

His eyes narrowed. That paranoid, everyone-was-stomping-on-his-parade feeling choked in his chest. "When else would you have—you know, it doesn't matter."

God, he was shaky. And wired. And losing his damn mind.

She cut a glare at him that clean sliced through him. "Why are you so freaked out?"

Good question. "It's a trust thing. Doesn't matter though."

"Trust. Ha." She threw her head back. "And you've laid all your cards on the table? You're pissed because you think I checked up on you, and what? Didn't tell you? Waste of my time."

A professional intelligence gatherer had her hands on him, and she was too hot for him to say no. "You've worked me over since I met you. Hell, Cat, at least own up to it."

She smirked at him. "Says the guy who ran off on me today and won't tell me why."

"It's need to know. And you don't." No one did. "End of discussion."

Hurt flinched across her face. *Piece of shit, dude. You're a POS.* "Fuck." Rocco scrubbed a hand over his forehead and into his hair. "Cat."

The Spanish tirade started. She took a step forward, another and another until a finger poked him in the chest, and her mouth was moving a mile a minute.

"I have no idea what you're saying."

She kept going. Probably calling him every name she could think of.

"Cat."

The tip of her finger poked his chest over and over. Damn, she had a point. How could he expect her to be totally honest with him when he was hiding a huge secret?

"Kitten."

That just made her angrier. Her words gained speed, volume, and fury.

"Oh for Christ sakes. Ay carrumba, chimichanga. I have no idea what you're saying, but shut your pretty pie hole."

Her mouth froze, mid-foreign curse. She blinked and closed her mouth, almost delicately, which was funny, given the tizzy she'd been in. "*Chimichanga?*"

Yeah, no shit. Chimichanga? He was one bullet short of a full clip tonight. "Got your attention, didn't I?"

"Pie hole?" Her voice teased.

"*Pretty.* Pretty pie hole."

Caterina covered her mouth, failing to hide a grin. She turned away and looked back without turning her head, trying to not laugh and failing. "You're a piece of work."

He shrugged, just to make her smile again. "Better than a piece of shit, I guess."

"Ah, you're a funny guy, Rocco Savage."

"Shhh. Daniel Locke." He stepped closer, mimicking her earlier in the hotel room. "First kiss. First fight—" His phone rang, and she smacked his chest. Not many had his number, so he grabbed it, checking the screen. "Saved by Boss Man."

TEN

Rocco and Caterina walked out of the bar as Rocco answered the call. Jared spoke before Rocco even said hello. "Parker pulled a miracle out of his ass. Might as well start looking for the British equivalent of Cuban cigars because you're gonna owe him. Big."

Well, hello, good news. About time you showed up. "El Mateperros is ready to meet us?"

Caterina's brows raised, and she mouthed, "*really?*"

Jared grumbled. "Bigger."

Rocco shook his head at her. What was bigger than that? Supplies were, and more supplies made him a happy operative. "Sugar filled my shopping list of guns and ammo, and I can pick up my goods in the morning."

Caterina rolled her eyes as they boarded the elevator.

What was that about?

Jared continued, "Almost, but not why I'm calling. But you should know the girls talked. Not sure how that turned out. You know Sugar. No telling how Caterina took her."

Maybe that's where the tattoo tidbit came from? What would Sugar have said? Something about his ex? Sugar was hit and miss in the nicety department. Maybe that was Cat's problem? Girls liked to chat. So she got busted gossiping? That was the issue?

Rocco looked at Cat. Her arms were crossed, and a textbook *mildly annoyed* was painted across her face. Yeah, he might have to dig into the

Sugar-Caterina connection. They arrived on their floor, but he hung back in the hall because when he walked into their hotel room, he didn't want Jared on his mind, but rather Cat in his arms.

"All right, all ready, Boss Man. What's the deal?"

"We've got a solid lead as to where El Mateperros's has a residence. Country estate, not too far outside London."

"You're shitting me."

Jared chuckled. "Dead serious."

Caterina tapped Rocco's shin with her foot. "What?"

He covered the phone. "Got a surprise for you."

Her face lit up. If he could get that smile on her face at least once a day, he'd give himself a grade A in the temporary hubby department even after today's failures.

He turned his attention back to Jared. "Send me what you got. We'll handle it and get back to you."

"Roger that." The call ended.

Rocco pocketed his phone. "Good news."

"Tell me."

"Better—I'll show you. Let's get in our room." He threaded his fingers with hers. "Besides, it's a surprise."

She bumped her shoulder into his and smacked his chest. "Surprise me now."

"I don't know. You did say some awful things to me a few minutes ago."

"Stop it! You have no idea what I said. Besides, you were bagging out on me. I should still be mad."

"Can't stay mad at a face like this." He smiled and watched her focus on his dimple. For all the attention it'd gotten him over the years, it was the first time he cared.

She squeezed his hand, dragging him toward the room. "Come on, tell me."

He scrolled through new messages and handed her his phone. "Feast your eyes on this."

She stared, stopping in the hallway. A little line furrowed above the bridge of her nose. Looking up, back to the screen and then up again, she titled her head. "Is this what I think it might be?"

He nodded, taking the phone back. "I'm your favorite person. Ever."

The screen was dark green with the outline of a house, a few cars, and a narrow road. There were three light colored blips inside the house.

"You got me thermal images? We know where El Mateperros is? *Ay Dios mio.*" Her smile was megawatt. That must've been her kind of present. "How? Never mind! Not important."

She bounced down the hallway. Amused, he followed. Her mind must've been racing. Her mouth sure was going back and forth between English and Spanish. Seconds later, they were in the room, excited to the max, and sex had nothing to do with it.

"I'm not as crazy as I look." She reached for his phone again.

"You might be. But I kinda dig it." Yeah, he was kinda digging her like she was kinda obsessed with El Mateperros. The more he thought about her, the more he wanted her. Any plan to keep away for the sake of the job was quickly becoming pathetic. He tossed her the cell. "Guess that makes me nuts too. Want to go stake the fucker out or plan our next move?"

Catching the phone, she held it against her chest, angling her head so that her eyes did that look-through-the-lashes thing that he was quickly realizing was one of his weaknesses.

"You dig crazy?" she asked, a little too quiet, a little dead-ass sober.

"I dig you." He let the words hang. She didn't move.

Everything tensed. The room slowed. He might always remember that look in her eyes, but he couldn't define why.

Rocco cleared his throat. "So let's follow up on the fucker."

"I've never been this close before." She sucked in her bottom lip. "Love this. Really. This is just… amazing."

Breaking through their heaviness, Caterina jumped forward, locking her arms around him, hugging tight. "Thank you."

The physical impact of her hug shocked the hell out of him. Fevered awareness shot from her toes into his hair. Everywhere in between burned red hot—just because she touched him. He breathed in her spiciness, mouth watering. He closed his hold around her, hugging her back. Keeping her tight against him.

Not thinking, only feeling her curves, he blinked and found he had her against the wall. Pinned. Blood rushing to his cock, he pushed against her flat stomach. His mouth slanted over hers, then journeyed to her jaw, her ear. Kissing her neck. Sliding his tongue down her collarbone. The insane taste of her skin and the intoxicating smell of her hair consumed him. Pushed him to the brink of coming undone. Just couldn't think straight.

"Caterina, sweetheart. I need you." He throbbed, pulsing in place and dying to be inside her. Carnal need, raw and unabated, pulsed through him.

She nodded, breaths hitching. "Yes."

There was the job, then there was her. And the job was supposed to come first. Always. But with Caterina, it didn't.

"Thank God you said that." His hands ran over her, everywhere. Groping, feeling, caressing, owning. Fingers memorized her feel. The touch revved his senses. Tension fueled his lust, which was stronger than he'd ever experienced. More powerful and potent. It was a hunger. He wanted her. Thought about her. Avoided her. Fell to her. And now he was drowning in her. Caterina was his vulnerability, his thirst. One look. One shot. One taste. He was done.

"You're dangerous, Kitten." He could barely breathe for kissing her. "The devil himself couldn't make me stop right now.

She shimmied up his thighs. "I'm an angel. Don't know what you're talking about."

The room spun. Sounds crashed around him. But it wasn't a hallucination. No. This was different. Her voice echoed in his ears.

Angel. *Angel.*

Scary familiar. Rocco pinched his eyes closed. He came crashing down hard. Reality scratched at his perception. A hard and fast detox from a Caterina-fueled oblivion. "Angel?"

"What?" Her breaths were as uneven as he felt. "Rocco?"

He closed his eyes, flashing back. Carpet swirling. Walls melting. An angel by his side. God, he was losing his ever loving mind. "I can't..." *do this.*

Can't breathe.

Can't make sense of anything anymore.

"What." Her voice dripped over him, cold as ice. The *what* wasn't a question. More of a verbal slap in the face, and it stung. Caterina's legs dropped. Her cheeks pinked. From embarrassment or fury, he had no idea. Didn't matter because it took a serious dick move to make her react that way. She was a rock. Completely collected. Man, he was on fire today. One wrong move after another.

He stepped backward. "The job. I'm here for the job."

"Right." The word was a brutal jab.

But he deserved it. "I'm…" *losing my grip. Reliving daydreams. Or nightmares.* He rubbed his eyes. "Jet lag or something. It's been a crazy couple of days, and my head's bothering me—"

Alarm registered in her eyes. "Your head?"

"I'm…" *Unable to complete thoughts… Making moves that I can't cash in… Acting like a bitch-ass pansy. Or, all of the above.*

She smoothed the front of her shirt, unintentionally drawing attention to her killer rack, and if he could've kneed himself in the nuts for pulling a stunt like this, he would've.

Caterina cleared her throat in a cute little way. "Fine. I'd really rather talk about El Mateperros anyway." Her pretty little lips lied to his face, and Rocco knew he would chalk this moment up to one of his biggest losses, ever.

Fuck. He shook his head. Now he was the embarrassed one, watching her try to make him feel better. "Bullshit, no need to make me feel better. Asshole move, I got nothing to say."

"Well, maybe." Her half-smile teased him, and she almost looked shy. *Almost.*

"I'm going to pay for this one, aren't I?" Again he closed his eyes and shook his head, thanking God she was being a good sport about his major poor form. "Don't hurt me in my sleep."

"I won't." She made a cross over her heart. "*Lo prometo.*"

"Look, we've been up forever. I'm dying to get to the ACG house, but I want to do it right. Let's call the night and hit it hard tomorrow?"

She was absolutely giving him an out. Despite what he wanted to do, he needed to take her up on that one. Mental exhaustion wouldn't help in the hunt for the Dog Killer.

She grabbed some clothes from the dresser. "I'm going to jump in the shower, then we can go to bed. Get some sleep. I promise, you'll wake up in the morning and feel so much better."

As Cat walked to the bathroom, all he could picture was the shower-steamed mirror. *Hope you feel better, Handsome.* And he'd never been more excited to crawl in bed and just sleep next to a woman.

ELEVEN

Eyes still shut, Caterina yawned and rolled over in the sea of blankets. Solid man surrounded her. She was tucked under his arm, wedged against his side, and he smelled like heaven. It'd been too long since she'd woken up next to a man. Well, that wasn't true. She'd spent more than a few nights camped out at random covert locations around the world. But knapsacks and a team of black ops dudes didn't count. They were always on the job. She was never interested in them. Plus they knew she could castrate them with a piece of dental floss, so they stayed away. Smart.

All that time spent on knapsacks near stinking men taught her that Rocco wasn't sleeping. She knew it without opening her eyes. How long had he been awake? Carefully, she blinked. His chest was bare. A huge bicep acted as her pillow, and he was watching her. "Morning, sunshine."

As soon as her head had hit the pillow the night before, she'd been lights out, which was a miracle because he had her worked up and ready to explode. A little talk about his head bothering him had taken her down a notch. Yes, she worried about him. But how on earth did she miss out on a moment like Rocco heading to the shower after she got out, then crawling in bed with her? There was no excuse for missing out on that show.

"It's almost nine in the morning. You always such a late riser?" Rocco's voice sounded whiskey rough.

Closing her eyes again, she let it rumble over her. "I wouldn't have killed you if you got up early and made a coffee run."

"Done and done."

"Wait. What?" She propped up on her elbow, her eyes tracing the pinkish scar on his chest, wondering how someone so tough was so considerate. "You got out of bed? Left, then got back in bed?"

"Yeah. You sleep like the dead. Coffee's in the kitchenette."

"Why?" No one ever got her coffee. True, most times there wasn't some place to grab any, but there was always a coffee maker somewhere. Or Instant and some water.

"Why, what?"

"Why would you do that? It's so..."

"Nice? I'm a nice guy. Sometimes." He had her on her back before she could blink. "Yesterday sucked big, hairy monkey balls. Forget about it. Okay?"

"Big hairy monkey balls do nothing to get me naked."

He half-cocked a smile, and his dimple waved at her. "Yesterday sucked. Erase it from your memory."

His forearms were on either side of her head, and his eyes were inches from hers. When he spoke, the words tickled her lips. Heat raced through her. His erection pushed against her as he fell into place between her legs. What she would do for her skin to be bare. To feel him like this against her. All that male beauty made her crazy enough to beg.

"Okay." She nodded, embracing her swirling emotions. Too fast. Too soon. So right. So now. Even after the stunts he'd pulled, her need for him was desperate, and if he didn't touch her soon, she was likely to hurt him.

"We're starting over." The morning roughness still scratched his voice no matter how long he'd been awake. He shifted his weight, and his shorts-covered length rubbed her pajama pants. They had on far too many clothes. She wanted to say something about that, but pure desire colored his expression, such a dominant stare, a face used to giving orders. No doubt he'd take care of that issue on the quick. Adrenaline pulsed in her veins, rushing in her neck, tightening her chest. Need throbbed in her core. She angled so that their friction would torture her in the best of ways. She'd never wanted to be touched more than she did in that moment.

Wait. "Rocco." She lifted her hips, arching into him. Her body and her mind were having a stop-go disagreement. "You're okay?"

"Don't ask me that again, and I'll be fine."

They were a go.

He crashed full lips onto hers, picking up where they'd left off the night before. Suckling her mouth. Revving her from sleeping to sexy with the speed of a morning kiss. Hunger ravaged her. Blinded her. All she could do was feel his hard body and crave every minute caress she could glean.

She nodded, her bottom lip dragging over his. "I won't say another word. Totally silent."

Rocco tore her shirt straight down the middle. Its fabric ripped, and the sound echoed in her ears. He chuckled, cavern deep. "I didn't say *that.*"

He devoured her neck. His massive hand cupped her breast, thumb toying with her nipple and sending a whirlwind of sensation cycloning from the tip to the farthest reaches of her nervous system. Every nerve. Every synapse. They danced and fired and shouted in insane excitement.

"I want to hear you. Feel you. That hot little attitude of yours, I'm dying for it to come out and play."

"*Por supuesto.*" Of course.

"Don't know what you said, Kitten. But damn, that's hot."

Nothing about this was sweet. It was rough, and it was what she wanted. Rough hands. Rough mouth. Rough can't-get-enough-of-you sex.

She arched off the bed, and his kisses trailed to her other mound. He sucked deep into his mouth, rolling his tongue and growling. An earthquake of reactions nearly blew her mind. Skin shivering. Pussy begging. Mind tumbling so fast and hard for Rocco that she didn't know which way was *like* and which way was *lust.*

"Roc." They were moving fast, exchanging real rings with pretend meanings, but she'd take it. His hips flexed, and she met his move. "Take your shorts off."

"You first, Kitten." His lips tickled her nipple. Gasoline to her fire.

His hips shifted, and her body's begging and pleading magnified. She shucked her pants, grabbing his along the way. Made her giggle, made him smile. Made for the perfect moment.

They were naked. Tangled. Hot flesh and wild need. The stalk of his erection was far past impressive, hot and in her hand. She stroked her fingers down to his balls, letting her other hand trail.

"First time I saw you, I wanted this," he growled.

She nodded because she was choking down the same thoughts and so much more, scared it would make him run. Again. And then she might kill him.

He grabbed his wallet from the nightstand drawer, found a condom, and slid it on.

Smoothing his hands over her folds, he teased the nub of nerves with a stroke of his knuckles. "You are so damn sweet."

Why sweet? She was anything but. Hard-shelled. Hot-headed. And when he looked at her like that, touched her without slamming into her, Caterina believed him. They would do both wild and unrestrained, but they could rock a moment that might just qualify as special. He ran both hands down her thigh, cupping behind her knee and angling it, dragging the heel of her foot back. Rocco leaned over and kissed the knee, sliding her other leg up.

Exposed to him, she fought for contact, but Rocco simply slid his hands down her thighs, watching her face. "Prettiest pussy I've ever seen."

Heat flooded her face.

"You don't think you're all that sweet, do ya, Kitten?"

"I have my moments."

He laughed and she grabbed him around his neck, pulling close, chest to chest. One of his hands clamped to her bottom, squeezing the cheek, making her back buck. The hot steel of his cock positioned, pushing and parting. Her nerve endings screamed, and spectacular sensations wicked from her core to her clit.

"Sweet, sweet." He buried his face into her neck, biting and scratching her skin while he stretched into her body, joining them.

Breaths stolen, her mind spinning, Caterina bit her bottom lip and let him take her. "*Dios.*"

"That's my girl."

Her mouth parted. She moaned, "Rocco."

Pressure and perfect pain. It'd been so long since she'd felt this. She wanted to groan and growl, shout his name and beg him to fuck her, but it came out a desperate hush.

He paused. A ragged breath tore from his chest as he retracted only a fraction and eased into her again. Biceps crushed her to the wall of his rock hard stomach.

She forgot the world in his strength. "I need this."

"I need *you.*"

Vibrations buzzed across her skin, and she rocked her hips, rubbing herself against him and experiencing every thick thrust. She came alive for him. Slickness coated his shaft, her juices heightening the sensations. Her mind memorized the deepness in his eyes, the concentration and determination playing across his features.

They locked eyes, and vicious tension clawed just beneath her skin. She nodded, agreeing. And that was it. He dropped her back against the mattress, diving deeper into her sex, filling her when she thought fullness had long been achieved. Caterina pushed her head back, moaning as Rocco thundered into her. Her body flowed with him. They were a frenzied mix of penetrating, panting, cursing, and crying out for more. Relief and release seemed too far away. He pulled back, on his knees, grabbing her legs and spreading her wider. The dedication in his jaw was too powerful not to notice.

He lifted her ass off the bed, shoved a pillow behind her tail bone without missing his stride, and—oh hell, that angle…

She cried his name. Sucked in oxygen and savored the passion, the picture, everything before her. His chest was massive. Defined. His broad shoulders were enough to support a tank. Taut skin covered perfect abs. Sculpted. Muscles bunched and corded. Rocco thrust into her again, deeper, until possession was no longer a question.

"Yes," she ground out the word, ready to repeat the truth. Sweet bliss started. Thinking about him, them, this…that would make her come.

"Caterina." He sucked her name through his clenched teeth.

She didn't recognize herself. Losing control had never happened, but now it was. Rocco met her stroke for stroke. The bastard would kill her with pleasure, she was sure of it, but she'd die happy. This was too good to just do once. She'd live to fall in bed with him again. It was a promise to herself.

"Roc." She couldn't catch her breath. Didn't want to try. Breathing was for wimps. This was the major leagues, and if she was going to survive, it had nothing to do with oxygen. "Help me." Breath. "Hold me. Push me over the edge."

His jaw worked. Resolve painted across his face. Sweat beaded on his forehead as her juices wept from her, coating both of them.

"So close." Her fingernails ripped into the sheets.

His hips pistoned, driving until she couldn't see. Fireworks exploded behind her eyes, between her thighs. Her muscles tightened until…she combusted, rippling over his cock. Pulsing. Tensing. Extraordinary flashes of satisfaction blew through her veins, and when she thought it wouldn't last another second, when she was too sensitive to be touched, Rocco slowed his roll and kissed her through the amazing intensity. His head rolled to the side, dropped back, then he inhaled, expanding his chest wider than she thought possible. Slowly, he brought his gaze back to her and lowered himself down, his face mere inches from hers. "I need you close to me."

She nodded; she might've been crying, might've been cursing. She didn't know what she was doing.

"Let me hold you close." The tinge of sadness in his voice brought her back to his arms.

Her heart clenched. There was something about that gravelly, forsaken sound. "Rocco?"

He shushed her with a kiss. Soft, again. Back to where they'd started. He was wounded, though he'd never tell. Required loving and caring, but he'd never ask. She knew that about him, just like she'd known who he was when she first set eyes on him on that bench weeks ago. And right now, she knew that the couldn't-wait-another-second frenzy had morphed into a couldn't-crave-you-more-than-now dance.

Rocco's chest pressed against hers. A fine mist of sweat kissed their skin. Her legs wrapped around him, then her arms did the same, hugging and holding onto all the power and strength that made him loom so large. His hips rocked her slowly over and over. The intense, overwhelming fullness short circuited her brain until all she could think, see, and believe in was them. Her tongue explored his skin. His saltiness seared her taste buds, and the sweetness of the man holding her stole her heart.

"Damn, you are amazing," he whispered into her ear.

Amazing?

Her? Not really.

Them? Absolutely.

His body swallowed hers; his embrace all-consuming, so powerful and delicate. Easing and penetrating, slow and steady, thrusts that made her mind desperate for their interlude to both last for hours and demand relief, again.

"Roc." Shivers swirled over her sweat-dampened skin. All she could do was repeat his name. And beg.

"What do you want, Kitten? Tell me what you need." His teeth scratched her neck and chipped away at her sanity. Rough hands swayed over her back, cupped her ass. She could feel him all over.

"This. You." Their passion flooded her. "I want nothing more than you—" *Handsome.*

She almost said it. Almost did it again, where she showed her hand and told him the things she was keeping to herself. *Like the tattoos.*

His mouth took her, languidly. Tongues dancing and dueling. He kissed the side of her mouth, her cheek.

Drowning in his scent, succumbing to emotion she would never admit to, Caterina embraced another incoming climax, wanting nothing more than for him to come with her. Waves of pleasure hit them both. His hips surged. With spastic thrusts, he shuddered, holding her to him. A heavenly second of watching him completely lost in her was all she needed to come again. Lost in a dream of what a normal life could be, she memorized the feel of his arms and pretended he was her lover, not her partner. The idea was entirely too tempting.

TWELVE

Caterina fell back asleep in Rocco's arms. He scrubbed a hand over his head. Last night, she'd been asleep when he crawled into bed, and he'd stared for hours before somehow falling asleep. It was wrong not to tell her where he'd gone, what had happened to him yesterday, if for no other reason than he might endanger her life. A bad trip in the wrong location. Hell, any trip at an inopportune moment could get them both killed. Guilt was a wrecking ball. And he'd had the opportunity to walk out. He'd had the chance and intelligence not to strip her down and dive onto her naked body, but he had ignored reason.

Damn.

He rubbed his head again, scared to look down at her. It hadn't been all fast and hard, not at all, and that was some scary shit. Something between them rocked his sensibilities, making hot sex that could have been nothing more than an adrenaline-filled free for all into something he'd memorized. Every move, sound, sigh, and climax, was scored into his memory. He'd dragged it out because fucking her was insane. Goddamn, this was bad news. He liked it. A lot.

Get your game face on, man.

The internal pep talk didn't work.

Rocco sat up, tucking her against him, and grabbed his barely warm coffee off the nightstand. Dark, mussed hair covered the side of Caterina's face, and he moved a few strands to see her better. He'd let her sleep because if she woke, he'd talk to her about op jobs and torture tactics. About how Titan and whatever drove her to this line of work always came first. Cat was different. His job was the most important thing in life, and Cat would totally get it.

Yeah, if she woke and opened her mouth, saying something all sexy like *let's go blow this up*, or *wanna catch a terrorist today*, in that killer accent, he would fall for her.

They'd check out El Mateperros's location later that day. Focusing on that terrorist piece of shit was a solid plan. Playing the part of Daniel Locke was part of bringing that POS to justice, but working this op was an eye-opener. It made him realize that it was possible to have as much passion for something that wasn't Titan. And that was Caterina Cruz.

• • •

Godforsaken rain had drenched the entire city for the past few hours. Out of habit, Rocco's eyes searched the sidewalks and front entrance of the hotel, always looking for threats. Nothing caught his eye. Travelers. Tourists. Bellhops. All looked ordinary enough. After shutting the door behind Caterina and throwing their gear bags in the back seat, he circled the front of the Audi. The hood was warm in the cold weather thanks to the valet bringing it up.

He tapped on the quarter panel, slid around for his door, and slipped into his seat. "You ready?"

She smiled. "Haven't been this excited in so long."

Raising eyebrows, he raked a look over her, intentionally reminding her of just how excited she'd been recently. "I might take offense to that, Kitten."

A gorgeous blush lit her cheeks. "You play the newlywed card well."

"I'm not the only one. Let's do our recon then get back to it."

A taxi cab cut in and idled in front of their car. He mentally cursed the backward way everyone drove, checked his mirrors, looked over, and—the passenger caught his eye. Rocco's mind lurched.

"Give me a sec." Opening the door, he cautiously stepped out.

No way.

He angled to the side, backing a step for a better look at that fellow. Tall. Broad. Business attire. Maybe strapping, judging by the bulge at his back. If Rocco could just get a better look at the guy paying his fare and talking to the bellboy.

He shook his head. That massive dude looked a lot like…

"Hang tight." He held one finger up to the window.

Cat nodded.

Two steps later, and he cut the guy off. "What the fuck?"

It didn't make sense, but nothing had on this job.

Roman's eye narrowed. "You owe me."

"What are you doing here?" Rocco looked at Roman from head to toe to baggage and back again. "Are you wearing loafers?"

"Yeah, this wasn't my idea, buddy." Roman pulled at his collar.

Button down shirt. Pinstripe tie. Sports coat and slacks. "You look fuckin' ridiculous."

"As do you, asswipe."

Rocco looked down. His outfit mirrored Roman's. Fuck. He did look like a tool. "For the job."

"Same. Since your ass apparently needed a Brooks Brothers hand."

"No way. Get out. Go home."

"Not my orders. Take it up with Boss Man."

"Shit." Why was he so pissed anyway? One of his main concerns was their manpower limitations. Taking out El Mateperros with just the Cat-and-Roc twosome seemed borderline insane. Still, his chest felt tight. The urge to grab his girl and run took hold.

With Roman around, spending every waking second in bed with her wasn't going to happen. He and Cat could play husband and wife to a certain point, but with his boy there, he'd have to take the charade down a notch or two in the hot and heavy department.

"We're on our way out."

"No problem. I gotta check in, do my thing." Which probably meant grab a couple beers so he could handle to the suit and tie. "Here."

Roman reached into a *brief case*. And now, Rocco had seen it all.

"Is that a purse?"

"Jared would understand if I pummeled your face in." Roman kept searching. What did he keep in there, anyway? Wasn't as if it was an actual, in-use briefcase. "Read this, jackass."

Rocco laughed, watching Roman tug at the tie and smooth his jacket. "More paperwork. I've never been on an op that required this much reading."

"Glad I'm not alone." Roman handed him a folder of papers then undid the top button under his tie. "Find me at the bar later."

"It's going to be a few hours."

"Trust me. That's where I'll be."

Rocco slapped his shoulder. "See ya."

A bellboy nodded to Roman. His bag sat stacked on a cart. Rocco thought about giving him hell for not caring one stupid bag, but then again, he'd done the same thing. Both them were trying to fit into the role of having more money than God, earned behind a desk. Titan paid well, but they absolutely didn't have to wear suits and ties.

He rolled the folder and turned toward the Audi. Caterina's gaze followed Roman until he went through the hotel's sliding doors. Then it shot to him. Rocco rolled his eyes, shrugging, then got in the car.

"Here you go, Kitten." She could be in charge of their reading assignment.

"What's that all about?"

It was a freakin' buzzkill was what it was. "And then there were three."

"I don't understand."

"Me either. Read that, and see if we learn anything worth a damn."

They pulled out onto the main road, and he followed the directions that he'd memorized to the location that Parker swore was El Mateperros's English home base. Caterina paged through the folder, and the sound of papers shuffling made him more anxious.

"We know all this. Duplicates of the images Titan pulled. The only thing new is the addition of the Locke's *bodyguard*, who was your friend, I assume. It's a backup plan."

Jared never made backup plans without a reason. There could be a hundred reasons, and none of them were great for Rocco.

"His name is Roman."

"Well, the paperwork says his name is Liam Laird."

Rocco drummed his fingers on the steering wheel. What was Jared's move, and why didn't he see it? The next forty-five minutes of their drive was silent, and he searched for the reason Roman had shown up.

"Here we go." Nothing came to mind.

He pulled onto a bumpy side road. Trees reached high overhead and arched over their jangled pathway. As long as Jared didn't know Rocco had slept with Caterina or that he had a serious mental mishap, he was golden. He pulled the Audi over into a location Parker had scouted via satellite images. The site would leave the vehicle out of sight unless someone was really looking, and far enough away that it wouldn't be a red flag to anyone working with the ACG. Without saying a word, Caterina slid into the backseat, stripping off her clothes. It'd be so wrong not to steal a glance, and before he opened the door and changed, Rocco watched in the rear view mirror.

"Pretty, pretty, Kitten."

Long black leggings covered her legs. She lifted her ass to scoot them on. "I thought it was pretty pie hole."

"Never livin' that one down, huh?"

"Get dressed." She slipped on a skintight black shirt, dropped the clip out of her Beretta, and inspected it before sliding it back in.

If he wasn't careful, they'd slip onto El Mateperros's property while he was sporting a hard-on, and that would be a bitch to run with. He shucked the khakis and button down, donning camo cargos and an UnderArmor shirt. Suddenly, he could breathe again.

"Looking good." She jumped back into the front seat and handed him two handguns plus a package with activated listening and tracking devices. "Here."

He tucked a Glock into his back, stuck the other into his leg holster, and looked over. Caterina held a serrated blade between her teeth as she held secured a 9mm into her waistband. Forget *Fantasy Island*, and screw porn. That was about the sexiest thing he'd ever laid eyes on.

Her cheeks pinked again. "What? Why are you looking at me like that?"

Words wouldn't come. A blade between the teeth turned him on far more than anything soft and see through, not that he would complain about that either. The whole image was just something else. "I've never—you're freakin' badass, Kitten. Hot as hell."

She took the blade out of her mouth and sheathed it. "And don't you forget it."

He reached across the drive shaft, grabbed her around the waist, and pulled her sweet body into his lap, kissing her until he couldn't think straight. There. He'd needed that. Maybe now he could breathe. "Goddamn, you drive me crazy. Let's roll."

They tumbled out the car, a mess of arms and legs. His heart beat heavily, and dread tapped him on the shoulder. Suddenly, he wasn't thrilled that Caterina was within a click of a terrorist known for offing families for fun.

THIRTEEN

The gray sky misted. Rocco studied Caterina's face. Her eyes were bright, searching down the road they would take to El Mateperros's British HQ. According to the reports they'd read, the ACG hadn't spent much time here until recently.

With a suspected attack imminent, the terrorist leader had been making waves, though no one could pinpoint from where. Well, they were about to blow the lid off that intelligence blockage. If they could accomplish their job today, intel would feed straight to Parker's room of bitchin' binary shit. Jared would make sure analysts got their hands on every piece of data they found. All in the name of justice.

That fucker-in-hiding—going around the world and blowing crap up while pumping up the ACG's reputation—would have his day of reckoning soon enough. Rocco couldn't wait to drag him out of his little country bumpkin estate and sling him up. How many countries would fight over who got him first?

He double checked that their Audi was out of sight. It was. "Ready?"

Caterina nodded and was already moving toward El Mateperros's place. It took them five minutes to reach the outer perimeter. A stone fence. Good look, but poor defense. Give Rocco a charge and a few blocks of plastics, and he could make the fence fall like stacked dominoes. It'd be quite the show. Cat would like it, but impressing her wasn't on the agenda. Nor was making a scene. But still… she'd like it.

Really? He rolled his eyes at himself. Between wanting to impress her and wanting to have her tucked away safely, Rocco's attention was distracted at best. He cleared his mind but still smelled her perfume. Shit. With her an arm's length away, he considered recalibrating their plan. They had to slip in, scout the scene, plant a couple of bugs, and get back to the car. But the idea of separating from her didn't sit well. He looked at his watch. Their goal was in and out in forty minutes, and they were already ahead of schedule. He frowned, mind clouding with thoughts of her. They could get in and out and home before—

A hotel room isn't a home.

"I don't see anyone," Cat whispered over her shoulder as they slunk closer.

She'd taken their forward position. A cutesy-fancy country house came into view. Couldn't the ACG find a manlier place to call British HQ? This place looked like his grandma's dream come true. It screamed doilies and banana bread, not international terrorist. But Rocco had to give credit where it was due. This was a great cover.

Caterina looked equally unimpressed. "You sure this is the right place?"

"Coordinates match."

"Maybe your boy Parker is wrong."

Rocco laughed. "Yeah, nope." A smaller stone fence surrounded the two-level house. Ivy grew up the walls, and there were outbuildings behind—probably a barn, though it didn't look in use.

"Same plan?"

Unless she decided to call the job off, his mouth was sealed, no suggestions for her to hike it back to the Audi. He nodded. "You take right, I'll head left. Meet you in the back."

Caterina took off before he could tell her to be careful or watch her back. It would've made him an ass, but a little name-calling didn't hurt. Besides, what would he say? *I don't like you running around with a couple guns and a knife the size of your forearm.*

The truth would earn him a piece of her mind, most likely in Spanish, which would get him all bothered and make him want to leave her someplace safe. Or someplace they could be alone. Their circle of banter would commence. But his reasoning was well thought out. Hand-to-hand battle wasn't her specialty; breaking a man's mental barriers was.

Rocco continued to watch her instead of moving to his first location. Fuck, man. That Spanish beauty was giving him heartburn. She was out of sight in seconds, and he was still squatting behind the fence, wasting time. Ducking, he ran to the first of the three spots that he needed to check while dropping listening bugs and location trackers.

First, he hit the Jaguar in the driveway. No cover, but it would only take him a hot second to stick the homing device in the wheel well. He activated it, sidled up to the exterior wall, and waited for Caterina to take her position opposite him. If she gave a thumbs up, he could plant the device. Thumbs down, he had to move on.

What was taking her so long?

Seconds ticked by. Anxiety built in his chest. Something had happened to her. Someone had seen her. Captured her. Hell, if someone hurt her, Rocco was going to go ballistic. Maim and kill. What the fuck? Where was—

Dressed in all black, sexy and stealthy, she appeared in her designated spot, arm out and…thumbs up. He had a go. He dove to the Jaguar, slipped the tracker onto the dirty underbelly near the tire, and busted ass to his next location. Looking over his shoulder, he couldn't see her anymore and decided he should've kept her with him. They could've swung through the property together. It'd take twice as long, but why did that matter?

The next twenty minutes were a blur. One location to the next. He set the listening and tracking devices then hauled back toward their rendezvous spot. She was there waiting, and soon as he set eyes on her, he ran faster. His heart pounded, not from exertion but anticipation. A cherry-colored, megawatt smile and exertion-flushed cheeks painted her absolutely gorgeous. But that didn't matter. Unneeded risk on her part jumbled his mind. Honestly, he didn't need a thumbs up or down. He could get to that Jag without her help, and even if he couldn't, they didn't *need* to have a tracker on El Mateperros's vehicle. They could survive without it.

"Let's go." He moved past her, leading the way this time. If a threat was jumping out, he was taking it down.

"Job well done to you, too."

Over his shoulder, he glanced at her pretty pout. "Come on."

"What's your problem?"

"Nothing." *Everything.* If his freakin' hallucinations weren't a problem enough, now he had a chick messing things up in his head. He'd thought he left girl problems back in the States.

She's your partner. Act like it.

She's a woman you're digging. Protect her.

The two lines of thought battled, and he ignore Caterina's barrage of questions as they jogged back to their hidden Audi. He opened the driver's door and got in, turning over the ignition. They could disarm later. They were far too close to the ACG for comfort, and he wanted to hit the road. ASAP. Caterina stood outside his door, hands on hips. Not moving.

"Come on." He rolled his hand. "What's up?"

Her damp hair was smoothed back, and her skin glistened from the falling mist. "Out of the car, Rocco."

Dropping the name. She meant business. Too bad. "No time, Kitten. We gotta roll." *And I have to get your cute butt farther away in a hurry.*

"Get out of the car, Rocco Savage. Now." Oh, first name, last name, she was pissed.

He had zero idea what could've gone wrong or what he'd done, but an anxious pressure weighed on him. If he appeased her, they could leave sooner. Rocco got out. It'd only take a second. Maybe. "Cat—"

"What the hell is your problem?"

Maybe longer than a second…

"Nothing. Let's go." He turned back to the door, but she snagged his arm and bent it back. The woman was a pro. Kind of made him proud of her. "Seriously, Kitten. What—"

"You first. What's your problem?"

He could overpower her, break free. But—hell, that wasn't the point. "I don't have a problem. Cut it out."

She turned up the heat, wrenching his arm further up. "Spit it out, big boy."

"Okay already. Don't make me drop you, Cat."

She let go, and he turned around to see her pace a tight, angry circle. "Rocco."

"I wasn't thrilled you were out there. That's all."

Her mouth gaped, and she stared at the sprinkling, spitting sky. When her gaze leveled back, her eyes were narrowed damn near to slits, and she was ready to kill. "You cannot be serious."

"What?"

She rubbed her temples. "Tell me that you would've said that twenty-four hours ago. That you would've pulled this crap *yesterday*."

What was she talking about? "I don't—"

"Tell me that you didn't conjure up this uber-protective junk because we had sex this morning."

Bull's eye. She'd nailed it, and he hadn't even known that was dead center of his issue. Kissing on her seemed a lot better than working with her.

"I don't know if I can, babe."

"Yesterday afternoon, you would've told me to go after El Mateperros."

He nodded "Yeah, well, that was yesterday. Life changes."

Fire exploded in her eyes. The browns went nearly black. Anger. Fury. Passion. They collided on her face. Her arm roared back, and her fist slammed into his jaw.

"As you Americans say, this sucks."

She had a hell of a right hook.

Working his jaw side to side, he had to give her credit. That surprise packed a wallop. He ran his tongue along his teeth and rubbed his cheek, tasting a hint of blood.

"Fine. Sleeping with you was a game changer. Get over it." Soon as it came out, he knew it was the wrong thing to say.

"Get over it? No I will not." She stormed to the rear car door, shucking off her weapons. Holding that blade in her mouth again, she opened the car. He watched as she stripped down to her bra and underwear.

Mother of God, did that woman have a body he'd kill to touch. Lick. Kiss. Worship. She stood in the drizzle, wearing silky, lacy underthings that were perfectly see-through. "Too bad, girl."

"Too bad?" She growled at him, pulling her dress back on. "Too bad?" That time she screamed. "You sexist, chauvinist piece of—ugh!" She tore her hands into her wet hair. "You have no idea—*no idea*—the hell that bastard has caused me. And one time in bed with you? You're all of a sudden going to try and change that? No. Hell no."

What? "El Mateperros is...what? Personal?"

Red-faced and pacing, she blew out a breath. "It doesn't matter if he is or if he isn't." Her hands went back into her hair. The light rain caused her hair to curl. She stared into the sad sky. He watched while she stood still, her dress beginning to soak and cling to her curves. "Why, Roc?"

Now he was beyond confused. "Why, what?"

Confusion, hope, anticipation—he didn't know—crossed her gorgeous face. "Why's it a game changer?"

Well, shit. He asked for that one, didn't he? "Come on now, Kitten. We're married and all. I have to protect you. My role's going to my head."

"No. Answer me." Rounding the backside of the Audi, she wobbled in the gravel and mud until she hit pavement. It wasn't nearly enough time for him to come up with an answer. "Sleeping with me was a game changer. *Por que?*"

That Spanish of hers was like a truth serum. "Because you're beautiful. And in my head." The thick beat of his heart pounded. He craved her body against his. "I'm liking you a lot, and I never know what will come out of your mouth. Half the time I don't understand it, but every time, I'm dying for it to happen again."

"Roc..."

He grabbed her around the waist and pinned her against the Audi. She gasped, and he loved it. While he was still in camo and armed, she teetered on ridiculous heels and wore a fancy wife dress. Didn't matter. He breathed her in. Spiciness wrapped around him, making the air hang heavy with a sensual aroma that he craved.

Possessive need strangled him. "Tell me you want to be kissed."

She nodded, her eyes wide. "I do."

"By me. Say it."

"I want you to kiss me, Rocco."

He crashed his mouth against hers. Couldn't taste her enough, couldn't get as close as he needed to. On her, around her, in her. His mind rushed. His cock jumped. The world tilted, listing to a halt, waiting for him to sate an urge, a craving that he couldn't describe, with only a simple kiss. He pulled back, and his heart pounded, punching his lungs, tightening his throat. There wasn't enough oxygen, and he didn't care about breathing, living, dying. He cared only for the woman whose sweet taste lingered on his lips.

Caterina gasped, her breathing just as erratic as his. Rocco swallowed, trying to wrap his mind around the woman in his arms. That he could feel this way…

That she could look at him like that…

His mind was blown. The thick ridge of his pants-covered erection pressed against her. She had to be cold. Had to be turned on. Her nipples showed through the wet dress. Dark and erect, and Rocco would feast on them soon enough. His mouth brushed her neck. His tongue traced across her flesh, and she wilted in his embrace, still pinned against the car.

"Tell me, Caterina Cruz, that this morning wasn't a game changer."

She shook her head, and the delicious smell of her shampoo filled his nostrils.

"Tell me," he growled. "Damn it."

"We both had a crazy day yesterday. Blowing off steam. That was this morning. I swear." She shook her head again. "But no game changer. Nothing can be different."

"Bull-freakin-shit, Kitten." He kissed her neck, nuzzling his cock against her, drawing out a little moan. "Crazy doesn't begin to describe my day yesterday. But I know how it ended, how I woke up, and so do you. Game changer. Now, tell me."

Her chin jutted up, and her gaze fell away. "I don't want to lose El Mateperros."

"Forget that fuck. Forget that I'd rather stand between you and any enemy. Or hell, that I'd rather leave you home. Forget all that, then focus on me."

Her gaze was far away, but her eyelashes fluttered.

"Look at me, Cat. Now."

Eyelids shutting. Caged against him, she softened and nodded, whispering, "Game changer."

The words were quiet, almost sad, which he could take a thousand different ways. But the only thing he would focus on was her and him and how a just-for-fun fuck had ended up far more than a hotel room romp.

"Glad we agree." He kissed her, ignoring the cold rain that fell harder. "And whatever your beef is with El Mateperros, we'll deal."

FOURTEEN

The green countryside rushed by, and the songs playing on the radio were the only thing that kept Caterina's mind from spiraling. She sat in the passenger seat, watching Rocco drive back to the bustling streets of London, his huge muscles in a tailored shirt. Business GQ wasn't her thing, but Rocco made a compelling case for dress shirts. He had the cuff links off and the sleeves rolled up, baring thick forearms. And when he drove with a wrist tossed over the steering wheel, the man couldn't look any more confident.

Game changer.

Too bad she couldn't feel any less confident. Her body betrayed her life's mission, leaving her turned on and quickly losing focus on her prize. A dead Dog Killer. She couldn't shake her arousal. Vivid memories of Rocco pinning her to the cold, wet car door and nudging his hard-on between her legs all but made Caterina straddle him while they drove. She was far too obsessed with connecting to his touch again.

Rocco's phone buzzed in the center console. She grabbed it. "It says Jared."

His hard jaw sawed back and forth.

"What? You don't want me looking at who's calling?"

"No. I don't know. Not used to it."

She wasn't sure if she liked that response. He wouldn't be talking about game changers if he had a girlfriend at home. Or would he? Was that what

88

a game changer meant to him? Whatever. She did like the way his biceps bulged when he took the cell from her. His undone collar emphasized how thickly the man was built, and the fabric around his chest begged for mercy. She closed her eyes and felt the press of his chest, the kiss of his lips. Every time she spoke in her native tongue, his desire made her feel beautiful from the inside out. When his arms wrapped around her—even when he simply tossed an arm over her shoulder—she felt safe. Those were new feelings, and she wasn't going to mess them up because he had a problem with her picking up his phone.

Rocco had the phone perched on his shoulder. "All right. If there are any problems, have Parker let us know."

Her complete fixation on El Mateperros wasn't as strong of a driving force as usual. Rocco had been talking about the trackers and bugs they'd just planted, and she was having fantasies about his body. A little guilty that she could focus on anything besides El Mateperros, she tried to ignore how sexy Rocco was. Not the easiest thing to do.

He put his phone back in the console.

"Careful. If it rings again, I might look."

He shook his head. "I don't care. I don't know why I did that."

"Because you don't want me seeing who calls?"

"Trust me, it's not like that."

"If you say so."

He cleared his throat. "*Previously*, I had someone who wanted the title of wife in a major way. She had something to say every time a job came up."

"Like what?"

"Like, don't go. Let Titan calls go to voicemail. Get a nine-to-fiver. Stuff like that."

"Sounds like she didn't know you."

"Does, doesn't it?" He looked over, almost smiling. His gaze set her insides on fire all over again, catapulting her stomach into cartwheels. He cocked half a grin, flashing that dimple. "You might be the hottest little thing I've ever laid eyes on. Even in that dress."

"What? You don't like my dress?" Flirting was good. Flirting played down how she was unconsciously re-prioritizing major life goals, the fact that Rocco was, at the moment, far more interesting than El Mateperros and whatever started feeding from the bugs they'd just left.

"I do. But, holy hell, woman. That black getup when you're ready to get your badass on? Hot. Covers you head to toe, but leaves nothing to the imagination."

Sex. Completely superficial. She could handle that because it meant she wasn't putting Rocco above El Mateperros—if she could just distract herself enough.

She un-clicked her seatbelt. "That's a pity. Surprises are fun."

"Didn't say you—what are you doing?"

She unclicked his seatbelt and ran her hand along the plain of his chest. Solid wall of brute force. It was a total turn-on. Her tongue ran across her bottom lip, and he was watching her instead of the road.

"*Tu me vuelves loca, Rocco.*" And she would at least get some kind of fix now. Her hand ran over his cock, feeling it thicken through his pants. "And I want to drive you crazy too."

A deep groan vibrated through the Audi. They'd drifted hard to the shoulder, and he righted them on the road. "Yeah, that mission's been accomplished, babe. But—"

His eyelids sank shut as she rubbed his length. He forced one eye open, then the other, dropping his head back against the headrest but trying to watch the road. "Feel free to try any new torture moves you have up your sleeve."

She pulled at his zipper. So slowly. The teeth unhooked one by one and echoed around them like an erotic promise of what was to come.

Rocco shifted in his seat. "Wicked little vixen."

With the zipper down and him raring to go, she slid her hand into his boxers. Strong as steel, thick as a branch, and hot, silky, smooth. She pulled him free.

"God, Caterina." He repositioned himself, his breath catching with the slide of her hand. Her thumb caressed the crown of his cock. "I'm gonna run off the damn road."

"Liam Laird will be with us for a while?"

"Roman?" His head dropped back. "Please don't say my buddy's name with my dick in your hand."

She stroked him. "I'm just trying to get a sense."

"Of?" His voice hitched again when she applied more pressure.

"How much alone time we might have."

"I'd assume next to none."

"Pity." She leaned over, taking just the head of him into her mouth. Her tongue licked and when Rocco groaned, she sucked tight.

"Vicious move." He blew out a breath.

Her teeth teased him lightly, sliding up and down his shaft. Then she trailed her tongue. "I think you can handle it."

A deep rumble escaped his chest. "Not complaining."

"Good." She took him in her mouth again, sucking him deep.

Rocco clenched one hand into her hair, steering the Audi with the other. His hips flexed. "Christ, we're gonna get pulled over."

"Stop?"

"Do. Not. Stop."

She laughed with her mouth still around him.

He groaned. "You're killing me."

Taking him like this had started as a distraction for her, but now… it reaffirmed what she wanted to be distracted from. Desperate hunger filled her. The taste of his flesh, the saltiness of his precum, the sexy masculine sounds he made with each slip of her tongue and curl of her fingers. She loved this.

"Your mouth…" He sounded even rougher, and that urged her on.

Rocco made her want normal like never before. Normal life. Normal man. Maybe even normal love. Roots and a relationship were something she'd only wanted once her search-and-destroy mission was over. But was Roc the type of man she hoped for?

An American? That would be unexpected. Private military type? Not on her most desired qualities list, but she wouldn't have to hide her past from him.

She pulled back, licking, tasting, stroking, exploring, then looked up and lost herself in his eyes, in the pleasure of making him come apart. Completely helpless in her desire, she prayed that this feeling would stay with her. Her hand cupped his sac, dragging her nails lightly over the tight skin. Needing his release, she tormented and tortured, until he was strung so tight she could count the seconds until he climaxed.

His head thumped back against the headrest. Thighs tightening and straining in dress pants, he growled her name, pulsing and throbbing deep in her mouth. Wet warmth came as he lost himself to her, and she swallowed, hungrily, greedily, savoring the power and perfection that was them together.

Erratic breaths and a hand laying haphazardly on her were the only things she noticed. Slowly, she came up, dabbing at her mouth. Everything made sense when she focused on Rocco.

"Game changer." He winked. His lazy smile and sexy dimple hung on his face.

"You've got jokes." But she couldn't hide her smile.

"Nope." He grabbed her hand and kissed it. "But I do have you."

Consider her heart stolen. She had no defenses for that. "I like you."

"Good. Glad you finally admit that." His dark eyes were satisfied and shining. He rubbed a hand over his jaw and blew out, then readjusted and zipped his pants. "We should take more long drives in the countryside I might become a proponent of those 'long walks on the beach' lines you ladies always dream about."

"Pretty sure that's not what that's about."

He gave her a look that would melt a glacier. "Pretty sure I'd go and find out."

Just when the moment couldn't get any better, it flip-flopped and couldn't get any worse. "I grew up on the beach. It's not all that it's cracked up to be."

"Can't be that bad."

She tugged her hand back. "I hate the beach."

He chuckled. "Some guy break your heart beachside?"

Her stomach turned. Her father's screams echoed in her brain even this long after the massacre. "Something like that."

She watched the passing trees and the sad gray sky, and ignored whatever Rocco was saying. An aching heart and a guilty conscience drowned out the rest of the world. If she hadn't asked for her birthday to be on the water. If she had asked for her daddy to stop saving the world for just one day, just long enough to eat cake and play games with her, then her family might be alive. Her throat burned with uncried tears. She pinched the bridge of her nose, willing the tears to evaporate before falling. Instead a memory certain to make it worse rose up. Such bad timing.

"No, daddy, no. Not today. Today's my day." She sat on his lap trying to take off the badge he displayed so proudly.

"Every day is your day, my little one."

She shook her head. "This is the big one. Ten years old!" She snatched at his badge again, and he let her take it this time. "Please," she begged. "Mama hates the guns. Leave this at home." She tossed the badge.

"Mama hates the gun runners," he corrected. "Not guns."

She hated the guns. They scared her. Her bottom lip came out. "Please."

He sighed, shaking his head. "But today, we'll make it just us. No good guys and bad guys."

"No guns." Caterina smiled, triumphant.

He smiled and kissed her cheek. "A birthday present to you. Only cake and presents."

"Cat?" Gravel spun in the wheel wells, and the car jerked to the side. Rocco tugged her arm, dragging her from the wretched grip of her real life nightmare. "What's wrong?"

She blinked, dazed. Where to begin? Streams of sadness fell down her cheeks. It may've been seconds ticking by, but they felt like lifetimes. When she did look up, Rocco's surprised concern melted into gentle prodding.

"Caterina." They were stopped, the car in park. He faced her, his fingers brushing her cheek. "You're crying. What just happened?"

The memories were too much, and she couldn't tell him about her family. She never told anyone. To voice that day, to explain what had happened and how she'd survived...that was too much. Too much regret. Too much sadness. She'd never survive the pain. Remembering was all she could stand.

"I can't—" Her throat cracked. She couldn't even say no.

Her head shook, and her mind shut down. She swallowed away the lump in her throat and pictured the country house they'd just left. *El Mateperros. El Mateperros. El Mateperros.* Channeling her lonely misery into hatred, she fueled her obsession, vowing once again—as she had every time her heart hurt—that she would end El Mateperros's life. Slowly. Painfully. And he would know why he was dying at her hands, just as her family had died on his order.

"Where you at? Come back to me." Rocco's strong voice reached her, sturdy and safe, comforting, as his warm hands cupped her face.

She took a breath so deep her lungs might explode and let it drift out. "Guess you don't end up where I am without a little crazy."

"That wasn't crazy. That was…awful."

"Same difference." They sat in long silence. "I'd kill for a Diet Coke."

"Funny, I think you might."

"And Funyuns."

He wrinkled his nose. "Nice combo."

"Don't knock it 'til you try it."

His thumb caressed her cheek, maybe searching for any last minute tears. "You sure you're okay?"

A weak smile was all she could muster, but she righted from his hold and clicked her seatbelt into place. "Okay enough. I'll be better once I get my soda."

The gear shift clicked softly, and he eased them back onto the road. "You'd better warn whoever hurt you on the beach bad enough to warrant that kind of reaction because, baby, once you tell me, I'm gonna kill them."

Not if I get to him first.

FIFTEEN

Rocco walked into the hotel bar, sweeping his eyes over swanky décor and a piano he was intimately familiar with. Roman sat the bar wearing a sports jacket, and it looked so absurd Rocco had to muffle a chuckle. One false move and the expensive fabric over his buddy's back would split at the seams. They weren't meant to wear the corporate getup. A tie was a noose, slacks, shrink wrap, and don't even get him started on the lack of convenient places to carry a weapon. He nodded to the bartender to bring him whatever Roman was drinking, then dropped onto a barstool.

Two of them in collared shirts. The odds were unreal. Rocco cleared his throat. "So that file you brought explained nothing. What's the real deal?"

"Guess Boss Man thought you might need an extra set of hands; it's easier to have someone stationed by if shit goes down. Use me, don't use me. That's your call."

Made sense. Jared hated solo jobs. Even though Rocco was working with Cat, no one else from Titan meant no one else at all. "Fine."

Roman's brow furrowed. "*Fine?* What's got your boxers in a bunch, dude?"

Rocco's drink arrived, and he took a sip, grimacing. "Fuckin' gin?"

"Should've asked what it was first, dick. Liam Laird happens to love gin."

"Liam Laird. Christ, what a name."

Roman shrugged. "Whatever. How's the job going? That Mrs. Locke of yours is something to look at. Whoa, buddy."

"Watch yourself."

Two hundred pounds of soldier-in-a-sports-jacket turned in his chair, eyebrows raised, and tilting his head. "Is that right?"

Rocco took another sip, confirming that gin tasted like bark off a pine tree. Pine was for household cleaners, not liquor. "Eyes off the missus."

"Come on now, *Daniel*. What fun is it to bust your balls if you act like a prissy bitch, all sipping your drink like it's high tea over at Buckingham Palace?"

Rocco ignored him, taking a larger gulp. Goddamn, he hated gin. "She's a cool chick. I happen to dig cool chicks, so it works out well."

"You two playing house?"

He held up his left hand, showing off that prime piece of jewelry that, only days ago, had made him cower in his camo. "Married for the job."

"And you're avoiding the question. Not bad, man. Not bad at all."

"Shut your face, Roman."

"Liam."

"Dick."

"And—" Roman's eye twitched as he looked over his shoulder. "I do believe we are in play. Guy at your four o'clock has been on my radar, and he's on the move. Three, two—"

Rocco turned his head. "Can I help you?"

"Message from El Mateperros. He will send a car for you tomorrow afternoon." Dark hair. Dark complexion. Dark suit. He fit in the pricey hotel but had a definite ACG quality to him. "Be ready."

The messenger retreated without waiting for a reply, leaving Rocco and Roman holding their highball glasses. Rocco turned to face the bar and set his glass down, grumbling.

Roman tilted his head toward the exit. "Bossy little fuck, wasn't he?"

"Something about this rubs me the wrong way. We've been tracking El Mateperros, Parker's been watching him, but I knew that fucker was watching us."

"Everything about El Mateperros rubs me the wrong way." Roman threw back the rest of his drink. "He's a bad guy's bad guy. Did you read Parker's intel briefing? You know why a North African Muslim has a Spanish nickname? Shit's fucked up."

Rocco had been shocked reading the report on his way from the States. El Mateperros had earned his chops breaking open seaport cities for a gun runner. He slaughtered families, even their dogs. El Mateperros had been their slang for the Dog Killer. That name had started in Spain and worked its way out. "That's a hell of a message to leave for your enemies to think about."

Roman signaled for his check. Anger bunched the muscles in Rocco's shoulders. "Someone's gonna fry him." He shook his head. "As long as half of Europe doesn't file for extradition."

Roman nodded. "Let's knock this op into the done column and hightail it on home."

"Yeah." Rocco rolled his shoulders, antsy to get back to Cat and not think about how quickly this could be finished. What was his little game-changer up to? Getting ready for bed? Cleaning her weapons? Drinking Diet Coke and eating Funyons?

Roman signed his bill and stared at him. "You know you got this look on your face? Like you're falling for your partner and don't know what to do with it."

Rocco drained the rest of his glass. Tasted like crap, but the burn was good. He rolled his shoulders again and rubbed the back of his neck. "She's a lone ranger. I'm based on another continent. Nothing to fall for."

Roman slapped him on the back. "And another one bites the dust."

"Let's not get carried away with the impossible." He smiled, shaking his head but his insides hurt—ached—and that was something worth thinking about.

• • •

Caterina had transformed the hotel bathroom into a spa. Satellite radio played Flamenco guitar. The scent of exotic fruit burned from scented candles. Caterina had one leg hung over the side of the tub when she heard the bathroom door click open. Bubbles covered up to her chest, a warm cloth covered her eyes, and an empty wine glass sat on the edge of the tub. She peeled up a corner of the cloth up. With the overhead lights turned out, the candles glowed. A book she'd nabbed from the hotel's lobby sat on the bathroom floor, and a man that she couldn't ignore stood in the doorway.

"Kitten." His eyes smoldered, and his body was a testament to the hard work of his job. He leaned against the door jamb, elbow above his head, forearm hanging down, so relaxed when everything on his body was perfectly carved and sculpted.

Deep within her stomach and so much lower, warmth spun and spiraled.

"*Hola.*" Hi would have been just as easy without it, but she knew how to make his eyes dance. His dimple appeared, and she wanted to press her lips to it. "I was just getting out."

"Don't."

A rush of adrenaline made her heart and lungs teeter-totter. This husband-and-wife routine was becoming much more than an act.

Rocco shucked his shirt, revealing that pinky, fresh scar and kicked off his shoes and socks. "Met with Roman. One of El Mateperros's men made contact."

Her heart raced, partially because his hand rested on the buckle of his belt and partially because their target had found them, just as they had found El Mateperros. She and Rocco were so close, their cover as the Lockes holding up amid the ACG's scrutiny. This time she would catch the Dog Killer. They would find him, then she would kill him. Simple.

"They made contact…and?" She wanted to know more, but her stare was transfixed by his hand. He worked the thick leather belt open, unsnapped his pants, and nothing outside the room mattered.

With his pants hanging open, precariously clinging to the solid curve of his buttocks, Rocco took a step toward the tub. "And we have a meeting scheduled."

Her eyes shot up. "It's happening?"

"Tomorrow."

Too much hope obscured her thoughts. Too much Rocco skewed her priorities. She needed to jump out of the bath and plan the next day to the most microscopic detail. Rocco took another step forward, hooking his boxers and sliding them over his solid erection. His clothes dropped to the floor, and she leaned forward, reaching for his hand.

He nodded. "It's happening."

So much was happening. Her head was spinning. Distracted and focused. Confused and certain. So very soon she could sink her claws into her family's killer. A smile broke her cheeks. Then her heart crashed, sinking past the bubbles in the oversized tub. When El Mateperros was dead, after she had killed him, Rocco wouldn't be around. The job would be over, and he would be disappointed in her. He liked rules.

Didn't he?

At least she thought he was the kind who frowned upon assassinations. Murder. He'd never know about her family. Jared would never tell. So Rocco Savage, all-American hero, would think that she pulled the trigger like a mercenary instead of turning the terrorist over to be tried, judged, and punished.

Trickles of bubbles dripped off her arm, quietly splashing in the water. His hand found hers, and shocks of excitement rushed at his touch. She inhaled and embraced everything they would share. When it ended, it would end. She wouldn't regret any decision she made, either bringing her closer to him or chasing him away.

"Why the long face?" He stepped in, sinking chest-and-tattoos deep in water and faced her. The splish-splash of lapping water made the bubbles wave around them. Their legs scissored underwater, and the coarse hair on his thick legs brushed her calves, her thighs. Somehow, surrounded by bubbles and candles, he still looked Titan tough.

"You look unbreakable." She stared across the valley of bubbles. Impossibly broad shoulders spanned the end of the tub. He spread out his arms, resting them on the sides, and she couldn't tell if he had relaxed or was preparing to propel himself across the sudsy water.

"That's not a bad thing." His dimple flickered on and off. "Come here."

He reached forward, hands gripping her hips and pulling her close. Each of her breaths weighed heavier than the last. Her cheeks and chest warmed, and he folded her legs behind his back, leaving her weightless in the water and bobbing against the hardened length of his cock. Rocco smoothed her against his body.

She wanted to feel him everywhere. Inside. Outside. All over.

Her tongue licked his neck, savoring the delicious taste of his skin. Hints of his cologne made her mouth water, and her eyes closed as she tried to memorize his smell.

"You are battle-hardened." Her fingers explored, stroking over the taut skin, touching the old wounds and scars that he claimed didn't bother him. She fingered his tattoos, the colors dark against his wet skin.

"I'm a lot of things." His wet hands slid down her back, cupping her cheeks.

She took a breath and traced the lines permanently drawn on his bicep. A flag, an eagle, letters that looked as deadly as their promise.

"May God…" Her fingers slid over the first words.

As if he knew exactly what words were where, he whispered what she touched. "Have mercy on my enemy."

Moving her finger over. "Because—"

"I won't." The gleam in his eye spoke the tattoo's truth. "Patton."

She pulled back. "I bet General Patton would think it better for us to jump out of the water and plan for our meeting with El Mateperros tomorrow."

Rocco's smile disagreed. "He liked good fights and calculated risks." He kissed her, his tongue opening her mouth and stopping the world on its axis. She tasted how familiar he was becoming on her tongue. "And *I* bet he might agree that staying here, with you, is a risk worth taking."

Safe from the outside world in his arms, she didn't have an argument. Five o'clock shadow made his cheeks scratchy and sexy. The flecks of strength in his eyes, his strong jaw and powerful shoulders promised her that all the world's problems could be handled tomorrow.

Caterina lowered her forehead to his cheek. "A risk worth taking... maybe."

"We'll be ready for tomorrow." His chest flexed when his arms hugged her, highlighting the jagged pink scar standing out against his tan skin.

She pressed a tiny kiss to her fingers and ran them along its edges, almost scared it would hurt him. "What happened?"

Her hand pressed tight against his breastbone. The *thump, thump, thump* of his heart beat against her palm.

"Don't worry about it."

"Tell me anyway." She didn't want to move her hand. "*Por favor.*"

A long sigh fell from his mouth. His brow furrowed, then he dropped back against the edge of the tub, staring at the ceiling and pulling her closer, so the deep water covered her back. Rocco stroked her spine. Her chin rested on the scar.

"A job in New York City went wrong, but the girl's safe, and I got a new war wound to add to the collection, end of story."

"I think there's more." Her cheek moved to lie against his chest. Warm water teased her neck, her hair. His body tensed underneath her. "I want to know. I want to know everything about you."

"Everything about me?"

"*Sì.*"

"*Sì?* Oh, Kitten, you know that's my weakness. Don't you?"

She did. Playing up the one-syllable accent, she reached between them and grasped him, stroking long and slowly. "*Sì.*"

He chuckled, rough. Velvety. "What do you want to know?"

"Why Titan?"

"Gotta love a job with the good guys. Bouncing all over the world. Great team. Good jobs." He sucked a breath when her thumb covered the crown of his cock. He tilted his head, breathing in and flexing his hips to smooth his length against her submerged palm. "I met this lady once, had to work with her, pretending we were hitched. She liked candles in the bathroom. Bubble baths. Crazy girl stuff like that."

She smiled again. "Really. Sounds like torture."

"You know, you'd think so."

"But?"

"But she was pretty damn incredible."

That was more than enough to make her forget about planning their next day, but she wanted to keep going. "Tell me more."

His palms rested on her butt and massaged. "She had this Penelope Cruz look to her and an accent that brought me to my knees. Think she knew it. Used it against me."

"She sounds smart." One of his hands drifted to her hip, sliding on her skin. Shivers erupted under the water. Her sex throbbed for his touch.

His fingers found the vee between her legs, teasing. The pads of his fingertips parted her, stroking, sliding, testing, and tantalizing. Focusing on her clit, he put her through agony. The little bundle of nerves seared her from the inside out.

"Yeah, smart. And ruthless."

Still lying on him, still with her hand wrapped around his erection, she stroked him as he stroked her. His powerful legs held hers in place. His other hand cupped her ass, squeezing tight.

He pushed into her. Two fingers delved deep, and she gasped. "You're the ruthless one."

"And the sounds she'd make before she came—they'd be the only thing I could focus on all day long. Getting to that moment again."

She shushed him, tightening her grip. "Don't say that. You'll embarrass me."

"Sweetest sound I've ever heard was when your tight pussy milked my cock, Kitten."

Her cheeks flamed, but the rest of her did too. Fingertips to toes. Even her shoulders burned. Ragged breaths and racing blood. She could barely hear him. "Rocco."

Fingers curving, the water splashing between them. "Love when you say my name."

She nodded, biting her bottom lip, near blinded by a tidal wave that was about to crash over her. Panting, she tried to say it. Whispering, hoarse and hot. "Rocco."

"Fuck, yes."

She moaned, unable to stop it. The sound reverberated off the bathroom's wall. Her insides were building, building…

"You're gonna come on my hand. On my face and on my cock." His hand pumped, diving deeper, and he sucked a deep breath, cursing. "You have a long night ahead of you."

She couldn't breathe. Couldn't think. The fireworks had been lit, the sizzle was getting ready to explode, and she wasn't going over the edge alone. Her hand stayed with his rhythm, working him over just as he did her.

"Cat." He gasped with her. "Caterina."

She bucked in his arms, feeling his erection pulse in climax. They fell apart together, water splashing and bubbles melting in the wake of their heat. Breaths mirrored, gasping and rasping. Lips, legs, lives tangled. The moment lasted forever, and it was perfect.

"That was worth waiting until tomorrow to plan our attack." He hugged her tight, letting her stare at him.

Those eyes melted through her. Powerful and passionate. Nothing hidden. He was in the moment, so raw it was a thing of beauty. And she would ruin it all with her lie.

Rocco wanted justice.

She wanted vengeance.

SIXTEEN

Another day living large in luxury. As much as Rocco wanted to complain about wearing business suits and not firing weapons, he couldn't. Waking up with a gorgeous girl, planning a terrorist take-down, acting like this was his normal life—wasn't a bad way to live. He slammed back the last of his black coffee and double checked the .45 he'd decided to use as his sidearm and the 9mm subcompact tucked into his ankle holster. Both weapons were concealed, not his preferred way of carrying. It was much easier when those babies were easy-access, strapped to his hips, thighs, chest, wherever. But wearing weapons like they were some Armani accessory didn't go with the designer labels.

The morning ticked by so slowly. He stood, glanced in the mirror next to the kitchenette, and didn't recognize himself. Yeah, he needed to get back to camouflage and ditch his collar stays. Caterina swayed in, looking every bit her part: elite, untouchable, and all his. The room brightened when she walked in, and that had zero to do with his mind trips. He checked his watch. "It's go time."

"Almost ready." With a quick tug that nearly stopped his heart, she propped up a long leg on the coffee table and hiked a clinging skirt thigh-high. A serrated blade was already secured to her thigh, and she was repositioning a subcompact .22. After a moment of up, down, all around—he would've killed to be that gun—she smoothed the fabric down as she stood, grabbed her Diet Coke off the table, then did a spin. "Can you see anything?"

Man, he saw all kinds of stuff, mostly a woman he couldn't spend enough time with, both in and out of bed. He saw a deadly intelligence gatherer with a Northern African knowledge base that made him proud and an operative who'd been an independent operator for so long that she seemed to ping-pong between taking El Mateperros down and simply taking him out... but none of that was what she meant.

His palms itched to slide over her curves. "Nope. Don't see a thing."

The soda bottle hung limply in her hand, and her chin fell back when he stepped close enough that their stomachs kissed.

"Good."

Damn, that accent would be his undoing. "Let me tell you what it does to me, knowing you're all geared up under that pretty little outfit of yours." He slipped his arm around her waist, letting his hand drift down the sway of her back and settle on her perfect ass. Her subtle perfume teased him, intensifying how extraordinarily feminine she looked and mocking how absolutely dangerous she was.

"But you didn't see this. Did you?" From between her breasts, hidden by the silk of her blouse, she produced a blade. The thing was thin as a letter opener, sharp as a razor, sexier than all the lace lingerie in the honeymoon suite. All the blood in his chest dropped, rushing straight between his legs. Sporting wood and having no time to do anything about it, he laid a kiss on her that did little to tame the snap, crackle, pop rushing under his skin.

He brought his lips off hers, just enough to still feel their heat. "You don't actually want us to leave the room, do you?"

Her melt-in-his-hand chocolate brown eyes turned to concrete. All the gauzy softness she'd been seconds ago stiffened into a starched soldier. "Of course I do."

Alrighty then. She had a serious hard-on for this job. A knock at the door took both their attention. They were a few minutes behind, and Roman wasn't having it.

"*Vamos.*" His fake-newlywed-wife turned hardened-operative detached herself from him and power walked in killer heels toward the door. She threw it wide as if she couldn't wait to leave.

Roman leaned against the wall, eyeballing them suspiciously, then shook his head. He stepped closer and discreetly motioned toward the elevators. "You're being watched."

"You sure?" Rocco asked.

Caterina glanced down the hall. "We should confirm."

Roman nodded. "Agree."

"Got it handled." Rocco took Cat's hand, and Roman led the way.

Passing the housekeeping cart, Rocco paused in front of the woman fiddling with a bed sheet. "Excuse me."

The woman looked up, putting the sheet on her cart. She wore a uniform and name badge like she worked there. "Yes, sir?"

"I lost a button." He gestured to a sleeve cuff that was hidden by his sports jacket. "Do you have one of those sewing kits?"

Caterina laughed and rolled her eyes at the attendant. "Like he would sew anything."

The woman nodded, surprise that they'd approached her written all over the lines scrunched on her forehead. "Of course. One second." She searched the top of her cart, the sides, and a few pouches. "I'm sorry. I'll have one left in your room."

"That'd be great. Two doors down on the right. Thanks." Rocco winked and wrapped an arm casually around Caterina.

She whispered into his ear. "We're in play."

"Ten-four, darlin'." Because seriously, housekeeping didn't know where their supplies were? He expected better from the likes of the ACG's people.

Roman punched the elevator's call button, and a minute later, they stepped in. "Too easy."

"Or sloppy."

Cat shook her head. "Not El Mateperros. Never sloppy."

"So they wanted us to know they were there?" Roman walked toward the door as they neared the lobby's level. "Why?"

"*He* wanted us to know." She chewed her bottom lip. "The bastard has a thing for mind games and power trips. The Lockes are a new vendor. He wants the upper hand. I'd be surprised if he didn't pull something else equally as bold."

Caterina made a good point. The elevator car slowed to a graceful stop, and they hit the lobby looking every bit their parts. Rocco and Cat, Mr. and Mrs. Locke, arms-dealing lovers, and their bodyguard, Liam Laird. They were an imposing bunch. Even clothed like urban sophisticates, he and Roman looked like a two-person football team—the American, pigskin kind of football—and Caterina like a movie star billionaire heiress. Looks and money. And she was his. They pushed through the doors and merged onto the bustling, London streets. The crowd moved about them.

Roman slipped on a pair of shades and lagged behind them. "I make this bodyguard work look good."

Rocco rolled his eyes. "If you say so."

Caterina went up on tiptoes to kiss his cheek, whispering. "See anyone?"

He shook his head. They wanted to avoid the sitting duck routine while waiting for El Mateperros to send for them. The right offense was a good defense, and that meant getting to where they were out in the open and on neutral ground.

Well, not neutral.

Parker's intel from the devices they'd planted said Big Ben was the ACG's ground zero, and Titan was on their way for an offensive strike of the head-fuck variety. If the ACG had plans to strike Big Ben, and no one was supposed to know, then they were playing their own version of obvious-maid-in-the-hall-watching-a-room, which was kind of a long name for a game that should've been called *one up, fuck you.*

They needed El Mateperros unsteady and ready to make a mistake. They needed more than to just stop a single terrorist attack or remove a single terrorist leader from power. What they really needed was to learn more about the ACG's behavior, future plans, and then when the opportunity was right, they would take El Mateperros into custody, after learning every possible tidbit of intel. Then the ACG would no longer be one of the world's most secretive groups.

"We've got company," Roman gruffed behind them.

Caterina linked arms with Rocco, and they put their best tourist-foot forward, because what else would honeymooning, arms-dealing couples do before a meet-and-greet with an elusive terrorist? Just a normal day in their made up world. She pointed to a store front filled with candies, then spun to his chest, arms around his neck. "Got one. Your four o'clock. White male. Khaki jacket, white shirt, blue jeans."

Damn, she played the newlywed wife gig well. She repositioned to his other shoulder, and Rocco held her close, just for a moment to breathe her in... and let her look for other ACG groupies. He eyed Roman, who nodded.

Rocco flagged another and whispered her ear. "And your two o'clock. Black hair, dark skin. Same clothes. Jeans, white button-down. No jacket."

"That's a lot of people to set up a sit down. El Mateperros means business." She shook her head. "I've got a bad feeling."

She was right.

Roman came closer, hand on the butt of his sidearm. "We've got more company."

"This isn't a meeting invite." Rocco stopped, unwinding Cat and grasping her hand. He narrowed his gaze. "They're closing in."

"You got this?" she asked.

She might have had some moves, some training, but field operations weren't in Cat's repertoire. He knew that, and if he'd had even the slightest suspicion the ACG would play like this, Cat would be locked safely in his *other* hotel room.

Roman moved in front. "We got this."

Big Ben was within sight when Roman led the charge, leading them to a location where they could get a bearing on their defenses. Rocco and Cat powered behind him, ignoring the ACG men who had them surrounded. Their goal was Big Ben. If they could get there before confrontation, their message would be sent.

And... they had arrived. Roman stopped and turned to face one side of their attack. Rocco took the other, sandwiching Caterina between them. An ACG man came from the front and another from the back.

"Nice spot. Ever been here?" Roman quipped.

Clear as the uncertainty on their faces, they didn't like where they were. *Big Ben, fuckers. We know.*

Even though they had Cat enclosed, she was cool as the metal barrel on his favorite Glock. He felt the energy radiating from her. The strength and focus. Roman sidestepped into the closest ACG man's line of sight, cutting him off from his target—Daniel Locke.

"Back away, buddy."

"Daniel Locke." The man stood down but leaned to speak around Roman's shoulder. Apparently, he had a death wish. "Come with me."

Roman had him turned around, arm jacked behind his back. "How about some manners? Fucker."

Two ACG approached from behind. He had them, and Roman had the others. But when one fucker put hands on Caterina, Rocco's whole world went red. For split second, he worried that this was the worst piss-poor timing for a hallucination, but then realization slapped his senses into gear. Someone put hands on his woman. She happened to be schooled in the art of pain and torture, but that didn't matter. She was his, and that man might die because of a mistake.

Caterina's hand went to her breast, extracting the hidden ice pick of a knife and throwing it into the man's foot. His head snapped down when Rocco's fist knocked it back up. Blood sprayed down to the sidewalk.

"Don't touch my wife," he growled, rabid and wanting more.

Around them, the ohs and ahs of startled passersby started a commotion. Someone had surely called the cops. Not exactly how their plan was meant to go but not the worst thing that could happen.

A new man approached. The other ACG assholes appeared to back off and take their cues from him.

"Your wife will be left alone." He extended his hand to Rocco. "It's time for you to come with us."

He let it hang in the air, unanswered. "This isn't my usual way of doing business."

"El Mateperros is expecting you."

"You aren't making any friends, asshole."

Cat stood beside him. "I am fine."

Rocco took Caterina's hand in his, decided not to create a bloody scene on the streets of London, and sawed his teeth together. "Anyone touches my wife again, they won't live another day on *El Mateperros's* payroll. Understand me? I don't care who he thinks he is."

"Not her. You."

That was exactly what he wanted, to leave Caterina safe with Roman, but she'd probably de-ball him later if he tried that move. Taking longer to respond than he should have, Rocco shook his head. "She goes where I go. Package deal. As does that man." He pointed to Roman. "I need assurances that she's safe after your thugs made their move."

The man stepped forward and placed his palm on Caterina's shoulder. She didn't react. Didn't have to. Rocco's muscles surged forward. His shoulder caught the man before his brain caught up and said not to attack. They slammed against a storefront. The man's head smacked back, and spider-webbing cracked the glass. Trickles of blood ran down his neck.

"Never touch her." His body pounded. Unanticipated fury caught him off guard, but he channeled it. His hands cupped the man's neck. "I'll tear your throat out if you lay hands on her again."

Sweat beaded on the man's forehead, and lack of oxygen turned it a gonna-die-soon shade of fleshy red. The other ACG men approached cautiously from behind but didn't engage. Roman hovered, ready for whatever Rocco needed.

"Got me, dickhead? Touch her and die." Rocco rippled his fingers then released.

SEVENTEEN

The familiar sing-song of adrenaline rushing through Rocco's veins centered him. Amid the coughing and hacking, Caterina stood next to him, unfazed. There may even have been the slightest smile on her face, though she tried to downplay her amusement. Funny how he was getting to know her slightest tics.

Rocco glared at the other men and returned his gaze to the cougher. "We prefer discretion. *I* prefer a blanket of anonymity. That is how I do business. I don't care if it is *El Mateperros* or not. Understand me?"

Sirens roared.

Rubbing his throat, the man stood down and walked toward the other men. A quick nod and a mumble, then two Mercedes sedans rolled up.

Rocco turned to Caterina. "You okay, darlin'?"

"Never better." Her eyes twinkled.

He squeezed her hand, uncomfortable with the anger bubbling in his chest. "Someone touches you like that again, prepare for the unexpected."

In her heels, she went up on her tiptoes again and whispered into his ear, "*Un segundo.*"

There she went with her Spanish again, as if he could ever say no. At least he understood this one. One second. Got it.

Caterina stepped to the disoriented man who still rubbed his throat. She let loose a fury of words he didn't know but would pay to hear again. Tearing him up, then down, verbally assaulting him for laying a finger on her. Shock pinched the man's face. He seemed even more surprised at the finger poking than at the scuffle.

Cat turned back to Rocco, went back to her tiptoes and kissed his cheek. "Had to get something off my chest."

Talk about a proud moment. He chuckled, shaking his head. Roman tried to hide a laugh with a cough, and the ACG men were either embarrassed or in shock, but all parted as Caterina walked toward the waiting Mercedes. Her lips screwed, and her head tilted, letting dark brown hair fall over a smoky eye. "Are we leaving?"

"We are." Roman moved toward her, and Rocco followed.

The driver of the car held open a door for Cat like some pleasant terrorist chauffeur. When Roman took the front passenger seat, Rocco slipped in the backseat with Caterina.

She whispered close enough that no one else could hear. "Temper, temper."

Lacing his fingers into to Caterina's, Rocco tried to focus on their goal. They needed details on the ACG's upcoming attacks—not just Big Ben—in order to prevent them. They had to find out how extensive the network was and if the rumors about their financing had any truth. They had to do everything they could to take down El Mateperros, bring him to justice, and dismantle the ACG.

Easy enough.

The driver handed each of them black silk scarves. "Eyes, please."

That was expected. Caterina took hers without questioning and fashioned it over her eyes. Roman glared from the front passenger seat, but did his too.

"Between the two of us—" Rocco glared at the driver. "If something smells wrong, the ties come off, and you'll be in a world of hurt. You feel me?"

"El Mateperros prefers anonymity."

"As do I. But I'm only willing to play this game up to a point. That stunt outside earned the ACG no goodwill with me."

He donned the blindfold, then listened and anticipated every move, memorizing the turns and traverses. They were going back and forth. The luxury sedan clipped carefully over railroad tracks at the same crossing more than once. Made sense. The driver was being careful to keep their precious Dog Killer hidden. Rocco didn't much care since he already been there. A couple of blindfolds and beefed up ACG blowhards trying to touch his woman wouldn't keep him from mission accomplished.

Caterina's hand found his again. Cloaked under the black silk blindfolds, they sat in the back seat. He stroked his thumb over her delicate knuckles. It never failed to surprise him how soft she felt, even when the image of her in black, wielding sparking electrical wires was his favorite memory of her. Well, of her *clothed.*

Her lips found his earlobe. "You okay?"

Rocco jerked back to look at her even though he was blindfolded. "Yeah. You?"

She eased closer, and her lips tickled his neck, then his ear. All part of the man-and-wife charade, but the pinpricks running across his skin wasn't faked.

"This means more to me than you will ever know." She held her breath. He couldn't see it, but he could feel it. Feel her. "I need you to know that."

He shivered. "Understood."

"I wish you did."

The black tie blocked everything out. No sun. No outlines. He imagined her biting her lip, looking lost, but he didn't know why. He would rather she work that sinful smile and bat those thick, dark lashes. He wanted her try to convince their onlookers of their newlywed spark, of their deep connection. Too bad he was already convinced. Hell, well past convinced and on his way to believing his own BS. A couple in love...

Caterina whispered, "If things don't go as planned. If... something happens, we're partners."

Something? Like what? Nothing could happen that they hadn't prepared for, with the exception of a trippy freakin' mental breakdown.

He wouldn't have an episode. That simply wasn't an option. He'd kill himself trying to stop it before he left her alone with El Mateperros.

Wait. He wasn't alone. Suddenly, Roman made much more sense. Which meant Jared knew. Maybe. And what did Roman know? Rocco would deal with that line of questioning ASAP, but in the meantime, he had Cat talking about vague what-ifs and partnerships, and he needed her to focus.

"We're married, Kitten. You're stuck with me." He brought her knuckles to his lips. "Nothing to worry about."

A few more turns and curves and the engines stopped.

"Blindfolds off." The driver exited and opened Cat's door. Rocco and Roman snagged theirs off. Cat twisted her silk tie around her fingers. Nervous? Not this lady. No way.

But something was bothering her. Then all of her fidgeting stopped like she'd flipped a switch. "This may be the best and worst day of my life."

EIGHTEEN

Caterina had been at El Mateperros's quaint house just the day before, but it hadn't had the same effect as it did that moment. Today, she would face him. As she exited the Mercedes, her head spun. She balanced on her heels and stymied the overwhelming urge to run into the house, find El Mateperros, and put a bullet between his eyeballs. Quick and easy wouldn't do. He needed to suffer, and Titan needed to find out everything they could about the ACG before she ended the Dog Killer's miserable existence. That was the right thing to do for London, but more importantly, that was the right thing to do because Rocco wanted Titan to assist in dismantling the ACG.

It wasn't lost on her that his motivations were playing into her plans.

The ACG men exited the second Mercedes, and they all began the walk toward the house. She couldn't wait to meet El Mateperros. What did evil look like? And what made him hide? Horribly disfigured? Humpbacked and covered in mangled warts? That was a little clichéd, but why else would a man hide so deftly?

Rocco and Roman flanked her. She barely noticed. They had spoken to her, but she had no idea what they said. In seconds, she would be face to face with the man who'd ordered her family's massacre. The man who'd earned his name on her family. The Cruz family's massacre had started El Mateperros's rise to fame, if the local rumor mill was to be believed. The ACG had been a fledging group the day they'd killed her family, leaving her alive. It was the first day that monster had started his reign of brutality.

Yesterday, the country house and all its cuteness had irritated. Today it was almost unbearable. Potted flower boxes lined the first floor windows, and the stone path they walked on was smooth, surrounded by manicured grass. Surrounded by the ACG men, Rocco took her hand. Roman walked ahead. Her pulse raced while her mouth went dry. Just feet until she breached the door. Five. Four. Three. Two. And she was inside the home of her prey, her target, her life's obsession. She trembled in the waves of adrenaline. So very close. Inside the door, nutmeg and allspice hung in the air. Her irritation quadrupled.

"Weapons." The man Rocco had skirmished with beckoned his hand at them. "You'll get them back."

Rocco growled. "Again, not how we do business."

"Then we'll take you back."

A standoff ensued. Long seconds felt like decades. Caterina shifted, trying for nonchalant but drowning in impatience. Rocco shifted too, then nodded to Roman. They disarmed. She waited for him to motion to her to do the same. A quick nod gave her the go. But with all their eyes on her and her gun way up her thigh… *Screw it.* She hiked up her skirt, unholstered the gun, and placed it in the hands of a man who might've just come in his pants.

"Check them." The lead ACG man gestured to them.

Rocco stepped between her and the men. "Touch her and you already know what will happen."

Someone manhandling her might cause Rocco to lose his mind. Last thing she needed was for him to hallucinate. Lord, what would happen then?

"One more." She pulled out a serrated blade from her other thigh, and every man in the foyer stared, jaws hanging. "I expect this back."

Roman gawked at her, then at Rocco, who knew what he was thinking. She could've done a strip tease and not bagged that reaction. Men loved their bloody toys, and when a woman hid them on her body, she had the upper hand.

The ACG men shuffled, glancing everywhere but at her, all looking as though they'd been busted for peeking up a girl's skirt. Not too many gun-and-knives-toting ladies must have crossed their paths.

"*Sí?* I will get that back?"

Their heads nodded. Even the lower-in-command looking ACG men, who she was sure had no say. All right, already. Time to get this meeting rolling.

The one who'd ordered their disarming led them down a hall. Knick-knacks decorated shelves. Rows of books lined the walls and were stacked on the floor. Maybe this wasn't El Mateperros's house. A grandmother's, maybe? Caterina's teeth sawed together. His family lived comfortably while hers had been buried, murdered by his order. Bastard.

"Wait here," the lead man said, and she noticed red welts on his neck.

They were left in a sun room. Fresh herbs grew in labeled little planters along the expanse of windows. Her temples throbbed. What kind of terrorist headquarters was this?

"Sage?" She scowled at the plant. "Mint?"

Rocco meandered around the room, poking and reading their labels, then nodded to the books lining the halls. "Didn't take the guy for an avid reader."

"Stephen Covey, Steven Levitt, and Jim Cramer? Dude's got a whole lot of economics books." Roman picked one up. "*Looking for Fame* by Lady Gaga? Really?"

Her brow furrowed in such a way that a migraine was sure to come. El Mateperros was a pig. A terrorist. What was he doing with lavender and lemon basil decorating a room that was this… gorgeous? Sun streamed in. Loungers and chairs begged visitors to take a seat, relax, and soak in the breathtaking view of greenery. She hated it. Hated him.

Rocco sidled up to her. "You okay?"

"Never. Better." The pressure in her head was going to make it pop off. Today *had* to be one of the best days of her life. She'd finally have a face to go with the name.

"If you say so." He picked a label from a container. "Lemon basil? Who would've guessed?"

Her fingernails dug into the palms of her balled-up fists. Maybe she could emit enough hatred that Rocco would stop commenting on fucking herb blossoms. Roman looked equally intrigued.

"Daniel Locke." A smooth voice surprised her from behind.

Rocco and Roman turned. Bile rushed into Caterina's throat, coating her tongue. She coughed. Choked. Sputtered. That moment, that very second she'd been waiting for the better part of her life was at hand. The monster had graced them with his presence.

Her heart pounded too loudly, enough that it drowned out the initial pleasantries between the men. She didn't hear a thing—too busy succumbing to memories. Shouts, gunfire, and the taste of the blood from her bitten lips. Chewing the inside of her mouth. She didn't understand why, on her special day, the world was falling apart. Rocco touched her back. She still hadn't turned around. Her eyes threatened to water, but she refused. She would not let it happen, so help her God. Not for El Mateperros. No signs of weakness. No telltale vulnerabilities put forth for the asshole to enjoy. Fuck him. She wanted his pain. His sorrow. She wanted to capture it, to bottle it to look upon and draw from when she was at her worst.

Her pseudo husband's hand walked around her waist, reassuring her with just a touch. He stepped back—smart not to take his eyes off their enemy—and leaned over, his lips at her ear.

"You okay, Kitten?"

No. She was falling apart on so many levels. That goddamn second, she couldn't breathe.

"Kitten?" He stepped closer, and she blinked back the burn of painful tears.

Cat swallowed. Swallowed again. Her nose wrinkled, and she inhaled as deeply as she could manage in a blouse and bra that had turned into a vise.

"Fine." She cleared her throat. God must think her a badass because he'd handed her this moment, and he didn't dole out shit she couldn't handle. That was a fact taught long ago by that miserable bitch called life. She nodded. Stronger. Her family deserved better than a pathetic public breakdown.

Balancing on one heel, she pivoted and looked up. Rocco, Roman, and El Mateperros. *El Mateperros?* Her lips parted. Fury fell. Shock. This had to be... shock. *El Mateperros?* The Dog Killer looked... smart, even debonair. She choked back bile because some might even call him...gorgeous. Strength came back to her in droves, reminding her of all she'd been through. She wanted to tear his face off, shred his tailored suit, and rip out his perfect black hair by the fistful.

NINETEEN

El Mateperros extended his hand toward Caterina. It hung, looking pampered and soft. His eyes were the color of brown sugar, crinkling at the corners, dancing like he knew he was *the man*. It made her sick.

"Mrs. Locke, the pleasure is all mine." The hand continued to await her.

A storm raged in her chest. A thick blanket of suffocation wrapped itself around her.

Rocco's grip on her tightened, and his throat cleared. "Kitten?" He was a little louder that time, evidence to her mini-public breakdown. This was so bad. "Okay?"

Okay? No. She wasn't okay. She expected a mass murderer with pocks and scars and gouges. A monster. With horns and a snarling snout snorting toxic breath. This was her meeting with the devil. He was *supposed* to be evil incarnate. But, dapper and distinguished? No. Just… *No.*

Money and power reeked from him. Confidence oozed. He winked at Rocco and Roman, and focused back on her. His smile screamed that he could have any woman he wanted. Any woman but her. The only thing she wanted was his head on a wall and the rest of him six feet under.

"Is your wife okay?" El Mateperros asked, pompous and self-assured, pulling Rocco and Roman's gazes back to him. The Dog Killer clearly misread her silence. Instead of shocked surprise, he saw silent interest. Her molars pressed together until her temples hurt.

Rocco's eyes narrowed, his shoulders straightened, but he reached for her hand. "I'm sure she's fine."

Caterina didn't move, didn't acknowledge that they spoke to her. Her life's mission was going down the crapper all because she was choking.

"Caterina?" Rocco tugged her to his waist. "Kitten. Come back to me, girl."

His breath was on her neck. His grip steadied her. She blinked, rolled through the disgust and surprise, ignored that this was the most embarrassing moment of her life and that she was falling apart in front of Rocco, then painted on her best smile. "I am so sorry. I just... got dizzy. Please—" She stepped from Rocco toward El Mateperros. "Accept my deepest apologies."

El Mateperros took her hand in his. "No need, Mrs. Locke."

Repulsed shudders rocketed from her lungs into her limbs. He brought her knuckles to his lips, lingering over her skin, and nausea taunted her. Vomit was fast approaching. Her mouth was too wet and her stomach too weak. But she gave a curt nod and snatched her hand back, swallowing the noticeable taste of bile. "*Gracias.*"

"Sit, please." El Mateperros gestured with the same hand that held her knuckles to his mouth. He needed to experience pain. A hurt that stole his life's happiness.

Caterina dropped into the chair with no grace, just pure, undiluted hatred driving her every move. Rocco touched her shoulder and then slid into his chair, keeping her within reach. Roman stood behind them. She tried to smile, tried to keep her cover, but things weren't looking bright and shiny. The guys were going to question her after this and deservedly so.

Rocco cleared his throat. "Like I was saying, the goon squad was unexpected and unappreciated. If we're going to conduct business, I expect a business relationship."

El Mateperros watched her for a few seconds too long then smirked. "You're new to the game. I don't believe you get to make the rules, Mr. Locke."

"I'm your only game in town right now. If you have any hopes in purchasing weapons grade explosives in short order, I'm your seller.

Your distributor. Hell, I'm your God at this point. Your people botched the London job, and no one wants to touch you."

"Hiccups happen." His gaze flicked upward. "And I doubt that no one wants—"

Rocco leaned forward, mighty and menacing. "You're too hot to sell to, but here I am. With my wife. And you're talking about rules? Guess what? I just rewrote the rule book, and whatever parameters you thought we were playing with went out the door when your muscle grabbed us off the street."

El Mateperros leaned forward, matching Rocco's stance. "I've guarded my existence, my reputation, since I began this journey. I wasn't about to have some newbie gunslinger out me just because he could sell me weapons quickly."

"Two hundred thousand US dollars was our agreed upon asking price. I'm throwing on another hundred thousand dollar fee for fucking with my day and with my wife. After that, we'll pretend this little shitstorm of a business relationship didn't happen. If you want to do business again, we'll start new. Until then, I'm your only option."

El Mateperros threw his head back and cackled. "That is a strong threat from an *unfindable man* who my men picked up with ease."

Rocco popped one knuckle at a time. "I'm here to make money, not friends. You're here because you need what I sell. Simple. You want games, go elsewhere, though that'd be impossible at this point."

"You're far more colorful than I expected." El Mateperros clapped his hand, eyes dancing, then looked at Caterina with more interest than she cared for, tilting his head at her pseudo-husband. "I like him." His eyes drifted down her blouse, and a smile curled onto his despicable lips.

All the things she wanted to say, and she couldn't. Instead, she reached for Rocco's hand and narrowed her eyes. "As do I. Think I'll keep him."

The smile he'd been toying with exploded into full out amusement. "Oh, that's too bad."

Rocco leaned forward in his chair. "Your pain-in-my-ass fee just went up again. Three hundred fifty thousand, total. Wire the money to this account by noon tomorrow." He pulled a slip of paper from a pocket and handed it to El Mateperros. "One more look at my wife, and don't bother. You won't be alive to accept delivery of the goods." He stood with her hand in his, and she melted into his side. "Kitten? You ready?"

More than he could ever know. She nodded, not trusting her voice and hating that Rocco spent more time checking on her than digging for dirt. She had failed.

"Pleasure doing business with you." The acid in Rocco's voice and the annoyance on El Mateperros's face made their visit the slightest bit more survivable. Roman led their way, and Rocco pulled her even closer. A lifetime's worth of pain eased off her chest under his arm. He nuzzled his lips into her hair, and the day suddenly wasn't as jarring. El Mateperros wasn't as shocking. Rocco guided her out the door, past the ACG henchmen to the running Mercedes. He opened her door, sat her down, and leaned forward to brush a strand of hair off her face. "Doing okay?"

She tried for a smile, but it was nothing more than a tight-lipped failure. She wanted to scream and punch the seat in front of her, but instead, she growled out her frustration, poured out her fear of failure, careful to keep quiet from the listening ears of the ACG.

Estoy perdida. I'm lost.

Lo odio. I hate him.

Fallé mi familia. I failed my family.

Rocco waited her out. His dimple was there, egging her on. She went on, cursed El Mateperros, not by name, but none the less, talked about the devil.

"Feel better?"

"Ha." She scoffed, but yeah, the weight was lighter. Having another person to share with had advantages.

Again, he pushed a strand of hair off her cheek. She wasn't even sure there was one, but loved how his fingers felt. "Sounded good, whatever you said."

"Maybe." She puffed out a breath. "I'm frustrated."

"You'll tell me later what happened to you back there?"

"Probably not." She shook her head. So much to say but never anyone she trusted enough to tell.

"Cute, though."

What? She shook her head. She went on a tirade about wanting to kill a man, her first round of doubts ever, and Rocco thought it was cute? She covered her mouth. That was insane. "You have no idea what I said."

"Like I said, it sounded good."

Roman walked up. "You two almost ready?"

"Almost." Rocco nodded him away.

"I could've been talking about murder and mayhem." Actually, that was exactly what she was talking about.

"Even better." The dimple teased her. Rocco dropped to his knees, peering up at her. "Let's ditch these goons soon as we get to civilization. Time to take advantage of our marital status."

Her jaw dropped, and she smacked his shoulder. The solid wall of muscle guarded her. "You're awful."

A one-sided smile curled on his face. "Oh, come on. Get your mind out of the gutter. Friday night TV. PJs before the sun goes down. It'll be all laid back and without a care. No one to impress. And room service."

"Maybe." She shrugged, but if he'd been talking about mind-blowing sex, she'd take him up on that too.

"Hell, Kitten. If chillaxing doesn't help, you can go back to your Spanish cussing bonanza. *Donde. Grande. Escargot.*"

"Is that all the Spanish you know?"

"I'll never tell."

"You know *escargot* isn't—"

He closed the distance between them. Surprise morphed into something more, something hot. Soft, full lips brushed over hers, and her stomach tumbled. That was it. She was done for. She'd fallen for her partner, her fake husband. Fallen so hard she knew it would hurt when she landed. How could she have thought this wouldn't happen? Because it couldn't happen. The husband-wife routine was a game. A ruse. They could kiss, fall into bed, but none of the emotion was supposed to be there. Too bad it was.

Her arms wrapped around his hard muscle and broad shoulders, and her fingers crept up his shoulder blades, along the strong slope of his neck, and into his hair. Soft and silky and thick, strands threaded between her fingers. She'd had many kisses before—many unmemorable moments—but this kiss? Need blasted through her, searing her veins and scrambling her senses. This kiss was a memory-maker.

A low groan vibrated from Rocco. It made her hungry for him, naked and crawling all over her. Flesh on flesh, legs and arms twisted in a fury of abandon. Trembling for his touch, she tightened her fingers in his hair. Pulling him to her. Wanting desperately for this kiss to last forever. It was just too good. Impossible to replicate if it ever stopped. His palms rasped down her cheeks, the callouses so different from the softness of El Mateperros's sick handshake. The contrasts between the two men boggled her mind. One, she'd die to have between her legs, the other she wanted to kill for even looking at her like that. Rocco was all man. The Dog Killer was nothing but a vile excuse for a human.

"Let's go." The driver opened his car door. "Blindfolds are in your seats."

Rocco's lips stilled. Her eyes opened to stare deep into his. Warmth covered her cheeks where he kept his cupped hands. Staying still, they locked in a moment.

His smile blossomed against hers, and he chuckled. "*Ay. Dios. Mio.*"

"*Ay Dios mio?*" He was too much fun.

He smacked a kiss back on her lips, lifted her knees, and swung her legs into the car. "That's about the only thing I know what you're saying."

He winked and shut the door. Unable to wipe the glow off her face, she looked out the window before she pulled on her blindfold. El Mateperros stood in the window, watching. His evil eyes nearly glowed. His gaze was on her. No one else. Not the car. Not Rocco. Then his lips moved. She couldn't read lips, but she knew what he said. *I know who you are.*

TWENTY

All his time at Cambridge and the London School of Economics had taught Yassine how to take his fledgling group and turn them into a money-making organization. Growing up homeless on Algerian streets, he hadn't had much outlet for his anger other than what the outside world deemed terrorist groups. He'd started on the coast of northern Africa with a fanatical mission, but that had changed long ago. All it took was new life experiences. He was intelligent and street smart. Made a profit running guns between his home and the Spanish coastline. Even though the ACG started as a terrorist organization, it was now nothing more than a means to an end. He, ironically enough, was a capitalist. He liked money, liked to earn it, loved to spend it. Plus, he was smart enough to realize that living as an angry idealist was pointless. His goal was to be rich and soon enough, famous. The cloak of anonymity had been useful for creating an international allure, but now it was time for his great reveal.

Daniel Locke held the key to his next job. Big Ben would be London's disaster. An attack on the old clock tower would propel him into the limelight. The newspaper headlines would read "The Search for El Mateperros," while the tabloid headlines whispered about sightings with his favorite footballers and the like. The ACG would leak his photo. His looks had always worked to his benefit. And move over, FBI Top Ten List; he was gunning for the number one position. The ladies would clamor for this attention. And this all started by moving small shipments of guns through tiny coastal towns. Not too bad.

Yassine stood in the window and watched Daniel Locke with his wife, kissing her as though it were the first time. His stomach turned. That was something Yassine had never enjoyed, the kissing. He never enjoyed the warmth of a woman, feeling her move underneath him, or worse, on top of him. He liked them cold and still. Eyes open. Pleased to be with him. Caterina Cruz wanted him, and he knew it within seconds of meeting her. It was the way she stammered through the introduction, how her eyes widened and her hand shook in his.

As Daniel walked to his side of the Mercedes, Caterina stared at the house. At him. Obviously, wishing that it had been Yassine to kiss her instead. "I know what you want." He put his hands against the window glass. It was cold and lifeless, just as he liked most things.

• • •

An hour after Caterina, Rocco, and Roman had returned to the hotel, she had on Rocco's sweatpants and oversized cotton t-shirt. She was sans makeup and had her hair in a messy bun. Her toes curled as she pulled the comforter around her on the couch. Who was she kidding? There was no doubt that kiss at the Dog Killer's house was for real and not to put on a show for the ACG. There was no doubt she'd fallen for Rocco, desperately, terribly hard.

Roman had left them soon as they hit the lobby. Rocco ditched her for the hotel gym. Not once did he ask what happened when she met El Mateperros. He simply made small talk on the way back to the hotel, helped her sweep for listening devices, then ordered everything on the room service menu for her to spend the night with, along with her thoughts. Forty-five minutes had passed since he'd left, wearing a shirt and shorts that clung to his body. That vision stayed in her mind. Surrounded by plates of food, she should have brought up her meet-the-Dog-Killer freak out, could've explained why she'd gawked and couldn't manage a basic hello. She took a giant scoop of half-melted chocolate ice cream and watched it drip off the spoon. For all she knew, he was at the gym trying to figure out how to continue on with a partner who got stage fright.

Her cheeks burned again, and she shoveled another scoop of melting ice cream into her mouth. What if he was speaking with Roman about how foolish she'd looked? About how she talked a big game but was nothing more than a flake? She blew out a breath over sticky lips. *Get up. Go talk to the guy. Explain what happened, and you won't feel like such a moron.*

Maybe the guilt and embarrassment would go away. Another bite of soupy ice cream. Maybe not. Maybe she'd just stay here with the ice cream and everything else she'd been picking at. Sampler. Soup. Sandwich. *Get up and go.*

She didn't change out of Rocco's clothes. After all, tonight she'd been practically ordered to pull the old married couple act, sweatpants and all. A quick ride to the lower level of the hotel and she followed the signs for the gym. Hotel gyms always smelled the same: plastic and sweat and disinfectant cleaner, all trapped on a lower level.

The sound of one person working out prickled her ears. Of course. It was a Friday night, and the gym wasn't a happening place at that day and time. She peeked around the corner.

Shirt off and wearing those sinful gym shorts that hung off his hips, Rocco Savage had a body that froze her in place. His biceps and triceps bulged as he pumped in time with a hard run on the treadmill. Her eyes followed the taper of his shoulders down to the curve of his—

"Kitten?" Rocco's gaze nailed her in the mirrored wall.

Her cheeks flamed. "Hi."

He planted his feet on either side of the revolving ramp and punched a few buttons to lower the incline. Chest heaving as he wiped his face with a towel, he studied her then drained a bottle of water. She studied the newish scar on his chest.

"Did you need something?" He stretched arms overhead, and every muscle, from pecs to torso, rippled.

Those shorts hung dangerously low. Did she need something? Um, yeah. *I need…*

Caterina shook her head. Now wasn't the time to fess up about El Mateperros. "I'm going to bed. Just wanted to say good night."

He jumped off the treadmill, seared her with a glance that probably wasn't meant to be as hot as she took it, and he meandered to the free standing weights. Taking two that weighed about as much as she did, he pulled them to his chest. Those biceps curls made her weak in the knees.

"You came all the way..." Biceps curl. "Down here." Biceps curl. "To say good night?"

"Should you be doing that? Your chest. That wound looks too fresh—"

Thin smile and a biceps curl. "All good. Ignore it. I do."

Sore subject. *Got it.* "Like I said, good night."

"Sweet dreams." He turned back to the mirror and let her go without another look.

She huffed in the elevator, then again at the hotel room door, frustrated with herself. She hadn't known where to start, and his bare chest made her dizzy. Now she stared at the bed and remembered how he powered over her and into her, making use of every inch of that king size bed.

"How am I going to survive him?" She stared at the bed.

"Who says you have to?"

She jumped out of her skin, spinning around. "Rocco!"

Her mouth started running before she could stop it. Startled, the Spanish flowed, and that look, *that dimple,* appeared on his face. She took a breath.

"Don't let me stop you. You're on a roll." He still had his shirt off, and she couldn't be any more aware of how gorgeous he was.

"Bad habit." She took a deep breath again, always trying to catch her breath around him.

"That's all right. I like it." He walked toward the bathroom, shrugging, and threw his shirt over his shoulder. At least he admitted to liking it. She watched him, so confident and unaffected. He could say anything. That was brave, the exact opposite of how she was feeling.

"I have to tell you something." She tried to put a blast of gusto in her voice, but it didn't sound as strong as she wanted to.

"What's up?" He turned and threw his sweaty shirt at her, hooking a landing on her head. The shirt smelled masculine—sweat and cologne—and it made her throat go dry.

"Um." She snagged the damp shirt. Gross, yet she didn't want to let it go.

"Want a divorce already?"

"What?" Her jaw fell, and his dimple appeared when he smiled, amused. "No, Roc." She wasn't letting go of him until he walked away. "I'm being serious."

He raised his hands in surrender, and the colors tattooed on his biceps flexed, distracting her from the dimple. He walked into the bathroom but didn't shut the door. "Jokes are done. What's up, Kitten?"

She wilted. Plan B: make something up, change the subject, maybe pick a fight. She could just start with the Spanish again. That'd throw him off. "I'm..."

"I won't tell anyone you snore."

"Rocco!" She rolled her wrist, staring at the ceiling.

His gaze raked over her, and she felt the caress. "Come on. Just playin'."

"I lost my train of thought."

He stared, unconvinced. "Nope. Bullshit. Spit it out."

"Seriously, it will come back to me. Go. Shower. You need it." She needed him out of sight for more than one reason. First, to avoid the discussion. Second, to avoid staring. She wanted to kiss his chest, the scars, the muscles, all the way down to where his shorts hung precariously. And, third, she was exhausted. Standing there, exhaustion made her delirious.

"Whatever you say." He turned his back to her.

The shower faucet turned on, and she shut the bathroom door for him since she would've otherwise sat there ogling.

The sounds of water splashing preoccupied her. She killed the lights and listened from the edge of the bed, ignoring the images of what he looked like naked. Her imagination was creative, but the real thing was so much better than anything she could have come up with. Sleeping with a man like Rocco was instant distraction and eventual heartbreak. There was a reason she had nothing. No roots. No home. No loyalties. She didn't deserve him. *But what about after El Mateperros was gone?* Well, then she would figure out how her life could change. Maybe they could see each other. But right now—

The door opened, shedding light into the dark room until he flipped the switch. "Heading to bed?"

"Maybe." Feet away from Rocco, she'd never felt more alone, more vulnerable, or more interested than in the dark. Instead of watching him, she crawled across the bed and pulled up the bedspread, then peeked back at him as she tucked herself in.

At least he'd worn his sweatpants out of the bathroom. She wouldn't be able to survive—*oh no*—his fingers pulled at the drawstring of his pants.

In the shadows of the dimly lit room, he raised an eyebrow. "Keep making sounds like that, and you're not going to bed. Consider yourself warned."

She covered her mouth to stifle a giggle.

"I heard that." The bed dipped down as he pulled back the covers and joined her. Freshly showered and smelling like soap, Rocco burrowed next to her. Every muscle tightened. She laid straight-pin straight, unmoving, not breathing. Her hands were clamped to her side, and she stared toward the ceiling, eyes wide open in the darkness. All she had to do was tell him about her family.

Just a simple tale. It'd been so long…Simple enough to recount cold, sad facts.

He moved under the covers, and she would've sucked in a distracted gasp if she had been breathing. Which she wasn't… Her will to stay blocked off was slipping like an emotional rock slide. It'd be so easy to let him in. "Roc."

"Yeah, babe?"

The words froze. Seconds ago she could do it. Now, no. She couldn't share tonight. Not until El Mateperros was gone.

"You're going to fall off the bed if you hug the edge any closer." He reached for her, and the sheets made a swishing noise as his hand found her bare shoulder. "What's a matter?"

"I'm fine." *I'm so not fine.*

"Then scoot your cute ass over." The palm of his hand rested on her stomach, rubbing a circle around her belly.

Cute ass? "I'm trying to sleep. Don't touch me."

He did anyway.

She smiled, unable to help it. "I bite."

"Now that, I'd like." He laughed, and the sound echoed in the bedroom.

Sighing, she turned to him. He sat upright, pulling the covers off his bare chest and dragging free her protective layer.

"Caterina." Rocco had her tight against him. That was a terrific interrogation technique. Not one that she'd ever used before but it was effective.

Playing defense, she tugged the covers back and elbowed him. She hit a solid wall of muscle. His arms tightened, his lips so close to hers. "You're going to kiss me?"

Maybe if they fell back into each other's arms, he'd forget she was dancing around a conversation.

"Maybe." His arms wrapped around her shoulder and slid down her back. "I'm not going to do anything if you're going to lie there, holding your breath."

"I'm not holding my breath," she whispered. "Just a lot on my mind."

"Right." His fingers slid over her skin. "You want to talk about today? You're not used to field work, right? That's what happened?"

Her mind stuttered before her mouth did. "W-what? You think I can't handle a meet-and-greet?"

"Tangoes are delivered to you most times, right?"

She closed her mouth and swallowed, wrapping her head around his assumptions. "Well, yeah, but that's not why—"

Rocco continued, "God, that dude thought he was hot shit, all *I can have any woman I want.*"

"He's a monster."

"He thinks he's the center of his world, and he eyeball-fucked my wife. On top of the whole, he's a bad dude thing, I wanted to punch him in the face."

She smacked his chest and had the same reaction she did after elbowing him. Solid man. "So that's why you kissed me while we were there?"

"To bust the guy's balls? No way."

"Then why?"

"You already know that answer."

She did. The kiss might have been a surprise in that moment, but their connection was becoming more and more real. Their spark was electrifying, and that jolt of possibility was messing up everything she'd ever thought she knew.

TWENTY-ONE

Rocco shifted in the bed sheets but didn't relax his hold on her. Tension bore down on her shoulders. Anxiety mocked her attempts at trust. He was one of the good guys, the only person she considered trusting, but he had the situation all wrong. Caterina almost couldn't live with that thought in his mind.

His voice softened. "You freaked when you saw him, looking all like a terrorist-model-dude, making eyes at you and—"

"What? That's insulting." Shaking her head, her nausea and disbelief were almost too much. "No way."

"You almost passed out when you saw him, Cat. Kinda had a movie star vibe for him, if you like that type of thing."

"You have no idea what I thought." She bit her lip. "It's not like that."

"So explain."

The air conditioning kicked on. A gentle hum vibrated through the room, slicing the tension that choked her. A stroke of his hand across her back shot her straight into disarrayed confusion, all mixed with arousal and trepidation.

He nudged her. "Enlighten me."

"I don't know where to begin." She curled onto a pillow, and Rocco lay next to her, putting his arm around her. Against all reason, she scooted closer, turned into him, and rested her cheek on his chest.

The scent of lingering soap made her sigh. His chest rose and fell, as stable and calm as she might have predicted. Always reassuring.

"Start anywhere. It's better than this vague back and forth."

True. "I wear this armor that the outside world wouldn't understand. You might. I don't know." He lived in her dark world of terrorist interrogations and black ops missions, so he might get it. He understood her job. Maybe he would even understand her drive.

"Try me."

His trunk of an arm clasped her against him. A burning sensation teased the back of her throat and her eyes. Thinking about her family, her anger, the vendetta that she had carried on for years, made it too much to say.

He urged her on. "I can't understand if you don't give me a shot. Trust is everything." His chest rumbled when he spoke, and the weight of his muscled biceps locked around her made the world seem safe.

But if she told him, she'd have to say she would kill El Mateperros, and he couldn't know that. Not yet. Probably not ever.

"I can't believe in trust," she whispered.

"Can't?"

She shrugged against his skin. "Won't."

"Try." The tips of his fingers skimmed across her shirt, dancing over her shoulder.

"I'm not sure why I should."

"Maybe you should ask why you want to tell me to begin with."

"I don't…"

"We both know that's a lie."

Panic surged from deep within her chest. He was right, and it was unsettling. Caterina shot up, running away from him and a sea of blankets, fighting to get to the edge of the bed before she made any more of an ass out of herself. Rocco found her wrist and drew her back, snaking a hand over her waist and pulling her into his lap. Shadows covered his face. The smell of soap was that much stronger close to him. Warm wisps of his minty breath tickled her nose, and he held her wrist in his hand against his bare chest.

"Caterina, I need you to trust me. *Need.* In ways that confuse the hell out of me." The timbre of his voice ground against her nerves, and all over again, she wasn't breathing. "Trust me, Kitten."

"I don't know how."

"That's not true. We both know it." He released his hold on her, but she didn't move from his lap. Slowly, she became aware of the heavy thump of her heart, beating a rhythmic, sad song.

He traced her chin with the back of two fingers, starting at her cheekbone and sliding to her collarbone. "As soft as you look."

"There's nothing soft about me."

His fingers skipped across her lips. "Again, not true."

She sucked in a deep breath, trying desperately to find strength from within only to look up, into his eyes and feel the surge of fortitude. "I'm going to blow our op. There's no way we're turning El Mateperros over." Another deep breath. "Because I'm going to kill him."

He never stopped stroking her cheek, her chin. He outlined her lips. It was as if she hadn't promised a premeditated murder was eminent. "How?"

"I don't know yet. I needed to see what I was dealing with first."

"Fair enough."

"You haven't asked why. Or what happened." Curling into a ball felt like the right thing to do, but she didn't, perhaps because this wasn't the reaction she'd expected. "I've never told anyone what happened."

His hand cupped her chin, thumb directing her to look up. "Jared knows your end game?"

"Taking out El Mateperros?" A knot the size of their honeymoon suite choked her windpipe.

"Yeah." He nodded.

So she nodded too. "Jared knows everything. Just... everything."

Like flipping a switch, Rocco shifted. Warm to cold. Offensive to defensive. Angry? Annoyed?

What the fuck?

He petted her leg twice, and they weren't the reassuring type of pats. "Glad he does."

"Wait." Shock and pain hit her so hard her skin went cold. "Roc?"

He held her gingerly but shifted her back to her side of the bed. "Yeah?"

"I thought this was trust. My sharing. You're... I didn't mean to upset you."

"I'm not upset. You and Jared created a job so that you could—"

"No—" She shook her head, tears welling.

"Jared needed someone dead? You did? You're more than an interrogator? An assassin too? I don't care, but I don't appreciate being told the job is one thing when it's really another."

"Stop. Rocco. You've got it all wr—"

He turned off the only remaining light. "Good night."

She'd hurt his feelings. Chest tight, throat stinging, she *hurt* for hurting his feelings. A wave of anguish overpowered her. Tears streaked her face.

"He killed my father, my mother, my brothers. In front of me..." Her voice cracked, and she used the sheet to hide her tears.

Rocco sat back up in the dark. "Oh—"

But the dark was good, hiding her in the shadows. "El Mateperros ruined my life. He left me alone with my memories."

"Caterina—"

"There was so much blood. My dad and brothers were just trying to protect our family." She couldn't stop. After years of burying the story, it rushed from her.

"Kitten, stop. I was being a dick. A jealous fuckin' dick. You don't need to say it. I fucked the trust. I'm in the wrong. Just stop."

"It hurts so bad." She sobbed, completely out of control. The sheet did nothing to hide the tears or the excruciating pain.

Tossing the sheet aside, Rocco pulled her to his chest, shushing her, rubbing her back. Her jaw ached, her heart ached, and even her soul suffered under the tenderness of his touch.

"Jared only knows because US forces were in my little town, on a peace-keeping mission, or whatever they call those things. They were there to stop the guns." She wiped her eyes again, staring at the ceiling in the dark. "Jared had to have been eighteen, nineteen years old. It was my tenth birthday the day I met him. He scooped me up, all blood-covered and still holding a birthday present."

Rocco kissed her temple, smoothing her hair.

"He promised me that if I ever needed anything, I could ask him. When I grew old enough, I said I wanted the name of the man who ordered the hit on my father. El Mateperros. And searching him down, since I was just a child, over the last twenty years has been my fixation."

Rocco tightened his hold, and let her bawl. "Today, you didn't just meet El Mateperros. You met the man who massacred your family."

The tears slowed. God, she was an ugly crier. This wasn't how a life-long fixation was supposed to come to light, not pathetic and weepy. Rocco would run from this job as fast as he could. She couldn't blame him. It had all been a lie.

"Caterina…"

And here came the excuses. He would bow out. Good thing she hadn't fallen too deeply for the guy. Just a tease of caring, of liking and loving. Just enough that she'd shared her deepest, darkest desire. The tears welled all over again. The back of her hand did little to wipe the tears from her cheek, especially when they wouldn't stop falling. "You can go. I understand."

Rocco faced her toward him. "You, Kitten, don't understand anything where I'm concerned."

He thumbed the last of her tears away. His eyes blazed, and his hand dropped, fingers interlacing with hers. A kiss pressed to her forehead. He lingered, and her weight relaxed against him. How could a simple, benign forehead kiss make everything feel better?

Pulling her tighter, he kissed her forehead again, then her temple. Her cheek. Slowly. Letting his lips drag. So she was wrong about the benignity of it.

"Forget it all." He nuzzled her ear.

"I can't."

"Forget it now."

His teeth tugged at her earlobe like flames ripping through her senses. Caterina let the scrape of his teeth burn. An uncontrollable fire ran down her neck, down her spine. Her back arched, her head dropped. He took her weight in his arms as she melted into him.

"Rocco." No idea why his name slipped from her lips, but it made him shush her. That sound, the vibrations buzzing from his lips across her skin, cleared her mind. All the hurt and pain and memories, all the terror and anger she carried lifted off her chest. It was just her and him in bed, and that was the only thing she could focus on.

She'd never wanted anything more than to be kissed and touched by him in that moment. "Please."

His lips covered hers, and the same as earlier, the intensity overwhelmed her. He consumed her, captivating her with the velvet slash of his tongue and the strength of his hold. Her arms looped over his shoulders, and her fingernails bit into his skin. His thick cock strained beneath his boxers. His lips devoured her, working down her neck as his hands worked up, smoothing over her shirt, her shoulders, to slide under her t-shirt.

He wasn't gentle as he explored, and she didn't want him to be. His journey made her kiss him deeper, hold him closer, until she landed on her back and Rocco peered over her. His legs nestled between hers, and his erection rubbed between her legs.

"You taste so sweet." His lips caressed the top of her breast right above the neck line of the shirt. So slowly that she wanted to scream, he moved to her nipple, teasing it, tugging it through the cotton. His tongue stroked the tip, then moved to her other mound. Same action. Same reaction. Arousal pooled and need drove her dizzy. His calloused palms slid over her stomach, freeing her from the suddenly unbearable confines of her shirt.

Rocco drew back, and his cock angled out. His chest loomed, perfect and scarred. A steamroller of a man holding himself so carefully over her... but it was his eyes that stole her breath.

"You're fuckin' gorgeous." He cupped a breast and leaned back over, taking it into his mouth. His tongue worked over the swell, flicking and encircling.

Words of a response floated away. He was the gorgeous one, brute strength wrapped into one sex god of a man.

Her hips rocked against him, pressing her sweats-covered wetness against his shaft, and getting a hell of a reaction. Brows pinching. Head dropping. *She* did that to Rocco. All tough and impenetrable. It made her steady. *He* made her that way. Steady and stable and sexy in a way that had nothing to do with tight black pants.

"Rocco." She needed him more than she ever knew that she could a man, and it didn't make any sense. Her eyes, her heart, had never seen someone who took her, fatal flaws and all, and held her, trying to make her feel better. "You mean more to me than you'll ever know."

Because she certainly couldn't tell him. She'd only known him for a couple weeks, and he'd only known that she'd known him for less time than that, but she'd call it was it was. Her heart, her mind, had pulled a surprise on her, and falling for him was happening fast.

"Right back at you, Kitten."

She'd started out hating *Kitten*, but damn if she didn't love hearing it tossed off his lips.

Unclasping her hands from around his neck, she slid them over each ripple of his abdomen. Taut muscles smoothed under her touch. At the waist band of his boxers, she slid her hands around his waist. With powerful thighs between her legs and the delicious curve of his backside under her hand, she moaned when his mouth rasped over her neck again.

He had her naked and underneath him again before she could even pretend to argue. Talented. "God, your curves are killing me."

His hands ran from her chest to her hips to her bottom and back, fingers kneading into her flesh along his path. Powerful. Masculine. All she could do was nod and experience him. This was normal. Two people in bed, sharing secrets. She loved it. "Sometimes I swear I'm going to change. Forget and move on."

He pulled back, and caramel eyes warmed down to her soul. "You can't change it."

"Maybe."

"You decided what you're going to do, and I'm not getting in your way. It'll either help or it won't. But right now, you're with me, not thinking about your history or the future."

Our future. "Just us."

"That's right. Just us. Right now. Nothing else."

He reached for his wallet, found a condom, and put it on. The tears that had disappeared were back, emotional but different. He hadn't said anything that should overwhelm her, but she was on the edge of losing it. Rocco took her hand, lacing his fingers with hers and pressed himself between her legs. He filled her, stretched her, sliding in and out, rocking until she gasped, until her lungs fought for oxygen. Sweat beaded along his forehead. The saltiness of his skin drove her crazy as her mouth kissed his sun-tanned skin.

"Caterina."

"Yes." He brought her back to the moment and pulled her close, eyes locked, hands laced tight.

He didn't blink. Didn't seem to need anything but her steadfast gaze locked on him. "Just feel for me. Don't think."

Don't think? Or don't remember? Don't plot and plan? The answer was simple: don't do anything except focus on him, his lips, their rhythmic plunges and escalating tension. All that spiraled inside her.

"Okay." Agreeing to anything he said was easy.

Her mind relaxed, and her body wound tighter. Anticipation and pleasure cried for release. She took his mouth, deepening their kiss, faster and harder, but somehow so sweet. She hooked her leg over his hip and was done for. Eyes shut and arching her back, she tightened on his cock. Caterina's climax rocked her from the inside out.

Her mind went white. Blank. Nothingness. It was spectacular, a perfect peace that she hadn't known possible.

Rocco wrapped his arms around her, pumping and driving and bringing his body into hers. His muscles strained. Low, guttural, gratifying groans poured from him, meeting her lips as he kissed her into a climatic oblivion. Finally, he slowed. Stilled. Their breaths and kisses intermixed, lost in the tangle.

When her eyes opened, Rocco still held her tight, and she couldn't live another moment keeping lies and love to herself. "*Te adoro. Te amo. Mi Galán.*"

His eyes darkened, serious and intent. But he didn't understand, and sadly, that was her point. She'd let him in on one secret and immediately picked up another. She loved him but wouldn't risk it all by telling him.

TWENTY-TWO

Rocco listened to the sweet hum of Caterina's breath as she slowly tumbled into sleep. Cuddling wasn't his thing. The word even sounded... odd to him, made him all tight-chested and uncomfortable. But holding her like this, all close contact and warm woman, this was the way it was to be done. Completely sated and spent, exhausted but reinvigorated, he could lie there all night long and not complain. The silence gave him an opportunity to replay her words in his head. *Te adoro-amo-what? Galán?*

It sounded like a confession. Maybe he was putting words in her mouth or hoping for something she hadn't said. But he knew adore and love, no matter the language. No idea about *galán*. But as long as it wasn't "I'll never," good things were happening for him.

Her body softened, completely turned over to sleep. One of the most dangerous women in the world lay naked and tucked to his side, her dark hair splayed over the white pillows. She looked angelic. Angelic? Angel... Like when his mind tripped and he imagined his angel... was he imaging Caterina? Maybe.

His fingertips tingled as he recalled the night he'd blacked out in London and woken up the next morning. His memory tripped, trying hard to place broken memories together. Zips and zaps of a hallucination threatened him now. Or was that just a memory? What had happened that night? And why was he suddenly so sure that Caterina had been by his side?

143

And the angel in his visions? The one who helped him to the other hotel room? That had to be in his head. *It had to be.* Because if not… Why wouldn't she say anything? So it wasn't her…Or was it? Damn his stupid episodes.

Rocco scrubbed his face and pinched his eyes, calming his mind down and forcing himself to remember the night in London with the guys. He'd left the bar. Stumbled onto a bench. Saw an angel who guided him to his hotel room, saving him from himself, and disappearing into the night. But not before writing a note on the mirror.

Handsome.

Only someone who played spy games would think about leaving an invisible message on the mirror, chancing that he might take a shower. Only someone who had brought up coincidence more than once. And only a woman who could read people as well as Caterina did would have seen him for what he was: not a drunk or a druggie, but someone like her who needed a hand in a messed up situation. He stared at her as his thoughts rushed, not sure if he was trying to put order into his chaos or if he was about to lose his mind again. Room five twenty-one wasn't that far away if it were the case, but he sure didn't want to leave the bed and let her wake up alone.

Deep breath. In, out, in, and then the threat of a hallucination dissipated, leaving him oddly relaxed. Rocco leaned over and kissed her cheek. "I just might be crazy enough to believe in coincidence now."

Sliding from the covers, he pulled on his sweatpants, tucked her in, and grabbed his phone, heading toward the mini bar. Glass-paned French doors separated the area from the bed, and the doors clicked quietly as he shut them. He dialed Jared's cell phone and cracked open the little fridge. Nothing but Diet Cokes. Made him laugh. Water from the tap would have to do, and while Jared's phone rang, he filled his glass and stared through the glass door at his girl. Gorgeous. Even in the dark, when he could barely make out anything. Fuckin' gorgeous.

He shook his head. Not his girl. But his partner—

"About time you checked in." Jared's grumble was so loud Rocco watched to see if he woke Caterina.

She didn't stir. And why would she have? It was a phone, not a PA system, and he was in another room.

But still Rocco faced away from her, keeping his voice low. "Hello to you too, dick."

He gave a quick update, mentioned Roman, but didn't play his hand one way or another about that, and gave up nothing that would tip Boss Man off to... what? The fact that he was playing house like a pro? That he'd gone from thinking about what was behind an MI6 partition to seeing what was under her clothes? He didn't kiss and tell, so Jared could stay in the dark.

"Anything else?" Boss Man was fishing. Maybe that was the reason Roman was sent out to help? Because Jared knew that Rocco was still hallucinating? Well, he wouldn't fess up to that. Too much on the line. Caterina had too much invested in this job, in El Mateperros, and if Jared pulled him out, she'd be stuck just shy of getting what she needed. That, and his ass would be benched, Titan-style. He rubbed his face. Losing his job should have been the bigger of the two concerns.

"Rocco," Jared snapped at him. "You still there?"

"Yeah. Bad connection."

"Right. Anything else?"

"Nope." Tension hung on the line. "All right then—"

"Did she tell you?"

Not where Rocco thought the conversation might go. With ninety-nine percent certainty they were thinking of the same topic, he agreed. "Yup."

"You okay with this job?"

Rocco chuckled. Leave it to Jared to make sure that, when shit got gray and murky, everyone agreed what was right and what was wrong. Rocco turned back toward the bed. Caterina was partially obscured by the comforter. Everything having to do with that woman was right. "Never more so."

"Good." Jared exhaled into the phone. "Good. Look. I may have turned that girl into a killer. She could've grown up to be, I don't know, an accountant or a doctor or something. Not... what she is. An interrogator on a mission."

Rocco pictured Cat with the live wires in her hand, touching the ends and smiling as the sparks ignited. Then the remembered the grief in her eyes and the pain in her words, recounting the massacre of her family.

"A woman with that kind of pain and that kind of drive? The best thing you did was give her an outlet. Pain like that has to be channeled." He shook his head. "If she didn't have that, then…I don't know if she'd be here today."

Jared didn't answer, and Rocco didn't hang up. Whatever they both had left to say, neither volunteered.

"By the way." Boss Man broke the silence. "Doc Tuska said you never followed up after you checked out of the hospital. Go see the doc."

Rocco dropped his head back and stared at the ceiling. So Jared and the doc had talked. That was all but a confirmation that if Doc Tuska knew what was going on, Jared knew. Too bad Rocco wasn't volunteering anything about his occasional, unpredictable electrical jab of zips and zaps that made him lose his mind. That was need-to-know intel, and no one needed to know.

"I'm all over it when I get home. Thanks for the reminder. Bye."

He ended the conversation before Jared could respond, then turned off his phone.

No one needed to know, but now he suspected everyone already did. Why hadn't Roman said anything? And what about Caterina? Had Jared talked to her? It didn't matter. At least not right now.

Quiet as he could, Rocco cracked open the French doors and crept back into the room. He took one long look over Cat as she slept, then he slid under the covers, pulling her into his arms.

"What do you know about me?" he whispered as she nuzzled against his chest.

"Not nearly enough." All sleepy and sexy without even trying. Her eyes didn't open. Her breathing didn't change. *Sleep talking.*

His fingers slid over her arm and across her collar bone, testing if she was awake. No reaction. Even asleep, she was always an operative, always listening. For whatever reason, that did it for him. Her sleepy confession was all the confirmation he needed to know he'd fallen in love.

TWENTY-THREE

Sunlight flooded the honeymoon suite when Caterina woke up, feeling like they had made good use of the room since they'd checked in. She rolled over, and her gaze crashed into Rocco's, warming her entire body in an instant. How long had he been watching her? "Good morning."

One side of his smile kicked up, and the dimple killed her. Rocco brushed his lips over hers. "Sleep okay?"

"Like the dead."

"Yeah, I don't know about that." He rolled back onto his pillow, tugging her with him. "I'm going to die if I have to put on a pair of khaki pants again today. Let's blow this place and go have some fun."

"Missing your camo and C-4?"

"Hell yes." He kissed her then stretched, surrounding her with a wall of muscle. "Go shower. I'll grab us some breakfast. Be back in twenty minutes."

"And coffee." She sat up, tugging the sheet around her. "Lots of coffee."

"Roger that, Kitten." Rocco crawled out from under her, off the bed, and headed for the closet. He passed over the clothes, grumbling. Finally selecting a shirt and pants, he was pulling on the shirt as he turned around. His eyes lit, watching her watching him. "Change of plans. I'm keeping you in bed. Then breakfast."

"Oh yeah?"

147

"Yeah. There's a *muy caliente* babe in my bed. You think I'm going to pass that up."

"*Muy caliente?* I'm rubbing off on you."

Rocco stalked over to the bed and kneeled on the mattress, making it dip under his enormous presence. "Whatever it takes to keep you talking like that." He kissed her, wrapping his hands around her waist and letting them drift to her bare back. "Most times, I have no idea what you're talking about. All I know is *dos cervezas, por favor.*"

He made her laugh. "Two beers?"

"Two beers, *please.*" He didn't pull his lips far from hers. She still felt both the heat and his humor. "Let's see what else I got... *Uno, dos, tres. Gracias. Adios. Arriverderci.*"

Spanish. Spanish. Spanish. Italian. "So close, big boy."

"I'm just testing you. Besides, I said most times I have no idea. Don't forget that sometimes I do."

Her skin prickled as his fingers danced up and down her spine. "Do, what?"

Because if *do* meant understand her, after she'd talked about loving him, she might die of embarrassment. That mumbled, Spanish profession of love wasn't for him to know about. Was she trying to get him to run? Hell no.

But right now, he wasn't running anywhere, and she couldn't keep her hands off of him. As quickly as he pulled on his clothes, she took them off. Their legs scrambled together, arms wrapping, holding each other. His breath was at her ear, her mouth at his neck. She loved him—needed him—the same way she breathed. Intrinsically. A basic requirement to make it through another day, sleep through another night. Rocco Savage was it.

Rocco pushed into her. "Goddamn woman."

Uh-huh. He was all she could feel, like sweet heaven. Hot like she'd never experienced. Not once in her whole life had she had sex without a condom. Never.

Her eyes opened. His did too. Locked together. "Please don't stop."

It could've been the wrong thing to say—the stupid thing to do—but their connection was too strong, and she'd had her birth control shot months ago. She was fine, and Rocco would never hurt her.

Tightening around him, Caterina prayed he'd keep going.

His breath hitched, mouth parting on a breath. "Okay."

Statement. Question. Who knew? "Okay."

Wrapping her in his arms, he pressed deep, breath catching. "Cat... You feel... unreal."

Caterina's hands gripped back, fingernails scratching and sliding down to the firm, flexing muscles in his backside. Rocco moved fast, driving and rolling. He owned her body. Possessed her mind. Everything, anything, he was the master. Together, they were almost more than she could stand. A hurricane of strokes and thoughts stoked her orgasm.

"So close." She could barely speak. "Please."

Rocco's hips pinned to hers, fast fucking within an inch of existence. All she could do was cling to his extraordinary body and reach into the depths of his eyes. When her core tightened, her body pulsed, and her mouth screamed his name, Rocco hugged her tight, spearing so deep, and he came in her, deliciously, insanely hot. Her climax embraced his, intertwining. The sexiest, most spectacular feeling and it was in his arms.

He collapsed on her, pulling her tight, and she needed to crawl into him. Being held like that, feeling him inside her, all was right in their make-believe world and spilling out into her real one. Fake relationship. Real relationship. It didn't matter, because she was in deep. Eventually, she unwound from him. She would shower in a few minutes, but now she'd rather just lay naked in their sheets.

"Still want breakfast?" His hair was mussed, and his lazy smile warmed her.

Sustenance. "Yes."

Rocco rolled out of bed, throwing on his clothes. One final kiss and he grabbed his wallet and cell phone off the nightstand. "Be back in a few. I—" He tilted his head, giving her a wink and the dimple. "You are something special, Kitten."

• • •

Yassine re-crossed his legs and set down his espresso, smacking his lips and embracing the burn on his tongue. His to-do list was growing at a rapid pace with the upcoming Big Ben event. But… was it big enough? Did it have the sticking power of, say, a meat dress or riding into an award banquet in an egg? God, he loved Lady Gaga. She was brilliant. His phone rang, and he tossed his magazine. The number was not only familiar, it was a pleasant surprise. "Hello, my friend. I thought I'd lost you."

His tried-and-true distributor laughed into the phone. "The last few weeks were a testament to my network. I have to say, when our last *project* didn't go as planned, I felt the heat."

Yes, he bet so. "But no longer?"

Half-waiting for an answer, half-distracted, he picked up an unread newspaper with a headline reading that the royal family and the US president had an upcoming event. An event like that would make quite the splash.

"But no longer, my friend." His pleased voice brought Yassine back to the conversation.

This was good. Buying his explosives and weapons from his regular dealer was more comforting, plus he had a sudden idea for a different project. An American project.

The man on the phone cleared his throat. "If you are still interested in making a deal, I am still interested in providing what you need."

"Perfect." He wouldn't have to use an unknown like Locke.

Yassine's mind wandered to Locke's wife. Her olive skin would be a perfect shade if she were paler and… icy cold. He took another sip of the scalding espresso and imagined the feel of frigid skin under his palms. Locke had the nerve to charge him more for *looking* at his wife? There were so many ways to teach that man a lesson. How would he break off their agreement? Something memorable. Something that said El Mateperros was to be respected and remembered. Several ideas came to mind as he scalded his tongue on espresso again and wished for an icy remedy. He ended the call, thrilled with the opportunities flooding his mind. His excitement raced. Time to go end the deal with Locke.

Slurping the last sips of his espresso and jittery from finishing it so quickly, he called for his men to ready the car. El Mateperros had business to take care of.

TWENTY-FOUR

Caterina lay in bed, buried in pillows, with a grin she couldn't wipe away. Last night had been amazing. This morning... she had no words and still hadn't recovered from being all love-drunk. Every time with Rocco was better than before, and where were his thoughts at—

Knock, knock.

She jumped. He hadn't been gone long enough to grab breakfast. A smile still painted on her face, she wrapped the sheet round her and nearly skipped to the door. "Forget something?"

No answer.

The hairs at the back of her neck stood a second too late as her hand turned the handle. Eyes focusing, she knew her instinct was right.

El Mateperros.

His smooth as sin features smirked through the cracked opening. All the terror from her childhood crushed her chest. She froze. Panicked. Unable to move. Unable to reason.

Until El Mateperros cackled, startling her back to a shell-shocked reality.

"Daniel's not here." She slapped her palm against the door—both hands—and used her bare foot as a fulcrum point. It didn't help as he pushed in. The sheet started to fall, and her elbows pinched it to her side.

El Mateperros wrapped his fingers on the inside of the door. "This is no way to treat a business partner."

Shaking her head, she tried to remember where the closest weapon was. Much farther than El Mateperros's, she was sure. "Come back later."

He pushed the door again, then his shoulder crashed onto it. Him against her, no contest, he had the upper hand, and she couldn't keep him out. All of her weight wasn't slowing the bastard's advance, and he didn't stop until he stood in the living room. "Mrs. Locke."

I know who you are. His watery eyes nearly glowed. Behind him, two of his thugs stood uninterested in her refusal of entry.

"*Por favor.*" The octave of her voice jumped, and she hated herself for it. "I can't let you in. *Daniel va a estar de vuelta en un minuto.*" Nerves were getting to her because the Spanish was coming on its own.

She had to play her part until Rocco came back. He'd confirm their cover. Mr. and Mrs. Locke. There would be no doubt. Their identities had been put together quickly, but they were primo. The room looked like a newlywed couple's: rumpled bed, lingerie in the closet, condom wrapper... somewhere.

There was just no way El Mateperros knew they weren't the Lockes. She'd been too careful.

He snickered. "I prefer not to wait in the hall."

"You should have called." She wrapped the sheet tighter around her, forcing away the disgust and alarm buzzing in her ears. She couldn't let years of training become useless. He could overpower her, but she could bring him within an inch of his life and make him beg for mercy. She just needed the upper hand. "My husband will be furious."

"Your *husband?*"

Maybe he did know. Shit. How? "Yes."

"Interesting." Two of El Mateperros's henchmen stepped into the hotel room and locked the deadbolt. "Say it again, *your husband.*"

This felt all wrong. He asked about her husband, but he wasn't angry. "Get. Out."

"I found another distributor. I don't need your weapons."

"They're not mine, and I don't talk business for my husband." She stepped away but didn't turn her back. What was that cadence to his voice? "Now, let me get dressed and—"

His arm shot out and grasped her bicep. "Not so fast, Mrs. Locke."

She clenched her teeth. "Let. Go."

A rip of her arm and he pulled her close, the sheet tripping her feet, and she slammed into his chest. He breathed her in. "You smell like smut."

Her stomach dropped. Arousal tinged his words. *Sicko.* She struggled in his grip, kneed for his nuts but missed. "He'll kill you."

"A beef-head arms dealer? No chance." He turned to one of the henchmen. "Start the water."

Water? What was this? Did he plan to work her over? And why did he sound turned on? *Ugh, disgusting.*

If she could anticipate his moves, then she could survive them. Waterboarding was more mental than physical. If that was his plan, she could last until Rocco came back. What else could he do with water? Soak her and shock her. That was a tough one too. Electrical shock was always hit or miss. It messed with the heart and fried the nerves. Her mind raced down the list of water-related ways he could elicit information from her. *Stop. Buy time.*

"No." She painted fear on her face, terror in her voice. Partially because it was already there, partially she needed to play to his ego. How long would it take Rocco to grab breakfast? "I don't have anything to do with his business. I don't know anything."

El Mateperros pulled her close. The mint on his breath was so different than the mint that'd been on Rocco's, and it made her stomach revolt. "I'm not here to talk business."

El Mateperros backed her against a wall. Her head hit. *Hard.* Pain exploded at the back of her skull, and he pushed into her. The crushing effort knocked the air from her lungs. His erection jabbed into her stomach. Her eyes went wide. The fear became real. Shit. Shit. Shit. The man who'd turned the water on came out with the trash pail. He grabbed the second one from the living room.

"I always like it better when they're married," El Mateperros said as the man passed and headed to the door. "Newly married is even more fun."

Caterina fought the hold. El Mateperros's perfect face was flawless, every pore microscopic, each eyebrow hair perfectly in place. Deep breath in and she slammed her forehead into his nose as hard as she could. Pain exploded between her eyes. Stars shone. A dizzying spin almost made her lose her balance, but she recovered, teeth snapping, hoping to sink into his perfect flesh.

"Bitch!" El Mateperros's nose bled. He roared back and smacked her face. "Fucking whore!"

Caterina hit the ground, scampering back on her bare ass, knowing she'd seen Rocco tuck a small caliber pistol under a couch cushion. Her attacker wiped his nose with the back of his hand, smearing the blood but not stopping the flow.

The man with the trash pails came back into the room, holding them differently—as if they were heavy—and went into the bathroom. The second henchman deadbolted the door. The tub's water turned off, and she heard a rush, like the sound of ice falling into a glass.

Ice?

Ice had filled the two pails.

Ice was now in the water. In the bathtub.

What the fuck?

She lunged to the side, hoping to reach the couch, but El Mateperros was on her. His fingers dug into her scalp and bashed her head against the carpet. Fireworks lit up the hotel room walls. The floral print on the wallpaper burst into an array of colors as she fought to remain conscious.

"No!" Her head pounded, but her eyes focused. She kicked and clawed. The sheet fell completely away. "Help!"

He laughed. His weight pressed on her, holding her in place. Caterina pumped her legs. Her arms wanted to swing, her fists wanted to find flesh, but he held her down on the floor and forced her to look up.

Beneath him, panic and fear paralyzed her body while her mind remained absolutely coherent. *No!* She snapped out of the shock, shoving her shoulder into his face; another direct impact and his bony nose might even have broken. He threw his head back and she lunged away, growling and grunting, needing to get to a weapon. Or simply get away.

"Help!" She wasn't too proud to beg for help. It was him versus her while his two men stood by. Three against her one. "Help!" Her voice screeched, throat ripping in pain, positive she had screamed loudly enough to make her vocal cords bleed.

El Mateperros clamped his hand over her mouth. Fast breaths tried to force their way out. But didn't. She couldn't breathe. Not enough air came through her nose. Panic. Oxygen.

They battled back and forth, and she had no idea who would win. Her nostrils flared. Moisture seeped out of her nose, her eyes, her mouth.

"Someone!" Hoarse, harsh pleadings didn't make it past the hand he held over her mouth. The room went hazy. Not enough air. Too much panic. And she was about to—

He moved his hand. Caterina gulped for air, drinking it in, coughing and sputtering, trying like hell to maintain consciousness. "Go away." It should've been an order, but it was a sad, weak plea. "Don't do this."

El Mateperros wiped his nose again and nudged her leg with his shoe.

"She's a fighter." One of his bulked up men step forward. "Ready for her?"

His bodyguards were ensuring he didn't need assistance? Caterina spat at him. "Fuck you."

El Mateperros's erection tented in his pants while he licked his lips. "No, that's my job." She could smell the mint on his breath when he got close. "Take her."

Take her? Take her where?

The other man dragged her away from the Dog Killer. She kicked and clawed, but it did no good. "Help. Help me!"

The more she yelled, the quieter she got. Her voice was gone. Blood seeped in her mouth from the force of overexerting her throat. Half-dragging, half-carrying, the man who held her smelled like sweat. He dropped her in a pile. She stared at the ceiling. The bathroom lights blinded her.

"Here you go. Chill out." And with a toss, she was off the cold tile floor and landing in the ice bath.

Frozen agony surrounded her, cramping her muscles and burning her skin as she fell underneath the water. She couldn't pull up, couldn't push out. Her legs flayed, arms splashed, trying to push above water and out of the deep two-person tub. A hand held her head down. Ice cold water rushed into her nose and burned, choking her. Ice cubes sloshed around the tub, covering her, bumping against her skin. She flailed. Every head turn, each push to come up for air was refuted. Her lungs ached. Her body wanted to gasp but only inhaled water. A hand pulled her head up, just enough to breathe and she gasped and choked, swallowing air. Coughing and sputtering. Her lungs couldn't jump start.

Where was Rocco?

Held up by the stinging roots of her hair, she shivered, shaking violently as she dangled from a hulk's grip. Ice cubes clinked against the tub. Her temperature was in free fall and serious hypothermia concerns poisoned her drive to survive. He pushed her in and out of the water a few more times until she was far past disoriented.

Just as fast as she'd gone into the tub, she was yanked out. Her head snapped back, and her limbs shook so severely she couldn't use them to defend herself. Hell, at that second, she couldn't use them to even stand. Sopping wet, bitterly frozen, she was held by one foot, on elbow and dragged to the bedroom, tossed onto bed.

El Mateperros lorded over her. "*Now* she's ready."

Licking his lips again, he turned them up.

She would kill him. She would. He'd murdered her family, and now he would rape her? Not without her tearing him apart as soon as she could move. Soon as she could run. Save herself and come back, just to slit him open knuckles to nuts and watch him bleed out. Slowly. Goddamn him.

The metal clink of the buckle brought her back to the hotel room, away from her plans for vengeance. He unbuckled his belt like he was putting on a show. A terrorist, rapist burlesque number, just for her. Every ounce of her strength shot into her ice-numbed limbs. She popped up and pushed back. Her feet fought to find the bed. She kicked, hitting him hard, the heels of her feet beating into him.

No effect. More kicks, screams…

It didn't faze him at all, and a predatory look of arousal blossomed on his face. He was growing more amused, more turned on by the second.

No. A growl roared from deep in her chest.

The bastard dropped his trousers. His erection pushed in his briefs, straining toward her, then he snagged her kicking ankles. "I love a cold, wet bitch."

His fingers squeezed too tight on her ankle. The bone felt ready to shatter under his strength. Fuck it. Let him break it. She pulled back, hard as she could, grabbing the comforter, the sheets, sliding in the mess of fabric while he laughed. And laughed and laughed. Wannabe necrophiliac bastard.

He pulled her forward to the foot of the bed and pounced between her legs, shoving himself into the vee of her body. Gorilla fingers gripped her flesh, bruising as he clawed up her body. Knees. Thighs. Hips. She tried to roll. Scream. Kick. His free hand fell hard, slapping her, and blood exploded in her mouth.

All went white…

…and she was back.

She shook her head for focus. Her eyes struggled to open. Then did. His fucking smile. His cock. Greeting her like some sicko jack-in-the-box, bobbing over her. Crushing weight dropped down, smashing her bare breasts, rubbing his vulgar, hard penis all over her.

He hissed, "Wet and cold."

Tears streamed down her face, and the blunt head of his erection pressed painfully against her sex. Her body clamped down. *God no. Please. No. God help me.* Her teeth steeled together. Blood filled her mouth. She swallowed and choked when he tore into her, sensitive flesh tearing with his invasion. Splitting muscle. Cries coughed out. Tears and snot ran down her face. And he thrust. And thrust. And rammed… grunting. Wrists pinned down. Vomit rose in her throat, into her mouth, stinging into her nose. Hot moisture seeped between them. Blood. She knew it without seeing it. The vicious tear of flesh. The raw burn and the blistering friction that she never could've imagined. She couldn't move her legs, her arms. Pins and needles from his physical restraint and dead weight. Complete desperation paralyzed her. And she sobbed. Harder and more, and her eyes cracked opened. His teeth were sealed together, lips bare, chin jutting every time he slammed into her. The tears wouldn't stop, and that deep, body-destroying hurt wouldn't quit.

His groan cried out, partnered with a thrust so deep that she almost passed out. He shuddered and pulsed, quivering his awful climax into her damaged body. El Mateperros stilled for a heartbeat. His teeth parted, mouth gaping, and his sick grin appeared. He pulled from her quickly, patting her on the chin. "Ice cold and wet. Does it every time."

His torso, his cock…. her blood stained his skin. He bent to pull his pants up, the belt clinking as he did, and she threw up, barely turning her head to keep from choking on it.

But that's all she could do. Lie in a pool of her vomit, bleeding between her legs and cry…

El Mateperros's voice smiled even if she didn't open her eyes to see it. "Good thing I knew what you wanted."

TWENTY-FIVE

Rocco strolled up to their hotel room, breakfast in hand, coffee balancing on his forearm. What a morning... Best one yet. He slid his key card into the door. It flashed red, but he pushed forward not expecting the deadbolt to be turned.

"Open up, Kitten."

Key card again. No dice. He knocked and knocked. Caterina wouldn't have used the deadbolt. Something was wrong. He pulled out his phone, direct connected to Roman. "Cat with you?"

Roman gave a quick nope.

Rocco's stomach dropped. "Caterina."

Nothing.

He tried the card again, same thing. The deadbolt was engaged, and no answer came from the other side. His gut twisted. Overreactions weren't possible when they were undercover. Everything could be assumed to be an attack.

"Come on." Their hotel door was coming down, or she was opening up. One last chance. "Kitten. Open the goddamn door."

Nothing.

He slammed it with his shoulder. Shit, he didn't have silencer on his .33. Blowing the door handle off would have the cops there in minutes. At least knocking the door down would give him slightly more time before someone dialed the British equivalent of 911.

Rocco charged the door. *Bam!*

Still on its hinges. Not for long.

Once more. *Bam!* And a third time—

The door flew open. Two men his size stood there. They looked like ACG, and they didn't stand a chance. He charged, ready to take them at the same time. One was on top of him, then the other. His fists flew. Theirs did too. Pounding. Flesh meeting flesh. The thud of muscles colliding charged him. Their two against his one was nothing. Right hook. Left. One grabbed a leg, and he used his knee to crack a nose, maybe break a jaw.

Out of the corner of his eye, Rocco saw El Mateperros. Clapping. Urging his men on. Like this was sport. Where was Caterina? He gritted his teeth together, and fists flew harder, faster, deadlier. A knife sliced at his chest, and fury ripped through his blood. He was done with damn knives stabbing at his chest.

Struggling to grasp it, to turn the blade away from his neck, Rocco growled until his temples throbbed and his vision began to shake. A knee to the guy's junk, and his attacker rolled, doubled over. Rocco brought down an elbow to his temple, and the dude was lights out.

Rocco hopped to his feet, snarling, beckoning. "Come on, fucker."

Now that it was one on one, El Mateperros had backed against the wall. Rocco would get him next. Then he caught site of the bed. Caterina. Naked. Not moving. White rage blinded him. He charged the man in front of him and tackled him to the ground. It took second to incapacitate him. Rocco swiveled around, searching for El Mateperros, but he was gone. Shaking, he stumbled toward the bedroom. Caterina's eyes were open. They followed him. But her head didn't. Blood...

Blood all over her.

And vomit.

She was crying. Bawling and sobbing.

His insides roared, guttural and grief-stricken.

"No!" The veins and tendons in his neck popped. Sweat covered him in an instant. Dangerous rage tore through. She needed a doctor, and he needed an outlet.

"Cat. Kitten." He threw a sheet over her, scared to touch her but desperate to take care of her. Aggression blinded him, and he couldn't breathe fast enough. Or slowly enough. Couldn't figure out which way was up or down. His world shattered, just fucking shattered, lying, bleeding on the bed in front of him.

Tears choked him. Anger fueled his madness. "What the fuck did he do to you?"

She wouldn't look him in his eye, even as he crouched in her line of sight.

"The police—"

"No," she croaked then cried harder.

Rocco clawed hands into his hair, desperate to release the violence. He was undone. Completely changed. This couldn't be happening.

"Cat. Please. Say something."

"I…" Her tears streamed. "Hurt."

Right then, a part of him died. "A doctor then. Something. Somebody. Fuck!"

Goddamn it. She needed help, and this cleanup needed more than just him. He touched her face. He'd slice El Mateperros to pieces. Dick first.

"Take me away from here." She choked on tears. "I can't be here."

He nodded, held her hand. "Can you move? Can you…" Can she what? Get up, get dressed? What did he want her to do?

"Whatever it takes. Take me away." The raspy heartbreak in her words would haunt him.

Roman. Rocco needed Roman because he couldn't think straight. Grabbing his phone, he direct connected again.

Roman answered immediately. "What's going on?"

Rocco couldn't form the words. Instead, he gave the shit-hit-the-fan call sign. "Code thirteen. Get up here."

"On my way." The line went dead. He knew Roman was running. Code thirteen was the bring hell, the world's ending call for assistance.

Caterina had curled into a ball. Her body shook and shivered, and muffled sobs came from behind the pillow she now had over her head. He placed a hand on her ankle, and she shot back, nearly jumping off the bed. The pillow fell away. Her eyes were wild, mouth wide open. Panting. She blinked.

"I'm… sorry." Head shaking back and forth, over and over. "I didn't—I'm…"

The hotel room door opened and closed. A curse joined the occasional groans from the downed ACG men.

Roman rounded the corner. "Whoa—" Then backed out, jaw clenching and eyes flashing to Rocco.

"Be back in a min." Rocco didn't know what else to say to her. Wasn't sure of how to comfort her or if he should even try. He walked out of the bedroom, over an ACG thug and nailed Roman with a look so full of uncontrollable hatred that he shook.

"Cat?" Roman asked, his throat bobbing. Silence ticked for an eternity. "The Dog Killer?"

"He. Hurt. Her." Rocco raged inside, twitching from unexpended devastation.

"She was…"

Grinding his teeth, he couldn't acknowledge his woman had been raped. He was going to be sick. And kill. He was going to fucking murder.

"Jesus Christ." The veins in Roman's neck stood out. Fury pounded through him too.

"We have to get her to a doctor. She's bad off."

"Calling Jared." Roman pulled out his phone. "He'll get someone good and off the grid."

Rocco stepped back to Cat. "We're getting you out of here. Give us a minute." He scrounged anything they couldn't leave behind and spent a minute wiping their prints. "You'll be okay. Promise you. I swear on my life."

She nodded.

"I have to get you dressed."

Another nod.

Tearing apart his closet, he found clothes that'd be baggy on her, and as carefully as he could, he slipped his sweatpants and shirt onto her. Too much blood. Her eyes followed his movements. "It's gonna be all right, Kitten."

It had to be all right. He'd found something special, and nothing would steal that from him.

Roman walked in, eyes averted though Caterina was now curled in a ball at the top of the bed, wearing his clothes and burying her head back into the pillows.

"Jared." His outstretched hand held the cell. "Needs to talk to you."

Rocco wasn't sure he could talk about Caterina, but Jared needed to bring down all the hell Titan was known for. That moment wasn't the first time he'd thanked God he worked for Boss Man, but it was the most important of those times.

"Whatever you need," Jared grumbled.

"Bring everything we got." Rocco seethed, stormed into the kitchenette, and swallowed the need to rip the hotel room to pieces. The pressure in his jaw would crush his teeth. His mind spiraled in shock. *Everything.*

He watched Roman drag the two ACG men, check pulses—they were still alive, damn it—and tie them together in a corner with curtains he'd ripped into ropes.

"What do you want to do?" Jared paused and told someone to shut the hell up in the background. Then all his attention focused back on Rocco. "What's your next move?"

Next move… Rocco sat on the bed, careful not to touch her without warning again. "I need a doctor. Fast."

"Parker's finding you a doctor." Jared yelled away from the phone. "Where's the doctor already?" He mumbled offline again, then back to Rocco. "You need to clean it up and get out."

"I know."

"How bad is she, Roc?"

An angry, cold sweat beaded on his forehead. He hurt for her. Pain wracked his mind. Tension in his fists begged for an outlet as he eyed the two men bleeding and groaning in corner. Just a few more punches. Anything. And when he got his hands on El Mateperros—

"Rocco," Jared snapped. "What's going on with our girl?"

He looked down and could barely describe his personal hell. "Tell me you've got someone we can see quickly." Turning away, he couldn't get the images from his mind. Whispering, he could barely take it. "A lot of blood, Jared. It's bad."

"God—I'm bringing the fuckin' cavalry."

"I'm not leaving her side until I know she's okay." He watched Roman clear the room of Titan-identifiers. "But I want that son of a bitch. You find him. I kill him. No discussion."

"Parker texted a doc's address and directions to you. About four blocks away."

Holy fuck, he couldn't breathe. She had to be okay. "Jared." He choked trying to talk. "I...Caterina is..."

"I got it. Get her to the doc."

The call ended, and Parker's text came through.

Roman walked over. "We gotta roll. Someone probably heard something."

"We're going here." Rocco tossed him the phone. Roman nodded. They both looked at Cat. The sobbing had stopped, or at least the shaking had. "She's not going to be able to walk."

"Fuck it. Someone tries to stop you, I stop them."

Right. "Kitten, honey. I've got to get you out of here."

"*No policia.*"

"I know. But you need a doctor."

She nodded.

"So I have to pick you up, sweetheart. Okay? I have to touch you."

She nodded again, and it shattered his heart. "Help me."

"I'm all over it. Just..." He slipped an arm under her shoulder and the other behind her knees. "Easy there." The clothes drowned her, and she buried her face into his chest. He sat down with her in his arms and begged God that something he would say could help. "That's my girl. Shhh. You're a survivor. You're the strongest person I know."

Roman tilted his head, nodding Rocco off the bed. He looked down at sheets and a comforter stained with blood. He stood. "I need you to be okay. Okay? Just look at me. Just a second."

She did, and his soul bled out. All he could do was nod, promising that he'd make this right somehow.

Roman stripped the bed, and then they headed to the door. Because of the number on the door Rocco had done knocking it in, the door was ajar and scratching when Roman pulled it open. He stuck his head out, then they were off. At the elevators, Rocco pushed the button, and Roman jimmied open the supply closet, coming back out with the soiled bedding in a bag.

The elevator chimed, and they got on. A family—mom, dad, two kids—took a step back when they boarded, but then got out. Good idea, but surely they would call the cops. Classical music played, and Roman held the closed door button down, skipping any floors that expected them to stop.

When they hit the lobby, tourists parted to let them exit. They were quite the sight, he was sure: Rocco bloody from the fight, torn shirt, busted face, a roughed-up, near comatose Caterina in his arms, next to Roman, holding a giant trash bag. They needed out of there before London coppers rolled up asking questions. Fists would fly if someone tried to stop them, or God forbid, tried to take her away from him.

The automatic front door opened, and they spilled out onto a crowded sidewalk. Rocco got his bearings, turned left, and checked on his girl. Caterina's eyes locked with his. She hung in his arms limp and a galaxy away, eyes bloodshot, lips swollen, and her nose red. Dried blood stained her cheeks and chin.

"I need you to be okay. Okay?" It was all he could keep saying.

A cold prickle chased down his spine. That spiky slide, like a thousand tiny shanks. It was fear, terror at losing someone he'd connected with. More than connected. He loved everything from her Spanish sass to the secrets that shaped her life.

She *had* to be okay. Had to.

His stomach turned. Passing a trash can, he ignored the urge to retch then watched Roman stop. Well, hell, now was as good a time as ever. Roman smashed the bag into the trashcan, pulled out a lighter, and lit it. It took a moment for it to catch. The comforter was probably flame retardant, but the sheets and bag weren't, and retardant didn't mean wouldn't burn. It only meant a pain in their ass. But it started to burn while he kept walking. Black smoke and burning plastic filled the air.

Cat's eyes flitted to the side like she wanted to watch her DNA burn away but couldn't control her line of sight. Concussion? The hell with walking. He broke into a jog, bumping people out of his way. Boots behind him said Roman agreed with the move. He broke in front of them, clearing their path on the sidewalk.

"Half a block, man," Roman called over his shoulder.

With Cat still cradled in his arms, Rocco pushed through the thick mob of bystanders. Her eyelids slid shut and jarred to open slits each time his feet pounded against the sidewalk. "Come on, Kitten. Stay with me."

I need you.

Her eyes shut, and her head lolled. No control. How much blood had she lost? Internal bleeding? Head injury? Combat mode took over. He saw no one, nothing but the end goal: the doctor's office. It was the only way she'd survive.

TWENTY-SIX

Caterina cringed as she drifted awake. Her memory was fuzzy. The film on her tongue made nausea roll. Instinctively, her body lurched to vomit. Bile and nothingness came up as she twisted on her side. Her limbs twitched and spasmed. Her abdominal muscles ached like she'd thrown up for days. Pain between her legs throbbed. Her abdomen was sore, bruised. Her insides—

The memory of El Mateperros above her, forcing himself in her—

Her stomach cramped. She dry heaved. Once, twice. Again and again. The memory made her retch. Relief seemed almost impossible. Her body disgusted her. She needed a shower. Needed to scrub and purge. Needed help…

Grunts and El Mateperros's voice. *No.* Tears fell again.

Her head spun, worsening with every remembered syllable of the disgusting memory. A headache panged her temples. Reality was awful. Hatred and misery took over. Why had this happened? Why couldn't she stop it? Strength and tenacity, impervious and impassable. That was how she would have described herself. Not pathetic.

Friction-burned flesh was raw between her legs. How had she— *oh…* a cool cloth pressed against her forehead. *Ah.* Relief. Only a small flicker.

But one ounce of it was enough to keep the maddening pain at bay for a microsecond. Disheveled strands of hair were tucked behind her ear, and again, the cool cloth. On her forehead. Her cheeks. Her neck. Opening her eyes was too much. Strong and stable warmth patted her hair, repositioning the cloth.

"I think she's waking up." An echoing, distantly familiar voice tugged her awake—*Rocco.*

The caress of his voice drew her eyes open. His chiseled face was furrowed. Soft caramel eyes had darkened and dulled. Her stomach twisted again, and her headache quadrupled, stomach roiling as the memories came back in jolting chunks, like flipping channels on the TV. A gap in memory, El Mateperros's face. Another gap, the ice bath. A gap, her sickening attack and—Rocco arrived. She hadn't seen him, but she heard him. All American-cartoon-style. Bow. Bam. Pop. The brute force. The sounds of the room being destroyed had screamed in her ears. Rocco had wanted to save her life, her *dignity*. One out of two at least…She gagged, wallowing until she boxed up the self-pity, hiding it from herself, and re-prioritized her feelings. Rage. That was better. If nothing else, it would make this survivable. Caterina would have El Mateperros's balls if it killed her. She'd castrate him with a toothbrush. Or a toothpick. Whichever one was slower and more painful. Soon as her body healed.

Hushed voices brought her from planning the Dog Killer's dismembering. A doctor. He shooed Rocco out of the room and gave her a onceover, asking questions and providing information. She didn't speak or listen, only kept her eyes partly open. There was nothing other than the obvious wrong with her, and she didn't want to talk about it to a stranger, even if he was a doctor. As soon as the exam was over, she curled back onto the bed and tried to sleep again.

"Kitten?" Rocco stepped back in, pulled a chair back to the bed, and his thumb smoothed over her cheek.

She blinked. Focused. Tried to swallow. Didn't work so much.

"Hello." Her whisper barely made a sound, cracking and aching in her raw throat.

His forehead bunched, and she saw a flicker of a smile, but then stress lines reappeared. "Hi."

Her eyelids burned as though she'd cried for days. They were swollen, and her eyes scratched with each blink. The cool cloth pressed on her temple again, and he smoothed it across her skin.

"How do you feel?"

She nodded. "Okay enough."

Rocco put the cloth down and took her hand. His dwarfed hers, and dropping down, he hunched over in a chair pulled close to the bed. Silence wrapped around them. The room was so quiet. Too quiet to be a hospital. Medical equipment lined the walls. A cross on the wall. Cabinets and medical supplies.

"Doc's been taking care of you…" He squeezed her hand as if trying to impart strength and brought it to his cheek. "Titan did a job for his medical charity out in—hell, it doesn't matter. Just know the doc here is good."

"Where is here?"

"Private residence, not too far from the hotel."

He scrubbed his bruised jaw and ran his fingers through his hair. "Damn, Cat. I never should've left you alone. I can't explain how sorry I am." His throat bobbed, and tears laced it. "I'm so fucking sorry."

He brought her hand back to the bridge of his nose and bowed his head. They fell silent. His breaths were irregular. Every few minutes, he moved, motioned, acted as if he had something to say, but nothing more came.

Finally, Rocco shook his head. "I don't want to make this about me, but hell, holding you to me… like I was the one dying. And I was. Dying."

What to say to that? She had nothing. Helpless guilt choked her.

Rocco continued, quietly, maybe talking to himself, maybe talking to her. "I'm sure there are special words I should say. Hell, or shouldn't say. Caterina… goddamn. I'm sorry. It shouldn't be like this."

Tears blurred her vision. She wiped at them, angry that they kept falling. Her body ached, soreness a vicious reminder of the attack.

"I forget what normal feels like, and I was normal…yesterday. Even hours ago." She gulped a breath. "How do you forget that?"

His jaw flexed. "Do you need to, ya know, talk? Want me to get one of the girls on the phone? Mia, Nic, Sugar, Sarah… I trust them. Someone else?"

"No."

"Cat…" She could hear him breathe. Swallow. A clock ticked somewhere nearby. "You want to talk to me?"

She didn't know what she wanted. Talking seemed awful. Silence was so much better. But even in silence, she couldn't get away from her thoughts. They replayed everything over and over. Licking a raw lip, she tried to find the words. "I shouldn't have opened the door."

"What?" His face twisted.

Forcing herself up, she pulled her hand from his and sat up. Emotions swirled. Guilt. Embarrassment. Anger. Desperation. Sadness. She was all over the place. Rocco moved to adjust her pillows, and she flinched, shrinking back as if he came at her with a baseball bat. Holy God. Her cheeks heated. "I didn't mean to—I know… I'm sorry. I—"

"Don't apologize." He moved so slowly, adjusting her pillows and delicately touching her arm to help her move back against them. His deliberate actions made her feel even more foolish. "There you go."

"What if—"

Slowly, his head shook. "You can't torture yourself."

"I've tortured people most my life. This is karma. I deserved it. And I was stupid. I should've looked, should've pushed stronger, fought harder." She dissolved into a mess of tears. "I'm stronger than this. I shouldn't have let it happen."

He wrapped himself around her. She flinched again, reacting even though she knew better, but it didn't stop him from enveloping her in the safety of his arms. Thank God, because she needed him to hold her more than she'd realized. She needed him in so many ways.

"This is *not* your fault."

Nothing to say to that. It might have been her fault. It *felt* a hell of a lot like her fault.

"Caterina Cruz." He pulled back, stealing his fortifying embrace. "Look at me."

But she couldn't. How would he ever touch her again? The worst person she'd ever met, the most awful monster that walked the face of the earth, had been *inside* her. She was disgusting. Awful. Just completely, absolutely horrific. And that bastard... She needed to hurl.

"Kitten." Slowly, he reached over, taking her chin in his hand and redirected her. Barely a whisper. "Just look at me."

She closed her eyes tight then opened to his warm gaze. Reaching. Caring. Loving. And it was too much. "I can't."

With eyes sealed shut, he sucked a breath, then leveled a stare as calculating as she felt cold and empty. He let her chin go and found her hand again, stroking her knuckles. "I'll get El Mateperros for you. Don't worry about a thing."

"No." She moved too fast. The room spun. Tugging her hand back, she shook her head, doing bad things for her nausea. "No. You can't."

"Kitten."

"No."

"Cat. Caterina—"

El Mateperros was hers. Especially now. No white knight was going to steal her revenge. "No."

"Lie down—"

"No." Panic flowed. She tore into a tirade, a mix of Spanish and English. She didn't even know what she was saying. It was all *El Mateperros is mine. You owe me. He owes me.* Too much hurt in her chest. In her memory. Anger bubbled up at Rocco, and a cold sweat broke out over her body.

"Caterina," he tried to cut her off.

But she couldn't stop. Her mouth ran. Her hands, her legs moved. She'd escape. Chase down her nemesis. Rocco couldn't take this from her. He just couldn't. El Mateperros, more so than ever, was hers to destroy. Mind spinning, she tried to hop off the bed. Rocco held her in place, saying something, but she couldn't hear him.

"What are you saying?" He turned behind them, talking to someone she hadn't seen. "What's she saying? Doc, a little help in here."

She couldn't stop. El Mateperros was her obsession. Her will to live, breathe, and survive rested on taking out the terrorist. He *took* from her, and he would pay at her hands.

Rocco's fingers snapped at her, but she couldn't look at him. No stopping her now. She'd walk out of the doctor's and find her attacker on foot if she had to.

A loud smacking sound stunned her. Rocco's hands were still together, hanging inches from her face after he clapped. Whatever she'd been saying stopped. Her mind went blank. Then she dropped back onto the bed, shaking her head.

"He's mine." She calmed down, needing to convey how much Rocco had to understand. "That bastard owes me. If El Mateperros took that much from you, Rocco, I'd say go ahead. Go get him. Take him down, tear him apart. Take what you deserve. If he hurt you—"

"You don't get it, Caterina," he growled. "He did."

No, no. He couldn't use her feelings against her. He couldn't play like they were feeling the same thing, all in the name of keeping her safe, especially when she knew so much was going on with him.

Rocco's hands on hers were steadfast. "He almost took everything I—"

"Don't say finish. Don't." Her mind reeled. Being in love with him was one thing. Being loved by him, a completely different thing. "That's... scary. Impossible to survive. Take your confusions and know that—"

"Can't help who you fall for or when it happens."

"Damn it, Rocco. Don't say anything else." She shook her head, defensive, wanting to protect *him* and her heart. "Not today. Not after this happened. I won't believe it. I can't."

"But—"

"Not today. I'm so fucked in the head. Even before... *this*. You don't understand what it's like to lose your mind."

"That's not true. You just don't know it."

And there it was, the only mention of what she had known was happening. Relief let her take a deep breath. Something to talk about other than what had happened to her. She could talk about him.

She'd *rather* talk about his freak outs. Her mind needed a break, and her heart needed to feel something other than fear and misery.

"Actually. I do, Roc." The night they'd met on the London park bench seemed so long ago. Somehow, she'd known they were supposed to run into each other. When it was time to force herself out of his hotel room that night, she couldn't resist leaving a note on the mirror. She'd thought he'd never see it, but she'd always know it was there.

She'd hoped maybe one day their paths would cross. Then they did. Immediately. She should've told him what happened. What she saw. What she knew. Or thought she knew. He needed to know whatever was happening to him was survivable.

His stare penetrated, wary. Its intensity burned into her. "You do? What?"

"I saw you when you left me."

Somewhere in the room, the clock continued to tick loudly. The slightest shift made her sheets swish.

"That was you." He didn't blink.

Caterina nodded.

"At our hotel?"

She nodded. "And…"

His head tilted, studying her. "The note in the mirror?"

"Yes."

His jaw gaped, and his eyes narrowed. "Somehow I thought it was."

Talking about this was so much better than talking about her. "I met you that night. You needed help, so I helped."

"I could've been on drugs, deranged. Just dangerous."

Her stomach dropped. Today had proven that she couldn't handle danger. When she'd looked at him, she'd known he wasn't. Both then and now. "You weren't, and I knew it. Down to my soul."

Rocco pressed his lips together, rolling the bottom one in for long seconds. "I thought you were an angel."

She thought back to that night. How vulnerable he was despite his size. Maybe she was his angel. Right now, he was hers.

"I thought I dreamt you. I…" He closed his eyes. Finally, they opened, darting around the room before landing back on her. "If anyone finds out—"

"They won't."

He rubbed his knuckles into the hollows of his eyes. "Remember that knife wound I told you about? The new scar?"

She nodded.

"I was dosed with some messed-up poison. I tripped my ass off when it first happened. Then I thought it flushed out of my system, but it keeps happening."

"For how long?"

"Weeks now."

"You should see a doctor."

He dropped his head back. "Yeah. True enough. Except I was worried about my job."

"Jared doesn't know?"

"Well, he might. I don't know."

"You haven't told him?"

"Nope. But the man has a way of finding out." He rolled his shoulders as if he were trying to relieve tension. "Think he already knows."

"You should tell him."

He sighed. "I should do a lot of things, starting with making sure *you* are okay. Forget about me, El Mateperros, this job. Let me get you home. Your *real* home, not some hotel room or short term apartment in a random city. Recuperate. We'll figure out your next move. Sound like a plan, Kitten?"

Her heart sank. Completely pathetic. The only constant in her life was a dedication to chasing down another person, and that person had violated her today.

She had no roots. She had nothing. No home. No address. Just… nothing. "That'll be tough. No home."

"No home?" His brows furrowed. "Where do you go between jobs?"

"I don't have a between jobs. El Mateperros is… my world. My obsession. I don't stop. Ever. And now that… he did this… I can't stop."

"Yes, you can."

"Let me rephrase. I won't."

"Caterina—"

"Earlier, when I told you to stop talking, that you shouldn't tell me how you feel about me? I am far more screwed up than you know."

"Not true." He reached for her, but she shifted back.

"Very true."

"I—"

"Rocco, I love you. But after today, maybe especially because of today, I wouldn't know what to do if you loved me too."

TWENTY-SEVEN

Years ago, Rocco had been in a Humvee when an IED hit. The armored vehicle flipped into the air, landing on its nose in a ditch, and everyone rolled and jarred with each harsh hit. Some were knocked out. Most were bleeding. He'd been bleeding and couldn't breathe. It turned out one of his lungs had collapsed.

Right now, he had the same feeling. Lungs aching. Breaths on hold. Mind all stuttering and coughing and trying to decipher what his next move should be. He didn't have one. Knowing he loved Caterina was one thing. It didn't make a whole hell of a lot of sense, but little did in his life.

Hearing her say it was another thing. Then, watching her say it as though it was something to walk away from, well, that was some bullshit. It took some balls to throw around the L-word. She had dropped it like a warning. *I love you. Stay away.* Like she wasn't sure where his head was. And that bit about not being sure what to do? Was that about him? About El Mateperros? About her next move in… life?

Rocco clawed his way to normal respirations. "I've never run from anything. Not gonna start with you."

Caterina pushed his chest and tried to get up. "*Oh Dios.* I'm not knocked up. No need to stake a claim or defend your—"

"Not uh. No way. You're not getting the last word in here."

On her feet, she swayed back and forth and needed to get her pretty ass back into bed. "So romantic."

His hands readied to catch her when she toppled, one near each hip, hovering. "Back in bed."

"No."

"Don't be stubborn."

"Then don't say anything else."

"What, like *I love you?*"

She smirked at him, and her mouth opened, then her eyes swung to the hallway at the sound of the front door. Roman entered. "*Hola.*"

Rocco took a step back as she settled against the edge of the bed.

Roman's eyes bounced between her and Rocco. "Boss Man's blowing my phone up trying to get an update."

Caterina bit her lip. "He knows?"

Rocco's phone had been ringing, but he had ignored everyone but Cat. "I'll hit him back."

"Roc, man, when you get a second." He tilted his head toward the door.

"Is it about El Mateperros?" Caterina asked.

"Not exactly—"

The sound of two more-than-familiar voices came in the front door of the doctor's residence. Heavy boots creaked on an old wood floor. The acoustics of the hallway amplified their presence, as if anyone in Titan needed amplification.

Rocco looked at Roman, then the dark hallway. "Are you kidding me?"

"What are you talking about, dude? You called in the troops. Winters and Cash were semi-nearby and got here fast as they could. Boss Man's wrapping something up, and Delta's flying in too."

Delta. That was good. That meant Boss Man was ready to bring it, and Roman was right. Where was his head? Every Titan resource was needed. But he really wanted to finish this I-love-you-but-you-can't convo with Cat.

Cash and Winters stood in the hall. No doubt, they were ready to get a move on. El Mateperros didn't know he had tried to attack someone within Titan, but after the show Rocco put on in the hotel room, the bastard had to realize he was dealing with something more than a mysterious arms dealer.

Caterina craned her neck. "What is going on?"

Roman nodded.

Yeah, she wasn't going to take this well. "Like Roman said, I called in the troops."

If looks could maim, she'd have had him strung up and bleeding out. "Why?"

"The husband and wife gig was up, and we know more about El Mateperros than has ever been known."

Her eyes narrowed. "We? Titan?"

"We, well, yeah."

"And me. Where do I fit into this? Because if you called in the troops, it doesn't sound good for me and what I want." Seething mad might not have been an adequate description of the vibes coming off her. "Bring them in here. I need to meet them."

Uh… *What to say? How to play this…* He nodded to Roman who walked out and returned. Cash and Winters walked into the room, nodding their hellos, and he wasn't in the mood to formalize the introductions.

Roman was, though. "That's my boy, Cash. I spot, he shoots. One shot, one kill type action."

Caterina nodded, not saying a word, which had to be bad. Experience said that if she was pissed, she was throwing down Spanish. If she was silent, then the woman was probably plotting his death.

Roman continued. "And that's Winters. Jack of all trades. Thinks he's a hardass. Comes in handy though."

More silence.

"Enough already. Out." Rocco had nothing to say to any of them. Except for Cat. "Now."

Cash nodded. Winters shook his head. Roman walked out with the guys.

Rocco grimaced. "Sorry about them."

They had left the room, but it didn't take away the tension.

She glared at him with thin, bruised lips. "You mean sorry for trying to take away my chance to kill El Mateperros?"

He took a step forward. "Cat, no. Look—"

"Stop saying my name, and make it happen so that I end this. *Me.*" She slapped the mattress. "Not Titan."

"We'll work something out."

"No. Not good enough. Promise me. *Promise me.* Titan can play a part, but I will get my revenge."

Her pleading shattered his heart. The sharp edges made him bleed from the inside out. "Get some sleep. You're worked up. I'm beyond exhausted. We'll work something out. *I promise.*"

Her skin was bruised, and her bloodshot eyes didn't believe a word he was saying. She knew how to read people, knew when the truth was presented. No matter his training, no matter how good he could make his promise look, they both knew he was lying. And there was no way in hell he was letting her anywhere near the man who had raped her. Hell. No.

She scooted back onto the bed, flipped the pillow, and pulled a blanket around her. Snuggling back down into the bed, a little too quiet for his liking, she finally closed her eyes. "Fine."

He walked over and kissed her forehead. "It'll all be okay."

TWENTY-EIGHT

With her eyes sealed shut, Caterina listened and waited, plotting her escape. Rocco stood watch. He didn't move. His breaths barely registered, but he was still there. First he wanted to talk love. Then he brought in Titan. Even if his motives were all warm-and-fuzzy, he was wrong.

What did she know about this place? It was the swanky private residence of some high-priced doctor Titan worked with. One of the many members in Jared Westin's worldwide network. Most likely one of the best doctors in this hemisphere. But that kind of doctor didn't have security to keep people in, only to keep robbers and the like out.

Titan's muscled-up meeting was happening down a short hall. A huge, curtained window with a slip of the outdoors showing told her they were on the first floor. It was one of those big windows, with panes large enough to crawl through...

Her clothes were a problem. She was in pajamas of some sort, nothing she could walk around in outside, and her shoes weren't sitting anywhere she had seen. One limb at a time, she made her body relax and slowed her breathing. Soft breaths, one after the other. All a ruse. Rocco had to be convinced she was asleep so he would join the Titan meeting-in-progress. It took forever. And if she didn't want out as badly as she did, she would have focused more on how sweet the guy was.

El Mateperros was her problem. No one else's.

Finally, Rocco stepped close, checked on her, and retreated out the door and down the hall. She counted backward from one hundred. Still worried he might pop back in, she slowly sat up, ready to play possum the second she heard footfalls coming back her way.

She heard silence in the hall and male grumblings in another room. She lifted her legs over the side of the bed and pushed up. The floor creaked, and she froze, ignoring the aching soreness that rocketed from her core. Caterina stood with arms out, knees bent like some teenager trying to sneak out at night. Hearing no change from the men, she searched the room.

Nothing under the bed. Nothing in the adjacent bathroom. But, oh—she looked lucky to be alive. Mascara circled her swollen eyes. Hair a rat's nest. She tried to smooth it down, but there wasn't a point, and she had to get out. Fast.

Another look around and she saw a plastic bag. Holding her breath with each step, she crept over and cringed when the bag crinkled as she opened it. Success. Rocco's oversized sweats and shoes. They were dark, and her blood stained them, but they'd work. No weapons, but that was probably asking too much.

She slunk over to the window and inspected the lock and alarm. Yes, meant to keep people out and not concerned with keeping anyone inside. With quick look around the room, she found her supplies. Tape. A long metal medical… stick. She could make that work. Listening once more, Caterina used the metal stick as a fulcrum, wedging it between the sensor and the frame and—

Clatter. The metal stick shot across the room, but the sensor released its hold on the window without pinging the alarm system. Tearing a scrap of tape in her teeth, she smoothed it in place, keeping the sensors together. Quickly, she shucked off her pajamas and pulled on what passed for regular clothes.

A noise in the hallway. A few footsteps and a laugh. She threw open the window, bracing for the alarm. Nothing. Good. Then she sat on the ledge, threw her legs over the window sill with a tremendous amount of pain and effort, and jumped. Her body was weak. The landing jarred her.

Head swimming and legs, torso, and crotch hurting, she took a second to adjust to her surroundings then took off.

• • •

In the back seat of the chauffeured Mercedes, Yassine sipped his latte and watched the brownstone, thinking over yesterday. There hadn't been a need to stay in the hotel room and watch his men get beaten into a bloody pulp. After slipping out and making way to his car, he'd witnessed quite the show. Daniel Locke, wife in arms, running down the street. The painful look on his face was seared into Yassine's memory, and over the course of the last day, the wife had become sort of a hobby that bordered on a compulsion. Knowing where she was, that his particular want, icy cold and unmoving, had been fulfilled left him wanting more.

So today he sat near the private home of what he had learned was a doctor, unsure what to do with this itch for a round two. He waited and waited. Interesting, everything that he saw while planning out his round two fantasy. It was enough to justify wasting time instead of planning his upcoming attack. People came in and out of the doctor's house. The Lockes' bodyguard. That made sense. Then additional men. All as large and deadly looking as the bodyguard and Daniel Locke. That did not.

Yassine took another slow sip of his drink and let the scalding liquid burn his throat. Always a thing with extremes for him. Hot. Cold. Life. Death.

The drape in a window moved. What—

Was that... the wife? Crawling out the window? He put his coffee in the cup holder and rolled down his window, as if the tinted glass somehow distorted his view. Free of discolored obstruction, the view was still the same. Fascinating.

Her hair was matted, a complete mess and not far different than when he'd left her lying on the bed. Oversized clothes swallowed her. How had the wife reacted in her husband's arms? Yassine's erection swelled. What had the husband said? Done? He never wanted someone more than once. But watching her sneak out, disrespecting her husband, and the hurt he'd inflicted upon her evident in her face... He wanted her again, wanted to find out whether she'd live or die in a second go-around. Now that was power.

A day's worth of dreaming about how he'd steal her back was no more. She'd presented herself for the taking. Again. Just like at his country home when she'd visited on her husband's arm. Lust fired in his veins as she wobbled on her feet, searching for which way to go. She was weak, half-way to how he liked a woman. Unmoving and barely conscious.

Everything had been working out well for him lately. His regular arms dealer was back online and working with him again. His plans to take down Big Ben and step from behind the curtain of anonymity were on schedule. And he'd found a possible way to expand his plans and claim more prestige for the ACG. A possible expansion to America.

• • •

This was a mistake. Caterina had a sixth sense when it came to being watched. With each unsteady step, the hot gaze of an attacker loomed close. It wasn't Rocco. Or Roman. Not that they'd attack, but both would certainly, carefully, drag her butt back to bed. The anxious tickle of dread screaming up and down her spine left only one option. El Mateperros. He wasn't done with her. Well, good. She swallowed away the automatic nauseated-angry reaction at his name. She wasn't done with him yet either.

But she *was* unsteady, She was also weak, injured, and in the worst condition she'd ever been in. She hadn't come up with an attack plan. Her mind was too fuzzy to form really any plan, and her psyche had been too desperate just to escape. The only thing she had come up with was to get to her London studio, change clothes, and arm herself. Hell, that plan hadn't even been planned. It only came to her when she realized how close the doctor's house was to the flat.

But it didn't help that her nemesis had sighted her and was tracking her, closing in. Readying for the kill. Or another assault. Probably both.

She spun around, ready to catch him, confront him. But she found nothing other than a roll of nausea. When she made it back to her studio, the first step would be to scour her cabinets for more painkillers and some Pepto. Outside a prescription for Valium, the pink stuff might be her only chance for easing the queasiness. She had to move fast, though. As soon as Rocco realized she was gone, there would be a very short list of places he would search: the hotel and her studio apartment.

He was going to be furious. Her heart seized, clenching in on itself with a dull ache that had nothing to do with the aftermath of a rape. He'd tear England apart to find her. She just knew it the same way she knew El Mateperros would come after her again. Would Rocco forgive her for sneaking out? Running away from him? She didn't deserve forgiveness.

Then again, he'd called in Titan to deal with the Dog Killer. That breach of their trust hurt. Guilt tried to edge in for leaving him like this, but she stomped it away. She hated herself for her preoccupation, but not enough to try to stop it. How long had she been walking? An hour? But she'd only covered a few blocks.

The studio apartment was still very far away. She had no money for a taxi. No one would pick her up looking like a beaten hobo. What was she thinking? The hotel was closer. New plan. Head there. Rocco had weapons stashed in every corner of that room. She changed directions and started walking. Each step dragged. Her bruised legs cramped, and her foggy mind dulled her instincts.

Wait.

She couldn't go to their hotel room. In addition to her attack, there had been a loud fight. Rocco might even have killed two men who could be connected to the ACG terrorist organization. Interpol likely had the hotel on lockdown. Pain killers were making this already bad idea a thousand times worse. Disorientation was beginning to take hold. Hazy outlook. Fuzzy mindset. Exhaustion had already set in. *Think.* Her on-the-fly plan was unraveling faster than she could say Dog Killer.

Slopping on the sidewalk, she took a breath, trying to figure where she was and what the right move could be. Her skin crackled. Instinct shook her senseless. She'd been stupid. Emotional. Medicated. And, now, unarmed and not ready, El Mateperros was coming for her, and there was nothing she could do. This spontaneous plan was now a full-fledged disaster. She could go back. She nodded. Yes, she would. Chalk it up to—

A black Mercedes pulled out of a driving lane and stopped in front of her. The window rolled down.

El Mateperros.

New plan: Suffer and survive but not die before he did.

TWENTY-NINE

A rapid rush of steps pulled Rocco's attention from their Titan pow-wow. The doctor hurried into the room, red-cheeked and with a furrowed brow. How did Roc not see this coming?

"Goddamn it." Even before the doc opened his mouth, he knew. "She's fucking gone. Right?" His molars ground together, and he spun, punching the wall. "Goddamn it."

"She's gone?" Roman's jaw hung slack. "The woman could barely stand."

The doctor pointed down the hall, eyes wide and sticking his neck forward like a pecking chicken. "The security system—"

"Disabled. That wouldn't stop her." Rocco's hand throbbed, but he wanted to punch the wall again because damn, that felt better than the fear shredding his heart. Instead, he ran his busted knuckles into his hair. What was Caterina thinking? He grabbed a fistful of hair and pulled. The sting bit his scalp, and he needed it.

Sudden concern that stress might trigger an attack sat on his chest. If he lost his mother freakin' marbles in front of the guys, it'd be a career-ender. Not to mention that it would slow down their search for Cat. A buzz burned in his ears. He wasn't sure if it was frustration that he hadn't seen her move coming, rage that some asshole who'd attacked her was still walking around *alive,* or some busted side effect from falling in love. Bad for the heart, bad for the head.

He'd always be second to El Mateperros, and if they didn't catch him and kill him, the Dog Killer would always be in their relationship.

"So..." Winters pushed off the couch.

"We go find her. This doesn't change us finding El Mateperros, and that's where she's headed. No question." Rocco paced. "Roman and Cash, hit the hotel. Winters, her apartment. Rendezvous back here in an hour, and we'll have a plan for our next move."

Now to decide what he would do. A thousand directions pulled him. The pounding in his head had nothing to do with hallucinations and everything to do with a sexy Spaniard. Man, she was gonna light him up, all spicy-sounding, and he couldn't wait. Just as long as nothing happened to her.

"You okay, buddy?" Cash asked as they readied to head out the door.

"No, fucker. I'm not."

Cash readjusted his cowboy hat. "Alrighty then. Someone else gets a shot."

Roman met Rocco's eyes. "Cash, I'll meet you and Winters outside."

Rocco pulled out his phone. He needed Parker to hack every damn traffic cam in London. They could pull every link, run it through whatever fancy technology Titan had, then Rocco could show up, throw Cat over his shoulder and enjoy the hell out of the tirade that was sure to come. Simple.

Roman held out his arm, hand bumping into his chest as he paced. "Hold up a minute, Roc."

"What?" He glared at palm that brought his distracted ass to a standstill, then at Roman's ugly mug.

"We gotta talk, man."

Talking? No thanks. Next thing, Roman would be Kumbayahing it, trying to get him to calm down.

"No time." Security camera feeds were more important than whatever Roman had on his mind. Rocco punched Parker's number. Jared would be the next call, but he couldn't waste time explaining to Jared that Caterina had run off on a suicide mission, barely conscious and recovering from a major injury, while Parker could be working. "Parker—"

Roman growled to get his attention. "I know."

Fuck. *I know?* Is that how that conversation would start every time? And this time, now?

Parker's voice carried from the phone. "What's up, Roc?"

"Hold on." He pulled the phone down and hit mute. "So what? Deal with it later."

"You need to tell me if you can handle whatever has been happening to you and still get your girl."

"Nothing in the world will keep me from getting her back safe and sound."

Roman's forehead pinched. "Do you even know what's wrong with you?"

"Don't know. Don't care. Not right now."

"Roc—"

"Move your ass, Roman. That's a goddamn order."

"Rocco. Chill, dude. Clear your head. We'll get her. She'll be okay. You're my boss. I get that. But you're my buddy too, and I'm not doing shit until I know you aren't going to get yourself, your girl, and everyone else here killed. You got me? Orders or not."

Rocco took a deep breath. Didn't help. Instead, his fist flew opposite Roman and the pain from hitting the wall was a perfect distraction from the jumbling BS in his brain.

Roman didn't look any more convinced. "Feel better?"

"A little." He shook his fist. Flares of sharp pain radiated up his forearm. "That's why Jared sent you here, right?"

"One of the reasons."

He spread his fingers then bunched them into a fist. Nothing broken. "Jared knows?"

"Yup. That's true, but he trusts you. As do I. So if you say you've got this, you've got this."

Fuck, man. Honesty would get this conversation over with. "Yeah. Not one hundred percent sure the how and why, but I've got this."

Roman scrubbed his jaw. "If you want to know what's going on, I can give you what I know. Titan's not exactly HIPPA compliant, and knowing that you were losing your mind everyone now and again was mission critical."

Rocco rolled his eyes. There were no secrets, medical or not, on their team. He knew that, even if he'd wanted to ignore it. Roc worked his throbbing hand, grateful for the distraction. "Tell me what Tuska and Jared said, and let's be done with it."

"The New York hospital didn't know what you were poisoned with. Sent it off to some high and mighty facility."

"Knew that."

"Report came back and ended up on Doc Tuska's desk. He called Jared—"

"What did it say, Roman?"

"It was a discarded government experimental drug. Meant to be truth serum but had a nasty hallucinating side effect. Random but eventually stops." Roman shrugged. "Until then, you've got a nightmare on your hands."

"Sounds about right."

"It sucks. You should've seen the doc, dick. He can't do anything about it, but at least you would've known."

Rocco shook his head. "Nah. Jared would've benched me."

"I think you don't give the prick enough credit."

Maybe. Maybe not. Why push his luck when he'd just landed his dream job? He needed to wrap his hand in ice instead of thinking about how Jared would or wouldn't have reacted. "What about Cash and Winters? They know?"

"Nope. Dude's not a gossip, if it wasn't mission critical, I wouldn't know either. So, no, no one but Jared, Sugar, and me know."

"Cat knows."

"All right. A select few who care about you."

Rocco's head bobbed, agreeing. "I'll scour the world to find her."

"Figured that out, buddy." Roman walked to a window and looked out. "Hell, I'd expect nothing less."

"But I won't put Titan in danger. Ever."

"Ten-four, dude. Ten motherfuckin' four."

"So we good?"

Roman turned and gave him a chin lift. "Solid."

They walked toward the door. Rocco's hand throbbed, knuckles bleeding, but he slapped Roman on the back. "No joke. Thanks for whatever we're about to do."

• • •

Excruciating pain woke Caterina. Hogtied and woozy, she felt her stomach jump into her throat. Her body wanted to wave a white flag in surrender. Every part of her ached as the floor vibrated beneath her. A steady whirring noise made an already impossible headache worsen. Turbulence hit the same second she realized it was an airplane floor that she kissed.

"She is awake." A thick accent called over the noise of a plane's propellers.

How long had she been out, and where were they going?

"Get her up."

Rough hands jerked her tied arms. Pain sprung in her shoulders and arm sockets. The raw burn between her legs pulsed.

Nothing can bring me down. Not pain or death. I will survive until I don't, but he will go first.

The seconds after she'd seen El Mateperros's Mercedes were a blur in her memory. A thug got out, grabbed her, wrapping something over her face. Then nothing. Whatever she'd been dosed with made her unsteady, but the man who'd grabbed her off the floor now propped her in a chair. She blinked, trying to get her bearings. Everything was gold-plated. Caviar and crackers decorated fine china that clattered with each bump in the air.

El Mateperros sat across from her, and her heart took off at a sprint. Sweat sprung across her body. He didn't lunge for her, didn't do anything but tap the tips of his fingers together. But still, he'd hurt her so badly that she reacted simply by seeing him. "Yes. She is awake."

Caterina hid her tears and her fear. Everything that boiled within her. "I am awake."

"You are not afraid of me."

Hell yes, she was. "No, I am not."

"Why?"

"I'm not afraid of anyone." Lie after lie spilled from her cracked lips while vomit threatened.

"Interesting. And tell me, how did you meet your husband?"

What was this? A conversation between old friends? "What do you want with me?"

"Humor me, Mrs. Locke." He cupped his chin in thought. "I do not even know your first name."

"And I'm not in the mood for small talk with the sick fuck who raped me."

El Mateperros's lips ticked up. Not quite a smile but there was pleasure there. A bevy of emotions rolled through her again.

Guilt. Rocco would kill himself looking for her. She searched the airplane cabin for any sign of where they were going. *Fear.* When he found her, would she even be alive? He would find her. Wouldn't he? Even if she were dead? *Denial.* She couldn't be sitting across from him. Damn it... *Depression and disappointment.* Titan was never going to find her.

El Mateperros finished off a cracker. "What is your first name?"

What did it matter? "Caterina."

"And your maiden name?"

Another round of emotion pushed through her pain. *Determination.* "Cruz. Ever heard of it?"

"Cruz? Commonplace, I suppose. But no, I know no Cruzes." He went back to steepling his fingers, and Caterina looked around the plane's belly and counted five things she could use to bring him to his knees if only she had the access and the strength. A water glass. A seatbelt. A Mont Blanc fountain pen. An apple. The rope wrapped around her wrists.

"Too bad you don't." She shrugged, trying to fake courage and strength. "You should know the reason I'm going to kill you."

Genuine shock crossed his face. His mouth dropped open, and his head tilted. "Tell me, Caterina Cruz Locke. Tell me why I will die."

She'd waited her whole life to throw what he'd done in his face. "You killed my family, and I will kill you."

He dropped his head back and coughed a doubting cackle. It crackled across her skin, washing away all of her wooziness and pain. She was a woman on a mission.

El Mateperros checked the time on his Rolex. "What you know of me may be incorrect. Rarely do I kill anyone. That's what I have people for." He stretched in his seat. "I was born poor and grew up realizing how I could escape the crappy streets in Algeria. I made a name for myself—"

"My family was murdered on the beaches of Dehesa de Campoamor by your hand, or your order. I do not care."

The sarcastic laughter stopped. He paused then strained a gaze at her. "You don't say."

"I do."

He dabbed a spread on a cracker and slowly ate it. After finishing the cracker, he finished the rest of his drink then raised the empty glass. "Allah's not what drives me. Maybe in the beginning. But your family's death—"

"Massacre."

He inclined his head. "*Massacre*. Their demise turned me into a household name in some circles. They were how I earned my nickname."

"You ruined my life."

He studied her while snacking. "Interesting. If that's what people need to keep my name on their tongues, let them have it. They're still talking about me, and that's what matters."

"Excuse me?"

His cold eyes fired, excited. "Do you know my favorite Lady Gaga quote?"

"Wh-what?" Her eyes pinched shut. She couldn't tell if she'd lost her mind or if this was some insane reality. "No. I can't begin to imagine your favorite quote by anyone."

"I've always been famous. It's just that nobody knew it yet." He looked out a window, stroking his cheek. "Soon they will know."

Her jaw unhinged. "This is all for...some sick kind of fame?"

"This? What I do?" He shrugged. "Yes."

She shook her head. "There's something wrong with you."

"Yet, I'm flying in a Lear Jet. Eating caviar. I've got a beautiful woman at my disposal. So it seems as if there is something right with me." He smeared another cracker. Ate it. Stared at her.

On the surface, he was a very pretty person. Some might even go as far to say a beautiful person. In a purely physical review, all the parts worked. But something evil and rotten festered in him, ruined his mind. He was a psychopath or a sociopath. Something.

And that something refilled his glass from a crystal decanter. "I had plans for you, but now they've changed."

"*Por qué?*"

"Good question. You will make an excellent addition to my team."

If she thought her stomach had bottomed out before, she was wrong. Now it had. "Excuse me?"

"Fool me once, shame on you. But fool me twice." He clucked. "I thought there was something special about you. After our visit earlier—"

"When you *raped me.*"

He smiled, and it was magazine model perfect. "After our visit, and when I saw your *husband* in action, he seemed less of a meat-head and more trained operative than I gave him credit for."

Visit? "Rape."

"A little more nosing around, and my researcher turned up a fascinating theory based on an interesting rumor. Have you heard of the Titan Group?"

"*Vete al infierno.*" Go to hell. He could rot there for all she cared.

"Titan, we believe, was responsible for kidnapping one of my lieutenants. And even more interesting are the rumors of a very attractive intelligence gatherer who worked my lieutenant over before his demise."

Oh fuck.

"The look on your face might as well be a confirmation. I don't believe you are a Locke, but I do believe you will come work for me."

THIRTY

Sitting on a park bench in London with his head hanging between his knees, Rocco crossed his arms over his head and wanted to puke. Twenty-four straight hours of searching and no sign of Caterina. No sign of El Mateperros. Titan had searched-and-destroyed El Mateperros's country house after finding nothing at the hotel or Cat's studio apartment. The ACG hotspot had been empty except for minions, and despite Titan's best efforts, the minion-fucks didn't have anything intelligent to share. The bench creaked. He looked up enough to identify Jared then hung his head back down.

Rocco had never failed. Ever. This was the most important job he'd ever had, and he couldn't have done a worse job.

"Keep your head in the game, Roc. Parker will figure out a location. Give him a little time."

Rocco shook his head. "You have no idea what the sick fuck did to her. Now he has her. Alone."

"She's tough. She's a master manipulator and trained to dole out pain. She can out talk, outwit, and out think anyone."

"Including me."

Jared's head shook. "I doubt that."

"I never saw this coming. She just walked out. Exactly what she wanted when she wanted."

"Nah." Jared shook his head again. "If she wanted to work you over, she would have, then said goodbye and used the front door. You would've waved and said, 'see ya.' Wasn't the case."

"Might well—"

"Shut down the pity party 'cause we don't have time for that bullshit." Jared's phone rang, and he looked at it. "Parker."

Rocco's head hung down, but he still looked over. "So answer it."

"I will if you get your head out of your ass."

"Christ, Jared. Done. Head out of ass. Answer the phone."

"Your head's messed up about a girl, and you need to right it. Now. Or this ain't gonna fly."

"Right it? Nothing to right. She walked out. What does that say to you? Because, to me, it says fuck you very much."

Jared leaned back. "Happily ever after doesn't come with a red bow. Doesn't mean perfectly ever after. It means shit sucks sometimes, and you muddle through it. Especially with that girl. She's tough, but she's a product of her life. Help her change that, help her accomplish what she needs to, then you're set. Love. Happily ever after. Whatever bullshit comes with that."

Rocco watched him, letting his words resonate, then shook his head. "Not her style."

"Give her a chance."

"Tried." He'd tried so hard.

"I would bet Sugar's sweet ass that you tried to fix Caterina's problems *for* her. Women like Caterina…" Boss Man shook his head. "It takes a bigger set of balls to say 'what the hell do you need me to do to? How can I help you?'"

Help her? Hell, Rocco hadn't tried to help, like *actually* help her. He had tried to take care of it by calling in his boys. That was real help. In his mind anyway.

Jared continued. "'Cause you gotta know Caterina's just like Sugar in a few ways. One of those is an independent streak as wide as this damn ocean we just crossed. When they need help, they *need help*. Not a fix."

"Not a fix." A fix was what he'd wanted. It seemed simple enough. Titan fixed shit. He was an expert shit-fixer. Easy.

"Fix their problem for them, and they'll fuck it up worse than before just to prove they could do it on their own. And they will *fix* it on their own, probably better than you did in the first place, but life's a lot better if you just give the lady what she needs the first time." Jared cracked his knuckles. "A little help."

Rocco sat back and rubbed his temples.

Jared cracked his knuckles again. "So that's lessons in love by me, volume one. You want the rest of that, you can buy the book."

His phone rang again.

Rocco stood up. "Answer your phone."

"Not so fast." Jared stood.

What the hell? Rocco glared, annoyed and confused. "What?"

"We gotta talk."

This again?

This was the *talk* from Jared, and the timing sucked. "Look, I know what you're going to say, so let's have this ass-reaming later."

The phone kept ringing. Jared shook his head. "We're having it now."

"Answer your phone, Boss Man." Lips flat, he pressed them tighter, trying to keep his cool and failing in a humungo way.

"Not until I know what's going on, and if you're with the team moving forward."

Rocco puffed out his chest. His elbows angled, arms pulling from his sides. A fighter's stance. "You'd better believe my ass is with the team. Say that again, and we'll have problems."

"Roc, man, we have problems now. And hell if I'm going to let you get yourself killed trying to save your woman because you're too stupid to stand down." He took a breath. "Funny thing about Titan: we don't run from shit, and I've seen enough of it. Hell, I've experienced it myself. We don't run from a fight, and we don't run from the right woman. Those are the breaks for taking it like a man. The right one comes along and we man up. No pussyfooting around. No 'I'm too cool, I won't be tied down, it won't happen to me.' None of that."

Rocco tilted his head. "Roman. Beth."

Jared shook his head. "Roman's not in love. Yet. That asshole's gonna hit it hard though. One day. Wait and see. But I'm talking about you."

He shrugged, trying to play it down. Trying to hide his clenched fists and teeth. "So talk."

"What's the deal? Are you sick? Having flashbacks? What is it, and how often is it still happening?"

Anxiety crushed his chest. "I'm not sick."

"Fine. Whatever you want to call it. How are you affected?"

He paced the length of the bench. "We need to get to Caterina."

"And I need an assessment of my team leader."

"Goddamn it, Jared. Fuck. I'm fine. My girl's in trouble. That's my problem. You mind if we move all this to some other time? Fuck, man."

"Status update or you're done."

He ground his fist into his hair, knotting it up until the roots burned. "I'm going more crazy now than ever before. It hits me out of nowhere. I trip balls. I don't see it coming. I'm just fucked. But nothing compares to right now." Rocco choked down a breath. He was more angry and more sure of his moves than ever before. Getting in Jared's face until mere inches separated them, he growled. "Bench me, and I'll still find her. Take me with you, and I won't have to shove my fist in your goddamn face."

Jared got right back in his face. "Are you going to be a liability?"

"The fuck if I know, but you aren't going without me." His head felt ready to pop, his muscles tensing, his voice bellowing with all the anxiety trapped in his chest.

Stop. Regroup.

He took a deep breath. "Now answer that phone."

Boss Man remained squared off. The phone rang nonstop. Finally, he nodded, stepped back, and touched the screen, pressing it to his ear. "Speak."

Rocco took a deep breath. Sweat tickled the back of his neck. His blood pounded, and he could taste the need to fight, to stake a claim to Cat and make sure that woman knew exactly how he felt.

Talking on the phone, Jared gave a few nods and a groan that did zilch to make Rocco feel better. After a few eternities, the call ended and Boss Man looked ill at ease. "We're going wheels up. Pull the team, and let's go."

They needed to fly somewhere? How had this spiraled from her wandering off to them needing a Titan jet to go *help*? "Where is she?"

Shifting in his boots, Jared hesitated. "Parker's best guess: Africa."

"Best freakin' guess? *Africa?*"

"You doubting our boy?"

For the first time, maybe. He wanted coordinates, her heat signature pinpointed on a map or an outline of her safe and sound and ready for pick up. "Africa's a big fucking place—"

"Somalia."

Rocco's jaw dropped, and his heart stuttered. Of all the places in the world, could it be any worse than that devil's armpit of a place? No. No it could not. American history in Somalia was painful. Bloody. And God love the Special Forces that had gone in, come out—or didn't— and the hell they'd been through along the way. Somali's record of operations-gone-wrong wouldn't be far from anyone's mind.

Rocco focused on his left hand. On his ring finger. The Locke job was over, but the ring was still there. It was simple. White gold. Maybe platinum. It wasn't something he'd have picked out to wear, but damn if he would take it off. Not now. Maybe not…

He shook his head. Scrubbed his face.

A silly metal band made him feel closer to her as if it symbolized everything they had gone through so far. The thing didn't have a start or an end. It just ran in perpetuity, very similar to his commitment to her and this job and taking out El Mateperros.

Rocco nodded to himself. "Somalia it is. Let's roll."

THIRTY-ONE

Fifty yards off the Somalia coast, Rocco dove through another crashing black wave. The Indian Ocean seemed content to drown him, but he ignored the churning water and threats of riptides and powered toward the shore. Nothing would take him down. Nothing would slow his stride. Certainly not Mother Freakin' Nature.

His team was on course and on time. Tonight, he was back with Titan, and it felt good to get back into gear and ready for war, especially with Delta lurking in the wings. Titan would find Cat, and he'd *help* with whatever she needed.

El Mateperros had to know they were gunning for him. Why else take off to Somalia? Bad things happened there. It stank of trouble, lawlessness, death, and destruction. But Titan was prepared. Between the two teams, they had naval back-up and air support. They'd pull Cat out after she eliminated El Mateperros. Simple. And that was the plan as they surfaced at one of the most deadly locations on earth.

Parker's words played through his head. "Statistically speaking, there's nowhere else in the world she could be, also nowhere more dangerous." Parker knew stats and numbers as well as he knew a good kill shot and evac plan. His warning didn't go unheeded.

If the extraction went south, both teams were ready to avoid a Black Hawk Down situation. They'd get out and get out fast. But they all wanted blood, and all involved wanted El Mateperros. Rocco was done for if they didn't bring Cat home. His feet found the sandy ocean bottom, and he ducked up the beach bank a dozen yards away from land.

Water dripped off him as he cradled his weapon to his chest, waiting for the cue in his ear piece. It pinged.

"My team, you're a go." The neck microphone picked up his whisper and he charged forward as a wave pulled then broke over his back.

Cash and Winters flanked his right, and Roman and Jared had his left. They rose from the murky depth, the dark bathed in night vision green. Perfect approach. No moon overhead. Roman and Jared fanned out, and minutes ticked by while Rocco crawled into position with Cash and Winters. Cash was on sniper duty, and Roman would feed him intel until they hit a planned radio silence. Rocco and Winters scurried through the brush, eyeing a small hut and taking their offensive positions.

A hundred yards back in the air, Delta team waited. The waiting killed him. Where were Jared and Roman? Where was the call? Why was this taking so long?

"Delta. You're a go." Jared's order triggered the nearby team's expulsion from the water. They did it without a sound, but Rocco knew it had happened with surgical precision and the viciousness of rabid Rotties. Four men on the ground and two men in the sky moved perfectly in sync.

The Delta go-ahead was also Winters's trigger. He had set up two blast zones, one on each side of a hut believed to house Caterina. There were several other buildings nearby, but Titan only wanted El Mateperros. Casualties were to be kept to a minimum, and blasts were to be used as distractions. Draw 'em out, so they could get their mark and his girl.

The minute mark passed. Rocco checked his watch. Three, two, one... and... Above, two helos dropped in, lighting the building as if dawn had broken. Winters's blasts went off in... three, two, one.

Bam. Bam.

Light. Smoke. Fire. ACG forces scrambled, taking the defensive and protecting their building like they protected their fort and king.

Rocco's breathing slowed down as he watched them perch on the roof. Burrow at four corners. The certainty of that Cat was nearby calmed him as he caressed that familiar curve of his trigger. The whirring of the choppers blew debris, dulling shouted ACG commands. Villagers screamed, and lights went out in nearby houses as if that would stop danger if it were coming for them.

The enemy might've expected something but not this type of arrival. Rocco and Winters pushed forward. Behind them, Delta's four-man machine provided cover, while Cash and Roman were sighting and shooting in tandem while Jared provided logistical orders. The operation was a thing of tactical beauty.

Tango free, their enemies scattered on the ground. Rocco breached the door. Winters rolled around the corner. First room. Clean. Second. Same. Third and—

Shackled, lying on the ground, hands pinned above her head to a cinder block wall was the love of his life beaten and bloody with her eyes shut against all the hell he'd brought with him. His lungs had stopped. Heart stalled. Throat clamped. Winters shouted over the roar outside that Rocco needed to get his bitch ass in gear. He hit his knees, tore off a glove, and reached for her neck. A pulse… It was all he wanted.

Blood-crusted lashes fluttered. Cracked lips parted. Caterina's unfocused eyes narrowed. "*Galán.*"

"*Galán?*" he asked even though that moment wasn't the time for a question and answer session. He'd heard the word before.

"You're mine. My beau. My Handsome," she whispered, ignoring Winters working on her shackled hands.

Handsome. She'd loved him as long as he had her, since the very beginning, when he didn't even know what he didn't know. "I fuckin' love you, Kitten."

A sparkle in her swollen eyes and an uptick to her broken smile was all he needed. She groaned. "I'm hurt."

He looked up. "Almost done?"

Winters nodded. "Trying. Another second."

Caterina coughed. "I didn't kill him. Yet."

By the looks of it, she had tried. He swallowed away the words dying to come out of his mouth. *I'll do it. I'll rid the earth. He's mine. I want his blood.* "Still can, Kitten. Just hang on."

She coughed, maybe trying to swallow. "Big Ben."

"Don't worry about it."

"He tried to make me work for him." She coughed again, and blood kissed her scabbed and scratched lips. "I couldn't. Wouldn't. But then I thought—" Cough. "If could find out. When. How. You'd come get me—" Cough. "And I could tell you."

Her hands dropped. Winters stood. "Let's roll."

Rocco wrapped his arm behind her, and she cried out in such agony his eyes burned.

"Broken ribs."

Rocco's blood boiled. This helping bullshit was over. El Mateperros would die at his hands. "Alright, Kitten. I'm taking you home."

"Big Ben. He has someone else. Not in weeks. Saturday."

"Saturday?" Winters looked at him.

"What day is it?" Her eyes furrowed. "I couldn't stop him. It's happening—" Cough. "What—" Cough. "Day is it?"

His stomach bottomed out. They'd been off the grid for about five hours. "Saturday."

THIRTY-TWO

Winters and Rocco helped Caterina to her feet in her jail cell hut. The room spun fast, fast, fast... and began to slow... slow... and stop. She swallowed, parched, a metallic taste in her mouth and the stench of dried blood staining each inhaled breath. She hadn't taken out El Mateperros, and now she hadn't stopped the London attack. Complete failure.

"Was there an attack?" Caterina asked, but she couldn't hear her own voice. It sounded muddled and echo-ish.

Neither of them answered her. They didn't know, or they didn't want to say? Her stomach sank again, cramping with the possibility of a terrorist attack that could have been prevented. She closed her eyes, thinking about all the missed opportunities to save lives. First her family, now Londoners. The guilt was suffocating.

"I don't know." One of them answered, but there was a distorted rush of blood in her ears masking voices that should've rung distinct and familiar.

Finally, she opened her eyes. They were just as sick over the possibility as she was.

Every move hurt. No doubt she had a couple broken ribs and a few bruises that went down to the bone. There wasn't internal bleeding. Enough time had passed that she would have been dead if there was, so at least that was ruled out.

"Can you walk?" Winters asked.

Now wasn't the time to play heroine. "Not really."

Winters reached for her, but Rocco enveloped her in a hug, an arm hooking behind her legs and the other holding her back. Somehow, he did it without moving her too much, then handled her like she weighed a tissue's weight. The hold hurt far less than she'd expected.

Outside there were blasts and bombs. A helo, maybe two, hovered and lit the night like it was a day at the beach. Beyond the faux safety of this shack, Somalian war lords were in the throes of battle. None knew who Titan was or why they were there, but this neighborhood specialized in terror, blood, and the trade of all things in between, every man running and gunning to safeguard his illegal lifestyle.

Tucked in Rocco's arms, the chaos barely registered. She was safer than she had been in days, even with the ping of bullets and rattles from explosives. Rocco equaled relief. Soon she could sleep, eat, drink—

"Where is he, Kitten?"

Well, she'd felt relieved until he brought her back to the moment. All her pain became vivid again. "Gone. To London." She took a deep breath and wished she hadn't. White hot strikes of agony pulsed in her ribcage. "They couldn't break me fast. He couldn't wait. Said he'd be back."

Rocco's face was tight. "Did he... again?"

"No."

"Thank fuck."

Her eyes watered. Once had ruined, her but she could see Rocco's point.

"There's going to be an attack." She couldn't think about herself now, and she'd done all she could but hadn't stopped the ACG's plan to strike Big Ben. People would die. Had died? Who knew what was happening in London at that moment? It'd been so preventable. Her throat seized as she tried not to cry over the enormity of a terrorist attack.

Pull it together. She sniffled but centered, channeled her inner badass and thought about her objectives. El Mateperros might be out of reach, but if nothing had happened in England yet, there was still hope.

Winters turned. "Ready?"

Rocco looked down.

"If London hasn't happened yet…" She licked her cut lips. "We have to stop it."

"Gotta get out alive first." He followed Winters, tucking her against his chest and somehow palming a combat pistol. The two men scanned their surroundings and motioned. Maybe an attack plan. Maybe an extraction plan. Whatever it was, it was fascinating to watch Rocco work with Titan. Undercover as the Lockes had been fine, but this was who he was, covered in weapons and camo and face paint. If he said he was getting her out alive, there was no doubt.

Her captors were all going to die. The team of ACG thugs who had worked her over weren't going to live to see tomorrow, and she was okay with that. But having met them and suffered at their hands, she could tell why El Mateperros wanted her to work for him. His men had no technique. Brute force didn't extract information. That was no way to gather intelligence. If she thought about her few days with them, she might have learned more than she gave up. Her mind was too tired to process that thought.

Rocco stared at her again. "Almost ready."

His eyes shone. Rough whiskers covered his cheeks, the result of not shaving for days. They took off at a jarring pace. She hurt like hell.

Rocco loves me. It was an instant salve and a flash of adrenaline. Above them, around them as they left the falsely protective walls of the hut, a fire fight hit full steam. Bright flashes. Rounds zipping. Winters and Rocco moved fast. Two choppers arrived directly above them. Whipping air beat down, gusting and blowing dirt in wild swirls. Tiny rocks and leaves hit her face, pelting her with tiny bites. The two aircraft separated, peeling in opposite directions. Air cover remained, and as far as she could tell, there was a never ending supply of ACG fighters. Knock one down, five more popped up, weapons firing in both hands.

Rocco and Winters pounded through brush and broke free. A clearing. The beach. She'd been vaguely aware of her surroundings, and even in the dark of night, she knew they were near the water.

The crash of the black ocean added to the sing-song of automatic weapon fire. Chancing a look up from Rocco's chest, Cat saw that the night was too dark to differentiate her surroundings. The water would be black as the sky, black as the trees that had surrounded them, their canopies obscuring the view of the choppers. Cupped in Rocco's arms, she took a deep, painful breath when his feet hit the beach. The men didn't stop—

A pounding boom hit behind them. Violent. Angry. Exploding. Yellow, red, orange lit the night. Rocco's body tensed, his hold squeezing her tight, digging into her bruises and breaks. Heat and blasting air hit them. The beach brightened. Everything morphed into a candlelit day. Lapping water and waves. Sand packed down. Trees and brush not as thick as they'd seemed but now on fire.

Winters spun, eyes wide, mouth agape. Both men watched. She watched. Their chopper had been hit. Black smoke filled the air as quickly as it took for her mind to understand the situation. The helicopter fishtailed left and circled. Shouts broke her trance. Rocco moved them, cursing.

Winters voice boomed. "Go. Go. Go."

"Bail out," Rocco shouted toward the sky. The un-rhythmic hitch of rotors not rotating coughed above. "Now! Goddamn it. Get out of there."

The chopper was too low. Too close. She knew that. No way could anyone in that bird could evac—

Like the effort had been too much, the slow motion disaster crashed into the night. The helicopter dropped sideways. Trees split. Metal bent. Smoke and fire burst. Rocco dove, shielding her as a giant burst of light exploded behind them. Toxic, acrid fumes poured around them.

Winters yelled at Rocco. Rocco yelled back. Then they were up, taking off into the water. Icy cold splashes shocked her skin. Her backside was submerged. Shock and shivers froze her mind. A fire raged on the beach, in the trees.

Rocco pushed her forward, and she looked up. A rigid-hull inflatable boat. A man grabbed her aboard. Pain rocketed from her ribcage, her bruised muscles, and cut skin. Rocco jumped in behind, and her teeth chattered. Her mind reeled.

"Wh-hhat—" She'd wake up. This was a nightmare. A visceral, bad dream. Any minute, she'd wake. A helicopter just went down *saving her*? No.

"Who—" She tried again, concentrating on the question and dreading the answer. "Who... What..."

She shook. Violently. Couldn't stop because she knew—just *knew*—what he was about to say.

Tight-faced and angry-eyed, Rocco watched the beach, and she watched him. Their boat took off farther into the water.

"Who was that?" She coughed. She didn't mean for it to come out like that, but forcing it was the only way it would come at all.

The edges of his eyes crinkled. "Delta Team One." His jaw worked side to side. "And they're gone."

THIRTY-THREE

Caterina lay on a hard cot under a pile of warm blankets in the massive operating center that Titan called a jet. The tension was thick enough to cut with a Somalian machete. She watched the table of men scrunched together. She hadn't said a word since she'd had a quick, cold shower, but silence worked because nothing came to mind. They'd lost two men because Titan came to save her. The guilt was more suffocating than her broken ribs.

Titan. Delta. One group, different teams. Rocco hadn't offered much in explanation, and she didn't understand the difference between Titan's main team and Delta. How were they related? Or not related?

She wished harder than she'd ever wished for El Mateperros's head on a shiny platter and that she could disappear into nothingness and never have to look any of them in the eye again. Their teammate was dead, and she was to blame. Just like her family had died, and again, she was to blame.

Voices had murmured quietly while Jared was on the phone. Rocco had been charged with questioning her soon as the shock had washed away. Nothing much materialized. It was as though she could remember everything but nothing at the same time. Watching the men who'd risked their lives for her... she couldn't stand her own skin and couldn't even offer intelligence after spending days with the ACG.

The terrorist attack in London hadn't happened, but it would. She was certain of it, and had nothing to offer. *Another round of guilt, please.*

"Caterina." The phone hung limply in Jared's hand. "We need you over here, hon."

Hon didn't sound good. It sounded like the handhold before a death sentence. Every person in this plane had to hate her. She hated her. So much hatred. Where had it gotten her? In love with a man who would surely never be able to look at her again.

"Okay." The lump in her throat nearly muted her response.

She stood shakily then folded the scratchy blanket she had tried to disappear into. Wet hair still tangled on her shoulders, so she pushed it back, praying that their conversation wouldn't make her want to jump out mid-flight. She needed more of the painkillers she'd been given but didn't dare ask. Didn't want to seem weak. Didn't want get dopey and lose control of her emotions.

Each footstep was a struggle. The carpet felt like wet sand and her legs like jelly. Finally, she stood next to Rocco. An empty chair awaited her as her eyelids burned with tears. A distant, probably forced smile crossed Rocco's lips, and he dropped his chin, encouraging her to sit.

"Lo siento." *I'm sorry.* She was, but no amount of apologizing would make this right. Falling into the chair, she couldn't imagine what they'd want with her. Avoiding their stares, she picked at her cuticle. Daring a glance up, she saw deep emotion flicker on their chiseled mugs. They were military. Special Forces. Elite of the elite. Retired. Discharged. They were all kinds of things, and they were all looking at her.

Sucking her bottom lip into her mouth, Caterina looked at Jared and wondered how bad this would be. "Yes?"

"Nothing was found at Big Ben."

She blinked. Was he questioning her intel? "Their plan was to attack the clock tower on Saturday. You said it's Saturday."

Jared rubbed his hands over his eyes, kneading at dark circles and then at cheeks covered with bearded growth. "What else you got?"

What else? They'd lost men, and now she had bad intel. Her hands knotted together, fingers twisting. "I don't."

"Think harder."

She shook her head, completely sick. "I... can't."

"ACG is going to strike. Is it the location or the date we have wrong?"

Scrunching her eyes closed, she rehashed everything she'd heard, but her mind was so foggy. "I'm not sure."

"Rocco." Jared's voice rumbled. "Walk her through it again."

Before he responded, Caterina left for the lavatory at the back of the jet. She slammed the door and heaved. Fire erupted in her rib cage. Cracked bones and disgrace-drenched dry heaves were a vicious combo.

The door opened behind her, and she refused to look up. "Go away."

"Kitten?"

"Just drop me in London. Hell, touch down wherever we are, drop me, and go."

"We're over water, so that won't work." His attempt to lighten her mood failed.

"That's perfect, actually."

"Come on, Cat." He crouched down, balancing on the balls of his feet, forearms resting on his knees.

"Your men died."

"God rest their souls, but it's not the first time. Won't be the last."

His curt nod killed her. The walls came closer, and the ceiling pressed down. The raging beat of her pulse punched in her veins. "*Ay Dios.* I can't breathe."

"Look at me."

"No."

"Cat—"

"No! I don't know what to do, what to say."

"There's nothing to say right now except for—"

Her stomach swam again. "Except for I had bad intel." She choked it out, covering her mouth. "Titan came to get me, but it shouldn't have happened. You should have left me with them. Never. Ever. Should have come for me."

Strong hands rubbed her back then pulled her into Rocco's chest. He rocked back and sat down, pulling her into his lap in the tiny space. "I think you know that never would have happened."

"Wasn't worth it."

"There's nothing harder than what we went through tonight. But I know those men; I've known them for years." His voice cracked, and his throat bobbed. "There was nothing they'd rather do then chase down some fuckin' terrorist piece of shit and make sure somebody's girl makes it home safe. Not a damn thing."

"Your girl?" Eyes wide, she pulled back in his arms. "Still?"

His eyes narrowed, and his head tilted as if trying to assess where her head was at. "Nothing's changed. If anything…" He pulled her back into his arms, and she melted even as she fought it. "If anything, everything seems more real between us. I meant what I said."

He loved her. "You can change your mind."

"Don't feel like it."

"Oh." She stared at her fingernails, jagged and dirty, then back to him. "Rocco, I…" God, she loved him. So much. So strong. "I don't know how to walk away from El Mateperros."

His eyes flinched almost imperceptibly. "No one's asking you to."

She nodded. "He's… I think it's a sickness. An obsession."

"You're not the only one who's screwed in the head. Right?" He chuckled, but it was more of a grimace.

"You're too good for me."

"You have sins. I have sins. We have secrets. But mix 'em together, and what the hell does it matter?"

It didn't. *They* did. "I don't know how to do this."

"My vote is for giving it a shot."

"I wouldn't know what to say. It sounds so foreign in my head."

He smiled. "Everything sounds foreign coming from you. Say what's in your head. No one's judging you."

She inhaled as deeply as she could, and it hurt like hell. But then she let it go and tried to free her words. "I fell in love with you along the way."

"Good. Glad you did."

"It may have been the night that I helped you and you didn't know."

"Bet I made hugging that bench look good."

He tried to joke, tried to lighten the moment, but now that she had started talking, she wasn't sure she could stop. "I believe in coincidence, and I believe in us. In you." He was the only way she could survive El Mateperros and the Delta team guilt. Deep breath in. *Hurts like hell.* Deep breath out. *Time for the truth.* "I love you."

"Hell, Kitten." Half a smile tugged his cheek, and the dimple appeared. "I know that."

Coughing a laugh that hurt her ribs, she didn't care and batted his chest. He buried his head against her neck, lips brushing her skin. For the first time, she felt human instead of like a machine only capable of chasing down her enemy and providing bad intel.

He let his lips linger and his tongue flick. "Let me ask a few more questions, just to jog your memory, then we can talk to Jared. After that, we'll get some shuteye."

Pressing her head against his shoulder, she sighed. "What is this, the slowest of the Titan jets? We should have been in London in after a couple hours."

He pulled her back, eyes sparkling "We're wheels down in about eight hours. I guaran-damn-tee that by the time we get off this plane, Titan will have a plan, and you'll have a new perspective—"

"Eight more hours?"

"Until we're wheels down on American soil. God bless the US of A. You might even like it."

"What?" Her mouth hung open until she snapped it closed. "But—"

"Look at it like this: When you don't know what your next move is, your options are endless."

In love. In America. With Rocco. He was right. The options were endless.

THIRTY-FOUR

Rocco watched Caterina's jaw open and close a few times, taking in the idea of heading home with him. He hadn't said that in so many words and hadn't quite worked through the logistics—like asking her if she wanted to live with him—but it seemed like a good start.

A good start to what? Hadn't he just politely asked his ex-girlfriend to get her belongings and leave? That he wasn't the type for commitment? And now he flying half-way around the world, dropping phrases like *Surprise! You're coming to America* while Cat suffered from the shakes—or maybe the stupids—any time the Dog Killer came around.

Hell, it didn't matter what he was asking, where his mind had been before he met her, or what she focused on day in, day out. With Cat in his lap, everything was working the way it should. He tried to kiss her cheek, and she flinched. "You okay?"

"I think the painkillers are wearing off." Caterina looked down. "I'm a little jumpy without them."

"Jumpy?"

"Yes…" Biting her lip, she let time float by. "Ever since I was attacked, if someone moves too close or touches me unexpectedly… I'm almost in tears."

Shaking his head, he couldn't imagine. "I'm sorry. Just—"

"Don't say that. I can't handle apologies."

"We are two people, crippled by mental what-the-fucks, talking love in an airplane bathroom." That was about as real as it could get in Rocco's world. "You sure you're down for falling in love with me? Because I'm blowing this romance thing."

Her cracked lips upturned. "I never had a choice."

Rocco pulled her gently off the floor. "You good with flying home?"

"I don't have a home."

Total come-live-with-me failure. He rolled his eyes and tugged her close. "Semantics. You good with coming home with me? Hanging with me—"

Until... He wasn't going to say *until* because he didn't want an *until.* Until she healed... Until they took care of El Mateperros... Until they were finished with spending time together...

None of those worked for him. He liked hanging with Caterina and loved her something fierce. Did that alone make a relationship? Hell no. But did he want to give it a go? Hell yes. She wasn't saying anything... Maybe he was getting in over his head.

Rocco rubbed his temples. "Caterina. This is all... Look..." He drank her in: sad eyes, scratches and cuts barely scabbed over. Their lives were complicated... Time for the truth. "I don't want to be here right now. Not like this."

"What?" she whispered, her lips making a little O.

"I don't want to be here." He was doing this all wrong. He looked at the ceiling then back to her. "With you, like this." Deep breath. "I want to be home, *with* you. Like an *us.* If that makes sense."

Flat lips and pinched brows. "No. It doesn't."

"Come home with me. Stay. With me." Damn it, he sounded like a meth head trying to say the alphabet, all hitches and pauses and stutters. Another deep breath. "You and me, Kitten. Together."

The corners of her lips ticked. "Are you asking me to move in with you?"

"Well, it sounds like a teenager asking his girl to go steady when you say it like that."

She tilted her head, laughing. "I'll come home with you."

"Thank fuck." Pressing his palms to her cheek bones, he let his thumb slide lazily back and forth. His lips found hers, quickening across her damaged skin, scared he'd hurt her but dying for another kiss. "Glad that's settled. All right. Let's go. We have to go back to the war room eventually."

She nodded. "All right."

Hand in hand, they pushed out of the lavatory and headed down a narrow hall. A high pitched whistle brought them to a standstill. *Jared.*

In one of the backrooms of the flying behemoth of a battleship, Jared whistled again to get their attention and stepped into the hallway. His hand was up, holding them in place with a silent order. A phone perched on his shoulder, and he rubbed his eyes. The man didn't look like he had slept in days. Probably hadn't.

"You sure? Cause if you're not, I need to know now." Jared waved them back and then ducked back in the door.

It was a tiny office space, and he paced a tinier circle. Rocco held Caterina close, an arm around her waist.

Boss Man grumbled and exhaled loudly. "All right. Thanks, Sarah. See you soon."

Damn, Jared would hear about that later. Calling Sugar Sarah? The names weren't *that* similar. Caterina didn't sound like any other name he could think of, so hopefully that problem would never come up. Not that he was married to Cat. Not that he wouldn't marry her. What was he thinking about? He needed sleep too. The way his mind was tumbling through stuff tonight was enough to give him motion sickness. Moving her in, thinking about marriage...

Jared pocketed his phone. "Caterina, you doing okay?"

"*Si.*"

He bounced eyes to Rocco. "She doing okay?"

And *that*, ladies and gentlemen, was a strategic move. Boss Man wasn't stupid, and Rocco shook his head. In the heartbeat of time it took for Rocco to realize she'd been baited, Cat laid into Jared, saying God only knew what. Sexy as it was, it was still a verbal ass whipping. Jared's shiteating grin grew as wide as Rocco had ever seen it.

Cat stopped, damn near de-balling him with the razor edge of her stare.

Rocco threw up his hands. "I only said he was smart enough to figure out our next offensive attack."

She flashed her glare from him to Jared, and thank God that laser beam of anger was focused on someone else. Taking a step toward him, she growled. "Do not test me, Jared Westin. I said I was okay, so I am okay."

Jared's lips fought another grin. "Needed to know how okay you were, and judging by those beauties spewing out your mouth, I'd say you're pretty okay." Jared turned his attention from Cat to him. "We have a situation, so listen up."

Well, hell. That order was full of all kinds of shit-gone-wrong.

Jared paced again with furrowed brow. Something weighed on him. Whatever it was, Rocco was about to bear the brunt of it.

"Brock's coming back as a team leader."

Rocco's blood turned to sludge, thickening in his veins to the point that he couldn't breathe. His head dropped back, scanning the ceiling, until he righted it again. He focused on Jared and the job that was about to be stripped from him.

"Right. Brock... Right." His hands went clammy in Cat's, and she squeezed, empathizing with him. His chest caved in on itself. And this was in front of Caterina. Nothing like getting booted out of a job in front of the lady he loved. "Cat, why don't you give us a second."

"Of course."

Soon as she'd slipped away, Rocco crossed his arms, pissed at himself, at Jared, at Brock, and at the whole world. Brock, he had no reason to be pissed at. Things happened, and Rocco understood that the guy had his balls in a trap. But fuck, man.

"What?" Jared scowled. "Not the right move? You're a smart guy. You know the players, the situation. Not exactly what I want to do, but with circumstances the way they are, he's the guy."

Rocco worked his jaw, gnashing his teeth. "Yeah, he's the guy."

This was because Jared thought his mind was still weak? That he could trip out at any moment? Or was this punishment? Rocco hated his psychedelic episodes, hated that he still had poison in him. Hated everything about losing control.

"What the hell is your problem, Roc? Tell me another solution."

Shut up, Jared. Stop antagonizing. Stop pushing.

217

Zip. Zap. Fuck, no. Not now. Not now. The pull of a wicked hallucination tickled his consciousness. This was the reason he was losing his job and probably losing his place on the team. All he'd ever wanted was to rise in the ranks, to lead a Titan team, and before Boss Man's freakin' eyes, Rocco was giving him the picture perfect proof that he was unfit for the job.

"I need a minute." Did he say it out loud? Did it even matter? He had to at least save face with the guys. Rocco powered to the lavatory, planning to lock himself in there and break the handle so he couldn't get out or make an ass out of himself. He reached the bathroom, opened the door, and barricaded himself within. He waited with his eyes shut for hell to strike.

THIRTY-FIVE

Heavy footsteps pounded behind Caterina. Fear curled up her spine. Knowing she was in the safe confines of Titan's jet was one thing, feeling that she could be attacked at any moment was another. She turned too fast, making every bone and bruise call out a reminder of her injuries. Jared's stern face was more serious than it'd been when she'd walked away from what seemed to be a very uncomfortable conversation.

"Caterina, your boy's got an attitude problem. So you and me, let's rehash what you know."

Ignoring the irrational flight or fight response from Jared coming up on her from behind, she shot him a kiss-my-ass look. Cat knew she shouldn't be like that toward him. No one on this plane would ever harm her, even if they blamed her for the Delta team deaths. On the other hand, Jared had gone out of his way most of her life to make sure she could be where she was today. He should expect her attitude to be tripwire sensitive.

After he hurt Rocco, the mama bear in her wanted to attack. That was the part of her Jared had best cultivated from afar, so maybe it was okay to let him have it. "What more do you want?"

"A ton. Move. Let's go." He spun and back tracked. "My office. Now."

"No."

He spun back, stunned. Obviously, he didn't hear no too often. "We've got a problem. I'm not asking. I'm telling. Now move your ass, Caterina."

"No." She turned back toward where she was going, which was a room of men who hated her. If she had anything that would help save lives in London, she'd already said it. Jared and Rocco could ask her all the questions they wanted, phrase them in a million different ways, but it didn't change her answers.

No, he didn't. His hand grasped her shoulder and stopped her, somehow without aggravating the pain from her injuries. Jared would never hurt her. No one but the Dog Killer would. Still, she roared on the inside. She would've jumped him, hit him, strangled and kicked him, but it wouldn't have done a thing to make her feel better. Molars steeled together, she tried to keep her cool and focus on the Rocco-Brock issue. "Why'd you fire him? That's so far past poor timing and bad form. You, Jared flipping Westin, are an asshole."

Two little lines appeared above the bridge of his nose as if he couldn't quite understand her accusations. "What?"

This wasn't a translation problem, and she wouldn't let him get away with playing dumb. "Demoting Roc. Firing him, whatever you just did—"

"Stop." Jared's eyes narrowed, and his head angled. His gaze flitted from her then down the hall. "What are you talking about?"

She sneered. "Brock."

His hand went to his forehead. "Well, shit."

Well, shit? What did that mean? It didn't matter. "I've known your reputation most of my life. Hardass. Can accomplish the impossible. Hell, you saved me, offering a solution to my problem that no one else would ever have dreamed up. But failing Rocco when he probably has never been more committed to you and Titan…" She shook her head, devastatingly disappointed in the man she'd all but idolized.

Jared crossed his muscled arms over his broad chest. "Brock's taking over Delta team. I lost a team leader tonight. You don't know Brock, or our history, but he's coming back, leading a different team. Rocco's staying as is."

"As is?"

"Christ. As is. Yes."

She faltered for an apology. It was the second time tonight she wanted to offer that and the second time the simple phrase wouldn't adequately convey how she felt. "I don't think either of us thought that's what you meant."

His phone rang. "I have to take this. Find Rocco. Report back to the war room. And for God's sake, tell the man what I meant." He grumbled before taking off and snapping a greeting to the caller.

Where was Rocco anyway? Retracing her steps, she passed empty areas. The lavatory was the last place to check. *Knock. Knock.* The light didn't show there was an occupant, but there was nowhere else he could be. "Roc?"

Silence.

Knock. Knock. "Rocco, you in there?"

The door opened with an easy pull. Rocco leaned against the wall, near where she had been earlier. His fingertips massaged his temples. She stepped in, closing the door behind her and shutting out the rest of the world. "*Galán.*"

His smile was exhausted but triumphant. "I win."

"What?"

"I win. I win, goddamn it. I'm stronger than this mind fuck. I refuse to let it happen again."

She didn't think it worked like that, but what did she know? "It...?" Not knowing what to call his reaction to the last bits of poison in his system, *it* seemed as good as any faux technical term she could make up. "It was happening again?"

"Yup. But I pinched it out. Forced it to stop."

She was really not sure he could stop a chemical reaction within his body but it had stopped, and that was important. "So it's leaving your system?"

He scowled at her. "Whatever you want to call it, this time I win. I stopped it. I willed all the zips and zaps and lightning strikes in my brain to shut up and go away. I am the goddamn winner of this round."

He was so serious, so cute, and she couldn't help it. Her lips upturned. "You... sound a little crazy. Just so you know."

The harsh lines on his brow softened, and amusement flickered in his gaze. "We dig crazy. I thought that was our thing."

She smiled and laughed quietly, resting her palms on his flat stomach. "I dig crazy."

"Two peas in a pod, or something like that."

Caterina leaned against the wall, and Rocco lugged an arm over her. Anxiety blasted through her veins at the sudden movement. Hiding her reaction from him, she focused on the good. Rocco was so warm and so safe... Then she remembered why she'd come back to find her missing white knight. "I was wrong, Roc. You were too."

Rocco squeezed her close. "What about?"

"Brock."

His muscles tensed around her. Claustrophobia struck. "How so?"

She swallowed away the irrational feelings and concentrated on their conversation. "He's replacing your fallen Delta leader."

Rocco's hand stilled, fingers locked in place. "No shit?"

That made her grin. "No shit."

"Huh." His hand dropped, and he slowly began to relax. "How about that."

"Who's Brock?"

"Someone whose wife is never going to let him—" Rocco's head dropped back against the wall with a thud. "Sarah. Brock's wife is named Sarah."

"Okay..."

"Jared was on the phone with *Sarah Gamble* not Sugar." He went back to rubbing his head. "Long story short, Boss Man and Brock butted heads. Brock's a good dude who's been through hell. Way complicated."

"Complicated is not my thing."

"Yeah. Me either. But look, there's something you need to know."

"About complicated?"

His head dropped down even while he kept his arm slung around her. "Yeah, I guess."

Great. Because she wasn't at rock bottom yet? "Hit me."

"Before Titan came to London, when we dropped dude off at that MI6 hotspot…"

"*Sí?*" Suddenly she had a bad feeling, and it had nothing to do with the post-rape apprehension she was hiding from Rocco.

"I had just walked away from a girl. Relationship. Whatever you want to call it."

The pit of her stomach bottomed out. It was less jealousy and more anticipating bad news. "All right."

"Wasn't anything serious. Well, I guess she saw it differently."

Sadness crept into her chest. Still not jealousy. But it still didn't sit well. "We all have a past."

Actually, she didn't really. Caterina had never let herself get close to anyone. She wasn't in the same place long enough, and no one understood what drove her day in and out. Besides, when she lived her life tracking an underground terrorist, clipping articles and scouring pictures of what El Mateperros could've looked like, it wasn't conducive to inviting a man to come over. Newspaper clippings and maps with dozens of tacks across the world didn't say "stable woman."

"She wanted something serious. I didn't." He cleared his throat. "Honestly, with some of the guys settling down, I'd thought maybe a regular girl in my life would be, I don't know, interesting. But it wasn't. Things moved faster than they probably should've, and she started talking rings and the future. So I…said no thanks and hightailed it to London."

Caterina stopped the urge to balk. Did she want him to want a ring? A future? What did she want? "Okay." She wasn't a rebound girl, but still, self-doubt crept out of nowhere and joined their conversation.

"Why bring it up now?"

"Because no one else would sit here and understand how freakin' on top of the world I feel right now, not succumbing to a tripped-out mindfuck, and keeping a job that I'm crazy about. I don't want to have any secrets between us."

"An ex isn't exactly a secret."

"Well, I don't want you to be uncomfortable."

"Why would I be?"

"I wasn't kidding when I said I ended it and left on a job. You know how it goes. Anyway, we came back from London, but I never went home. Crashed over at Roman's place. There's a good chance some of her stuff is at my place." He groaned. "Like a toothbrush or something."

Yeah, jealousy was trying to make her first trip to the US suck. She wouldn't let it. "A toothbrush I can handle."

Throwing his other arm around her, Rocco pulled her tight against his hard chest. "Pretty flippin' cool chick, you know that?"

"I try."

He kissed her temple, and she took a deep breath, handling their closeness with less of a problem. She nuzzled against the scruff on his cheek.

"You doing okay, Cat?"

Every muscle from her calves to her shoulders locked. *No, I'm not.* "Yes."

"The further we get from Somalia, the jumpier you are. Even before you knew it wasn't London."

Just tell him the truth. It wouldn't be so bad. Maybe. "I know you're not him, but sometimes, I feel…claustrophobic. And hot. Like I can't breathe. It doesn't make any sense."

"Hell, Kitten. It makes a lot of sense."

She shrugged. "I feel stupid."

"I bet you're going to feel a lot of things."

Pushing her hair back, she agreed. It'd been a roller coaster. "I keep trying to forget, but the clearer my head gets, the more I panic." She closed her eyes. "It's like I can't take a breath sometimes."

"What do you need? We'll park this jet if you need some fresh air."

What did she need? So much. "I want to look toward the future. I want to visit America with you. Just… tell me about it. Distract me, and then eventually it won't be a distraction. It will be life."

He went to kiss her but pulled back. She hated herself for being thankful that he stopped short.

Rocco licked his lips and looked like he was trying to reorganize his thoughts. "You'll like where we're going. Titan's based in Virginia, but Jared's got business in Baltimore, a couple hours away, so we're landing there. Let's just stay put. We'll get a doctor to come check you out. Maybe bind up your ribs. Then, if you want, we'll hit the Inner Harbor. Do a chilled out date night. Get a hotel room and relax—"

A shiver ran over her skin but it wasn't panic. "Wait. What did you say?"

"Dinner delivered. Movie on the TV. All-American Friday night. Think of it as a welcome to the country."

Now it was her turn to rub her head. Something he said triggered a recent memory. Fuzzy. But it was there. "No. Wait. Where?"

"Baltimore."

Come on. She was so close. On the tip of her tongue. "No."

"What's going on?"

"I just—something—I'm trying to remember something. I swear it has to do with the ACG. I just can't—God. This is so frustrating."

He turned to her, hands on her shoulders. She flinched but didn't care. "Virgina. Jared. Baltimore. Dinner."

"No."

"Inner Harbor. Hotel room—"

"Inner *Harbor.*"

"Inner Harbor? They're going to hit a harbor? A—"

"Harbor." So close. That wasn't it. What was she trying to remember?

Memories pushed from the edge of her conscience. Her time with the ACG was rough. Mentally, she blocked out the physical pain, toughening her exterior. *Harbor. Harbor. Harbor.* There was something there. Something she should remember. What...was it? She groaned, trying so hard. Just on the tip of her—"Harhour!"

"What?"

"Harhour? Harhour. *Si.* Yes. Harhour."

"What is?"

"His name is Harhour." Her stomach cramped. Remnants of the conversations raced through her mind. "Yassine Harhour. And he wants to be famous."

THIRTY-SIX

Caterina had come up with a first and last name for the Dog Killer. Rocco was up and on his feet before she could continue her thoughts, moving them down the hall as if he were Secret Service headed toward a bunker. Spanish flew from her lips. Eventually, he'd have to learn more Spanish, but if he had to guess, he figured she'd just said, "Slow the hell down."

He burst through the doorway of their flying war room. "Got something else." Nodding to her, urging her on, he nudged her in front of him.

"Yassine Harhour." Her breath was a little rushed, and damn, he should have been more careful because she was hurt. "He wants to be famous."

"Famous?" Jared asked from the head of the table.

"Yes. He was obsessed with planning his… coming out."

Roman slapped the table. "Lady Gaga."

Boss Man swung his gaze over. "Excuse me?"

"At the ACG compound, El Mateperros had some how-to-be famous book written by Lady Gaga."

"So either something more newsworthy hit today, and they put their plans on hold, or…" Jared cracked his knuckles. "Something more newsworthy is coming up."

Cash had been balancing on the back two legs of his chair, but he let it fall forward. "There's a big royal thing happening at home."

226

Jared grumbled. "A big royal thing?"

"Yeah, Nic and the girls have been following it. Getting all excited over some—"

"Where?"

"DC."

"When?"

"No idea."

"Fuckin' A. Someone call Nic and find out when the big royal thing is so I don't sound like a dick when I call the Secretary of Homeland Security."

"Roger that." Cash grabbed the phone from the middle of the table. A few button pushes later, he lounged back in the chair and everyone waited for him to find out whatever the royal thing was. "Hey, sweet girl."

A few groans and eye rolls followed.

"Hold on a sec, Nic." He put the phone to his chest. "You fuckers mind?" Then back to the phone. "Remind me what you and the girls were blabbing about? A prince or something."

A few uh-huhs later, he smiled and hung up the phone.

"Well, lover boy?" Jared cracked his knuckles. "What says Nicola?"

"There's a prince and princess, a new baby prince, and they'll be at the White House in two weeks. That seem big enough to make an elusive terrorist mastermind come out of his shy shell?"

"That's worth a phone call to make sure it's a known threat even if they can't find chatter on the wire to collaborate—"

"We've got a good source." Rocco tilted his head toward her.

"True enough." Jared nodded. "Good job, Caterina. Told you, you'd remember something. Not get some sleep. You did good."

● ● ●

Baltimore, Maryland. In America. The painkillers had worn off, and sun cracked its sleepy, morning light into the hotel room. It seemed odd that she'd been all over the world and never swung by the States, but neither had El Mateperros, to the best of Caterina's knowledge. Funny how, once she stopped chasing him, even if it was for one night, he would end up in the place where *she* was going. To the United States. To Rocco's home.

Jared took what she knew and fed it to the American protective agencies. Homeland Security. FBI. The CIA and her friends at MI6. While this was planned for US soil, it was the royal family and those agencies and so many more had been chasing El Mateperros.

Her ribs were wrapped tightly after a Titan doctor had shown up in the middle of the night to give her a medical evaluation in her hotel room. The doctor knew Rocco, too. By the time they went to bed, both she and Rocco had been expertly inspected, dressed, and prescribed to, and good thing. She hadn't noted her fever, nor had she realized that the pain was masking a possible infection. Their doctor made her promise to get a full work up at his office in the coming days and gave her a heavy dose of antibiotics in the meantime. He also suggested that she find a counselor. Uneasy pinpricks moved across her skin. No. She didn't want that. She wasn't ready to deal with her attack. Only her retribution.

More sunshine spilled into the hotel room. The smell of coffee pushed her further awake, and she stretched every tender muscle. "You did it again, didn't you?"

"Yup." Rocco's voice was sleep drenched.

She wouldn't complain about his habit of slipping out of bed to get coffee as long as he made it back under the covers by the time she woke up. "God, you're a good man."

"You just use me for your caffeine."

"Least you know the truth." She burrowed into his chest. "So now what?"

"Room service."

"And after that?"

"We go home."

"What's your home like?"

"Well, if you're staying there, you can call it your home too."

A blush crept through her cheeks. It was more than just him extending that to her. "I've never had a place called home before."

"Sure you did. You just haven't in a while."

"Spain?"

"That was home, wasn't it?"

"That was a nightmare."

"Maybe you'll go back one day, and it won't be so bad."

She shrugged. "Probably not. Only if I had no other place to go."

"How about this: we go home, you get the lay of the land, and we make our next plan after that."

"What about El Mateperros?" She flinched. Seriously, she couldn't help it. No matter what she did, he was on her mind. "I know. That's all I talk about. I'm trying."

Rocco's hands were far away from her. Every time he touched her unexpectedly, or God forbid, romantically, she jumped out of her skin. It was weird, wanting someone to touch her so badly but yet feeling so panicked by the idea. He must have picked up on it, so while he was bringing coffee into bed, he wasn't doing much more. It broke her heart, hardened her heart, then broke it all over again because a kiss was all she could handle. A touch and hug when she saw them coming. But nothing more. *Pathetic.*

He shifted from her. Maybe he saw on her face what was in her head, and that was why he spent more time smoothing the sheets between them than running his hands over her. "If he's doing what we think he is, Titan can help, but the US government's all over it."

Tears welled. She was freakin' sick, wanting to hurt someone and feeling such loss at losing the chance. But it was for the best, letting the government stop a terrorist attack, protect the heads of state, and hopefully catch the major players in the ACG.

Rocco picked up his hand and deliberately brought it down, stroking her arm. "I know. It'll be okay though. I promise."

The tears fell for so many reasons. "I just want him so damn bad." *And I'm destroyed that he took something from me—from us—that I may never get back.*

"You'll get your revenge one day. I'm sure." With exaggerated, careful movements, he pressed his lips to hers, and her crazy urge to maim drifted.

"Okay. Take me home." Between wanting to forget about El Mateperros and remembering that Rocco had an ex-girlfriend whose stuff might be lying about, she was less thrilled than she should've been but happier than hell she'd handled the kiss without reaction. Maybe she'd summited Mt. Freak-Out and could go back to loving him without problems, maybe even by the end of the day. Yes. She could do that.

The alarm clock blared. Rocco reached over to shut it off and the butt of her hand shot up, catching him in the jaw.

Panic. She had flat out—no thinking—panicked.

So much for summiting Mr. Freak Out. Nothing was changing by the end of the day.

• • •

Rocco's gut churned as he unloaded a pretending-not-to-be traumatized Cat from his truck. The last few weeks with her had been on the job, but today he was introducing her into his personal life. No job. No Titan. No terrorists or jets or playing a role for the sake of a job. Not that he'd ever hidden himself from her. But here, at home, there were no distractions from real life, and that was what he wanted with her. A real life.

He wished he could do a once-over of his house before Cat walked in. No need for real life to start with his ex-girlfriend's stuff strewn about his place. Well, he'd politely asked her to get her stuff and leave the key, but he hadn't checked. It hadn't been as though he planned on going on a job and bringing home a girl to live with him.

"Why are you smiling like that?" Caterina stood in the driveway, watching him lost in his thoughts.

"Excited." *Or not sure what's on the other side of the door.*

His stomach twisted. Worse, what if his ex was waiting for him, wanting to convince him to give it another go? All tied up in a bow or something.

Cat would probably kill her. Or at least torture. Because that's what she did well, and for as cool as she played it, he'd accidentally made her jealous. He'd seen it in her eyes. It was kinda cool that she was staking a claim but kinda sucky because he didn't want her doubting them for a hot second on top of everything else she was dealing with.

He rubbed his chest, trying to knead away a sudden tightness like heartburn but dull. Caterina had never been tied down before. Never had a place to lay her head long-term. Making her jumpy, startling her with baggage from an ex on top of recovering from an attack, wasn't a well thought-out plan.

Cautiously, he took her hand, lacing his fingers with hers. "Let's go, Kitten."

"Okay." Her scratched cheeks blushed, and she was the most beautiful thing he'd ever laid eyes on.

After some quick code-punching and deadbolt-unlocking, the door swung open, and Rocco placed his key in her hand. "All yours."

And now they were walking through his foyer while he was on hyper alert for all things feminine.

"Nervous?" She dropped his hand. "What do you say? Cold feet?"

"Hell no. Just…"

"Ah, worried about love letters and rose petals left around your place?"

He coughed. "Not my style."

"So what then?"

He leaned against the wall, pulling her carefully to him. His forehead kissed hers. His lips followed. "You're kind of feral. And this is pretty damn domestic."

"True."

"So how does it work?"

"You *do* have cold feet."

His chest tightened all over. "No way."

"So? What?"

"When the adrenaline wears off, where's that leave us?"

"Hopefully in bed." She laughed.

She joked, but he knew that was sugarcoated, at least for the foreseeable future. "Say it in Spanish."

"*Esperemos que en la cama.*"

Every. Single. Time. Sucking both his lips into his mouth, Rocco focused on flirting without taking it anywhere. "Tell me something else."

"*Estás loco.*"

His hands dropped to her waist. "Calling me names?"

"Maybe."

He wanted to take her to his room, make her his in their bed. Make *their* bed. His breath hitched, practically panting for wanting her and scared like all hell that he'd get close in too fast and scare her. The erection between his legs wasn't helping at all. Sadness floated in her eyes, and she had to be thinking a variation of the same thing. "I'm in love with you, Caterina. You need to know that."

She nodded.

"So whatever it is that you need. Waiting or talking or—"

"Killing."

His eyes sank shut. The chance of her finding revenge against El Mateperros was nil. "Whatever it is, we'll get through it."

"Okay." She was so sad. It stabbed right into his heart.

His phone buzzed with a text message, stopping the conversation, which was good because he had no idea where to take it. A quick look at the text made the moment even worse. *Assignment up. Get to HQ.*

He brought her to the States, brought her home, and now had to leave her with all the baggage and no one to help. He'd be lucky if she was still here when he came back.

THIRTY-SEVEN

Caterina's first night in Rocco's house and she'd spent all alone. One text message and he was gone. It was expected. She'd known this came with his job, and now she was surrounded by all-American normalcy.

Until he came back, she had his house, his truck, and strict instructions not to mess with his DVR. But he didn't say anything about his Frosted Flakes, and she was on a second bowl and completing the children's maze on the back of the mini milk box when the doorbell rang. Looking more like a kid in a giant's clothes, she slid across the kitchen floor in his oversized socks, which matched his oversized shirt and shorts. They smelled like him and swallowed her whole, making her smile every time she thought about him.

Cautiously, she peeked through the peep hole. A blonde stood there, hands on hips, with lips and boobs that had more than a little bit of enhancement. That couldn't be the ex-girlfriend. Could it? Three deadbolts and a security system that took more than few button pushes, and she had the thing disengaged and the door thrown open.

"Hi—"

"You have *got* to be kidding me." Blondie's chin jutted out. "Who. Are. You."

A living, breathing Barbie doll was about to get a face full of fist. "I'm Cat."

"I bet you are."

233

That particular American phrase wasn't lost on her. It roughly translated to *I hate you, bitch.* "Rocco's not here."

"His truck's here."

"Right." Maybe Barbie didn't have a lot upstairs. "But, like I said, he's not."

"Let me guess. One of his super-secret, I-can't-tell-you-anything work outings. Classic."

"Work *outings*?" Outings didn't do justice to all the shoot 'em up, knock 'em down that Rocco did. Nothing in that word that said he'd give his life trying to do some good in the world.

"Yeah." She eyed Cat's oversized pajamas. "But I didn't expect him to—"

"Be very careful about what comes out of your mouth next. I'm more than familiar with his outings because we work in the same *industry*. That makes me very, very adept at shutting your mouth for you."

Barbie's mouth dropped. "You think he's so into you. Well, he was going to marry me, and that wasn't that long ago."

Cat lifted her hand. The Locke's wedding band was still in place because she'd forgotten to take it off. She wiggled her fingers. Not that she was *really* married to Rocco. Not that it was a good idea to pretend she was. It just happened. "Go. Away."

Barbie's mouth fell again, hanging open much longer. "No, he didn't."

True. No he didn't, but Cat was keeping that to herself. "You need to leave."

"I have stuff here."

"It's gone." Rocco had said that his ex might've left a toothbrush. A toothbrush she could handle, but not tall, blonde and perky going through his house and claiming items. "I'll tell him you stopped by."

Barbie smirked. "He's not that great of a catch. His stupid job always comes first. You're all alone, waiting, talking to me, and it's because he's out there where there's a ton more of you, wherever you came from—"

"Classy." Wow, did that sound familiar—something else always coming first.

"You're nothing compared to his job."

"*Adios.*" Nudging the door closed with her Rocco-sock-covered foot, she waved her left hand, flashing the ring again.

Barbie's words stung, not because Cat believed them but because that was the attitude she'd pulled since day one with Rocco. He could never compete with El Mateperros. Everything else she wanted was secondary. After the Dog Killer died at her hand… how did that reshuffle her priorities? Caterina peeked through the peephole and watched the woman shake her ass as she left. Blondie McGee had choked matrimony down Rocco's throat. Maybe Cat's disinterest in everything other than a certain terrorist was her selling point.

She was safe. Holy freakin' matrimony wasn't her number one priority, but what if she wanted it to be… And where had that thought come from?

• • •

Rocco had been gone for days, but someone didn't know that. The cell phone he'd left her rang constantly. Ringing and ringing and ringing—driving her absolutely bonkers. *Probably Busty Blonde Barbie.* It wasn't her business who was calling, but for sanity's sake, she was about to answer and tell them to trust the voice mail. It would do the dang job.

It rang again, the same number that been calling for days. This time she was done. "Hello?"

"It's about time you picked up the phone." The woman's annoyed voice sounded familiar, but Cat couldn't place it. "Christ, I was *thinking* about getting worried."

What? "Who is this?"

"Seriously?"

"*What?* Yes. Seriously."

The woman huffed. "This is Sugar."

"Oh. Explains so much." Cat rolled her eyes.

"He doesn't have me programmed in?"

"Guess not."

Sugar scoffed in her ear. "Just me, or in general, he doesn't have people programmed in?"

"I don't know, *Sugar*, I haven't gone through his phone."

"Wait, what? Seriously? What's wrong with you?"

Caterina didn't have an answer for any of those borderline rude questions. "Um—"

"Whatever, answer the phone from now on. How else am I supposed to get a hold of you?"

Me? "Why? Everything is okay?"

"Hell, nothing's ever *okay*, but there's nothing to complain about at the moment. Get dressed. We're heading your way."

"What—" Caterina pinched the back of her neck. "We, who?"

"The girls. We're headed to dinner at Mia's, and you're coming. Like it or not."

"Why?" Not that she didn't want to make friends, but was Sugar friend-making material? Cat didn't know her, didn't exactly trust her.

"Why not? Mia cooks crazy awesome. We're all very curious about you."

Cat laughed. At least Sugar was honest. A bitch. But an honest one. "Curious?"

Knock, knock.

"Well, when I said on our way, I meant pulling into the driveway. Open up, Senorita."

Caterina closed her eyes. It was the first time that she'd smiled in quite a while. She pocketed the phone and went to the door. Her hand stayed on the locks longer than it needed to, as if she were considering turning out the lights and ignoring what was certain to be a carpet-bombing of phone calls. But she turned each lock, disengaged the security system, and was greeted by everything a woman named Sugar might look like, except with dark, almost black hair. Sugar's stiletto boots, in-your-face boobs, and badass attitude made Caterina like her just a bit.

"Well, come on in." But Sugar was already strolling by. Three ladies followed, all apologetic smiles and pleasant hellos. The four of them formed a little semi-circle around her, and Caterina wanted to feel uneasy about them but didn't.

"You're pretty damn cute." Sugar assessed her from messy bun to flip-flops and back.

"Glad you think so." She did the same once-over on Sugar. Leather pants and a shirt that left nothing to the imagination. She turned to other women. "I'm Cat."

Sugar pointed and ticked them off. "Nicola. Beth. Sarah."

Cat smiled, recognizing two of the names. "You're all married to someone with Titan?"

Sugar, again, pointed at each. "Yes. One day. Sort of."

A blonde with an easy going smile and no problem rolling her eyes at Sugar stepped forward. "Sorry we're barging in. It was *our understanding* that you knew we were coming. I'm Nicola Garrison. This is my friend Beth, who isn't anywhere close to 'one day,' and Sarah *is* married to Brock. Sugar just likes to be a pain in the ass."

"Oh." Cat sucked in her bottom lip. Rocco had given her the ten-second story on how he had Brock's old job, Brock and Jared had gone to war, but now Brock was picking up the reins of whoever was Delta. The details on that were sketchy at best. Rocco had also told her the Sarah didn't want Brock working ops and had even left him for a while.

Sarah waved her hand. "I know what you're thinking. Don't. Brock and I are handling this fine."

Sugar walked toward the kitchen. "I'm getting a bottle of water. Go change, and then you can tell us all about Rocco in bed. Curious minds want to know."

Her mouth dropped open. "What?" Her cheeks had to be neon pink. Nicola and Sarah shook their heads; Beth's jaw hung open just like hers. They all apologized for Sugar, but the more Caterina interacted with Sugar, the more she liked her, even though the lady drove her batty.

THIRTY-EIGHT

Their mission had been grueling—into Mexico to rescue a woman from a cartel thug—but it was done, and Rocco was ready to come home. He about jumped onto the plane and volunteered to fly the thing home, all so he could see Caterina. Finally, it all made sense, all the time Winters and Cash and Jared ran back toward domestic tranquility. Well, as tranquil as anything could be with their particular brand of one-and-only.

As soon as he had a second, he called Caterina and was ten degrees past shocked when she was at Mia's after Sugar had scooped her up. Mia was doing a big feast, not out of the ordinary, and he'd never wanted to get over there so much in his life. Now, with Roman and Cash by his side, Rocco walked through the Winters's garage and into their kitchen. Parker, Winters, and Jared brought up the rear.

The room smelled like lasagna, and familiar voices filtered in. Mia cooked a helluva meal whenever they were coming in hot from a job. It had become some sort of a tradition: bust ass then eat until they popped.

The ladies were all there. He heard them in the living room and scanned for Cat. Winters's daughter Clara ran into the kitchen, hooking herself onto his leg, and he grabbed her, tossing her into the air.

Clara giggled and screamed, kicking short little legs in the air. "You stink, daddy!"

The living room erupted in laughter. But a laugh that he'd memorized wrapped around him the same moment he set eyes on her. Caterina smiled at him, and his stomach jumped into his throat.

He was by her side in an instant, ignoring the jibes from the guys. "Hey, Kitten."

Relaxing on the couch with an iced tea in hand, she was the only thing he wanted to see. His chest felt lighter. Content. Having her there worked in a major way.

Caterina cocked her head apologetically to the side and watched him watching her. "Sugar kidnapped me."

"Glad she did."

Right when he was about to drop down next to her, she pushed off the couch. Conversations quieted. No one was blatantly trying to listen, but it was too obvious that they were. He didn't care. He threw his arm around her waist, pulling her close before he thought better of it. She didn't pull back though. Maybe time had helped the slightest bit. Maybe she saw his bear hug coming.

"You do stink." She wrinkled her nose.

Goddamn, she was cute. With more caution than with his hug, he kissed her. "Mud and sweat will do that."

"You don't care that I'm here?" She eyed the room of people watching them.

"Why would I?"

"These are your friends," she whispered. "And their *wives*."

He laughed, pulling her out of the living room for privacy. "We're living together. That should count for something. Besides, Beth's here, and she's as single as they come."

"Oh, I know all about the Beth-Roman connection."

"Not addressing the we-live-together comment?"

She moved closer, whispering, "I've never...had a real boyfriend." Her cheeks turned pink. She blushed all the time when it came to him and them. He loved it.

"Don't want to hear about real or fake, but I'll let you use it as an excuse for easing into whatever." He kissed her again, this time with a little less warning, and she did fine with it. "But only if you fill me in later on Beth. All I know is Boy Wonder over there would die for her to smile at him, and our favorite single spy girl hasn't noticed a thing."

She rose on tiptoes, whispering into his ear, "I'm not used to lots of people and lots of love."

Mia called out from the kitchen. "Grub's on the table."

Like she'd thrown a bone to a pack of wolves, the living room emptied past them with Titan leading the charge and the ladies lagging behind to take a last peek at Rocco holding Caterina.

Rocco shrugged. "It's not so bad. People and love."

"It's different."

His hands flexed around her waist. "But not bad."

She shook her head. "Takes some getting used to."

"You still wanna give it a try?"

"I'm here, aren't I?"

"But you were kidnapped." Damn, he'd never been surer of anything in his life than of her with him, hanging with his buddies, living in his home. "Kitten, I want the people I love around me, and that's you. I love you."

Her mouth opened, but he kissed her quiet. Just when the moment was perfect, distraction waved its ugly flag. There were so many things he needed to talk to her about and so many he couldn't. Guilt rushed through him when she opened her mouth to him. It'd been too long since she'd been comfortable enough to pull him against her and just let go.

He should've thought about how sweet she tasted or how good she felt finally leaning into him just a little, but all he could think of was that Parker had located El Mateperros within a day's drive, and he wasn't passing it along. Rocco had made the decision. He was going to find El Mateperros. Kill him. Be done with the entire thing.

Caterina wouldn't know until it was done. She wouldn't be able to take the kill shot she'd always dreamed of, but she wouldn't chance her life either. Keeping her safe from her own demons was worth not telling her. At least that's what he kept repeating.

Brown eyes fired brightly. "Say it again. Tell me that you love me."

"I love you, Cat."

Her lips covered his and his guilt increased. The front door opened and he pulled away from her.

I'll be damned. Brock's here.

He gave Cat a squeeze before taking her hand. "Now things are starting to get back to the way it should be."

Brock lifted his chin, nodding hey. Sarah walked out of the kitchen and over to her husband, went up on her toes and kissed his cheek.

"What's up, man?" Rocco squeezed Cat's hand. "This is Caterina."

Typical pleasantries were exchanged and it felt good to have her by his side, introducing her like she was his girl.

Well, not like. She is.

Sugar was making all kinds of noise in the kitchen. Sarah and Caterina smiled and escaped for the kitchen. Rocco hadn't seen Brock in a while. Most everyone understood the why and how of the Brock debacle. Jared had been the only holdout and understandably so, but now the deep Brock freeze was over.

"You cool with this?" Brock asked. "It could be awkward and all."

Rocco did have Brock's old job. Brock used to be his team's leader, but more than that, they used to be boys. A lot went down under rapid fire, but his opinion of the guy hadn't changed. "It's the best damn thing Boss Man could've done, given the circumstances."

He nodded. "Delta team seems okay with me too. Given the circumstances."

"I'm glad you're back, Brock."

He looked around. "Yeah me too."

Mia stuck her head in the living room, baby on her hip. "Stay out here much longer, you'll both be out of luck. Cash and Roman are eating everything."

"Holy shi—"

Mia clucked. "Mouth, Brock."

His familiar smile flashed as though he were thrilled Mia was on his case. "Ace is huge. Huge."

"Well, if you and Jared hadn't got your camos in a twist, you'd know that." She winked. "Come on. Grub's on. Eat or starve."

Rocco nodded. "Be in there in a sec."

241

Mia walked further from the kitchen. "Cat's a good one, by the way, Roc."

Wasn't that the truth? He nodded. "I know."

"Don't screw it up. That last girl." Mia shook her head. "What were you thinking?"

No kidding. What had he been thinking? She'd acted like he was the greatest thing since laser-sighted rifles, but there was no spark. No interest. He'd been bored out of his mind. Then she was there all the time, shacking and staying and dropping megaball hints about carats and cuts and clarity. The girl wanted a big ole rock, and he wanted a way out fast. Not that he'd led her on. He'd promised her marriage and long term weren't for him.

He was wrong. Caterina was long term for him. And marriage—

Brock slapped him on the back, walking toward the kitchen. "Time to get this over with." He rounded the corner and joked. "I'm back!"

The ladies clapped, the guys busted his balls, and Rocco stood, stuck, thinking about the difference between wanting Cat long term, and wanting Cat married.

THIRTY-NINE

Sugar hated mornings after Jared came back off a job because he woke before the crack of dawn to catch up on office duties. But he'd been gone for too many days, and she wasn't about to let him just disappear the first day he got back. Being the rock star of a wife that she was, she'd readied Asal for school and grabbed them McDonald's for breakfast. At least she was nursing a gigantic cup of coffee and had her McMuffin fix.

Coffee steaming in her hands, she watched Jared pace while talking on the phone and housing a McGriddle. Pieces of the conversation pricked her interest, but every time he turned in his office pacing loop, she lost parts of what he said. Whenever he rounded back toward her, she pressed into the leather chair in front of Jared's desk, petting Thelma the bulldog, and studying her coffee like the steam was spelling secrets.

Thelma groaned, and Sugar clucked at her. "Shh, girl." Quiet… because if she thought she'd heard Jared correctly…

Jared grumbled. "Yeah, Roc knows. El Mateperros—"

He turned and mumbled, talking while he finished off his breakfast. What was he saying?

Then back again. "We're waiting, probably tomorrow, oh dark thirty. Damn ACG—" Another bite. Couldn't he wait to finish breakfast?

She lost the conversation again. She leaned over, disguising the action as petting her dog, just to pick up missed words.

"Either way, Roc gets what he wants. Homeland Security gets what they need. It's decided."

Sugar leaned back into the chair, and Thelma jumped up, thinking she was a lap dog. Sixty pounds of lap dog, but Sugar didn't care. She was lost in thought. It *sounded* a hell of a lot like Titan had found ACG, knew where El Mateperros was. Jared had been studying thermal images before bed and again this morning.

Jared looked her way, and she pretended to fidget with her coffee and pet Thelma. The dog made her snotty bulldog noises, which helped Sugar's cover. But Jared looked... guilty?

He'd told her Caterina had been raped and gave her as many of the details as he knew, which basically boiled down to Cat wanted to kill El Mateperros for killing her family, but then after he'd raped her, it became even more of a life goal. Rocco had been feeling a serious need to avenge his woman's attacker. Jared said he could imagine that...

Titan was going after El Mateperros, letting Rocco do what he needed to. Taking care of it for Caterina. Didn't they know any better? Or was their male chromosome constantly fucking with their brains?

Jared ended his call and tossed a folder on his desk. "Gotta hit the head. Be back."

Yeah, he wasn't thrilled with whatever they were doing. He had that whole better-of-two-bad-options face on.

"Have fun." She grabbed a handful of Thelma's wrinkles and gave the pooch kisses.

When the door closed, she was up and going for that folder. A quick onceover and she saw that they were definitely thermals and scratch page of notes. *Numbers... Coordinates.* She snapped a couple pictures with her phone and dove back to her seat. Thelma jumped off as Jared walked back in, still looking up to something he shouldn't be. *Well, yeah, El Mateperros was Cat's!*

"Going somewhere?" he asked.

"Errands. Work. Guns aren't going to build themselves."

His forehead wrinkled as though he knew she was up to something. His knuckles cracked one at a time. "All right. Thanks for breakfast."

"Anytime." She kissed his lips then wiped away her lipstick mark. "I love you, J-Dawg. Don't you ever forget it."

Because by the end of the day, she would have to remind him of it, she was sure.

• • •

Caterina sucked down her second Diet Coke of the day. Idling in a parking lot, she sat in Rocco's truck under a big sign that simply read GUNS. Her fingers tapped the steering wheel. Sugar was a tricky one. Cat had a good feeling about her sometimes, but absolutely not all the time. She had no reason not to trust her, but Sugar was intense and aggressive. A bit of a try-me attitude. A wrought iron door swung open, and out walked Sugar. Cat guessed waiting outside was no longer an option. She reached for her bag, turning off the ignition. When she looked up, Sugar tapped brightly painted fingernails on the window.

"Out."

Always the conversationalist, wasn't she? Caterina nodded and took a calming breath. Anxiety made her so jittery. Couple that with her second finished soda, and she was shaky.

Caterina opened the door. *"Buenas tardes."*

"Yeah, good afternoon to you too, senorita. Get your butt inside. We need to talk."

Typical Sugar. Caterina shook her head but followed through the parking lot, then through the very secure front door and down a long, dark hallway. Voices and live fire filtered from the gun range. The inside of Sugar's place was both tactical and comfortable.

"Nice place—"

They walked into a fuchsia office. "Let's get down to business. Sit."

Caterina looked at the chair and watched Sugar take her desk chair. "I didn't know we had business."

"Just sit. Please."

Please? Not typical and it made her anxiety jump. "Sugar—"

"Look, I'm not good at the whole soft, nice thing, so please sit your senorita ass in the chair. I need to talk to you. *Please.*"

Caterina chewed the inside of her mouth and then sat. "Okay. Talk."

The confidence on Sugar's face flickered. Her lipsticked lips faltered, alternating between a forced smile and a comfortable frown. She took in a deep breath then puffed out her lips when it escaped. "I..." She gestured her hand, rolling it in a circle. "I know what happened." Sugar sucked in her bottom lip. "To you. Even though I guess I shouldn't."

She knew? Oh...Cat's lips flattened, and a full body heat covered her in embarrassed discomfort. "Okay."

"And I wouldn't bring it up—"

"Okay." Discomfort moved aside for anger. Caterina wanted none of this conversation. She hadn't wanted to talk to a therapist. Hadn't wanted Rocco to set her up with any of the Titan ladies to talk. None of that. She wanted one thing, and it had nothing to do with verbalizing the inner workings of her mind. "If that's all—"

Sugar pushed back from her desk and ducked underneath, returning with a large black case and a sheet of paper. "Unmarked. Unregistered. Untraceable."

Cat stared at the case for a long time, her heart pounding, soaring, hope and terror fighting for top billing in her chest. "What is this?" She picked up the piece of paper then looked at Sugar, confused and hoping her mind wasn't messing with her. "These are coordinates?"

"Si, senorita."

"Could you just call me Caterina? Cat?"

A painted, genuine smile cracked on Sugar's face. "What fun would that be? Anyway. Yes, that's a little lodge in West Virginia."

She tapped her teeth together. "And that's...where?"

"Well, we're in Virginia. So west."

"Now's not the time, Sugar. Work with me." She shook the paper. "What are you saying here?"

"I'm *saying* nothing because I'd like to *stay* married. *But*, this is a... present. Welcome to America, where all your dreams come true. You deserve it." Sugar patted the case and cleared her throat. She stared at the case, and when she looked up, there was a cold, hard strength in her eyes that Caterina respected. "Look, Senorita. I'm not the girl you talk to about feelings or whatever. But I *am* the girl who will sit you down and say that fucker needs to pay for hurting you. I know your history, your family and then… he *rapes* you? Fuck him. I'm giving you the one-way ticket to send his ass to hell."

A lump formed in Cat's throat. Sugar pushed the case to her side of the desk, and Caterina stood, tracing her hand on the case. When she looked up, Sugar nodded, and Cat popped the buckles. It opened but not all the way, and her hands rested on its top. Looking inside was almost too good to be true. She'd been so close so many times that it scared her how close she was again. A location and a weapon. Caterina could do this.

"Open it. It's all yours. And whatever else you need. *Comprende?*"

She lifted the case lid and pulled out an assault rifle.

"From my personal stash." Sugar pointed a pink fingernail at the weapon. "And you can't go wrong with a—"

"You made these?"

"Well… yeah." She shrugged. "It's all mil spec quality, and shit, Caterina. I don't know. This is what I'd want if I were you. I'm not assuming to know how you feel. I just." She nodded to the case on the desk. "I'd want someone to load me up with a whole lot of firepower and point me in the right direction, so that's what I'm doing."

Caterina glossed her hands over the weapons, and Sugar pulled a black bag onto the desk. It made a heavy noise when she set it down. "And ammo. Grenades. A pistol and a backup. Some holsters. And a flashlight. Every girl needs a good solid Mag light in her pack."

Grenades? Her mind couldn't wrap around the enormity of the gesture. "This is the nicest thing anyone's ever done for me. I don't know what to say."

"Say this will stay between you and me until I tell Jared. Say that you'll engage and eliminate, and it will make you feel better."

"I promise."

"Smart girl. If you need to talk feelings, talk to Mia. If you need a drink, call Nicola. But if you ever just need to pull a trigger until your ears are bleeding, your body's aching, and you're spent, call me."

"Okay."

"If you want help or even someone to road trip with, I'm game."

A genuine smile curled on her lips. "No, this is all me."

"Figured as much. I'll help you load up and see you off."

Five minutes later, both the case and the bag weighed down the back of Rocco's truck. She slammed the tailgate up and pulled the bed cover back down, securing it into place. "Sugar?"

"Senorita?"

She scowled, rolling her eyes. "You're a pain."

"I know. But I'm the best kind of pain to have."

True. "I've been out on my own for so long. It's nice to have people to talk to and have them accept me."

"Takes some getting used to. Trust me, I know. But we get you."

They did get her. It was nice.

Friends, a man, and a house to call home for the foreseeable future. Her hands still rested on the back of the tailgate. Well, it was nice, at least until he found out what she was about to do. Then, there was no telling.

FORTY

itan HQ wasn't that close, and when there wasn't a job, they didn't
really hang out at the office. Well, Jared and Parker did, but they had
office work. When there wasn't a job to plan or debrief from, they all
trained, slept, and caught up with life. But Jared pulled them in this
morning with a text message reading, "*get your asses in*," and Rocco was
more than familiar with what they would discuss.

El Mateperros.

They'd all arrived, and Rocco knew only what Jared had mentioned. Parker had found the Dog Killer. Titan had been contracted
to provide intel on any upcoming attack on the royal family's visit to
the White House. They hadn't been contracted to specifically locate El
Mateperros. All the ACG intel on potential threats had gone straight
to Homeland Security.

Yesterday, Jared had been ninety percent sure they'd found where
Yassine Harhour was bunkering down. Today, Rocco had no doubt
that Jared was one hundred percent certain. Rocco had already told
Boss Man that he wanted El Mateperros, and Jared had agreed with no
discussion, and now it was time for a game plan. But he was starting to
second guess taking the kill from Cat.

The team gathered around the war room table. They'd spent
enough time there that they all had unspoken assigned seats with
Jared at the top of the table. Brock was back in his regular seat. He and
Rocco flanked Jared.

"Brock's bringing Delta in a little closer to home than they've been," Jared started. "So while not on this job, the teams will be working together in the near future."

Roman, Winters, Cash, and Nicola nodded.

Boss Man continued. "I've never been one to sidestep situations before. You all know we've been contracted to monitor chatter on ACG. Parker's all over it. Other than feeding Homeland Security any intel we find on the Royal family-White House shindig, we're hands off. Not our job. Not our mission. No contract, nothing."

A huge *but* loomed.

"But. Parker found the Dog Killer. He's remained stationary for almost twenty-four hours, and we got a visual confirmation. I gave Rocco two options. We pass the intel along today, or we pass it along *tomorrow*. Taking down Yassine Harhour tomorrow won't endanger anyone, won't move up the timeline on their presumed attack."

All eyes landed on Rocco.

A gift from Boss Man. Jared slapped his arms across his chest and waited.

Rocco nodded, ready to repeat what he'd already told Jared. "And I said we tell them tomorrow." His hands formed fists under that table as he thought about El Mateperros and how he'd worked through the real complication of Jared's offer: did he take care of that asshole, or did he let Caterina? Because there was no way he or Cat would just let the federal government arrest the bastard.

Rage, white hot and blinding, grabbed hold of him. For a hot second, Rocco thought maybe it was a flashback, acid trip-out from before. But it'd been weeks, and this was different. This was internal pain, anguish, and a bloodthirsty need to take revenge out on the fucker who did his woman harm. That was simple enough. Guilt too. Caterina had wanted her whole life to end El Mateperros's. And that was before the son of a bitch hurt her.

Help her. Jared's words from weeks ago rang in his head. Doing this on his own was most likely the wrong decision, but that was the way it had to be. Or was it?

"Let's do it and be done with it." Helping her might just kill him. His alpha gene stoked a caveman urged to go fix shit, Titan-style.

Jared nodded, tight-lipped. "All right, we'll do this one overnight."

They nodded, talked logistics, and disbursed. He had to be ready to go in four hours, but until then, he'd at least spend time with Cat. Hell, it may be one of his last times doing so because, when she found out, she'd walk.

Rocco dialed her as he drove home. One phone call went unanswered. Then another. He was on the fourth unanswered call when he pulled into the empty driveway and the fifth when he heard the phone ringing in the kitchen.

The house was empty. It wouldn't have been alarming—Cat had taken to using the truck when she went out—except for the abandoned phone. He circled around the table, staring at the phone, wondering where—

A note taped to the fridge had a heart at the bottom of it.

I'm sorry. I didn't have a choice.
XO

He rocked back on his heels, a sudden restlessness taking hold. Rocco snagged the phone off the table and scrolled to her phone log. Other than his number, the last call in was GUNS.

Everything moved too quickly in his mind. All the what ifs and maybe nots. But Caterina was gone. Phone at home. And the last person she spoke to was Sugar? Bad news. Bad fucking news.

Using her phone, Rocco hit redial. The phone rang once.

Sugar answered immediately. "Everything okay?"

"Goddamn it, Sugar. What is going on?"

She sucked in a breath. "Rocco."

"Yeah. What's going on?"

"Well…"

"Spit it out, Sugar."

"No."

He choked out a harsh, angry laugh. "I'm not playing. What the hell is happening?"

"I don't know what you're talking about."

"Bull."

She huffed out again. "Fine. Whatever. Titan knows where El Mateperros is."

"I know, damn it." He scrubbed the scruff on his chin. "Why do you, and what have you done about it?"

"I overheard and told Cat," she rushed out her words. "She needed to know."

"I fucking know. I—" Rocco slammed his palm against the wall. "Damn it, Sugar. Jesus fucking Christ. What'd you do, send her packing with a gun and some ammo?"

"Well, not quite, prick. I gave her a couple handguns, a rifle, some grenades—"

"What?" he roared. "Wait. What did you just say grenades? Are you out of your mind? We're in the fucking United States. You can't send her to West Virginia with a goddamn arsenal."

"No one said she's going to use everything, but she needed options."

He put the phone on speaker, sat at the table, and rubbed his face. "What the hell am I supposed to do now?"

"Nothing. Let her do her thing."

"Christ. Shit." He tore his hands into his hair. "How long ago did she leave your place?"

"Like five hours."

"Five hours..." He did the math. Assuming she'd stopped at home to write the note and was driving reasonably, she'd be nearly half way there.

"So... Are you going to mention this to Jared?"

"Am I going to *mention* this to Jared? I'm going to freakin' ask him to warm up a chopper." He blew out an exasperated breath. "Bye, Sugar."

He ended the call and grabbed a Diet Coke out of the fridge. Fake sugar wouldn't kill him today. He cracked the top off and flung it into the sink. Without looking at the screen, he called Jared and already hated the conversation that was about to happen.

"You think twice about leaving Cat out of this?" Jared barked into the phone.

"I made the wrong choice. She should be the one to do it. But now we have a change of plans, Boss Man, and I need to get to West Virginia before she gets herself killed."

FORTY-ONE

A half kilometer from the coordinates, Caterina pulled off the winding highway and down a steep mountain road. The sun had set, blanketing her in the cover of a dark dusk. No one could see her. Wearing black from head to toe, she strapped on a thigh holster, secured a pistol onto a tactical belt, and holstered two combat handguns with enough ammo to blow up a West Virginia trailer. Then she slung the tactical rifle over her shoulders. Tucked into her ankles were her two favorite knives. She was ready.

The forested space between her and El Mateperros was dense. Thick trees decorated a sharp incline. She'd be going up on the way there, making it easier to retreat. Her blood rushed. Excitement tingled in her palms. This was the day she'd waited for. Running the first thirty seconds was smooth—graceful and exhilarating—as if she'd been meant to end up there, on the side of an Appalachian mountain, armed from ankles to collarbone.

The quiet *thump, thump, thump* of a stealth helicopter registered before she could even identify the sound. Cold shivers sliced down her spine. A waterfall of anger and apprehension streamed into her limbs. She picked up a steady run, hopping over downed limbs and ignoring the scratching bushes and branches.

Had Titan come to stop her? Had the United States government decided that tonight would be the night they showed up and dismantled the ACG? She ran faster, the steep incline slowing her down more than she'd expected. The rhythmic thump of quiet rotors soared above her, passing.

No! She was too close. Caterina pounded the ground faster, running harder than she should with barely healed ribs. She wasn't losing El Mateperros. Not this time. She'd get to him first if it killed her. Whoever was in the chopper could have the ACG. She just needed El Mateperros. Was that too much to ask?

Outrunning a chopper was impossible. She lost track of the whirring of blades as they bounced off the mountain walls. Straining to hear… Maybe she didn't hear it anymore? Maybe paranoia was getting to her, and the noise had been an echo of a farther away aircraft. She listened. Not much. She pressed forward again, attributing the sounds to road noise from the nearby highway. Or it might've been a commuter plane, a puddle hopper or a—

The stealth copter swung back over her head at the same time she hit a clearing, dropping… One. Two. Three. Three men. They melted into the ground, away from her line of sight, and the helo disappeared. Holding her breath, she looked at the house El Mateperros was likely in, waiting for lights to come on or gunfire to erupt. Her heart slammed in her chest, pounding her sore ribs. Nothing. No lights. No gunfire. No—

A solid knock to the back of her legs took her down. A hand clamped over her mouth.

"Oh, Kitten, we have to talk about this later." Rocco's soft lips brushed her ear. The warm moistness of his breath tickling her neck made her blood rush all over again, and that had nothing to do with him knocking her down and catching her fall.

She pushed him away and rolled to her stomach in the damp grass. Her strapped weapons dug into her thighs, hips, and chest. Uncertain apprehension made her stomach drop. Rocco wasn't going to let her take the shot, and she'd resent him for the rest of her life.

"Sorry about that. Didn't want you to scream." His voice rumbled over her.

"I am not a screamer."

He chuckled low. Rocco's hand slipped off her cheek, down her neck, over the ammo and guns strapped to her, and ended around her waist, pulling her close. "I'll have to disagree with that."

She huffed, not in the mood for his jokes. "Go home, Roc."

"What are you doing out here all alone?"

"I didn't have a choice."

"Wrong, woman. It might have taken me until the last second, but I want this for you. I want you to be happy, and fuck it, if this does that, then that's what I want to."

"But—"

"But nothing. You'd better believe your sweet ass, I'm not going to let you get killed, and you sure as hell aren't going in alone. Guess that's love between the two of us. Your fight is my fight, and baby, I want you to pull that trigger." He pulled in heavy breath. "As much as it kills me not to be the one, it's your fight."

She swallowed the knot in her throat. "But you brought a team."

"Jared'll be back when we need him. Winters and Roman are in position."

Her eyes went to the sky. Jared was manning the chopper. She wasn't sure if she wanted to face him after this. "I don't know how to operate with a team."

"You're not going without strategic cover."

"I'm not going in to take him out alive."

"Not a problem, but I'll be with you. Partners."

She shook her head. "No."

"Cat, it's not a debate, and we don't have time."

He was right, and she had no idea how many ACG were inside. She needed their help. "Okay."

Rocco took her hand. She expected a kiss or a hand hold. Something. Instead, Rocco handed her a comm piece. "Mic and earbud. You'll be live to all of us. Jared too."

She slipped them on. "Test."

"There's our girl," Roman whispered.

"Crystal clear," Winters added.

Her ear piece crackled, then Jared came on. "I'm not happy with you and Sugar, and don't give me any of that *lo siento* bullshit."

"Ah, don't be mad."

"Whatever," he grumbled. "Get it done then get on board."

She looked toward where she came from. "Your truck's here."

Rocco nodded. "No prob. We'll drive back. Let's do this." They advanced. "Roman." He pointed to the south side. "And Winters."

Thirty seconds later, they'd ducked and run to the back door, pressing against the wall and sidestepping. She came to the back door and rested her hand on the knob, testing. "Locked." She pulled a lock kit from her pocket, slipped out two toothpick-like pieces, and slid them into the lock. The night was quiet. Cool. She listened for clicks and felt for tumblers, adjusting her tools. Time flew. Pressure made her hot, as if all of Titan watched her pick the lock. Working alone had its benefits: her own schedule and lack of a peanut gallery.

Click. The last tumbler moved. She tried the knob and it twisted.

"Good girl."

His praise soothed her nerves. "You go high right."

He nodded, spoke to Winters and Roman, pulling them in to join them, then nodded. Four of them versus whatever was in the house. A twinge of guilt surfaced. They'd already lost Delta men because of her. Now they were walking into an unknown situation because she'd decided to come here alone.

"We're good when you are, Kitten."

She pocketed her kit and withdrew a high-powered handgun, twisting a silencer into place. Fingers counted down. *Three. Two. One.*

Rocco charged in from behind her. She dropped, scanning, gun outstretched. They cleared the room. Not a peep from the house. Were the occupants asleep? It'd be an early night, but they had a big couple of days coming up. Or had she missed them? Was it an empty house?

Rocco pointed, and they crossed a kitchen. Leftover food sat on a counter. People had been here recently enough. Great sign. Stairs ahead. She chopped her hand through the air. She would go up; he could cover. Rocco nodded, and Winters and Roman rolled in behind them. The first step creaked. She cringed and looked at Rocco. He was positioned at the base, gun pointed up, watching out for her. Another step. Another. Creak. She swallowed a groan. In her head, the sound was a trombone blaring, but no one came running. At the top of the stairs, she motioned Rocco up. She eyed four closed doors and guessed which one was the master bedroom. Rocco summited and *creak*—

That wasn't him. Or her. She spun. A man in his boxers walked out of a darkened bathroom. Their eyes met. His mouth opened, and a single yell hollered before Rocco's silent shot dropped him. But a silencer wasn't silent.

Lights turned on. Men called out, muffled by the four closed doors. They were surrounded, but ACG was split and unaware. Straight ahead had to be the master bedroom. She moved fast, kicked open the door—El Mateperros. He was pulling on pants. Their eyes clashed. He lunged for the nightstand, and she pulled the trigger. The bullet met his hand in a muffled explosion. It was the same hand that had held her down. That had touched her naked body.

"That was for touching me."

She pulled the trigger again, smiling as the round ripped into his knee, dropping him to the ground with a roaring cry of pain. "And that was for holding me down."

Now it was her turn to be the sick one because it felt way too good to have that power. She stepped forward, weapon pointed at his chest. His twisted, flawless face screwed tight in pain. In shock. Mouth agape, silently screaming. The bloody pulp of a hand stretched out in front of him.

Behind her, shots poured rained from and toward Rocco, Roman, and Winters. She heard it all through her earpiece: their voices, commands, warnings. So loud, so chaotic, but somehow so organized. She pulled out her earpiece, wanting to be alone, wanting it to just be her and El Mateperros in this little room.

He writhed on the floor. One steady footstep at a time, she had him pinned to the ground, weaponless and bleeding out. "I've waited so long."

She pulled the trigger again. The bullet whizzed by his head. Intentionally. "You feel that?"

The Dog Killer moaned. "Stop! No!"

"Feel that fear? Imagine being a little girl. Imagine the sound of death and the sight of loved ones, dropping all around. Imagine that hell."

The crack of bullet whizzing through the wall, into the room made them both jump. Excruciating pain exploded in her shoulder. She cried out, slamming her teeth together, absorbing the bite of a stray bullet. El Mateperros lunged off the floor. Her 9mm scattered across the room.

Hell no.

A punch hit her cheek. His good hand found her bleeding shoulder, grabbing into the wound. She screeched. Stars exploded in her eyes. Caterina grabbed another sidearm strapped to her, pulling the triggered as his already bloodied hand slid over her skin.

El Mateperros pushed the weapon down, reaching for it—needing to steal it to survive—and there was no way she was giving it up. Caterina growled. Thrashed. Cursed. They were blood soaked, and his hand found her grip on the gun. They struggled back and forth.

Bam! A round exploded, lighting the darkened room and slamming through an outer wall. Grunts and growls. She bit into his shoulder and kneed him as hard as she could. The gun skittered across the floor. Both reached for it. Neither found success.

His unwounded leg pinned her thigh. Her leg was at such an angle that she could reach the sheathed knife at her boot. Grabbing it, Caterina pulled it fast, and El Mateperros drew up, arm angled to slam his fist into her face. The knife was new to her but with practiced precision, its handle comfortable in her grip, she slammed the blade into him, sinking through his clothes, into his flesh.

He stilled. Shouted. Hollered. Fell back. The knife stuck out from his groin.

That hadn't been planned and wasn't fatal. But it was karma.

He looked down. Horror. Complete and total terror. She stared, mouth open, thinking it more traumatic and appropriate than a kill shot. But she still would take one. In a minute. She just needed to absorb the perfectness of their violent collision.

The door opened behind her. The fire fight just feet away sounded as though it had finished. She'd know more if she'd had kept her earpiece in, but Cat wasn't at all concerned that Titan had been taken out. Nothing would happen to them. She believed it.

El Mateperros's teeth were bared. He hissed. Rage burned in his eyes. "Fucking whore!" He rolled to the side, ripping the knife free. A shout fell from his lips like that of a wounded, dying bear. She grabbed the gun from across her chest, blood coated fingers trying to find the trigger and sliding as his knife wielding hand dropped toward her.

The gun fell into place in her sticky, wet hands. Finger on the trigger.

A blast exploded.

But—

She hadn't pulled the trigger.

El Mateperros, knife in hand, dropped to the floor.

Her head dropped back, hitting the floor. Breaths and sweat and blood poured out of her. Rocco stood above.

He'd made the kill shot. He'd taken out her nightmare and saved her. Too bad he had stolen her moment. A wild, desperate mixture of gratitude and jealousy ripped through her, tearing her into conflicting persons. She should've said *gracias*. Should've thrown her arms around him and asked for help with bandaging her arm.

But instead, she stayed on the floor, panting, bleeding, closing her eyes, wondering if it were really over, why didn't she feel closure? Or at least better?

He dropped to a crouch. "Kitten, you with me? You okay?"

Her shoulder pounded, throbbing pain and pulsing blood. But that was not what was on her mind. "No." No on so many levels. No because she'd been shot. Not because she didn't get what she'd wanted more than anything. Not because she'd never have a chance again.

Just… No. No. No.

Rocco gave orders in his comm piece. *He* was supposed to be what she wanted more than anything. *Rocco*. She needed Rocco. Wanted him. But right now, she hurt for wanting to be mad, hurting for her vengeance.

He scooped his arms under her and lifted to his chest. Their weapons knocked together. Her blood seeped into his clothes.

"Well then, let's get you out of here." He spoke into his mic. "All clear. We're coming out, and I need a medic kit."

The conversation continued, but she ignored it, watching El Mateperros's dead body leak blood onto the floor as Rocco carried her out. "There's a knife in there," Rocco said to Winters as they passed. "Leave anything else identifying?"

She shook her head, making her shoulder flare. It felt good, a distraction from herself. They walked out of the house as Jared brought the chopper down.

"Your truck."

"Who wants to drive the truck home?" he said into his mic, then to her. "It's taken care of."

That easy. Everything in Rocco's all-American life was always that easy. He made it look easy, as though she should've been able to do it long ago. El Mateperros was gone. Taken away by the man who said he loved her—who *did* love her—who'd put his life, his team's lives, on the line for her sick, sad desires. And now she was ungrateful that he'd saved her life? What the hell was wrong with her?

"I'm completely fucked up," she whispered. It wasn't for his benefit or really even for him to hear. He just happened to be there. But it was an acknowledgment of all that was wrong with her.

FORTY-TWO

The chopper lifted quietly and sailed into the black night sky. Caterina was tucked under Rocco's arm, asleep after a quick bandaging and shot of antibiotics and pain killers. They'd get her a doctor, let Homeland Security clean up their mess, and be done with this chapter in their lives. More often than not, on ops like this, Rocco manned the chopper. Sitting back there, away from his comfortable panel of controls and gauges, an empty feeling filled his chest. He'd seen it in Cat's eyes. As soon as she'd realized El Mateperros had been shot, and not by her, her eyes went cold. Distant.

Goddamn, he wished he could've given her that shot, but if he'd waited another second, it wouldn't have been a terrorist who died in that room. Rocco pulled her tighter, trying not to cause discomfort but scared that when she awoke, she'd be done with him. Split second decision. He'd had no choice and had acted before the consequences weighed in his head. That was how he was trained: see, react. If he had taken the time to bask in an indecisiveness, to think about how badly shit would go if he took this away from her, then he'd be mourning her. If Cat walked away, at least she was alive to do it.

The next few hours passed quickly. They made it to the hospital without problems. Caterina was wheeled away, asleep as he held her hand until they passed through double doors. Roman had to hold him back because, even though he knew better, Rocco fought the docs and tried to stay with her. There was nothing he could do but wait. It was a simple surgery to remove bullet fragments. She'd be in recovery before he knew it. He just had to wait. And wait. And it was taking a hell of a long time. Roman sat with him, and they waited.

"Fuck, man." Threading fingers in to his hair, Rocco dropped into a seat after another lap around the waiting room.

Cash joined Roman, and they took turns trying to say the right thing and telling him to calm down. They just didn't get on how many levels he was scared of losing her.

"She's tough as she is hot."

Rocco glared at Cash, but it wasn't about her living through a routine surgery.

Roman threw hands in the air. "You get my point."

"And you've missed mine. She wanted that shot, and I stole it."

His buddies had nothing to add because there was nothing to say. They sat there and watched middle-of-the-night reruns until the morning shows came on. Roman and Cash fell asleep in their chairs. Rocco's head hung down after asking a nurse for yet another update. It'd been too long, and Jared wasn't answering his phone—

Jared and Mia walked in the door. *Mia?* She held bags of fast food and coffee. Rocco's gut twisted. *Mia the therapist.* She was all *let's talk about feelings because that's how we survive nightmares.* Her cute face wasn't empathetic or pitying. She was all business, and she was facing him.

"Roman. Cash. Out."

Rocco's head dropped back. "What's wrong?"

"Rocco." Mia sat in Roman's vacated seat.

"Yeah, whatever. Say what needs to be said."

"She's having some trouble—"

"And that's why you're here, to help me understand." He rubbed his hands on his thighs. "News flash. I don't need help to understand. I'm sorry Boss Man dragged you out of bed. No need to prep me, let's go see her..."

"She needs time."

What the hell did that mean? He shook his head. "She needed a kill shot. I took it. She doesn't need time. She needs that notch in her belt. She'll never get it. So where the hell is her room? No one will tell me anything. She can yell at me. You can yell at me—"

"Roc, it's not that simple."

"The hell it isn't."

"Rocco—"

"She's alive. That's all that matters." He slapped Jared on the back on his way out. "So if that's all you needed to say, I'm gonna go break down some doors until I find my girl."

"Cut the crap, Rocco."

He spun, walking backward. "No crap to cut. I wouldn't change a damn thing. I saved her life. I'll chalk it up to my good deed of the week. Let her bust my balls."

"Don't. She doesn't want to see you." Jared's face was tight. "I'm sorry."

He hurt like hell because the woman he loved couldn't even tell him to his face that it was over. Screw that.

"Rocco." Mia's professional face faltered. "It's not you, and it's not over. You just need to give her a chance to sort things out."

"But—"

"Rocco, look man, given… how everything is, you've just gotta walk away. Give her a day. Or something. Don't make me toss your ass out of here. Trust me on this one. Just do the right thing."

His jaw hung open. "You're telling me that's… to walk away. You want me to walk the fuck away."

Boss Man blew out. "I need you to."

Rocco slapped the door. Fuck it. "Totally fine. I don't give a shit. I'm gonna go home. Watch some *Duck Dynasty*. Work out. Get back to a normal freakin' life. No head trips. No women making themselves at home. Nothing."

"Roc—"

He punched a vending machine on the way out, accidentally shutting Mia up in the process, but not giving a fuck. Sure, he would hear about that from Winters later, but screw it.

FORTY-THREE

Antiseptic and pancakes. Caterina woke, groggy and uncomfortable. In the background, the sounds of everyday life unfolded. Sugar was laughing. *Jared* was laughing. Their adopted daughter, Asal, was laughing. Everyone seemed to be having a great Saturday morning. She'd had no place to go after she'd left the hospital—well, she could have gone home, but she couldn't face Rocco—so she's asked Jared and Sugar to borrow a guest bedroom. Even that was a mistake. Clutching her stomach, Caterina wanted to fade away. Life was just too complicated.

Knock. Knock. She didn't answer, but why would that stop Sugar? It was her house after all. And even if it weren't, Caterina didn't think Sugar cared much for permissions.

"Up and at 'em, Senorita."

Caterina rolled over. "Later."

"Thought you might say that." Sugar flounced on the bed. "Pancake. Eat."

"Not hungry."

"Don't care."

"Sugar, seriously."

"If you don't want to eat, let's call Rocco."

God she wanted to call Rocco, and she would just die if he walked in and gathered her into his arms. He might just make it all better. But no, who was she kidding? Nothing would be all better. This was life, her new reality. She was happy about it—she had to be. No excuse for

265

not being… Really, she had to get out of there, further away from him so she wouldn't be tempted. "Fine. I'll eat."

Sugar shook her head. "Does you no good to run from him. She *hmm*-ed.

"He would absolutely understand."

Understand. Ha… "Maybe. Maybe not."

"He loves you."

"Me, yes. Agree. But what I've done…"

"Oh, Senorita. That's insane. You haven't done anything."

"Maybe that's the other half of the problem. I never do anything. Things happen to me. I try but fail."

"You're emotional. Not thinking straight. Eat. Food is fuel, and you need your strength. Then call."

She had to get out of there. "Fine. Maybe." Agree or the conversation would never end. "Eat. Then call."

"*Mommy!*" Asal called from the hall.

Sugar tossed Cat a cell phone and went out the door, just as Caterina's mom used to do when she was that age. Laughter erupted followed by too much fun, too much family and love for her to handle. Caterina ached on so many levels. She chewed a few pancakes, not tasting but knowing she needed to eat, and then stared at the phone.

The one good thing about never having a permanent residence was that Caterina never had the ability to store important documents and files. She'd never received a bank statement or had a check book. Everything was wireless, and everything was memorized, including her bank account numbers and contact lists. She picked up the phone, dialed her favorite North American mover, wired her funds, and had a seat on a cargo plane that would wait for her, just soon as she could wander away from Le Casa De Westin.

• • •

Asal Westin waved from the fence line, and Caterina knew Jared would kick her ass for pulling a move like this if he ever looked for her, which didn't seem like a realistic possibility. Caterina had offered to play outside with their kid, and reaching the edge of the property without setting off too many alarms, she asked Asal to count backward from one hundred before telling her parents thank you for the hospitality.

Feeling like crap on every possible level, Caterina broke into a jog, breathing through the pain in her shoulder, stomach, and heart, and finally she pushed to a run, going until she hit a road with traffic. It took her a few minutes to catch her breath and look less like the psycho she apparently was, then stuck out her thumb. The first trucker who saw her hit the brakes, and minutes later, she was headed toward a highway before Jared and Sugar could say leaving was a bad idea.

"You running from something?" The trucker seemed nice enough. Mostly looking for company. "Lots of times I see women running, they're trying to get safe."

"No." More like keeping someone away from her.

"Where ya from, anyway?"

"Puerto Rico." She lied. Why tell him Spain? There was the slightest chance that Titan, or more specifically, Rocco, would track her. She didn't need to make it easy for anyone. Maybe he would just give up.

"Puerto Rico." He nodded. "I had a girlfriend from Puerto Rico once."

The trucker continued to recount his stories of Latin lovers and his appreciation for accents. Rocco loved the way she sounded, and she never told him, but the way he sounded, all American and alpha… He was perfect. Time passed with each new trucker tale until she waved goodbye at a strip mall near the airstrip. She walked along the road, through a security gate, and boarded a waiting cargo plane. Her seat was between wooden pallets, and it would be a long flight. At least she had a small bag from Asal packed with the pancakes they had needed while they played and explored.

FORTY-FOUR

A week had passed since Rocco had seen Jared. No jobs were on the books, so there was no reason for Boss Man to blow up his phone. Finally, a text came through. One look and he hit redial.

Rocco's lunched about heaved on the floor. "What do you mean, have I seen Caterina?"

"She left." Jared sighed. "She grabbed a handful of pancakes, went outside with my kid, and never came back."

"So… she left."

"Maybe she's headed your way?"

Rocco shook head. "Yeah, no. She would've just borrowed a car."

"Look, Roc, there's something you need—"

"You know what, Boss Man? No. There's nothing I need to do. I am tired of letting others call the shots. Letting her say, I'm done. Letting Mia say she needs space. Whatever. Fine. Everyone can say what they want, and I've had enough of not saying shit."

"Roc—"

"I'll call you later."

"Rocco—"

"What goddamn it? You wanna tell me to give her space? To be her friend? Whatever you want to say, shove it. I'm going to find her, and she can say it to my face. She's pissed I killed the fucker. Fine. She can say it. She hates me for ruining some lifelong dream of murder. Whatever. It's true. She was gonna die. So I don't give a fuck. Bye."

He walked into his room—*their room*—and grabbed a bag. He wasn't coming home without her. A promise. A vow, and damn, he sounded like a crazy stalker, but that was what had to happen. She loved him. He knew deep down in his soul that she loved him. And he would talk her ear off until she remembered, then he make love to her until she screamed his name—well, soon as she'd wrapped her head around the idea of sex again. That was his plan. Getting from their relationship's point A to point B had a lot of logistical questions, but those could be figured out along the way.

Bag packed with a few changes of clothes, he grabbed a box of granola bars and his passport on the way to his truck. He had no freakin' idea where he was going. Rocco jumped into his truck, threw the gear shifter in drive, and peeled down the driveway. First up, call Parker. He reached for his phone. Wasn't in his pocket or on the dash. Not in his bag. He remembered throwing it aside to pack. Hell, he wasn't turning around for a phone. If he needed one, he'd buy a burner.

Before he knew it, Rocco had parked at Dulles International Airport and was staring at the listing of out bound flights. London. London. London. Several options. He needed the quickest one.

Standing in line took forever, and no doubt, scratched the earliest flight off the list of possibilities. Commercial flights were a nightmare. Finally, he made it to the top of the line and was directed to a kiosk. He punched the buttons. Check-in flights. Change flights. Where was *departing flights*? He looked up at the girl manning the counter, advising a dozen kiosks on where their gates were and strapping baggage claim stickers on suitcases.

"Excuse me? Emergency over here."

Kiosk Lady put up a finger, and Rocco cursed. He wouldn't make any of these flights. He'd memorized every flight to London by the time she waltzed over, smile painted on and flirting a bit too much.

"I need to get to London, ASAP."

"You don't have a ticket?" Confusion slowed her flirtation.

Come on, already. "No ticket." He waved his passport and a wad of cash and credit cards. "But I do have this, so make it happen."

Looking at his hand, then him, a saccharine look crossed her face like this was some romantic movie, and he was the hero chasing down the girl. "Is this about a girl?"

For Christ's sake...Well, that was kind of true, and Kiosk Lady seemed happy about it. "Yes. Help me."

He'd go along with her delusion of what might be happening, no need to mention killing off a terrorist who'd raped his woman. *Fuck.* The urge to maim tore through his veins again. He breathed it out, trying like crazy to keep his head.

She typed on her computer. "Hmmm...."

Hmm? He was about to jump the security line and board a plane by force. He could fly almost anything. A commercial plane wouldn't be a problem. "Tell me you got something." Otherwise, he would carjack a jetliner. Titan would make the news. Jared would be pissed after trying to help Rocco get out of that little problem. "It's really important."

"I'm sorry. Nothing available until—"

He rubbed his forehead. "I've got to get to my girl. *Have to.*"

A few more types and clicks. "I really want to help. There just aren't any seats until tomorrow."

"I'll try another—"

"I checked all carriers leaving here today." Her sweet smile made him want to punch the screen. "But tomorrow—"

His head lowered, his shoulders slouched, and defeat mocked him. Rocco turned, ready to kick his negative thoughts and find another plan of attack. How hard could it be to get a plane to Europe? How sure was he she was going home?

Home.

Home... wasn't London.

He raced back to the front of the line, cutting in front of a much older couple dripping in money. The man mumbled something about diamond-platinum status. *Whatever.* "Spain. Can you get me to Spain?"

The airline woman's smile faltered as she silently apologized to the couple he'd stepped in front of. "Sir—"

"Get me to Spain. Today."

"I was helping our *premier* guests." She all but curtsied, trying to make her apology stretch on his behalf.

"I have to get to her."

Another curtsey, apology thing to the premier people, and she focused on him, if for no other reason than to get rid of him. He knew that and didn't care.

"Um, do you have a particular city?"

Shit. Geography would kick his ass today. Where had Titan worked? Where did she say she'd lived? He was going to—what—wander around a country until he spotted her?

Think...

Southeastern Spain. Near Algeria. "Grenada. Murcia. Valencia. Just get me in that neck of the woods." He closed his eyes for a second, praying to God whatever she typed would give him a shot at finding Caterina. "Please. Just..." He cracked his knuckles and realized how quiet it was around him. Rocco looked over his shoulder. Dozens of people watched him. "I have to get there."

"Murcia?"

"Done. I'll take it."

She frowned, looking at her wrist watch. "You'll be cutting it close."

The hoity-toity premier woman butted in, her gray hair coiffed but her eyes dancing with the thrill of his moment. "Look at him. This boy can run. Get him that ticket."

Rocco heard murmuring beside him, behind him. This was turning into a spectacle, but who the hell cared. "I can run."

More clacking on the keyboard. "Baggage?"

"No." *Come on, come on, come on.* He pulled out his wallet. "How much time do I have?"

"Not much. Passport, ID?"

"Here."

"This computer system is taking forever. Sorry about this." She tapped the side of the screen a few times. "Um, I think it froze. There's another flight... um, give me a minute to find it."

The woman next to him elbowed her hoity-toity husband, who grumbled. "What?"

She raised penciled eye brows at him, tilting her unmoving, styled hairdo his way.

"How much time?" Rocco asked again.

"I'm working as fast as I can. Soon as it reboots, we'll get you paid up. There we go—"

"Oh, fiddle-sticks." The older woman next to him blew out. "Print him a boarding pass." She nudged her husband. "Honey, get his ticket."

"Get his ticket?" Kiosk Lady gaped.

Rocco gaped. "*Get my ticket?*" Somewhere in the back of his head, he heard Caterina talking about coincidence and everything happening for a reason.

"Yes." She smiled, nudging her very much less than enthusiastic husband. "Get your ticket."

"I can't—" Rocco stuttered, not exactly knowing why she offered or what to say. A last minute international ticket was some serious cash.

"You won't make it through security and the shuttles. This old beau had to chase me down. All the way to Paris. I've waited fifty years to pay it forward. Go."

"I don't need a free ride. This should cover it." Rocco handed her a wad of cash and a business card that simply had Titan's logo and a phone number on it. "If you ever need anything, it's on the house."

The woman nodded. Gold and diamonds sparkled on her. "Go."

From behind the counter, Kiosk Lady picked up the phone. "Hey, I've got a VIP coming your way. Get him through security." She handed him a hand-punched ticket, pointing down the terminal. "Good luck."

FORTY-FIVE

The tide was pulling out. Cold water lapped up to Rocco's ankles, and his feet made a rhythmic slapping-sucking noise as he walked in the rushing water. He'd arrived in Murcia, Spain that morning with little in the way of a plan. As he walked through the terminal, advertisements for tourist hot spots and transportation flashed at him. *The resorts at Dehesa de Campoamor?* He picked up a brochure filled with pictures of white, sandy beaches. Her hometown had been the alias she used? His plan immediately clicked into place, and he had a good idea of where to track Caterina down once he found Dehesa de Campoamor.

A sun-bleached fence was ahead at the top of the sand dunes. Behind it stood a one-room church with a steeple that had seen better days. The building was whitewashed, and everything looked as he'd thought it would. His eyes followed along the fence line to the open gate.

It only took a moment to reach the opening, and when he did, he dropped the shoes he'd been carrying and slipped them on. Grass surrounded the church and the small graveyard behind it. Above him, an old church bell began its angsty tolling, one loud clang after another. The hollow noise floated toward the sea and disappeared.

He scanned the grass, the graves, until he spotted her, sitting in front of a nondescript marker. Caterina's hair was down, floating in the breeze. She looked content talking to the gravestones, almost serene, and not at all how he normally felt when walking toward graves. Hands in his pockets, he silently crossed closer and watched her.

Whatever she was saying, it looked important. He remembered that Caterina had made a vow not to go home until vengeance had been exacted. Even now, his actions pained his heart, but he wouldn't have risked a do-over. He never would have risked her life. So here he was to explain that, and she could either take it or kick him back to America.

He held his breath and waited.

"Hi." She didn't turn around.

Her gauzy dress softened her. The white of the fabric stood out against her olive skin and dark hair. He could stare at her all day. Even now, she looked more beautiful than he'd ever seen her, cloaked in white and glowing.

"Kitten." He didn't move forward, letting her stay with her family and do what she needed to do. Then he'd bring her home, and they could start a new life.

Silent minutes later, she looked over her shoulder, pushing the loose hair away. "What are you doing here?"

"What do you think?" His words floated in the wind.

She dropped her chin, but then raised it to look at him again. "How did you know where I was?"

The distant sadness in her voice made his heart ache and arms hurt for wanting to hold her. "Wasn't that hard to find you, Cat."

"I would've come back. Eventually."

"Eventually would've been too long."

"Want to sit?" She patted the ground next to her, gathering the skirt around her knees. "My parents, my brothers."

"I know." He nodded, watching her stare at their graves.

"You would have liked them."

Slowly stepping closer, he dropped next to her on the grass. The graves were white and worn, the lettering of the names and dates weather-beaten. "Bet I would have."

"Rocco, I'm not the same person I was even a few weeks ago."

He inclined his head toward her. "I can say the same thing about me after meeting you."

"No. It's different. It's..." She bit her bottom lip and looked over the graves.

Damn. Something wasn't right. "Cat?"

"I'm pregnant."

"What?" The word just fell out. All shocked and... shocked. That couldn't be right. "But I thought..." He felt funny. Overwhelmed. Overjoyed. Damn, his head swam. "So... I'm going to be—"

"No." Her eyes welled. "I don't know."

"What?"

"I don't know." Pain flooded her words.

She wasn't pregnant? What?

"The same day, we didn't..." She sniffled. "The day I trusted my birth control was the same day I was attacked."

He didn't understand because there was no way she could be possibly saying—

"The baby, it might not—" Her voice cracked. She turned back to the graves and let her hair cover her face.

His windpipe squeezed. The baby wasn't his. Or maybe it was. Holy shit. He couldn't breathe. "It's..." He had nothing. "This... You... Are you okay?"

"Yes. No." She rubbed her temples. "This is not the way it was supposed to be."

"And you're going to k—"

"Yes," she hissed at him.

His stomach churned, not sure what he wanted the answer to be. Hell, this wasn't fair. Just—goddamn—wasn't fair. He inhaled and adrenaline rushed his system. "Okay." But that sounded forced. It felt forced.

His insides shook, muscles vibrating, teeth gnashing, shaking to the point of sickness, yet he looked down at his hands, and nothing moved. Nothing, and thank God because enough had come down on the woman he wanted to be his wife, and if he gave her an ounce more burden to carry, he might as well just walk away. It'd be better for them both.

"What are you thinking, Roc?" Her eyes searched his face.

"What am I thinking?" Repeating her question didn't help. For everything rushing through his mind, no words came. His tongue felt thick. "I'm thinking... Fight or flight or figure this out. There's nobody left to fight and..." He scrubbed his face. "And I'm not going anywhere..." Saying that out loud eased some of the pressure in his chest but not all. He was nowhere near being able to be okay, but it might be survivable. "I'm thinking, goddamn, Kitten, I hurt for you, but I want to figure this out."

"I thought you'd hate me."

"No way. Not possible."

She knotted her fingers. "Be repulsed?"

He shook his head. No, and that was the truth. He couldn't hate her. She'd done nothing wrong. "It doesn't work that way, me and you."

"How does this work? Because I don't know."

"What is there to figure out? We're having a baby. We—"

"We?" Her jaw hung open.

"Well, I didn't fly across the world for no reason. I want you to come home."

For the first time in what seemed like years, her lips curled into a smile, slight but there. "I never saw myself as the motherly type."

Yeah, he'd never thought about it either. Chalk that up to having a man-gene, but he was barely thinking past come-home-with-me. "How much had you actually thought about it?"

"Not much... And when I first found out... probably until I was sitting alone in a plane, somewhere over the Atlantic Ocean, I kept thinking that the baby might have his hair or eyes, or have whatever evil that made him the way he was." She shook her head, then whispered hoarsely, "That I couldn't love—"

Her voice cracked. Tears spilled.

Rocco had nothing to say because those thoughts were running ragged through his head, tearing up his guts. No way would he let her see his apprehensions. Hiding those fears might have been the toughest moment of his life. Nothing—not the challenges of war or his enemy—had ever tested him the way that love was making him work, hurt, and feel through their conversation. Didn't matter though, he'd suffer a million times over just to hold her hand.

Cat bit her bottom lip then straightened her shoulders. "But the more I kept thinking, the more I wondered about... everything else I might see in that baby's face. A smile or innocent happiness. Maybe a little baby girl who would grab my finger when she laughed. Or if I picked her up, my hug would be strong enough to soothe away her tears."

His throat ached. Trying to swallow a lump, he gave up and stayed silent.

"Maybe a little boy would have caramel eyes and a dimple. Maybe he'd run around trying to play superheroes with his dad."

Rocco dropped his head and rubbed his eyes. This was almost too much to handle. No, screw that. *Screw. That.* There wasn't anything he wasn't willing to do for her—

"If the baby's yours... but if the baby's not." She covered her mouth, head shaking. After a sniffle, she steeled herself. "I can do this alone."

No way. All he had to do was find simple words.

"I don't want you to." It was a promise, a proclamation. He thought he'd never want something more than bringing Cat back home, but he was wrong. He wanted to bring *them* back home. "Make no mistake, Kitten. Regardless of who the biological father of our baby is, this baby is *ours.*"

She didn't say anything. She wasn't agreeing or disagreeing, and silence, when it came to Cat, was bad news. But her jaw was back to hanging open, and the truth was, he didn't blame her. What was happening to her, what he was offering... that was heavy.

He cleared his throat and plowed forward. "Trust me when I tell you I didn't see this coming."

She closed her dark pink lips. "Me either."

"But I'm man enough to say any obstacle life drops on us, I want to figure it out with you."

Her eyes closed. After a minute, she looked at him from underneath thick, teary lashes. "You didn't know I was pregnant?"

"Nope."

Her sad smile upturned. "Mia and Jared knew."

Another bomb dropped on his chest. How did they not tell him?

"I'm not sure what to say to that." He thought back to Jared on the phone before he left for the airport and Mia showing up at the hospital. "You found out after you were shot?"

She nodded.

"I thought you left me because I stole your kill shot, everything you ever wanted in life. It killed me. But I had to."

"Now, I know that's what you had to do. That night, I was destroyed over it, would rather have died trying to kill him. Then finding out that I was pregnant—I couldn't handle it."

"So… You're pregnant. You're in Spain… What were you going to do?" *Were you. Not* are *you. Notice that and agree. Just come back home.*

"I was going to find a home, a place I could call mine."

Home was with him. "There's already a place like that."

She didn't answer, and the reminder drifted in the waterfront wind, floating away.

Tugging at a handful of fabric from her skirt, he pushed her to answer. "You're saying no?"

She sighed. "I'm saying I don't think I'm very good mate material. I went from being obsessed with the demise of a man to maybe carrying his baby, and I'm not even sure I could live up to being a good… *woman* to you."

"That's insane. I've never met anyone more woman than you."

"No." Her cheeks turned red, and she stared at the grass. "I have nightmares. I don't think I can do *that* ever again. Nothing has changed. I can't—I don't think I can be a good…woman."

"Kitten, nightmares we can handle."

"It's more than that." Her brow furrowed. "I'm… ruined." She jabbed her blade of grass with each word.

Oh hell. How could he be such an insensitive shit, focusing on one issue and forgetting about another. "Look, I love you. Love. Nothing about you is ruined. And nothing about you isn't worth loving."

"Now you're lying."

"When you were at Jared's, I was in hell. I hated it. I hated *him,* and he's practically family. But I never hated you. Just like you knew we were destined to meet, I know we're destined to never stay apart. You wanna skip town, jump continents, run from me? I'll find you. It's what I'll always do. You belong with me."

"I…"

"*You* love me like I love you." Two simple facts. She couldn't refute them.

"Yes."

"This seems simple enough. You have two options. Stay here and I'll stay." He looked around. Not a bad view. Beach living could be okay or at least something he could get used to. "Or we go home. What's it going to be?"

"There are more options than that."

"Not from my point of view."

She avoided his gaze.

"It's simple, Cat. Don't make this complicated. Everything else can be screwed up. Everything else, we deal with. You and me? Simple. So simple question, simple answer. I stay or you go. What's it going to be?"

"I guess…"

"You guess? Nah, that doesn't work. Just tell me. Which is it? Just say it."

"We go home."

He smiled. Relieved. "Good answer."

Her eyes lit up, and he felt his soul for the first time. His woman and his baby.

"Come here." He pulled her into his arms and kissed the top of her head. They faced the water, her back against his stomach and her loose hair blowing around his face, tickling his neck. She smelled like the outdoors, like the beach and the wind rolling off the Mediterranean. The church bell clanged again overhead, and birds soaring off the water squawked.

Her hand squeezed his, and he looked at it, small in comparison to his. "You're still wearing your band."

She shrugged against him. "Never occurred to me to take it off."

"Me neither." The bell finished clanging for the twelfth time and broke into a faster pace, a song, celebrating the day, announcing noon had arrived. A minister walked through the graveyard. "Let's not take them off."

Sighing, she clasped her hand in his. "Okay."

The gravity of his suggestion hit him but clearly had missed Caterina completely. "I'm serious. I don't want to take this ring off, and I don't want you to either."

Her head dipped back, leaning onto his shoulder. "Are you asking me to marry you?"

He laughed. "You plan on saying yes?"

Huge smile. Happy eyes. "Yes."

"I saw a minister." He spun her in his lap. "We already have our rings."

"And I *am* wearing a white dress."

Rocco stood, pulling her up with him. Her arms hooked around his neck, and her feet dangled. "Caterina Cruz, will you marry me? Today. Right now, where everything started and forced our paths to cross?" He kissed her. "Gotta marry me, Kitten. Has to happen."

The gauzy skirt billowed around them with a gust of wind. "I'm wearing white at a church when you show up? You know how I feel about coincidence."

"Say it, Kitten."

"*Si.* I'll marry you." And she kissed him with no hesitation, no need for deliberate caution and warning signs.

FORTY-SIX

"**Y**ou ready for this?" Rocco took her hand as they walked through the door.

"I'm never sure I'm ready for anything that Sugar's in charge of." Caterina could've killed for a Diet Coke that moment, but she had kicked the caffeine habit. "But bring on the Titan."

"Bring on the Titan." He laughed as they rounded the corner.

"Surprise!"

Caterina jumped. She knew it was coming, and she still jumped. When a half-dozen built-like-tanks men jumped at you, especially when they looked as deadly and daring as this bunch, all the warning in the world wasn't going to keep a girl from taking a step back. Lord.

She threw back her head, laughing, and Rocco held her out-stretched arm. "Surprise."

"Welcome home party, Senorita." Sugar stepped forward, handing her a glass of something sparkly. Maybe Jared never told her Cat was pregnant. Maybe she forgot. Hell, maybe she thought when Cat came home she wouldn't be anymore. Who knew? Sugar was a wild one, and Cat wouldn't waste time guessing her motives.

Catching her off guard, Sugar gave her a hug and whispered, "It's sparkling apple juice."

And that made Cat laugh. Always up to something, that one was.

They walked further into the Westin's living room, and she was comfortable. No one gawked at her. No one whispered, not as though they would have, but it was a little over-dramatic to make Rocco chase her onto the other side of the world.

Sugar and Mia ran around, making sure everyone had a glass, and instinctively Cat knew that Mia had cooked and Sugar supplied the liquor. She liked the idea of seeing the same people on a regular basis. That was odd, a foreign concept, but normal life took getting used to. Regular place to sleep and wake. Regular stream of constant people, also now known to her as friends... It could've been overwhelming, but it just wasn't.

"Told you, another one bit the dust," Roman called out.

"Cheers," Nicola and Sarah said at the same time, laughing. Clearly, their glasses weren't filled with sparkling apple juice.

"Cheers!" Asal mimicked, holding up her glass of something entirely different than the adults.

Jessica and Kelly, the Gamble kids, did the same thing. Then Clara imitated, copying Asal's actions exactly, and the toddler's voice melted Cat's heart.

"Cheers." Rocco laced his fingers in hers and held up her hand like she was a prize-winning fighter at the end of a round. "To my wife. Stuck with me forever."

Whoops and hollers rang out. Roman shook his head, muttering to Parker about the problems with love, even though Caterina had noticed in the five seconds she'd been there that his head followed Beth around. Nicola fell onto Cash's lap, and he was pulling out his wallet. A bet lost? With Brock wrapped around her waist, Sarah gushed to Sugar. And in the corner, Jared stood, arms folded, looking very pleased with himself.

Since they were making announcements... "And..." She tilted her head, her eyes meeting her husband's. "Rocco's gonna be a daddy."

All over again, the room rang out. The ladies jumped and screamed. Back slapping followed quickly with a bevy of questions. How was she feeling? How far along? What did he say? What did she feel? The answer to everything was perfect and loved.

Everything piped down after a few minutes. Mia ran off to change Ace's diaper. Clara followed Asal, Jessica, and Kelly around. Roman followed Beth. Parker was texting on his phone. Sarah and Sugar talked non-stop, and Nicola had stolen her husband's cowboy hat. Caterina was comfortable. She bounced between conversations with the ladies, trying to stomach food, but morning sickness seemed like it was raising its squeamish head. Jared kept watching her, saying little but Sugar more than made up for it with her snarky hostess humor.

After a few minutes of watching Jared watch her, she sidled up to Rocco on the couch. "Did you tell him?"

He shook his head. That was going to be quite the conversation, and Cat had no idea how Jared would react.

"No time like the present. Let's do it."

Her stomach bottomed, and that wasn't the morning sickness. It was the right thing to do—*the* only thing to do—but nerves were floating in her stomach, side by side with her baby-nausea, and she didn't want to get sick on Boss Man's shoes.

Rocco tugged her the last few feet. "Jared—"

"I need to talk to Cat."

Uh-oh. She gulped.

"Us first." Rocco moved her in front of him, and suddenly she felt like a little thing in an alpha-man sandwich.

Jared grunted. "Fine."

She took a deep breath and hoped Rocco would do it quickly, just like he'd ripped off the last of the bandages on her shoulder. "Cat and I had a lot of time to think this over."

She gulped, and Jared's eyes narrowed.

Roc kept going, "There's no other way to put it."

Get to the point already. She nudged him.

"We think you should be the baby's godfather."

Jared's jaw dropped. "Godfather?"

She smiled. "Seems like a job for Boss Man. I always thought of you as mine."

He uncrossed, then re-crossed his arms. "Well, fuck yes."

Caterina had to laugh. Only Jared. "*Gracias.*"

"Thanks, man."

Jared, apparently only able to handle one minute's worth of an emotional moment, nodded curtly. "One more thing for you."

She took Rocco's hand, always a smidgen nervous when Jared had that this-is-a-heavy-moment tone. "What is that?"

"Come with me."

He didn't wait for an answer and stormed off. They followed just like he probably expected they would, following him into a side room that looked like a home office. On his desk was a small box, wrapped in dry, blood-covered, faded paper.

The present.

It was straight out of her nightmares. No. Her memories.

"This is yours. I kept it. Don't know why. But there it is." He popped one knuckle at a time, and she stepped toward his desk, pulled by the little present.

She picked it up. Weathered. The paper was crunchy and aged, the ribbon flat, as if it'd been packed away.

"Open it," Rocco urged.

It was almost too much. She didn't want to disturb it. Curiosity encouraged her to tear the paper off, but it also felt like disturbing history. Carefully, she ran a finger under the taped sides, and they came up with ease. Twenty year old tape didn't keep its adhesive. She unfolded the paper without tearing and found a non-descript box. The top opened easily, and she found a bright red 1980s tape recorder and a cassette tape. The kind that allowed recordings off of her boom box.

"What is it?" Roc asked.

She pulled it out. All three of them studied it like they were preparing to disarm a bomb, and Rocco lifted it from her hands and turned it over, popping the back off. "Four double-A batteries."

Jared moved to his desk, removed the back of a clock, put it down, grabbed a remote,and opened it. "Got two." He tossed them to Rocco, who put them in. Jared continued through another remote, cursing when he found triple-As. "Give me a minute."

How many remotes could a man have?

Walking out the door, he was gone long enough for nerves to kick in over the homemade tape. The label read Caterina Cruz's Tenth Birthday in her mama's handwriting, as if she could ever forget that.

Jared stepped back in. "Bingo."

Two more double-As flew at Rocco. He snagged them mid-air and popped them in, closing the back.

Jared shifted in his boots. "I'm pretty sure I need to make sure Sugar isn't terrorizing people." After a couple of steps, he turned around, looking like his usual angry self. "Thanks for the godfather honor. You two blew my mind." Then he left.

Rocco sat in a chair, pulling her onto his lap.

She laughed nervously, remembering all the things she used to do with her family. Her brothers singing to the radio. Leaving silly messages and recording, re-recording over and over until the tapes wouldn't take anymore.

"You want to listen to it?"

Yes. No. Thousands of butterflies flew laps in her stomach. "It's probably nothing. Spanish radio, circa 1980s."

"So put it in, and press play."

"I can't."

"Hell yes you can, Kitten."

Without thinking about it anymore, she hit play. Spanish tunes screamed out. She jumped, and Rocco adjusted the volume. The music cut off.

"*Feliz cumpleaños!*" *Happy birthday!* A tidal wave of emotion hit her as her mama's voice sang into the air. "*Feliz cumpleaños! Feliz cumpleaños! Feliz cumpleaños!* Feliz cumpleaños!" Her brothers each took a turn wishing her a happy birthday.

The tape crackled. "*Feliz cumpleaños, mi pequeña!*" Her daddy's voice. *Happy birthday, my little one.* A full-body shiver started at her nape and spread. He kept talking, and she let the tears fall without bothering to wipe them away then hit the stop button.

"What?" Rocco's face shot up. "What'd he say? Why'd you stop it?"

She rewound the tape. Translating after her daddy. "Ten years old and you're turning into such a young lady. Your family loves you. Always remember, love is strong enough to survive anything. Even what you're about to hear." She took a breath. "That's where I stopped it. I don't want to hear—"

"It's your birthday present, not something awful." Rocco pressed play. She slammed her hands on top of his, trying to stop it. What would it be? Horrid family secrets? A reminder that she'd wanted her birthday party the way she wanted it, and it got them all killed? It was too much too—

Wham! blasted from the little speaker. Her brothers—the toughest boys she knew at the age of ten—broke into a booming. "Jitterbug." Four freaking times, singing along with George Michael and Andrew Ridgeley. Here brothers were singing along with Wham!?

"*Ay Dios mio!*" She slapped her hand over her mouth.

"What the hell is that?"

"I drove them nuts with that song. Non-stop."

All four of them sang, if it could be called that, at the top of their lungs over the music. "You put the boom-boom in my heart."

"That *is awful.*" Her husband was failing to keep it together. His lips sucked in. His chiseled cheeks reddened. His eyes danced. His chest rumbled, trying to suffocate hysterics.

"Awful! I love it!"

Hands covering her face, she couldn't stop laughing. Rocco couldn't stop laughing. It was so bad, and exactly what she needed.

FORTY-SEVEN

"I think I'm done." Caterina lay in bed, twirling her wedding band around her finger. "It's over."

Rocco rolled over, tucking his chin over her shoulder and slipping his hand over her swelling stomach. He couldn't get over how the bump kept changing. "Done, huh?"

"It's been a week."

"That's a long time?" One day, her stomach hadn't looked so flat. Then it had a little lull to it. Now it had achieved full-fledged baby bump status.

"It is when you have the world's longest morning sickness. It's been like a vacation."

"You may be the only woman ever to call pregnancy a vacation." He could feel her smile in his arms. His hand drew lazy circles on her growing belly, using it as more of an excuse to lay his biceps across her looking-fuller-by-the-day breasts.

She turned her head. "Are you excited for tomorrow?"

Tomorrow couldn't come fast enough. He never really needed to sleep and probably wouldn't get any that night. "Am I excited?" He kissed her neck. "Hell, woman."

"Me too." She nudged her head back and—he could've sworn—gave him the slightest bit more skin to kiss.

She didn't have to tell him twice. Her back arched, and he groaned. The erection he'd been carrying for two-months-going-on-eternity raged to life, and he shifted. Away. One day, everything would be okay.

He wasn't complaining. It would happen when he least expected it. At least that was what the pamphlets and counselors, and websites had all said.

"Boy or girl?"

"I don't know," she whispered.

Her hand rested on top of his. The big fat book of shit-he-was-supposed-to-know said that any day now, he'd feel the baby move. Any day now. He was waiting. She pressed his palm to her belly. Any day now could happen any minute now 'cause he wanted to feel his kid.

"Did you feel something?"

"No."

"Sorry." Her voice was feathery, and it tickled over his senses, just like her hand, no longer pressing but hovering, barely touching him, teasing his skin and drawing prickles that cascaded like thousands of shimmery bites, up his arm, down his spine. Straight to his groin.

God, he was going to die. Not wanting to be more obvious than he already was, Rocco tried to add a bit of space between them. He needed space, and she needed holding. It never balanced.

"Don't move away from me."

"Oh, Kitten. I don't want to. But I kinda have to." He kissed her neck as chastely as he could. "I'm sorry."

Her back arched into him again, her sweet ass backing up against his erection. The touch stole his breath, shut his eyes, and left him just savoring the closeness. Patience wasn't one of his virtues. Maybe he didn't have any. But he had been trying like hell to behave, and little moves like Cat was making weren't helping.

Her hand stayed with his, still drawing circles on her stomach. Tiny pinpricks erupted on her skin. Goose bumps. Her warm hand pressed his, taking the lead across her belly. His heart beat slowed down. Got louder. His shaft was painfully hard, and she was doing bad things to him. Guided by her hand, the tips of his fingers touched the lace top of her underwear. His hand snatched back, an automatic reaction, but her fingers caught him, moving his hand closer to the lace again. Closer. Then skimming across the top.

Holy hell.

His cock throbbed, and he held his breath. Unsure where to go, what to do, or what she needed. Unable to both think and feel, he thought too hard, and his hips flexed, feeling the curve of her ass through her pajama bottoms. His head lulled back. Hell, he could kiss her. That hadn't been a problem. Lips finding her sweet skin, he gently trailed a path to that special spot behind her ear.

Her hand still guided his as his palm smoothed back and forth over the lace front. His tongue swept, and her hand pushed down, stronger, surer, and further down. Again, further, such incremental moves, his breath held, coming in short bursts against her neck, and then her fingers cupped his against her sex.

"God, you are wet, Kitten."

"I know…" She nodded, her soft hair moving against his chest.

His fingertips curved against her, daring to touch and tease. Have mercy…

"Is this okay?" *Please let it be. Please…*

She nodded again. "Yes."

Thank fuck.

Sliding under the lace scrap, his fingers found her folds slick. His fingers caressed softly, carefully. She sighed, arching again, and he dared to part her folds and seek her clit.

She sighed, aroused, enjoying, and it made him bolder. His fingers explored. Little sounds he'd memorized months ago purred out of her lips.

Molding himself against her body, he inhaled the smell of her shampoo and savored the taste of her skin. "Is this what you want?"

"More than anything." Her voice was low, seductive, and seriously doing bad things to his control.

He'd kill to keep her and their baby safe for the rest of their lives. The amount of trust she'd found and placed in him made his heart clench. How was it possible to love so damn hard? He slid one side of the lace underwear over her hip bone. "Still with me?"

"Uh-huh."

His hand trailed her thigh, desperate to get back between her legs and wanting to make sure this worked for her as much as it was working for him. Fingertips dragging over her skin, goose bumps flashed against his palm, slowing him. Slower… Slower…

"Rocco." Her voice was husky and sexier than he could ever remember, and he'd spent an inordinate amount of time recalling every one of their moments.

He cupped her mound again, and she murmured and writhed against him. He abandoned her sweet pussy and hooked the lace from her other hip, dragging it down. To her thighs. Then over her knees, ankles, until she was bare to him. He didn't have a condom. But hell, they didn't need one. Breaths caught in his chest.

Caterina turned her head. "You've been so patient with me."

"If you're not—"

"I am."

"Thank God."

She wasn't turning around, and maybe that was how it had to be right now. Her hand drifted behind her, lazing across his thigh, crooking her arm under the covers. "I'm sorry it's been so long."

"Here and now, Caterina. Just you and me. Don't think about anything else."

She tugged on his boxers, and he made quick work of losing them. "Just us."

"That's right."

She kept her back to him. "Take my shirt off."

With pleasure. He pushed onto an elbow, running his hand over the jut of her hipbone, then back across the sinful curve of her backside. God, he'd missed her body. He spread his fingers as he drifted under her shirt and up her warm back. Following her spine, he trailed its valley to midway, then back down again. He toyed with the hem of her shirt then followed the same path, but with the fabric this time. The shirt bunched, and she shrugged out of it. Her hair pulled out and fell against him when she pulled her head through.

Completely naked. Such a luscious body. Rocco wrapped her in his arms, pulling her to his chest, his forearms covering her breasts. They were swollen, her nipples tight, and how he'd love to bury his face into her chest, teeth the tips until she bucked, delve his hand into her pussy, and make her moan. And that would come. He knew it. But now, he'd never been more turned on. She placed all kinds of trust and was taking a risk with him. It was almost too much to understand.

The bare length of his shaft pressed between them with the covers draped over. Her foot rubbed his calf, so delicate against the harsh hairs on his leg.

"You know how much I love you."

She nodded, her leg hooking back over his. The sweet taste of her seared his memory when hot moistness wicked over his dick. Dropping his arm, he again cupped her sex with one hand and palmed her breast with the other. His thumb flicked across her nipple, making her groan. The slide of their bodies swaying into each other guided his shaft between them, coating him, so hot and silky. Every single move brought him closer, and when his eyes closed, the head of his cock pressed into her like nothing else he could imagine.

She gasped. He froze, eyes rocketing open, muscles locked—fucking scared he'd screwed up.

"Please don't stop."

"Are you..." What? What would he say...?

"Here and now. With you, Roc."

Yeah, he was here and now as long as she was too. Rocco rolled his hips and bit his lip. Wet for him, she was too much. Absolutely perfect. He eased back, needing to connect them again. His chest went tight. Caterina's chest stuttered with ragged breaths. Fucking beautiful sounds. He thrust again. Stronger and deeper, and she mirrored the motion. The back and forth just about killed him. He could barely breathe, couldn't think, and was buried inside her. So fucking tight.

Flesh against flesh. No barriers, so smooth.

He rolled into her again, one arm underneath her, wrapped around her, holding tight, and the other giving him access to her clitoris. Pumping from behind, stroking her in the front, and holding his whole world in his arms, Rocco experienced them. So perfect, so in sync.

She tightened around his cock. Those pleas and cries that he'd missed so much fell from her lips. She'd strung tight, and he worked her, making her moan, owning each gasp. Harder. Deeper. She bucked, her muscles rippling, her body unraveling. He'd make her come a dozen times over if it felt this good.

"Rocco," she called his name with such intense satisfaction that his eyes sank shut, and he lost himself in her and came with her, hotness coating him with each tight thrust.

Best sex of his life. He kissed her shoulder and smoothed a hand over her stomach. Tomorrow they'd find out boy or girl, but tonight he'd finally found his wife.

EPILOGUE

Twenty years later…

Music boomed through the speakers. The drums beat a slow, patriotic march that brought tears to Caterina's eyes and a tightness in her chest. Two screens flanked a stage, a video montage of night vision attacks and folded flags to commemorate a soldier's sacrifice.

She couldn't hear any more. Too many emotions clogged her senses.

All went quiet. She sniffled, blinked, and wiped at her eyes.

"Ladies and gentlemen, this concludes the Special Forces qualification course graduation ceremony. The graduates will join you…" Cheers and applause ripped through the small auditorium, drowning out the rest.

Caterina threw her arms in the air, clapping overheard. She wrapped herself around Rocco while he whistled loud and proud. Their first born was a Green Beret.

Rocco snagged her in his arms and spun her in the tight aisle, laying a big, fat wet one on her kisser. Their brood of teenagers, two on each side, simultaneously groaned at their parents and cheered their oldest brother.

Cat kicked her feet until he put her down. "Let's go."

But they got nowhere. The audience's exit was blocked until all the Special Forces graduates had filed out. Too excited to wait, she considered walking on the chairs, but that would embarrass everyone. Though making her kids cringe was a favorite pastime, she wasn't trying to incite military social disaster protocol—teenage eyes rolling, husband teasing. Instead, she shooed them down the aisle. No go. No one moved. Bottleneck.

"Can you see him?"

Rocco searched over everyone's head. "Not yet."

His smile was as big as hers, and while he was playing it cool, he shifted in his boots, ready to push people out of their way. The Savage bunch wasn't a patient group. Then again, they didn't raise their family that way. Get in, get it done right, get out. Life was some variation of that, and having a pack of boys as honorable and driven as their daddy made it all work out.

She slipped on her coat, fidgeting, and shoved her hands into her pockets. The corner of what felt like an envelope scratched her knuckles. She pulled it out. Mom and Dad was scrawled on the front, and she tugged at Rocco's shirt.

He turned from crowd-watching, bottleneck-waiting duty, and she waggled it in front of him.

"What is that?"

"I don't know."

"Well, open it."

She did, unfolding the paper, and he read over her shoulder.

Dear Mom and Dad,

My entire life, you pushed me past what I thought I could accomplish. Today, all that paid off. The best of the best. That's been drilled into me. By you. By the US Army. And now by my peers. Special Forces. Thank you for everything you gave, sacrificed, believed in, and fought for to get me here because I know I didn't do it alone.

Love,

Jacián Arrio Savage

Jacián Arrio. His name meant a warlike healer, and it was a self-fulfilling prophecy. Their baby gave her peace, healed her from the inside out, and as he turned into a man, was everything she'd ever hoped for. Exactly like his father. That was it. She was done. Her heart seized up. Her throat ached. Happy tears spilled down her cheeks. When she looked at her husband, even he was a little misty. That'd be her secret. No one as tough and manly as Rocco would want that slipping out. Instead, she jumped up and kissed him again.

"*Ay Dios mio,*" he teased, and it never got old.

The crowd started moving, and it dragged her attention to the door. "Let's go."

Surrounded by her family, hunting for their graduate, Caterina beamed. A minute later, they were in an open area and searching, searching—

Jace.

She pointed, and the entire brood moved with the precision of a tactical team. Their daddy had taught them well. They moved swiftly through the crowd, and their target was surrounded. Her baby boy. All grown up. The boys slapped backs and punched chests. Roc jumped in too, but she hung back, watching all their proud excitement.

After all the testosterone emoting she could handle, Cat pushed into the knot of Savage men and grabbed her boy.

"I am so proud of you," she whispered but knew he already knew. It was her favorite thing to say. That boy might've been built like a cinder block wall like his daddy and was a feisty fighter like his mama, but he was something special on his own.

"I wouldn't be here without you and Dad." Jacián kissed her cheek. "I love you, Momma."

One of his brothers grabbed him, and before walking off with his brothers, he hugged Rocco. All their boys would follow similar paths, and the admiration they had for Jacián was a testament to how they lived their lives: strong and loved.

Rocco stood behind her, letting her lean against him as he always did. His hands cupped her hips, his chin fit down in the nook of her shoulder and neck. "You did good, Kitten."

"*We* did good."

They did perfect.

THE END

Rape is a crime. Talking about it isn't. Many resources are available if you need help. A portion of sales will be donated to a rape and sexual assault survivors non-profit.

COMING NEXT

SWEET GIRL

You know the story of how Cash and Nicola found love in Garrison's Creed, but what about a decade before *when they first fell in love?* **SWEET GIRL** is their prequel.

HART ATTACK

The next novel in the Titan series will arrive this summer. Roman and Beth have both flirted and ignored one another, dancing around their chemistry since they met. Time for them to find love.

Sign up for the newsletter to stay in touch about the Titan series.
http://bit.ly/11aWFzM

ACKNOWLEDGEMENTS

There are so many people I want to wrap my arms around and hug. Thank you to all the Titan readers who have supported this series. It means the world to me. A big shout out to all the ladies in Team Titan! I love chatting with you day in, day out. You make me smile so often.

Thank you to my family. My mom gave me a ferocious love of reading and writing, my dad a can-do attitude, and my sister, who is my role model and best friend, you push me each day to be a better person. Thank you to my husband who is my rock and my world.

To the team that helped ready Rocco and Caterina for the world, I adore you. The Red Adept editorial team rocks. A special thank you to Lynn and Karen for helping me. Thank you to Rihaneh Odde-Rivera for assisting with the Spanish phrasing. Thank you to the kick butt crit team that worked on this book: Claudia Haraway Handel, Racquel Reck, Sharon Cordes Cermak, and Jamie Salsbury.

Thanks to the design ladies that helped me on so many projects. Kim Killion, Jennifer Jakes, and Abigail Simmons at Hot Damn Designs, you three are simply amazing. Amanda Simpson of Pixel Mischief, you are my branding genius. Amber Haas of Phat Cat Design, you make simple ideas turn into visual fun.

Rox: You are a work horse. Thank you for your eyes.

Shex: You certainly made me look hard at plot lines, and I'm grateful.

Dia: You made me laugh when I needed it and helped me in more ways than you'll ever believe.

Sparks: I love ya, girl. We gotta keep dreaming big.

ABOUT THE AUTHOR

Cristin Harber is a USA Today bestselling romantic suspense and military romance author. She lives outside Washington, DC with her family and English Bulldog, and enjoys chatting with readers.

Facebook: www.facebook.com/CristinHarberauthor
Twitter: www.twitter.com/CristinHarber
Website: www.CristinHarber.com
Email: Cristin@CristinHarber.com
Newsletter: Stay in touch about all things Titan—releases, excerpts, and more—plus new series info. http://bit.ly/11aWFzM